The Brexit House

The
Brexit House

JULIA WINTER

Matador
Unit E2 Airfield Business Park
Harrison Road, Market Harborough
Leicestershire LE16 7UL
Tel: 0116 279 2299
Email: books@troubador.co.uk
Web: www.troubador.co.uk/matador
Twitter: @matadorbooks

ISBN 978 1803137 421

British Library Cataloguing in Publication Data.
A catalogue record for this book is available from the British Library.

Cover art by Rosie Galezia

Printed and bound by CPI Group (UK) Ltd, Croydon, CR0 4YY
Typeset in 11pt Minion Pro by Troubador Publishing Ltd, Leicester, UK

Matador is an imprint of Troubador Publishing Ltd

For my mother.

DAY 1

Monday 26th August 2019

They heard it on the radio as they were driving down to Dover.

The beginning of the end, thought Cecily. Although she had to rapidly correct herself: it was not the beginning at all. The beginning was forty years ago, or more. Really this amounted to just one more tiny, incremental slip – a slip and perhaps a spattering of loose earth and stones – down the proverbial slope.

The Prime Minister was considering, they said on the radio, requesting that the Queen prorogue Parliament. They didn't say, on the radio, that he would be doing that in order that the government could act without Parliament's consent.

Surely it could never happen? Not in this country. Perhaps somewhere like China; perhaps in South America; perhaps in the wild east stretching between Europe and Asia. But not in these gentle fields of England she could see flitting past the car window, soft-edged and self-contained within their bumbly hedges. It was just inconceivable that he could do such a thing. Proroguing Parliament! And even if – in some parallel universe – he *should* actually try it, well, even then, it still could never happen. Because, of course, the Queen could never acquiesce.

But she made no comment. And neither did her husband Florian, who was driving. What could anyone say, with a Brexiter in the back there, with the girls? Especially one who was their guest for the next few days. And Diana, the Brexiter, sitting in the back, made no comment either. Out of the corner of her eye, Cecily could see that Diana was gazing out of the window, apparently not listening to the radio. But with both hands she was holding her handbag on her lap, close against her stomach, and her thumb was tightly looped inside the metal ring that attached the strap to the bag.

Florian, having waited a decent two minutes so as to make it look as if there were no connection between the news and his reaction, reached out and switched the radio off. They travelled the last ten minutes of the journey without a word.

"Well, here we are!" Florian said when they arrived, crunching off the bumpy coast road and onto the gravel drive. His voice was startling, booming into the silence.

"Oh!" Diana exclaimed, in tones of warm, dawning curiosity, leaning past the girls to see through the window, "So this is your house!"

Cecily, looking at the limy, white house, with its low rooves and hobbity, lead-paned windows, cosy behind its curtains of honeysuckle and wisteria, felt a wave of mixed

2

pride and relief. This house, guarded by the host of tall chestnut trees that stood protectively about it, had been in her family for four generations. And though she had only ever spent holidays here, it felt more like home, more like *hers*, than any other house she had ever known. This was their last visit of the summer; their last August trip to the seaside holiday house, before the girls began at secondary school.

They began to clamber out of the car. Cecily watched Diana link her fingers, stretch her arms above her head and then twist her head from side to side, as if to loosen the muscles in her neck and shoulders. After that, she linked her fingers again and stretched out her arms behind her back, turning slowly in a circle as she did so. Watching, Cecily felt that particular feeling she often felt towards Diana: a protectiveness, a joyful spurt of generosity. It was something about the slight stoop to Diana's shoulders and a slight clumsiness about the hips, which seemed already to prefigure a frailty of old age; and a certain distractedness to her movements, suggesting her mind and movements were not entirely at one. Cecily suspected that, confronted with the house, Diana was experiencing a kind of social anxiety, and that this series of apparently calm, physical acts was cover for a process of mental preparation.

It was only when she had gone nearly all the way round, turning slowly like that, that Diana gasped, "Oh, my goodness!"

Like all guests when they first arrived, Diana had not been prepared for what she saw when she turned around: a sudden, wide expanse of glittering sea, way down at the

3

bottom of the cliffs. And you could actually see the coast of France, across the water. It was only a purplish-brown smudge on the horizon, far away, but undeniably France. Diana turned to Cecily with her mouth wide open in a comic show of wonder and admiration, and said again, this time separating each word emphatically, "Oh… my… goodness!"

Cecily felt a rush of pride, as if this view were actually an achievement of her own.

"Beautiful, just beautiful!" Diana said, turning her head from one end of the horizon to the other, and then to Cecily. "And you've been coming here ever since you were a child?"

"Yes. Well, my grandparents actually lived here back then; we used to come for holidays."

Diana was nodding; nodding and smiling as if she could just imagine. "You and your sister?"

"Yes, me and Victoria."

Just a touch wistful, Diana looked around at the house, so comfortably cushioned with creepers and lawns and shrubs and bushes, girthed with its mighty guard of rustling trees. And then she turned to look out again over the glittering blue spreading below. "I always wanted a sister," she said.

"Can we go in? Who's got the key?" Cecily's eleven-year-old daughter Julia was calling. She and her friend Olivia, Diana's daughter, had the boot open and were yanking out their cases. Interrupted, the two mothers moved back to the car to help them.

"Oh, wow!" Diana murmured when they entered the cool, dark hall, dropping her voice in slightly theatrical wonder. "What a lovely old hall!"

4

The hall was tiled in peachy old terracotta; quietly glowing as if it held some secret light within. Along the shoe bench and the central strip, the tiles were also buffed shiny by generations of passing feet. The walls were panelled in oak, up to about the height of a woman's shoulder, and whitewashed above that.

"Oh, it's so old-fashioned. I feel like I'm in a film!" Diana gushed.

Now Cecily felt a small, internal welling of discomfort. She hoped Diana was not going to be quite so effusively admiring about *everything*. It was a social mannerism; she realised that. And she also realised that it was quite standard, within their group of London friends, to ramp up one's reactions like this: "Oh, that's such a gorgeous dress! Oh my God, this cake is amazing! That's completely hilarious!" That was the way a lot of people spoke. The women particularly, although also sometimes the men. Cecily probably did it herself. What was more, she'd noticed before that Diana did it most of all when she was not entirely comfortable, like when meeting new people. But actually, that was the problem: this was how Diana behaved with people she didn't really know. Her behaving like that with Cecily put an unwelcome distance between them.

"I love the smell!" Olivia joined in.

Cecily caught Florian's eye. That smell had been getting worse for a couple of years now.

"Well, I'm afraid, Olivia, that's damp!" Cecily said.

"No! Really?" Diana protested, peering about the hall. "I can't see any damp!" She said it almost reproachfully, as if

Cecily had maligned the place and she was sticking up for it. Which was irritating when, after all, it was Cecily's house.

Not wanting to feel irritated, Cecily quickly led them all forwards. "So that's the study," she said, gesturing left. "And that's the sitting room." She gestured right. "And at the back there's the dining room and kitchen and larder and everything."

"So many books!" Diana marvelled, peeping through the sitting-room doorway as they all lugged their cases through the hall towards the stairs.

"Oh… yes, I suppose so," Cecily conceded. She'd stopped noticing, as they'd always been there. There were shelves and shelves of them, she saw now, looking through Diana's eyes. There were shelves all along the back wall, and on both sides of the fireplace. Old books, green and brown and burgundy with hard covers, acquired by her grandparents and perhaps even great-grandparents; and then newer ones with shiny fly covers, collected by her parents and herself.

Hovering in the doorway, Diana peered at the title of an old burgundy cloth-bound book on the shelf just to the left of the architrave. "*Folk-Songs of the Upper Thames,*'" she read. "My goodness! That book must be ancient!"

They paused there, but only briefly, as the girls were now racing up the stairs, and so they followed them. The stairs ended in a spacious landing, off which lay two bedrooms and a large bathroom. A short corridor led to two more bedrooms and another, smaller bathroom. Here again, the walls were lined with books.

"More books!" Diana commented admiringly as they passed through.

"This is where the girls are," Cecily said as they reached the doorway of the room on the left. It was large and square, and there was a small window bay with lead-paned faux-Tudor windows looking out over the sea. "We always just chuck the children in here as there's loads of mattresses that can be arranged, depending on the circumstances," she explained. There was indeed a haphazard pile of three or four mattresses in the middle of the room. "They'll be with Julia's cousin Zac as well, when he arrives. He's like… thirteen. Is that okay?"

"Of course, it's okay!" Diana responded effusively.

Next Cecily took her across the corridor to the master guest room. "And this is you!" she announced, throwing open the door. "Will you be okay sleeping in here?" she added a little anxiously as they stepped inside, as if she were uncertain about the standard of the room. It was only after she'd said it that she wondered why she had taken that tone. Was it false modesty? Because she knew full well that everyone always found the room impressive. It was another large room, square and light, with the same Arts-and-Craftsy window bay looking out over the garden. But here there was also a majestic four-poster bed, and the floor was spread with rugs in gentle 1920s colours: salmon pinks, browns and mints, and soft pale blues. Over by the window was a cherrywood writing desk; while two velvet armchairs sat, stout and portly, Tweedledum and Tweedledee, either side of a pretty fireplace tiled with mulberry and yellow art nouveau tiles. The room was impressive. But still she took that tone of vague, anxious solicitude, as if she suspected that her guests were accustomed to better things. And she didn't know why she did it.

Diana let go of the handle of her suitcase and looked about, letting her mouth fall open, once again, in a hyperbole of wonder. "It's amazing, Cecily! Is this really my room? I feel like an old-fashioned lady! Oh my God! Look at this lovely ditsy-print duvet!" She crossed the room to squidge the cool puffiness in her hand. "Is that real feathers inside?"

Cecily watched Diana run her hands over the fabric. It was not a duvet, in fact, but an eiderdown. "Probably; it…" she began. But then she caught herself. She had been about to say, 'it was my grandmother's' – but just as she opened her mouth, she began to wonder: had it ever been washed? It was a question she had, somehow, never considered before. Only Diana being there made her think of it. Olivia's school shirt was sparkling white and pressed every single day. Instead she said, "My grandmother bought it."

As she followed Diana's eyes around the room, she began to notice that the edging on the old velvet armchairs was coming loose; that the rugs were threadbare in places, and one of them had a dark stain along the fringe. And they must have been like that for years, she realised. But she could only really see it now that Diana was here. Also (although surely it had not been so bad before?), there was that large, bumpy patch of damp – swirly, browning yellow – on the ceiling above the fireplace that Florian was always fretting about. Diana's warm, modern house was spotless: sheer surfaces, shining windows, no clutter and no mess. She would not touch a yoghurt that was past its use-by date, nor consider scraping the mould off the jam. She wouldn't even let Olivia drink from the same cup as anyone else.

As she stood there, Cecily remembered now how once, when she was eight, she had heard her friend's mother commenting on the state of her school tights: Cecily's tights had often had holes in them, because her mother had never bothered about such things. She had felt suddenly mortified, standing there while two other mothers looked down disapprovingly at her tights. It had never occurred to her that holes in tights were something that could matter.

She had forgotten all about that until this moment. But now, looking about the room through what she suspected might be Diana's eyes, she recalled the emotion from back then. The realisation that what her family believed was perfectly acceptable could be – for other people – not acceptable at all. The sudden discovery of shame.

But Diana made no comment about the state of the room. She was crossing the carpet to look at the pictures on the wall. "Oh, who's that?" she asked, looking at the painting of Cecily's grandmother; a painting in mint-greens and browns, of a chestnut-haired woman seated with her hands in her lap, and looking rather uncomfortable in that oddly listless pose.

"That's my grandmother," Cecily said. "She was German."

"Aah…" Diana murmured, still gazing at the painting as if trying to glean something more from it. Then she turned to look at Cecily. "So I bet your grandmother was pleased when you yourself went on to marry a German?"

Cecily was touched. This was what she liked most about Diana: this genuine interest in people's feelings; even old, dead people in portraits. "She never knew, unfortunately," she said. "She died before Florian and I got together." Then she added, "But yes, I'm sure she would have been pleased." Although she was not really sure, in truth. Florian was also part Afro-American and part Togolese. His grandfather had been an American soldier stationed in Germany after the war; his father the son of a wealthy Togolese civil servant, sent to Berlin as a student in the '60s. And of course, she didn't say it, but she wondered whether her grandmother would have been quite so pleased about the African blood. Not that she had ever actually voiced any racial prejudices, but of course most people in Europe, of her generation, had been white supremacist to some degree; indeed, white supremacy, like male supremacy, had been so generally assumed that nobody had even thought about it.

"Aww…" Diana said. Then her gaze moved to the next frame on the wall, almost as if she were at an exhibition. "And that one?" She was peering at a group of schoolboys in cricket whites, arranged on a freshly mowed lawn. In the background there rose a splendid red-brick building with spires and a huge stained-glass window. "Who are they? Is one of them your father?"

"No, it's my great-uncle – the one in the middle, with the cheeky grin. He became the harbour master of Bombay, as it was then known."

"Oh, and these… what are these?"

Cecily went to stand next to Diana. She was looking at two small prints of pen-and-ink drawings of soldiers in red, with large, hairy Buckingham Palace changing-of-the-guard hats, running around a field. One was entitled *The*

Royal Dublin Fusiliers, 102nd and 103rd Foot; and, next to it, another, of brown men with large moustaches, dressed in white turbans and pantaloons and holding rifles and sabres, bore the inscription *No. 22 Mutinous Sepoys*. "Do you know what," wondered Cecily, staring at the two prints, "I've never in my life really looked at these before!" Once again, she felt suddenly ashamed.

They both laughed, slightly.

"I guess it's like that, in your own family," Diana offered. "Some pictures are just part of the furniture."

"Well, but it's just such awful imperial stuff," Cecily protested. "I should have noticed!" Now she felt decidedly uncomfortable, staring at those brown, moustached men.

Diana glanced at her, and then back at the print. "Yeah," she said, after a moment, not looking at Cecily, her eyes firmly on the picture, "but you don't have to be an imperialist to think… well, it's just quite incredible that such a small country managed to rule so much of the world!"

It seemed to Cecily that they were both aware of a tension gathering in the corners of the room. Because of this, she didn't mention what had just come into her mind, which was that Rome was a lot smaller, and that over the course of human history many, many other empires had risen and fallen from the most unexpected places. Instead she said, walking quickly across the room and gesturing to another picture, "And this is Dover Priory. It was an impressive Norman monastery before the monks were kicked out in the sixteenth century."

"Oh!" said Diana politely. But she didn't come over for a closer look.

Perhaps she had had enough of looking at paintings, Cecily thought. "Anyway, I'll leave you to settle in," she said, moving towards the door, "and then we should probably put some lunch together. And then we can go for a walk or something?"

"Lovely!" Diana said. But there was still a rift in the air.

"Great!" Cecily said, her hand on the door.

They smiled again at each other.

"No, that sounds *perfect*!" Diana said.

*

After Cecily had gone, Diana remained standing in the centre of the room, her feet on a line of pale green and gold hexagons that ran along the border of the fireside rug. She felt as if something had happened. She had an unsettled, lurching feeling in the pit of her stomach.

She looked around, admiring the room, attempting to ignore that lurch in her stomach. It was such a treat, she reminded herself, to sleep in a room like this for a couple of nights. It was almost like a nostalgia trip; back to a time when everything was simpler and infused with a slow, painstaking certainty – a sanctity that was lacking in today's world.

Although, to be honest, she thought, sitting down on the bed and looking around, she would have felt more relaxed if her husband had been able to come too. That moment – that strange moment between her and Cecily just now – had jolted her, and now she felt oddly vulnerable. If Steve were here, moments like that would not affect her so; she would have him as a buffer.

Everything, she had noticed as soon as she'd walked in, was in a fairly dilapidated state. Two of the floral tiles in front of the fireplace were cracked, the mirror was liver-spotted, and the edging on both armchairs was loose in places. But none of this bothered her the way it would in her own house. On the contrary, she found it almost uplifting; it made her feel free. That type of thing didn't matter here. It was something to do with a sense of history here that totally changed how she saw things. Each and every object here stored a story inside it, and if it was dilapidated, well, that was an integral part of the story too. That was how she felt here. Even the damp stain on the ceiling was almost romantic. How wonderful to live in a world where maintenance was unnecessary; where wear and tear and mess and dirt not only didn't matter, but positively added to the mystique!

She looked slowly about her: the leaded windows; the fireplace, framed with slabs of a creamy, yellowing stone which made her think of Canterbury Cathedral, which they'd stopped briefly to look at on the way here. She gazed about at the photos of old-fashioned school teams on green lawns, and the prints of imperial soldiers. On the bedside table was a bizarre collection of books: bashed-up airport paperbacks bundled together with small, ancient, stuffy-looking old hardbacks bound in dusty greens and blues. She went over to look through the titles: *Paradise Lost, The Pilgrim's Progress, Robinson Crusoe*… all names she seemed to half-remember, even though she was sure that they were not books she had ever read.

It was odd, but here she found herself in a world that seemed, in some ways, more like home than the contemporary world she actually lived in. Of course, in so many other ways, it was not 'hers' at all, this world. She had never in her life lived in a house with leaded windows, creamy stone fireplaces, and walls with this ancient, churchy smell of damp chalk. Neither as a child nor as an adult had her family owned Persian rugs and cherrywood writing desks, and none of her family had been to public school, served as army officers, or travelled anywhere in the Empire at all, like the people in these photos. And yet, this room seemed somehow familiar, so that, standing here, she felt the tug of nostalgia for a past she felt she had, in some sense, missed out on. She had a sense of being part of a national story; a history which reached out across the seven seas, bringing back treasures and wonder. They used to say, after all, that on the British Empire, the sun never set. And all of us British, rich or poor, could share in that; could bask in that reflected glory.

Of course, it was not politically correct to say that sort of thing now. No one was allowed to say a good word about the Empire anymore. Because we had exploited all of our imperial subjects, and because – worst of all – hand in hand with the Empire had gone the slave trade. But exploitation and slavery were as old as the earth, and continued all over the globe to this day, just as they had under the Empire. It was not, Diana thought, as if we British had been uniquely cruel or exploitative among nations; we had just been playing the same game as everyone else. The only difference was that – for a time – Britain had managed to play it better.

Besides, she also knew that, actually, where she

differed from the educated London people she mixed with nowadays was not in drawing pride and confidence from her country's imperial past, but in the fact that she was honest with herself about it. When she heard people – people like Cecily, in fact – disparaging the Empire, saying, "Oh, it was so exploitative!" or "Oh, it was so supremacist!", it was not that she disagreed. She knew very well that the Empire was both those things. It was just that to her, when people spoke like that, it seemed that, while they thought they were being humble, they were in fact bragging without even knowing it. It was a humblebrag, and that was what annoyed her. *Imagine, for example*, she thought, *a middle-aged man at a dinner party, talking about his schooldays. And what he says is that, when he was at school, he beat up everyone in the playground. He is very ashamed; he laughs about what a barbaric little sod he was: how unfeeling, how insensitive! How very different from his present self! He talks as if what he wants you to take away from this is how enlightened he is now, how sensitive, how ashamed that once he behaved like that. But actually* – actually – *what he really wants you to understand is so much more than that. Probably he is not even aware of it himself, but really he wants to make sure you get that, although he is kind and sensitive now, as a child, before he learnt that it was wrong, he was* able *to dominate everyone; that, of all the boys in the class, he was the strongest, the alpha male, and so – though of course he never would – he could probably still be dominant like that, if he wanted…*

*

While Diana was settling into her room, Cecily went downstairs. It was several months since they'd last been able to get down here. And coming back was always like... almost like returning to some well-loved childhood story; *The Magic Faraway Tree* or something. All bound up with the magic of childhood, this house was a secret, green and fertile refuge for her adult soul.

She went into the sitting room and sat down on the green velvet sofa along the back wall. At the other end of the long room, which had once been two, the windows looked out over the front of the house. From the sofa she could see light streaking in through those small cottagey, lead-paned windows. Constrained by the narrow panes, the light fell in narrow, Calvinist shafts, like the light in an old Dutch painting, beatifying with dazzling illumination just one chosen corner of the coffee table, and one narrow strip of the carpet.

It was true, what Diana said, she thought then, looking about the room: this house was literally full of books. Cecily had read quite a few of them over long adolescent summers, and even more after that. Here, for example, on either side of the window, were the shelves that her mother had put up to contain her university books when she graduated. She wandered over, and here they all were: the books from that first-year module *Reformation and Revolution in Early Modern England*, and the second-year module *Industrial and Social Revolution in Eighteenth-Century Britain*. She'd grown up with the happy assumption that, in England at least, all the great battles had now been fought and won, and by the right sides. But now, with Brexit looming, that security and harmony seemed suddenly at risk, and our hard-won rights something that could be taken away. And yet, standing there, looking at the books, she could hardly recall what the important battles were, who had taken part in them, or what principles they had established. She could hardly articulate, even to herself, what it was and how it had been built, this idea of England that Brexit was assaulting.

She was about to get up and see where Florian was and what he thought about lunch, when she noticed that something was missing. She couldn't think, at first, what it might be, until, moving her eye carefully around the room, she identified the problem. Her mother's two Italian vases! Great big vases! They should be standing either side of the fireplace, but they were not.

Florian peeped his head in then, from the corridor. He was wincing, furrow browed. She experienced an anticipatory weariness. Florian always did this when they first arrived here: finding things that were wrong and wanting to fix them.

"What?" she asked him, trying to indicate with her tone that very probably, whatever it was, she didn't really want to hear about it.

Not taking the hint he stepped into the room and – unusually – shut the door behind him. "There's a funny smell in the bathroom," he said.

"A funny smell? Which bathroom?"

"The one on the landing."

"What kind of smell?"

"Well… sewage, basically."

"Ugh…"

He stood there, looking at her expectantly. "Do you want to come and see?" he asked impatiently.

She didn't want to come and see. She wanted to have lunch, go for a walk with Diana on the beach, and look through these old books from her university days. But she knew what he was thinking, though he hadn't said it yet. He had told her enough times before. "You can't just hide your head in the sand," he always said. He'd said it when she'd failed to open their electricity bills until a penalty was due; when she'd failed to go to the dentist in the early stages of a problem and so ended up needing root canal treatment. Impingements of a quotidian world of mundane tasks that she could never quite believe was real until – suddenly – it was all *too* real.

And because he was right and it was hateful when he was right and she was wrong, she said, "Okay", forestalling him before he could actually voice his thought.

She got up and followed him upstairs to the bathroom.

The door was closed. But now he opened it, beckoning her in after him. He closed the door, and they both stood there, sniffing.

"I can't smell anything," she said, shrugging, after a while.

"Wait!" He held up a finger, slowly turning his head, as if he were listening, not smelling. He took two steps further into the room and sniffed again. "It's weird. It comes and goes." He sniffed again, shuffling to the left. "There it is! Stand here!"

She moved over to join him, and sure enough, there it

18

was: some foul ghost. Gone again for a while. And then, as she turned her head, it was back. Not just a smell; more like a drainage of energy, like when you're about to faint. And more than that: a wave of hopelessness, of decomposition, of corruption. "Ugh… what *is* that? That's not sewage!"

"It *is* sewage. That's *exactly* what sewage smells like!" Florian corrected her, with impressive certainty.

"*That's* what sewage smells like?" It seemed impossible.

He was looking at her as if she was slightly stupid. "What?" he said.

"I don't know… I guess I just never thought it would smell so… evil."

He laughed, teasing. "Yeah? You thought it would be a friendly kind of smell?"

"Well, no! But I didn't think a smell could have such… hopelessness about it."

He stared at her for a moment, and then rolled his eyes and continued, as if what she had said was so absurd he was not even going to discuss it. "Well, anyway," he said briskly, opening the door and stepping out into the corridor, "I guess we'd better try and find a plumber."

Cecily nodded, and then sighed. When her parents were still alive, when they'd retired here, they'd always been the ones to maintain the holiday house; Cecily and Victoria had never had to. It was not easy, she was discovering, when you only came up for the weekend or a holiday, to suddenly find contacts and deal with everything. Even back in London, it was hard enough to find a plumber nowadays, but here in Dover she knew no one, really; none of the family lived here anymore. Where did one begin?

"I just hope I can get someone over before we leave," Florian continued.

She looked at him in relief. He had said 'I'! She always found it hard to believe, but it really did seem that the solving of problems like this, which filled her with dread, was, for Florian, in some way energising. "Oh, do you think you could follow it up?" she said quickly. "Because I'm just hopeless at this kind of thing." She was trying to sound grateful and helpless in equal parts. It was low, she knew. But she also knew that he secretly enjoyed her appealing to his inner knight in shining armour.

"Yeah, yeah," he said, determinedly not looking at her. He was pretending to sternly survey the walls with a knowing, critical eye. He couldn't look at her, she thought, because he didn't want her to read in his eyes how much he enjoyed taking charge and saving her like this. He looked, as he scowled quizzically at the wall behind the loo, and at the ceiling, and then back at the wall again, like a boy pretending to be grown-up.

"Oh, thank you! Because I've got Diana and stuff…"

He nodded, still not looking at her. But, thinking of Diana now, she became aware of the more immediate social impact of this new problem. This bathroom was the one designated for her room and Diana's.

"It's embarrassing; it's such an awful smell," Cecily said. "I mean, with Diana here." To be honest, she was already uncertain what Diana would make of the bathrooms, with their rusty taps that produced only a choked little trickle of water that was sometimes weakly tea-coloured before it ran clear, and their lack of showers. Both bathrooms were freezing cold, maybe because the flaky old windowpanes were shaky in their frames nowadays. And the basins were so old that there were permanent brown stains where for decades the water had trickled down towards the plughole. Personally, Cecily loved these bathrooms. There was a magic in their coldness, their austere whiteness, and that iron tang in the air. The chipped white tiles; the long, long, brassy flush chains with their polished wooden handles; the childhood smell of old-fashioned camphor soap that still seemed to linger, long after her grandparents' great, waxy, cream-coloured bars of it had been replaced by liquid soap in plastic pump dispensers. But Diana might not feel that magic. She might notice instead the stains, the chips, the lack of fluffy bathmats, the dysfunctionally low water pressure, the fact that you needed all your strength to yank the stiff taps on. And, of course, the absence of a mixer tap: only a choice, when you washed your hands, between scalding hot and icy cold. And now, on top of all that, this insidiously evil smell. "Maybe we'd better ask Diana if she can share the other one with Victoria," she said.

"Well, yeah," Florian said, and then, as an afterthought, "And we'd better make sure that that bathroom's actually okay."

*

The other bathroom did seem okay, so Cecily went back to the guest room to tell Diana to use the one next to Victoria's room instead of the one on the landing. But Diana wasn't there; she must have gone to see the girls, or maybe to have a look round the house.

Cecily was about to leave Diana's room when she noticed that one creaky oak door of the huge, ancient, three-part wardrobe had fallen open. It did that quite easily, as it had dropped on its hinges over the years. She went to shut it; that section of the wardrobe was too crammed full of stuff for guests to use anyway. But as she put her shoulder to the heavy door, so that she could lift and close it at the same time, something caught her eye. Behind the cardboard box that contained her and Victoria's childhood dressing-up clothes, she spied a gleam: cream and yellow, and a glimmer of turquoise, that was uncannily familiar. She pulled the dressing-up box forward, to see better what was behind it. And there they were! At the back of the wardrobe, each wrapped lumpishly in an old woollen blanket from the laundry cupboard; wrapped so copiously, in fact, that the only reason she could make them out at all was that one blanket had slipped down to reveal a smooth china lip and a glimpse of a cool, shapely shoulder. Her mother's Italian vases!

In the 1960s their youthful mother had brought the vases back with her from travelling around Tuscany. She'd carted them all the way back to England in her car, and they'd been here ever since, which was close to half a century now. Her mother had been dead just over two years, now; the only person who could have put the vases here was Victoria. She must have wrapped them up and stuffed them in here the last time she was here. But why?

Once, Cecily remembered, Victoria had pushed her down the steps from the embankment to the beach. She couldn't remember why. In her memory, Victoria had simply shoved her, quite suddenly and for no reason, so that she careered and fell, crashing onto her knees on the flinty white pebble of Dover Beach.

Now she stood in front of the wardrobe unable to fathom quite what finding the vases there could mean, or even the nature of her own reaction. She was aware only of a turbulence inside her.

Then Julia's voice called insistently from downstairs, "Mummy? Mummy? Mummy!"

Cecily went down to see what was the matter.

"What time are Aunt Victoria and Zac coming?" Julia asked her as soon as she went into the sitting room. They were in there, the two girls, each sitting on one of the old bergère armcairs to either side of the fireplace. They looked so alert, so expectant, that they made Cecily think of a pair of bright-eyed little animals.

"Any time now, I should think!" she replied. Her stomach contracted slightly at the thought of her sister's imminent arrival. But that was absurd, she told herself. She was in her mid-forties now, for goodness' sake. It would be fine.

Hearing this, the girls looked at each other and gasped dramatically.

"Let's put them in the books!" Julia suggested to Olivia.

"What? Why? What are you planning?" Cecily asked them.

"We've got to hide our midnight feast before Zac comes!" Julia exclaimed, with camped-up drama. The two of them were already getting up, giggling at the excitement and the urgency.

"But don't you want to share it with him?" Cecily protested.

"*Share it* with *him*?" Julia repeated, outraged. "No, he's horrible!"

"But you can't just leave him out!"

"Mummy, you don't know what he's like! Last time he had a friend here, and I didn't have anyone, they had a whole pack of Celebrations and they didn't give me any!" Julia protested. "Apart from the Bountys, that no one likes!"

Cecily decided to leave the matter till later. Perhaps, she thought, when Zac actually arrived, the girls would change their minds. Because, despite certain antipathies, it seemed to her that there were still times when Zac and Julia got on very well.

She went into the kitchen to unpack the box of food they'd brought from home and to see what they could have for lunch, and when she came back into the sitting room she found that the girls had made a camp between side of the sofa and the bookshelf that lined one wall, and hung a sheet over it for privacy.

"Mummy?" came Julia's voice from inside the den. "Is that your legs?"

Taking this as an invitation, Cecily bent down and crawled over to the entrance to the den. Inside the girls were sitting on a nest of pillows and duvets, and between them they had a pile of dusty old books from the shelf.

"What are you doing?" Cecily asked curiously.

"We're hiding our sweets in the books!" Julia announced, her tone a mix of triumph and resentment.

"We're hiding our strawberry laces in the books, where he'll just never find them!" Olivia elaborated gleefully. Even though she'd never met Zac, she seemed to have already joined in – with gusto – on Julia's adversarial attitude.

Julia lugged one of the old books onto her lap. "You have to read the first line on whatever page you open," she explained to her mother, "and then you hide the strawberry lace inside." She looked back at the cover. "*Henry VI, Part Two*," she said, and then let the book fall theatrically open.

"Read it!" Olivia commanded.

Julia peered down at the tiny print. "'Ignorance is the curse of God; knowledge is the wing wherewith we fly to heaven…'" she read,[1] and then turned to Olivia, saying bossily, "Come on! Your turn!"

Olivia was looking at the picture on the front of the book in her hands. "Look – it's some woman being burnt on a fire!" She marvelled briefly, and then read the title: "*Foxe's Book of…*" Frowning, she leaned forward to try to make out the last word, but then shrugged, announced breezily, "Something!", and opened up the book instead. Running her finger along the page, she read, in tones of bafflement, "'I am persuaded that I am in the right opinion, and I see no cause to recant; for all the filthiness and idolatry lies in the Church of Rome.'[2] I have no idea what that means!" she announced merrily, before inserting a strawberry lace and banging the book down onto the pile.

"Oh no, there's Zac!" Julia whispered, peering out through the canopy of their little den.

Cecily turned to follow her gaze, and saw, through the front window, that Zac was indeed coming along the front path. She hadn't heard Victoria's car approach. With a hurried flurry of whispers, the two girls dived out of their den, dropping the flap behind them to hide the books. And seconds later, here was Zac coming through the hall and, seeing them all in there, straight into the sitting room.

Cecily, now somehow complicit in the girls' secrecy, hurried forward to greet him, "Hello, Zac! How are you?"

He grinned, taking in first her and then the girls, and hovered on the threshold, his eye flicking from her to the girls and back again, before coming on towards them. His walk, Cecily noticed, had acquired a self-conscious lilt; he had his hands in his pockets. He was thirteen now, and his upper lip was faintly shadowed with facial hair. Without taking his hands out of his pockets, he bowed slightly. "Hello, Auntie."

It made her sad, that bow. It seemed to come from a world she didn't want anything to do with.

Julia and Olivia, Cecily noted, were watching him from where they now sat, on the sitting-room floor.

Zac must have noted this too, because he flicked his hair, twitched his shoulders and said, in an affectation of insouciance, "Hi, girls!"

Julia recoiled, wrinkling her nose in distaste. "'Hi, girls? Hi, girls?'" she mocked. "I actually have a name. I'm your cousin, remember?"

Zac just grinned. Her scorn seemed to hearten, rather than unsettle him, which was Zac all over. He never took offence; he was supremely thick-skinned. Indeed, he seemed to positively thrive on criticism. It was an oddly attractive quality. "Yeah, but I don't know your friend's name," he said, grinning even more, as if this comment had won him a point.

"Well, here's an idea: you could *ask*…"

"I'm sorry!" Zac said extravagantly, and, turning to Olivia, held out his hand with a show of farcical deference. "I'm Zac. How do you do?"

Olivia, Cecily noticed, blushed.

Julia noticed too and was quite evidently annoyed. "She's Olivia," she snapped, "And stop showing off."

Zac beamed and chuckled, bashful, but as if being chastised like this was somehow pleasurable. "Hello, Olivia," he said. And then, still addressing Olivia, and lowering his voice, as if intimately, "And I'm really not showing off, by the way." He ran his hand through his hair again.

At this point, Diana came in.

"Ah! Diana, this is my nephew, Zac," Cecily said.

Once again Zac performed his languid, hands-in-pockets bow, which, Cecily now suspected, was the latest thing at his school. He then pulled out one hand and proffered it to Diana, smiling. "How do you do?"

Diana opened her mouth, and then she actually giggled – literally *giggled* – as she shook his hand. Though a grown woman, she seemed, Cecily marvelled, almost as bowled over as her eleven-year-old daughter. "What a little gentleman!" she remarked, admiringly, to Cecily.

"Yes," said Cecily, and rolled her eyes.

Zac smirked, and, encouraged by this, Diana nudged Cecily, chiding teasingly, "What's wrong, Cecily? Don't you like good manners?"

"I do like good *manners*! I just..." Cecily protested.

"It's just *me* she doesn't like!" Zac put in joyfully.

"Zac, you know that's not true!" Her indignation sent Zac off into delighted giggles.

In fact, she had always been fond of Zac. When he was three, they'd sat together on the terrace here, watching ants. It was only later, when he'd started school, that he'd learnt to squash them. Now, having progressed to a minor boarding school, he was – in Cecily's opinion – going rapidly downhill, which pained her.

"Oh, and by the way, Auntie," he followed up, "did you hear? Boris says we're going to be out of the EU by the end of October."

He'd recently taken to winding Cecily up. But because of Diana, she sidestepped this, saying, "Are you hungry? Where's your mum? We were just about to make lunch."

Victoria came in then, as if on cue. She was wearing designer wellies, and her hair was blow-dried, like an American's. She looked around at all of them, exclaiming, "Oh, my goodness! You're here already!"

Immediately, Cecily felt wrong-footed. "Well, yeah!" she said, trying not to sound defensive. "Why?"

"Nothing," Victoria said. "It's lovely to see you. Just… I didn't expect you until tomorrow!"

Florian came in then, to greet Victoria.

"I didn't expect you until *tomorrow*!" she said again, kissing him on each cheek.

Florian looked at Cecily. They'd definitely said they were arriving today.

"I was going to make up the beds for you and *everything*!" Victoria continued.

"Were you?" Florian said. He looked so surprised that Cecily almost laughed. When had Victoria ever, *ever* made up the beds for them?

"Hi, I'm Cecily's sister," Victoria went on, turning to Diana, all smiles, holding out her hand.

"Oh… and I'm Diana," Diana said hurriedly. "It's a very nice house!"

"Thank you!" sparkled Victoria. "And I'm guessing that this beautiful girl is your daughter?" She leaned in towards Diana with her smiles and her poise and her heavenly perfume, and gestured in the direction of Olivia and Julia, who were standing rather defensively in front of their camp. "What beautiful auburn hair!" she gushed. "And it's so long! When I was a child, I always wanted a sheet of cascading, long, auburn hair like that!" Her gaze flicked admiringly from Olivia to Diana, and back again, "Mine was just blonde…"

Olivia and Julia squirmed and shifted their feet. But Diana, Cecily noted glumly, looked charmed to bits.

"Oh, that's such a lovely thing to say!" she exclaimed.

Cecily experienced a bubbling, and then a hot upwards rush of anger. Poor Olivia, having to stand there and be talked about! And poor Julia: no one was saying how beautiful *her* hair was. This was exactly the difference between Cecily and Victoria! A few months ago, Cecily had made a conscious resolution to refrain from commenting on the looks of young girls she met. Women should realise that doing that all the time just reinforced the patriarchal message that looks were the most important thing about them. But of course, Victoria would have no time for challenging the rigged structures of society: she was far too busy working out how to climb them.

But even before she'd fully finished thinking this

thought, Cecily knew that that wasn't *really* why she was angry. It was just a justification she had come up with. Mainly, she was angry that Victoria still had the power to blow up her world; that within minutes of being with her older sister, she was already overcome by a childish sense of helplessness, of things being out of control, of being *not fair*.

"Do you know," she said, "I think I've left my phone in the car."

Outside, she made herself take a few deep breaths and contemplate two seagulls that were circling above the fields. Perhaps it was the place that made her feel like this, because here they were, at the corner of their grandmother's house, where she and Victoria had, on long-ago afternoons, played hide-and-seek, and horses, and being 'old-fashioned girls'. There, at the back corner of the lawn, was the rampant ilex oak they used to climb, and then the field where they used to go to see real horses. All around the terrace, the lavender bushes hummed with bees just as they had when Cecily was a child, and the feeling she was experiencing now was just as if she were eight once more. Eight years old and fuming with impotence, while her savvier older sister ran rings around her.

Once, Victoria had taught her how to hang upside down. It was on the lawn, here in Dover, where they'd had a climbing frame. A trapeze was suspended from its highest point, across the middle, and Victoria, who was good at gymnastics, used to hook her knees over it and hang upside down. It looked so clever, so sophisticated, that Cecily wanted to do it too. And then one day, when Cecily had her best friend Lizzie staying, Victoria agreed to teach them how to do it. She helped Cecily hoist herself onto the trapeze, and then supported her as she let go with her hands until she was hanging down. Cecily hung there for a bit, looking at the strange upside-down garden with its trees rustling against the sky, and feeling the increasing pressure of her blood tingling in her head. After a while, the pressure became too much.

"I want to get up now," she announced.

But there was no answer.

Frantically she twisted her pounding, upside-down head from side to side, trying to locate her sister. "Victoria? Lizzie?"

But Victoria wasn't there, and neither was Lizzie. Victoria must have persuaded her to run away and leave Cecily hanging. And the only way that Cecily could find to get down was to fall. She'd had to fall off on purpose and had landed so heavily on her stomach that for a moment she'd felt like she would never breathe again.

Why, Cecily asked herself now, had she come to stay when Victoria would be here too? And why, oh why had she brought Diana? She knew why, of course. She hadn't seen Victoria for months, and, back at home in London, she'd had this sentimental idea that, now their mother was gone, they could finally put all the sparks and fury behind them. And she'd imagined that Diana would be a sort of chaperone; a security against their sisterly rivalries getting out of hand. That was what she had been thinking. But already – and Victoria and Zac had only just walked into the house – she couldn't fathom how she could have been

31

so over-confident as to put herself into a situation like this. How could she have completely forgotten, in just a few months, what Victoria was really like?

*

"It's such an incredible house! It's so… oh, it's like Downton Abbey! It's like it's been here for a hundred years…" Diana was gushing when Cecily went back in.

And Victoria, flattering Diana in turn, replied, "Wow! You're *good*! It *is* just over a hundred years since it was built, in fact!"

"Oh, and it's been in your family since then?" murmured Diana.

"My great-grandfather commissioned this house himself, actually," Victoria said.

She was just awful, thought Cecily. She herself could never have boasted about all of this family stuff the minute she and Diana stepped into the house!

But Diana seemed enthralled. "*Did* he?" she cooed.

"Yes, it was built it in, like, 1908," Victoria was saying as Cecily went to join them.

"1903!" Cecily found herself correcting. She hadn't meant to, but there it was. And it sounded inappropriately belligerent.

Victoria let what Cecily had said hang there in a surprised silence. And, quite suddenly, Cecily felt like a gauche, aggressive, unpleasant person. How Victoria did it, she didn't know, but in front of other people that was the way Victoria always contrived to make her feel.

Victoria gave a delicate little laugh, saying, with arch, performative casualness, "Oh, was it 1903?"

"I think so, but maybe I'm wrong," Cecily said quickly, appeasingly. Actually, she knew she was right. But she pretended to allow that she could be mistaken, just because she suddenly needed to convince Diana that she wasn't what Victoria made her feel like: an angry, frustrated person who corrected people unpleasantly. She was tentative, thoughtful, considerate – that was how she had always felt with Diana, and how she wanted to carry on feeling. That was probably one of the reasons why she liked Diana's company so much.

Victoria smiled. "Well, whatever the exact date was," another little laugh; the gracious laugh of those who are unfairly attacked but take the high road, "my great-grandfather had it built and then left it to his children. But then later, my – *our*," and with this correction she reached out with a hand to demonstrate how she was generously including Cecily, "our grandfather bought out his siblings and then came with our grandmother to live here when he rescued her from Nazi Germany."

Their grandfather had *not* 'rescued' their grandmother from Nazi Germany. It was typical of Victoria to change the story to make it sound more sensational. Their grandfather had met their grandmother here in Dover, where he had had some minor role in organising the reception of refugees when she'd arrived. Cecily didn't correct Victoria this time, but she did wonder whether Diana had noticed the difference between her own account of her grandparents' meeting, and Victoria's.

"She was Jewish," Victoria added.

Partly Jewish, Cecily mentally corrected. Their grandmother had been partly Jewish by blood, though most of her family were practising Protestants by the 1930s.

"Wow!" said Diana. And then, looking uncertainly from one sister to the other, "It's a really amazing house."

"That's our grandad, actually," Cecily said, gesturing towards a photo on the mantelpiece. It pictured him in his youth, with his hair scrolled sculpturally into a side parting; wearing those very, very wide, gathered trousers that men wore in the late 1930s; and standing next to his father on a hillside, with one hand in his pocket and pointing at something or other with his pipe. *And smiling, for once*, Cecily thought. From what she remembered, he'd hardly ever smiled.

"Who's the other man?" Diana asked.

"Our great-grandad," Cecily said. She knew very little about what he was like, except one thing her mother had told her, which was that he would take an ice-cold bath every single morning, after performing a hundred press-ups. It was not the thought of the cold bath that had impressed this on her memory, so much as her mother's tone as she'd reported it. "A hundred press-ups and a cold bath *every morning*!" she would say, and Cecily had understood from the ring of pride in her voice that this was a practice that should inspire reverence, although she was never told precisely why.

In the little silence that followed, Victoria reached for the handle of the suitcase she had wheeled into the room.

"Well, I'll just take this upstairs," she said, "and then maybe we can see about lunch."

*

"I'm going to drive down to Dover Priory after this," said Victoria, putting down her fork after lunch in the dining room looking out over the terrace, and lifting up the glass jug.

The dining room shared, with the kitchen, the rear ground floor of the house. It had one set of double doors leading into the kitchen, another set leading into the sitting room, and, on its third wall, a pair of old French windows looked out onto the terrace and the back garden and then the field. It had hardly changed, this dining room, since their grandparents' time. There were still the burgundy spoon-backed chairs and the oval mahogany table. There was the Jacobean oak drinks cabinet, full of glasses with obsolete designations: thick-bottomed whisky tumblers, brandy bells, champagne saucers, snapdragon liquor flutes on long stems, small etched glasses for sherry, and tiny dolls'-house ones for port.

When they were children, Cecily and Victoria used to sneak out those curvy little sherry glasses with their delicate engravings of grapes and vine leaves, fill them with tonic water, lemon and sugar, and sip them out on the terrace. They'd pretend – ironic, giggling – to be grown-up mothers, sipping delicately with stuck-out pinkies and talking about their imaginary children.

On top of the cabinet stood a time-old collection of

spirits: cut-glass decanters with little labels on silver chains around their necks. The sunshine streaming in through the top pane of the French windows split and shattered in the prisms of the cut glass, casting itself in a ricochet of rainbow rectangles and rhombuses against the whitewashed wall.

As a child, over long Sunday lunches with her grandparents, Cecily had watched those rainbows come and go on the wall when the trees outside dipped and swayed in the sea wind, blocking and unblocking the light from the sun. They'd had to sit up straight during those Sunday lunches. But they were lucky, according to their mother, in that they were at least allowed to sit on chairs. When she was small, she'd had to sit on a barrel to improve her posture... or was it her character? Chairs, Cecily's grandfather had believed back then, encouraged both round backs and indolence in children. They'd had to eat everything on their plate during Sunday lunches with their grandparents. Victoria used to surreptitiously stuff her pockets with Brussels sprouts, which neither girl could stand, and tip them out into the loo in the break between the main course and pudding.

But now Victoria lifted the glass jug. It was a beautiful, full-figured jug – the glass deliberately crazed all over – that Cecily had given to their mother several years ago. Victoria lifted it to pour herself a glass of water, but at the last moment stopped and peered more carefully into the jug. She winced. "You know what," she said, standing up, "this jug is really smeary. Didn't you notice when you put it out, Cecily? I think I'd better wash it."

There was a slightly awkward silence as Victoria

squeezed past Florian's chair and went into the kitchen to wash the jug.

"Lovely day!" Diana remarked, looking up and out across the terrace to the garden, as if she had only just noticed the hot blue sky and the tall, slim aspen trees glittering in the sunshine.

"Anyway," Victoria said when she came back, "I'm going to drive down to Dover Priory."

"What for?" asked Zac.

"Dover Priory?" Diana asked. "What's that?"

"To get Dad from the station!" Victoria told Zac, and then turned to Diana. "There's not much left of the priory now, but the station takes its name from what used to be a huge medieval monastery. The remains are part of Dover College these days."

"It was all destroyed by Henry VIII when he *dissolved* the monasteries," Zac put in. He emphasised the word 'dissolved', articulating each sound slowly and mockingly, then looked around the room to see how this had been received. When no one much reacted, he said it again – "Dissolved. Dissolved... he *dissolved* the monasteries" – again pronouncing each syllable with a comically exaggerated elocution, revelling in the absurdity of the word, while his gaze travelled from person to person around the table with irrepressible delight. Bumptious as he was, thought Cecily, with that public-schoolboy confidence, his joie de vivre was still somehow disarming.

"*Dissolved* them?" Olivia responded as if on cue, wrinkling her brow in theatrical bafflement. "How can you *dissolve* a monastery? Isn't that where monks live?"

They all laughed then, except for Julia, who eyed Olivia suspiciously, as if she knew what she was up to.

"It's just a word they use, darling. It means he closed them all," Diana explained, although, even as she spoke, she turned hurriedly to the other adults for confirmation. "At least, I think it does? That was Henry VIII, right? That closed all the monasteries?"

"All those evil monasteries, what took our Peter's pence and gave it the Pope!" Zac continued, carried away now, in an excruciating cockney accent intended to suggest a belligerent John Bull proletarian.

Mortified, Cecily glanced at Diana. Had she noticed that Zac's attempted accent was a mockery of her own? Diana looked pink, but she was laughing. Cecily looked at Victoria to see if she had noticed her son's oafishness, but Victoria was not listening; she had begun reaching across the table and collecting plates.

Cecily had an un-auntly urge to squash Zac. "That's classic anti-Catholic propaganda you're coming out with, you know," she told him. "We've been brainwashed with it ever since the Tudor times."

"Propaganda?" Zac laughed. "They didn't have propaganda in Tudor times, Auntie! They didn't even have televisions."

Florian raised his eyebrows, "Goebbels didn't have televisions either. But did he need them?"

Cecily gained an unworthy satisfaction, seeing – from Zac's face – that he didn't know who Goebbels was. "The Tudors had preachers and they had pamphlets and they had secret police. It was all they needed to bring about a political and cultural transformation," she said loftily. She actually *wanted* him to feel out of his depth.

"Pamphlets?" Zac repeated, as if this word – like 'dissolution' – amused him. And then he turned quickly to say to Olivia, tongue in cheek, "My aunt is big on history." To Cecily he continued, with exaggerated amazement, "*Pamphlets*? Do you mean *actual* pamphlets? Like the little leaflets you get through the door?"

"Well, kind of. But—"

"What?" Zac hooted, "That was what they had instead of television?"

"The printing press had just been invented, and it was a whole media revolution; a bit like the internet today. If you had wealth, you could use it to influence people through pamphlets, just as now you can pay to influence people through electronic media."

"Huh!" said Zac. Sensing that he had in some way lost the upper hand in this conversation, he was also losing interest.

Still, Cecily continued. "Henry VIII disseminated propaganda to justify what he wanted to do," she said, "which was to transfer all the power, wealth and authority of the Catholic Church to himself. He pillaged the monasteries, which may have fostered parasitic, power-hungry, venal prelates, but also functioned as hospitals, hostels and soup kitchens, and as such were pretty much all we had in terms of social security. Well, apart from maybe guild associations, I suppose, and…" She stopped, realising that she was going off the point. She didn't even know quite what her point was; nor why it seemed so important to lecture Zac like this.

But it did. "He seized them," she went on, even though Zac was not actually listening; he was focused on arranging his face into a mock-angelic, mock-attentive expression so as to rile his aunt and entertain Olivia, "and all their money, land and possessions, and distributed them as patronage to his cronies. And he turned the monks and nuns who used to run them out on the street. And the thought paradigm that the propaganda justifying this brought about – the notion that Catholic Christendom is so corrupt and evil that we virtuous English Protestants must be free of its shackles – has been with us basically ever since."

Zac eyed her as she said this and then, realising that she had stopped talking, asked, "What? He did all that?"

"Yep," said Cecily. "It was a cultural revolution."

There was a pause while Zac arranged his face in showy appreciation. "Cool!" he said.

He was only thirteen, Cecily reminded herself. And she could half-remember a magical state between childhood and adulthood, where the world of grown-ups had seemed just another exciting game; where to be cynical seemed more sophisticated and more honest than the alternative. What were games for, after all, if not for winning?

Victoria came back in from the kitchen to get the pasta dish, and Diana hurriedly got up and began to help her clear the rest of the table. But even though she might, long ago, have partly shared it, right now Cecily had no patience with Zac's childish brutality. Not when this attitude was no longer confined to silly schoolboys but had become the guiding mentality of the adults who ran the country. This puerile social Darwinism seemed to be the creed of those driving Brexit. She was reminded of that quote from Marc Maron that someone she worked with had told her about:

> *If you can't afford the good food or if you can't afford health care or if you don't have a job or if your car is dangerous because you can't get it fixed and you DIE, you just lost the game – bzzzzz – thanks for playing extreme capitalism.*[3]

She just couldn't let this boy, her nephew, go unedified. "All the poor and homeless who had depended on the charity of the priory monks had nowhere to go," she said, fixing him with a stern gaze, at which he sniggered and then – mock-contrite – raised a hand to cover his mouth.

Standing in the kitchen doorway, Victoria looked at her watch. "Sorry to interrupt the history lesson, but I need to go or I'll miss the train," she said. "Does anyone need anything from the supermarket?"

*

Something thumped against the underbelly of the car as Victoria swung out of the driveway onto the coastal road. She stopped and got out, bending down and peering underneath to see what could have happened. But she couldn't identify anything untoward. Perhaps it was just a loose stone?

She climbed back in and drove on. This very expensive Land Rover was meant to be able to sail serenely over the bumpy limestone roads which plunged – even now, in August – into puddles in places. But as she drove, she could feel the lurch and jolt of each and every rut. It was hardly any more comfortable than sitting in Cecily's decrepit old Volvo. What was the point in paying out a fortune for an all-terrain car, she thought irritably, if you still had to swerve to avoid potholes?

Irritated, she checked her watch, and then became more irritated still: she only had about an hour before Dan's train was due in, so she'd have to be quite quick in the supermarket. She'd probably have got away at least ten minutes earlier if Cecily hadn't started going on like that. No doubt it was good for Zac to talk to her about these things, but really! The way she got so worked up about stuff; even a bloody Reformation that happened five hundred years ago!

Glancing down at the steering wheel, she noticed that her nail polish was becoming chipped. She needed to get them done properly, but somehow there hadn't been time this week. So she'd done them herself, and now, already, there was a chip, which added to her rising irritation. It was just this feeling of being blocked, constrained, frustrated. This knot of anger in her stomach; this feeling of not being able to be the person she normally felt herself to be. She knew this sensation; she always experienced it when she was around Cecily. A horrible feeling of being a teenager again, always made to feel that she was failing some test, that there was something wrong with her, that she should be different.

That Diana. In her current grumpy mood, it also irritated Victoria that Cecily had brought her here. It was actually quite hard to believe that Diana and Cecily could be good friends, as they claimed, when they were so obviously completely different. There was Diana, clearly – for lack of a better expression – uneducated. You could tell from the way she talked. She might be a PA, perhaps, or an estate agent, but she probably had no degree. And there was Cecily, who had gone to bloody Oxford, for goodness' sake. She had slipped down the socio-economic scale since then, it was true: their mother's golden child had not fulfilled her early promise and had ended up freelancing on the edge of the precariat, editing historical documentaries. But if not highly successful, there was no denying that Cecily was highly educated. She had a PhD, after all. So what someone with that background had in common with Diana, Victoria couldn't quite imagine. Diana was some pet project of Cecily's, she imagined. Knowing Cecily, it was precisely because Diana was lower class and barely educated that Cecily wanted to be friends with her. Just like that time, a couple of years ago, when she'd made friends with the Indian woman who'd been brought over from Goa twenty years ago as an arranged wife for some aspiring doctor, and had then talked about her all the time. Predictably, she'd got the woman to teach her how to make curries.

As Victoria approached the traffic lights at the crossroads in town, they turned red. And as she slowed to a stop she saw a runner, aged perhaps twenty-five, jogging up to the same lights. He was young, muscular and panting with luxuriant, dark wavy hair, sweating at his temples. Approaching the lights, he was tactically eyeing the slowing cars, and then looking over his shoulder to check whether any cars on the road perpendicular were planning to turn right into this road. Seeing none, he pushed forward with a glorious spurt of strength, and crossed in front of her car. Sitting at the wheel, Victoria experienced a thrill that dissipated into warm, tingling nostalgia. How sad that, now she was so very, very married, a vigorous, glowing young man like this, with such thick, glossy hair, would never again be a legitimate object of desire.

*

Dan's train drew in late, which was fortunate because Victoria arrived on the platform a little late herself and she didn't like to be caught out like that. Having been effectively overlooked in the family home for all of her childhood, she liked the feeling that nowadays, within her nuclear household, she was the central pin that held everything together. She was the centre of Dan's world and the centre of Zac's. She knew everything, anticipated everything, managed everything and almost never dropped a ball. It made her feel safe, appreciated, important.

She was on the platform when the train roared in, and she could see Dan walking steadily towards her, among the other commuters. He was looking tired, sweaty and untidy. His thinning hair looked particularly wispy in this perspiring heat. His shirt was also too tight: you could see the buttons straining over his gradually expanding stomach. Observing this, she experienced a twinge of discomfort: not quite – but almost – shame.

Funnily enough, it was only since she'd reached her

forties, and felt confident in herself, that she had begun to appreciate male beauty. It was only now, really, that handsome young men had begun to catch her eye, with their smooth, glowing skin and their taut muscles, and that bounce in their step. When she was younger those things had affected her less. It wasn't that she hadn't seen them; more that she had taken beauty more for granted back then. Youthful beauty hadn't seemed miraculous in the way it did now. And anyway, at that time she had been looking for something else. She had been basically lost ever since she hit puberty; and then there was that awful, druggy period after she left university, when she split up with Matthew. When she met Dan, she had been looking for safety, most of all.

Dan spotted her when he was about eight metres away, and raised his suitcase in one hand, waving eagerly with the other to signify that he had seen her. This, she noticed with a sinking of her stomach, had the effect of pulling up his shirt, so that it came untucked and his paunch popped out. It was lucky he earned such a lot, she thought; otherwise she didn't know if she'd be able to really stick it. That was a joke. It really was. Although she'd thought it, she really, really didn't mean it. It just happened to her sometimes: wicked thoughts flitting through her brain; thoughts she didn't really think were hers and that didn't in any way represent her real life hopes and desires in all their fullness. She had no idea where they came from. It was almost as if her mind was – even now, at the age of forty-nine – permanently experimenting with being somebody else.

When Dan reached her, he put his case down on the ground and wiped his forehead with a tissue. Taking her elbow, he kissed her on the cheek and then stepped back and raised his eyebrows, saying, "Have you heard the news?"

For a moment, Victoria imagined that there must have been some terrible violent occurrence: a terrorist attack in London was her first thought. "No! What? What's happened?"

"No, no – nothing's happened. But the rumour is that they're going to ask the Queen to prorogue Parliament in the next few days."

She felt immediate relief, together with a disappointment that shocked her. It couldn't be, surely, that she would have actually *liked* there to be a terrorist attack? "Oh, that! Yes, we heard about that, vaguely. So it's true?"

Dan shrugged. "Apparently," he said. "That's what they're saying at work." And then, shaking his head, he picked up his case again and looked at Victoria expectantly. "Is the car…?"

"Yeah, yeah. It's just out here."

They made their way to the car.

"Ooh! Did you remember to get the basil?" Dan asked, noticing the shopping in the boot. "I wanted to do that chicken with pesto; maybe tomorrow?"

"Yes, yes, I remembered. I got all that. And I got the stuff to make the little tapas."

"Great!" Dan said, heaving himself into the front passenger seat, and Victoria started the engine.

They were climbing back up to the coastal road when Dan continued, "Apparently it was all planned – the prorogation, I mean. Earlier in the summer, with some of the key backers of the Tory Party."

"Oh, was it?"

"You know, as the only way to really get the Brexit deal Boris wants past Parliament. Or possibly it's no deal he wants. There's certainly a section of Brexit opinion that thinks there are opportunities in crashing out with no deal."

"God!" Victoria said, glancing in her rear-view mirror and indicating. She turned off the roundabout and started heading up towards the cliffs. "So it's going to happen? No deal?"

Dan shrugged, "Possibly; it's hard to tell what the plan is."

She grimaced. "I hope that won't affect us."

"Well… you know, we'd be alright." Dan shifted comfortably on his seat, "I guess some sectors would be affected, but not us, as such. The value of our house might fall… but from what I've heard, probably not even that. I've also heard the view that it's mostly Chinese and Russian money fuelling the high prices, anyway. And Saudis, and that."

"Luckily, there are the flats in London. The rental income from those should be pretty safe, in any case," Victoria said. She leaned forward and tapped the dashboard with her knuckle "Touch wood!" And then laughed. "Well, there's just no wood around here!"

"Touch plastic!" Dan said, and chuckled.

They were out on the coast road, the sea stretching out on the right below them, when Victoria added, "Yes, I imagine we'd be alright really, either way. Brexit, no deal – I don't see why any of it should adversely affect us. I mean, my job's secure; your job's secure, I should think. We'll both probably have more work, if anything. And we've got quite a lot of money invested."

Dan nodded. "And that's the thing – this is what I tell my clients: as long as you've got a sensible portfolio, then Brexit shouldn't really affect you."

They'd had this same conversation before, thought Victoria as the countryside slipped by. They'd had it many times, in fact: repeating again and again all the reasons they had not to worry. But still, they were worrying times: Donald Trump in America; the upheaval of Brexit. And so it was comforting – periodically, and especially when there was a change of event, to just go through the checklist once again, to try and feel sure that they really were going to be safely cushioned from whatever might transpire.

Neither of them spoke for a while, both lost in their thoughts as the car purred along. And then Dan chuckled and rubbed his hand across his face, turning to his wife. "Are Cecily and co. here yet?"

Victoria nodded, staring at the road ahead. "Yep. She's with some mum from Julia's school."

Dan opened his window and leaned one elbow on the window frame "Oh, okay! We might be able to play some poker. I was thinking Zac should learn."

The lights changed and Victoria swung the car round, heading up the hill. "Cecily has been laying into him about the Reformation," she said.

"About the *Reformation*?"

"Oh, I don't know. The Reformation or *something*. I wasn't really listening."

Dan laughed. "*The Reformation*?" he said again.

Victoria said, "I don't know why; he wasn't even interested!"

Dan shook his head, chuckling. And then, a few minutes later, as if he thought he'd left enough time to change the subject, he said tentatively, "But speaking of Cecily. You know – did you ask her about buying us out of our share? Or vice versa?"

She didn't answer. Just as he'd said that, they'd turned the corner and the sea had come into view, sparkling, before they turned again. Part of her felt bad that she'd ever suggested to Dan that Cecily might want to buy them out, or them to buy up her share of the house.

"Presumably she'd like to have the whole house? You said so yourself, right?" Dan pressed, mystified by her silence.

"Yeah, yeah. You'd think so," she said vaguely.

"Or we could buy her out?" Dan went on, rehearsing this conversation, which they'd also had at least once before. "It's just that one way or another it would be really nice to have somewhere that we could renovate in our own style. Whether we buy up this one, or sell it and buy something else for ourselves. I mean... have you raised the subject at all?"

The house was just visible at the end of the road now. There was the front gate, where Victoria and Cecily used to swing. And there was the cherry tree that Victoria used to shimmy up easily, but Cecily could never learn to climb. Their grandmother used to send Victoria up to pick the cherries, and Cecily would act as her assistant: passing her the basket and pulling branches nearer with the hook. It

49

was about the only time Victoria had felt more able, more appreciated, more valuable in her family's eyes than Cecily. And, feeling generous from her vantage point in the tree, she'd picked pairs of cherries for them both to hang over their ears, and handed them bountifully down to her grateful younger sister.

She felt her stomach lurch, and cut Dan off. "No, no; somehow there wasn't the chance. I'll ask her later."

Thankfully, he didn't persist after that. He just looked out of the window again and nodded, saying affably, if puzzled, "Okay, no hurry!"

*

"Shall we go for a walk?" Cecily said to Diana, after Victoria had left. She felt, suddenly, that she just couldn't be contained indoors. It was about the vases, she thought. Or perhaps it was about this prorogation. Whatever it was, there was a turbulence inside her that needed to lose itself in the turbulence of the wind, the yearning of the sea, the vast expanse of the sky.

Diana looked surprised. "Okay," she said. And then, "Where shall we go?"

"Maybe just down to the beach?"

"What… the *beach*? Like… a real beach?"

"Well… yes!"

"Oh my God!" Diana let her mouth drop open, yet again, demonstrating amazement. "Can you just walk down to the beach from here? That's incredible!"

Zac looked up from where he sat on the sitting-room

floor with the girls. He looked at first surprised, and then gratified by Diana's tone of wonder. He stood up and ambled over to where she and Cecily were sitting on the sofa. "The beach is just, like, ten minutes away," he said, with a casual, proprietorial wave of his hand towards the window.

"No way!" Diana marvelled, and Zac raised a single eyebrow. Another mannerism, thought Cecily, that he must have picked up at school.

It had never occurred to him before, Cecily suspected, that it was anything out of the ordinary that from this house you could just walk down to the beach. Among the wealthy children at his school, after all, who probably had great mansions in places like Capri and the French Riviera, a four-bedroom holiday house on the cliffs of Dover was hardly anything to boast about.

"That's amazing!" Diana said again, this time to Zac, who shrugged again.

"I guess so," he said, and shrugged yet again, nonchalantly, laughing slightly. "To be honest, I've never really thought about it."

*

Out on the cliffs, Cecily and Diana watched the children run on ahead through the wind. Down below, the sea shimmered, but only in parts. In these parts it seemed almost flat, with only little wrinkles, like an expanse of silver foil that had been used and then inexpertly smoothed out. In the smooth parts it sort of shimmered in the sunlight, wrinkling and twinkling with endless pleasure, as if the sun were tickling its sheer surface. And yet in other places, there was no shimmer and no twinkle: instead there were little steel-grey surges that came rolling up behind each other, edged with foam.

Surely, thought Cecily, even if they tried, the Queen would not let them get away with it?

Nearer land, down on the beach, you could see the waves coming in one by one, only to overreach themselves and collapse, sprawling, on the shore. They came one after the other, predictably, rhythmically; each spooling in a line of lace-white spume that unrolled down the beach from left to right, before vanishing as the next curl came up and superseded it, rolling out its own little spool. And then there was the sound of those bigger waves, breaking on the rocks further up; the majestic sound of oblivion. Roar and then whoosh, roar and then whoosh, for ever and ever, amen.

And in fact, when you were out here, looking out across the timeless sea, it hardly seemed to matter anyway. What did it matter if the vulture capitalists and their enablers in the media stripped us of our human rights, our social protections and our environmental standards? What did it matter if they cut us loose from our European allies and protectors, and handed us over as friendless, defenceless serfs to the neo-feudal tyrants of corporate America? It was just a blink in the eye of time, after all; the sea would still go on.

"I never knew you could actually walk on them!" Diana was saying.

Cecily turned to her. "Walk on what?"

"The White Cliffs of Dover! I've only ever seen them from the P&O ferry, you know; coming back from France, eating my chips. Good old P&O! I thought they'd be too dangerous to actually walk on!"

They stood for a while, facing out over the waves, letting the wind blow against their faces, lifting their hair.

"Oh, look! We're just like two Botticelli Venuses! Our hair blowing in the sea wind!" Cecily said, striking the counterpoint pose.

"What?" said Diana.

"You know – Venus on the shell, floating in from the sea, cherubs trumpeting above her, with her hair blowing in the wind..."

"Oh, yeah!" Diana struck the pose as well.

They wobbled in the wind, laughing, united, for a few seconds, in a soaring spirit, until they felt the joke break and spool and dissipate like one of those little waves below, so that they were just standing awkwardly in a silly pose, each again separate from the other.

Diana sighed. "I want to be young again!"

Cecily contemplated, for a moment, her youth. She could almost hear it in the distance, like a piece of music: pink clouds and golden trumpets of glory! But mostly, she remembered now, she had squandered it on self-doubt; all of that desperate questioning about what mattered and what people thought of you. "I *would* like to be young again," she agreed cautiously, "but only if I could go back knowing what I know now. Being young was hell, in many ways."

Diana thought about this and then agreed. "Yeah."

"And I worried about the stupidest things!" Cecily continued.

"So did I!" Diana re-joined.

They turned from the wind and walked on, over the springy, mossy grass, bald in patches where the chalk and flint showed through. This was one of the good things about growing older that no one ever told you about: this finally becoming more at home in your own skin. It was like those dreams in which you find a whole new, beautiful, spacious room, in your own house, that you had never known existed.

"I saw a TV programme before I came," Diana said, after a while, "about Dunkirk."

Cecily and Diana had never once spoken about the referendum. The only reason she knew how Diana had voted was because the subject had just happened to come up, a few days before the referendum. At that point, *before* the referendum there had been no bitterness. But from the very first day *after* the referendum, the country had begun to split. In the subsequent days, weeks, months and years, the chasm between 'Leavers' and 'Remainers' had only grown wider and wider, until now, three years later, it had become a gorge that seemed impossible to broach or even approach. And yet now, suddenly, Diana was mentioning Dunkirk. Dunkirk! A pile of stones shifted and subsided in the pit of Cecily's stomach. In this new, post-Brexit England, even the casual mention of the defeat of the British at Dunkirk in World War II was entering dangerous ground. Dunkirk had – that summer, with the help of a much-hyped new film on the subject – become a centrepiece of Brexiter propaganda.

"Really?" Cecily said, keeping her voice as light and casual as she could.

"Yes; apparently it was all planned here, in a military complex underneath these cliffs – the cliffs of Dover. There's a whole military complex practically under our feet," Diana went on.

"Yes," Cecily said. Of course, she knew this. Her family had owned the house in Dover for four generations, and before that, some of them had lived down in the town. Perhaps as a child she had found it vaguely exciting, the history of the underground military command centre here. But now that the Leave campaign had requisitioned the Second World War for their propaganda machine, she certainly no longer did. In fact, she thought, looking out to sea so as to avoid Diana's eye, if Diana launched now into chauvinistic nonsense about the defeat that was Dunkirk, she didn't know if she would be able to contain herself.

"It was just incredible, the way they planned the whole thing," Diana went on. "They got ships and boats of all sizes; people of all, you know, *levels* involved: even local fisherman joined in the effort. And apparently it was seen as a completely desperate idea that had almost no chance of working: to try and get ordinary people to save an entire army!" she gushed.

Cecily nodded in a way that she hoped looked not unsympathetic.

"And you know, Cecily, I just... it actually brought tears to my eyes," Diana said, turning to look directly at her. The wind worried at the wisps of hair about Diana's temples, and her large, brown, slightly bulbous eyes were indeed shimmering a little.

Cecily felt she could almost see in them a history: the scars of past hurts, but also little, leaping, fiery hopes. "Oh..." she said.

"I just… sorry…" Diana stopped and wiped her eyes, laughing. "Sorry…" She fumbled for a tissue. "It's just being here and looking out over where it all happened… you know!"

But Cecily didn't know. In fact, she wasn't even sure what Diana meant.

"I just… well, maybe you don't see it like this," Diana said, "but for me, this is what Brexit is all about."

And there it was, out of the bag. Brexit, Cecily wanted to tell her, was nothing to do with Dunkirk. Dunkirk had been a government-managed expedition by civilians to rescue a defeated army during a war. But Brexit, she wanted to grab Diana's shoulders and tell her, Brexit was something else. Brexit was a coup. It was the first step in a plan to dismantle the existing political and legal framework in the UK and replace its government with minions serving a plutocracy that reaped the gains of unrestrained capitalism. And when Cecily thought about the war, in fact, she didn't think about Dunkirk. She thought about Poland, which had been ravaged. And Hiroshima. And the vast American military power and Russian troop numbers that had actually won it. And also, she thought about Churchill, who had said, at the end of the war which had taken millions of lives, "There is a remedy which… would in a few years make all Europe… free and… happy… It is to recreate the European family, or as much of it as we can, and to provide it with a structure under which it can dwell in peace, in safety and in freedom. We must build a kind of United States of Europe."[4]

But she didn't say any of this. She was experiencing a sensation not that different from the feeling she used to get when she was nursing, after the milk came prickling in her breasts. There was that same lurching in her stomach; the feeling of plunging blood sugar, of thirst, of exhaustion. She felt quite helpless. The fact that the Brexiters had now managed to link Dunkirk with Brexit in Diana's mind just showed that Brexit had become, over the past three years, a monster so ephemeral, so labyrinthine and many-faced, that you just couldn't even see which side to stick your spear in.

Neither of them said anything. And as they stood there in silence, against the booming of the vast tons of water heaving and hurling themselves against the shore below, Cecily became gradually aware of a new movement; an up-churning of emotion. And she realised then, to her surprise, that what she really wanted, at this moment, was for Diana to continue talking. That she had never, in the three years since the referendum, had an opportunity like this to try to understand what Diana understood Brexit to mean. But also, there was a sense in which Brexit itself hardly mattered anyway, right now. What mattered was a grand, dawning emotion of which Cecily was acutely aware; an opening up between them. It was like that feeling she used to get as a child here in Dover, when her grandmother took them to church and people sang the hymns. She would get it, sometimes, then: a momentous, glorious sliding and transforming and opening up.

She said, encouragingly, "Really?"

"You know. Back then we were really a nation," Diana went on. "We looked after each other and we all knew where we came from."

She turned, hands in pockets, towards the sea, Cecily found herself thinking, *This feeling now, of opening up,* this *is what matters.*

And then Diana gestured out across the waves. "You know! Think of it: all those little boats, rescuing those defeated, stranded soldiers. They turned a defeat into a victory!" She turned to Cecily and smiled, embarrassed. "I didn't make that up myself, by the way. That's what they said at the end of the programme: that 'They turned a defeat at war into a victory for solidarity.'"

Cecily looked out over the sea as well, and briefly, riding on the wave of Diana's emotion, she could see them. She could imagine those little boats, and for a moment she could grasp it; she was absolutely sure she could grasp that emotion of Diana's. She had felt it herself before, on occasion. She had felt it, quite suddenly, when watching *Casablanca,* funnily enough. A homesickness for a world in which everyone belonged and everyone believed in doing their duty. A nostalgia for noble standards of the past that were now lost. But she wasn't sure that such a golden age had ever really existed, and she would certainly never – never in a million years – have expected it to materialise as a result of this billionaire-driven Brexit.

"Back then, after the war, when they set up the NHS, was when people really cared about each other," Diana was saying. "Do you know what I mean, Cecily? We've lost that."

Cecily didn't answer straightaway. And then she said, "It's a shame that it took the shared experience of a terrible war, plus the threat of a communist takeover, to force the ruling classes to share part of their wealth and security with the rest of the nation. But yes, the establishment of the welfare state was a great achievement."

Diana looked at her quizzically.

"The trouble is," Cecily continued, "that since Reagan and Thatcher came to power and the Soviet Union began to unravel, the moneyed classes have been clawing back everything that they were forced to share in those post-war years."

"Oh, yeah!" Diana said. "It's all gone downhill since then."

There was a funny little silence.

But the welfare state is not what the Brexiters believe in, Cecily wanted to say. *The welfare state is what they want to destroy. The England they want to take us back to is not the England of the visionary 1950s and '60s, with its public libraries and council housing and the NHS. It's the England of the Industrial Revolution, when the rich did what they liked and the poor did what they had to.* But she couldn't say that to Diana, of course. It was tantamount to saying that Diana had been fooled.

"Whereas now it's chaos! So many people here that you can't get an appointment at the doctor's. You can't move for the squeeze on the Tube!" Diana declared.

It was true, Cecily thought. But that was because, though the population had grown and we had taken in millions of immigrants, the government, despite taking more taxes from more and more immigrants, had not provided a corresponding increase in GP surgeries, schools, houses or infrastructure. In fact, rather than growing state provision, it had been shrinking it. "For years governments have been cutting instead of investing in infrastructure," she ventured.

But Diana was saying, "And… well, you know I've got nothing against foreigners…" She turned to Cecily again, her bulgy brown eyes still watery in the wind, seeking affirmation.

Cecily nodded demonstratively, because this much she actually *did* know. Their circle of friends was very mixed. Within their group of shared friends, in fact, were one Dutch woman, one Nigerian, and one who was half British, half Iranian. It was true that Diana had nothing against foreigners. At least, not wealthy, culturally assimilated foreigners…

"But… well, my sister-in-law says she was talking to a mum at her daughter's school. She's Romanian and she's got a son, and she's living in a council property. Do you know how many people are trying to get council properties? And I've nothing against this woman; I'm sure she's very nice. But surely ours have to come first…"

"But under EU law, everyone in the EU needs to be treated equally."

The sea wind pestered them, so that they turned away and began walking along the clifftop.

"Well, that's what I don't like," Diana said, after a while.

"But if you were a British mother in Romania, say, and you wanted to take your child to the doctor, how would you feel if they said they had to treat Romanians first?"

"Well, I…" Diana stopped, temporarily flummoxed. And then continued haltingly, "I… well, I wouldn't be in Romania in the first place…" She said it jokingly at first, as if she knew it was a silly, irrelevant comment. But then, it seemed to Cecily, she realised that actually, in saying this, she really had a point. And she repeated it more confidently, almost indignant. "I mean, I wouldn't be in Romania, would I? Why would I be? Romania is a poor country and England is a rich country. That's why they come here and we don't go there. That's the thing. It's not fair. The Poles and the Romanians, they're all coming here. You don't see loads of British flooding over there. So it's our doctors and nurses and our schools and buses and trains and council houses that are overwhelmed, and it's *us*, the *British* people, who are losing out." She shook her head, roused by her own rhetoric. "Do you see, Cecily? That's why I want us to be able to make our own laws. I want to have sovereignty. I don't want to be told what to do by the EU."

But we're lucky to have these Europeans, Cecily wanted to say. *We didn't have to pay for their education but we are the ones who are benefiting from it. And they pay taxes. Florian pays taxes, just the same as we do.* But she didn't want to get personal, so instead she said again, "I think what's happened is that the government has opened the doors to immigration, but hasn't provided the social infrastructure to support it."

But Diana was also talking. "And it's our culture. I just want our culture back…"

Olivia came chugging breathlessly back up the hill then, her gangly legs pushing and her heels digging hard into the limy soil as she forced her way against gravity. Julia was behind her, moving somehow more easily. And away down the hill, Cecily could see Zac waiting. He was picking up flint stones from the path and shimmying them through the air.

"What is it?" asked Diana, her attention immediately riveted on her daughter, who, they could see, was clutching something in her pumping right hand.

"I found this!" Olivia stopped, panting, pulling up her sleeve and opening her palm. "Mum, is it a fossil?"

Diana peered at it. "Ooh... I don't know!" she said doubtfully. "I'm not a specialist on fossils!" She turned expectantly to Cecily.

"Well, neither am I!" Cecily protested.

But Olivia was already turning her hopeful, open, pink palm towards her.

"Okay, let's see..." said Cecily, making an effort to be interested. But she felt her disappointment sweeping up like an adverse wind in her face. She had been so hopeful that Diana would finally lead her to that mysterious vantage point from which she would be able to see it all spread out before her: Diana's view. And now, here was Olivia taking them in a different direction. And it might have been her only chance... She gazed down at the stone in the childish palm, while, rather amazingly, they all waited for her verdict. "It does look like one of those flat, curly shell things..." she said eventually. "I can't remember what they're called!" Looking at their blank, disappointed faces, she grimaced apologetically. "Sorry, I know *nothing* about fossils! I just remember that in books when I was a child, fossils did look a bit like that. You know, like a curled-up centipede?"

Olivia closed her hand and turned back towards Julia, saying, consoling, confidential, as if making up for the uselessness of adults, "We can search it up when we get back."

And they both turned back down the path to rejoin Zac, clattering and skidding on the steep, scrambly path of chalk and flint. When they reached him, far down the slope, the three of them paused and seemed to confer, before turning back to look at the grown-ups, and yell in unison, "Come on! Run!"

Diana and Cecily laughed with surprise, looking at each other and then back at the three little figures away down the slope. They felt embarrassed, suddenly, that the years had made them staid.

"I can run!" announced Diana.

"So can I!" agreed Cecily.

They ran, giggling and stumbling a little. The path was very steep and very uneven, so they had to really concentrate, so as not to wrong-foot themselves and fall headlong. The children watched them from below, but then, suddenly realising that the adults would soon catch up with them, they began to run again themselves, so that, by the time all five reached the final steps down to the beach, they were all breathless and laughing. *An uninhibited moment! A snapshot of light-heartedness!* thought Cecily, jubilant. And she noted that the happy, buzzy warmth still united them – comfortably, loosely – as they made their way, in single file, down the steep steps cut into the chalk cliff side. And that thought hit her again: *Only* this *is what matters.*

"And here's the sea!" Diana cried, opening out her arms as they reached the bottom of the hill and found themselves on the edge of the beach. "Is it warm enough to swim?" she asked, turning to Cecily.

When Cecily and her family had come down here in the holidays when she and Victoria were children, the sea had always been freezing cold. And yet – though it was never really said – they'd known that, if they didn't rush enthusiastically into the water as soon as they arrived at the beach, even if it was only Easter, it would mean they had failed some kind of test. In fact, it occurred to Cecily now, looking out over the sea, her family had had a bit of a thing about cold water. It wasn't just her great-grandfather and his cold baths.

Victoria had begun, from quite an early age, to rebel against these ordeals. She would refuse to approach the surge, or even set foot on the beach sometimes. She would park herself on the embankment steps, as far from the sea as possible, and insist, in her whiniest voice, "I'm not going in. Why would I even want to? It's not fun – it's just freezing!" But although such mysterious tests of character were a burden to Cecily too, she never tried to stake herself against her mother. It wasn't that she was a mummy's girl, like Victoria said. It was something else. It was that, unlike Victoria, Cecily believed her mother knew something; that there must be something important – something her mother, and her grandparents before her, and probably their grandparents before them knew – about the moral core of the universe, something which could be mystically communed with through such challenges. And so, while Victoria sat on the steps at the end of the beach, scowling, Cecily would dance in the icy waves and screech with pretend delight, revelling in her mother's approval, even though she knew that, at the very same time, this behaviour won her Victoria's contempt.

On the embankment by the beach, they passed one of those head-in-the-hole cut-out boards sometimes set up at tourist sites, so that visitors can insert their heads and be photographed. Here at Dover, on one side of the steps were painted a mermaid and also St George with his dragon. On the other side were two fat Victorian bathers: a woman and a man dressed in bathing caps and comic stripy bathing pantaloons with lace frills at the edges.

"Oh, look at these! Let's take a picture!" Diana dug for her phone.

Cecily's parents, she remembered, had always rather disdained these cut-outs. She didn't know, she realised now, why. Subliminally, she supposed, she had always assumed that her mother's disapproval was part of that same cultural inheritance, that mystic creed that drove her grandfather to take cold baths and seat his children on barrels. Was her wariness of what she perceived as 'mass culture' a stance leading back generations to some puritanical ancestral wish to be 'saints'; to set themselves and their children apart from the world with its greed and materialism? Or was it just socio-economic snobbery?

"Come on, Cecily!" Diana called. She was laughing. She had already photographed all the children with St George and the dragon, and was now waving Cecily over. "We've got to do me and you!"

Cecily didn't want to be a puritan...or a snob. And anyway, why shouldn't people have fun with the wooden cut-outs? "Okay! I'm coming!" she announced.

They all tried posing as St George and the dragon and as Victorian bathers, and took turns snapping pictures.

"That was so fun!" Cecily said twice, as they made their way to the beach.

Diana looked at her a little oddly. "Really?"

"Yes!" Cecily declared vehemently, and then felt the need to teach her daughter. "Don't you think, Julia? Wasn't that fun?"

Julia looked at her a little oddly as well. "Well," she said, "it was *quite* fun. But it wasn't *that* fun…"

After that, they made their way across the embankment and down the steps, until they were standing on the tumbling pebbles, facing the deafening sea. Diana and Cecily sat down on the beach, but the children went on towards the hurling waves and then took their shoes off at the edge and stood there; spume swirling around their feet, their toes sinking into wet sand. The girls paddled in, with shrill, thrilled shrieks at the cold, while the wheeling seagulls above emitted shrieks as well. Zac hung back, teetering on the edge. Finally, he ran in after them, with a great roar, but at the shock of the icy cold his battle roar twisted into a high-pitched shriek, and he ran out again almost immediately. He did this a few times, while the girls stayed in the water up to their calves and hunted for pretty stones.

"Aww," said Diana, watching the children. Rummaging in her bag for her phone again, she got up and went after them to take some pictures.

Cecily stayed sitting on the beach, watching each wave passionately prostrate itself upon the pebbles, reaching its foamy fingers up and up if trying to find something to grip on to, only to be dragged back out to sea again. She ran her hands over the pebbles, gripping them and rumbling them, enjoying their clattering against each other and the touch of their thirsty smoothness. She lifted a handful and let them fall between her fingers, clacking back down on top of each other. Curious how soothing it was to rake and clatter the stones like this. And then, tiring of this, she lay back and closed her eyes, listening to the lamenting sea.

St George was originally from what is now Turkey, she seemed to remember. And, if she weren't mistaken, he had spent much of his life as a Roman soldier in the third or fourth century or something. She opened her eyes, and with one hand began idly rumbling the pebbles again. Strange, how the English came to claim him as their own national dragon slayer, when England was a country he could never have even heard of; back then, it did not exist. But obviously his significance here and now was purely symbolic: a name and a face for humanity's eternal dream of Justice. St George, Jesus, Superman: the names and faces were as many as there were cultures. And always, even if a hero started off by representing Justice, he ended up representing more just 'Us'. And on the other side, the dragon. It was always the same story. The unjust, the Devil, the opponents, the enemy. That was Them. The eternal Us and Them. It was as if the human mind came with a Manichaean opposition already programmed in; as if we were born with two head-in-the-hole cut-outs in our minds: one for heroes and one for villains – the Us and the Them – so that we were simply incapable of seeing the world except in this binary way. We could put different faces inside the cut-outs, depending on where and when we were born. The baddie's face might be the Saracen Turk, the Infidel, the Jews or the Catholics; it might be the West, or communists, or the European Union. It was always changing depending on the where and when. And yet in the human mind the story was always, always, always the same: Us and Them. Us and Them.

She was thinking this, when Zac unexpectedly threw himself down beside her. "So what was the Reformation actually about?" he asked, his voice childish, eager, in a way it hadn't been at the table before.

This must be why she was fond of him. Despite his preppy mindset, despite his new fascist posturing, he had a curiosity that was, to her, disarming. This, here, behind all the bluff and the bravado, was still her round-faced baby nephew who had once, aged five, asked her, "If Jesus and Darth Vader had a fight, who would win?"

"In England? It was basically a power grab, like I said. A coup."

Zac looked puzzled. Now, with no one there but the two of them, he was more uncertain; less cocky. "But wasn't it about… *religion*?" His face was screwed up with cognitive dissonance, his brown eyes focused needily on her.

She was flattered. "Well, for some people it was about religion. For Martin Luther, for example; a German who framed the doctrines of 'justification by faith alone' and 'the priesthood of all believers.'"

"But what does that mean?" Zac said.

"Luther started the sixteenth-century Protestant movement," Cecily told him. "He said the Catholic Church hierarchy had brainwashed us into thinking that the Bible could only be understood and explained to us by priests and that we needed them to mediate between us and God. He said that the Catholic Church claimed this as a basis for extorting money out of us; making us pay for this access to and mediation with God, via the saints. Luther said that the clergy's special relationship with God, their 'expert' status, was a fabrication."

She looked at Zac. He was still listening.

"Many people had said similar stuff before, but one thing that was different about Luther was that he happened to say all this just at a time when the printing press had recently been invented, so his polemics spread all over Europe. The Protestant printing presses were like megaphones, announcing that we had no need of money-grabbing, power-hungry priests to tell us what God thought: the Word of God was evident for all to see, in the newly printed Bibles!"

"But that was in Germany?" Zac said.

"Well, it started in Germany."

"But what about England?"

"Well, Protestantism spread all across Europe and began to influence some in England as well, of course. But that wasn't really the reason why Henry VIII broke with Rome. He did that because he wanted a male heir and he and his wife hadn't had one, and he blamed her and wanted a new wife, but the Pope wouldn't let him. And because this happened when Protestantism was spreading across Europe, Henry realised, at some point, that if he turned Protestant, he could cut us from the structures of the Church on the continent and become head of a Church in

England himself, he wouldn't need the Pope's permission. If he did that, he could not only divorce and marry again and get an heir (or so he thought); he would also have his hands on all the Church's wealth."

"Oh, I see!" said Zac. He seemed to find what she was saying exciting.

She paused, eyeing him. She had an uneasy suspicion that what he was taking from what she said was not at all the message that she was trying to give him.

"So, he literally just kicked out all the monks and took their land for himself?" Zac said excitedly. "Did he have an army or something? How many monks and stuff were there? How much was all that land worth?"

"I don't know. But when he kicked out the monks and nuns, more than ten thousand became homeless. What he did was very cruel. But you see, Zac, what I'm trying to tell you is that in order to do such an unthinkable thing, Henry had to make it thinkable. He had to connect the Roman Catholic Church, in people's minds, with evil, which was no easy task because the Church was an age-old institution. From birth to death, life was structured by its rhythms and rituals. And however corrupt it was, it still benefited many people. There were great uprisings when he first began to attack the monasteries, and after he had stolen all of the Church's wealth, he had to get people to accept what he had done. Although what made it easier, of course, was precisely that he had seized all that wealth. The wealth he had stolen meant he now had at his disposal enormous amounts of patronage which could pay for support and propaganda."

"What's patronage?"

"Patronage is power – in the form of money or goods or favours – that you can choose to give to people in return for them behaving how you want them to behave. Henry VIII, for example, could sell or give profitable Church land to people who supported him, and then once they had acquired it, they too were invested in his revolution and became minor patrons themselves. There were large numbers of people, by the end of Henry's reign, who had personally acquired Church land and so had every reason to try and prevent any return to the Catholic Church."

"Oh, are you two at your history again?"

Cecily looked up to see Diana standing over them. With the sun directly behind her, she was a silhouette. She seemed giant, from this angle, and Cecily could not look at her without blinking, dazzled by the sun. And then she sat down next to them and became human-sized again.

Cecily was embarrassed. "I'm afraid so!"

She looked back at Zac. He was digging his toes in among the pebbles, and then trying to catapult them off by flicking his toes. His brow was furrowed.

"So, the Reformation wasn't about religion *at all*?" he asked, "I thought Protestantism was… you know… *better*?"

He was looking at her, Cecily thought, almost suspiciously; as if he suspected she was either wrong or deliberately misleading him. Gone was his puerile excitement about armies and winners and losers. He looked genuinely ruffled. She wondered what it was, exactly, that was bothering him. It seemed that she had touched a hitherto unknown priggish spot within him; that he found what she was saying almost offensive in some way.

"Well, there was a religious change as well," she said, "but it happened very slowly. Protestantism did spread, encouraged over decades by patronage from the newly moneyed Protestants who now owned Church land. I'm just saying that it was Henry's greed for power and money that initiated the split with Rome, and that, when he first harnessed the tide of Protestantism, it was only to realise his own ends."

"Greed for power and money," murmured Diana. She took off her shoes and stretched out her legs. "Well, it's always the way…"

Surprised, Cecily glanced at her, to try to gauge what she was thinking. *But greed for power and money were what drove Brexit*, she thought. Did Diana have no inkling of that?

*

The thing about Cecily, Diana thought, lying back on the pebbles and closing her eyes, was… well, she didn't understand. She didn't understand that if you keep on trashing and trashing your country, sooner or later you'll have nothing left to trash. A country with no pride in itself could not stick up for itself; it would be walked all over. The Empire was rubbish; the Reformation was rubbish – was there nothing good about England at all?

And it was funny, because in many ways, she had always found that she and Cecily saw eye to eye. There was that time last summer, for example, when everyone in that chat-messaging group they both belonged to because they lived on the same street started getting excited about a spate of burglaries. Nothing much was damaged or taken: just a broken window here; some money gone from a drawer or a car glovebox there. But people started saying that they had spotted the thief and they got so worked up about how to catch him in the act, and there was something… well, Diana had begun to find their excitement and obsession a bit… disgusting. She had felt that she just couldn't take part in a discussion like this, and noticed that Cecily was not taking part either, and when she phoned her, she had discovered that she and Cecily felt exactly the same.

"I just feel really uncomfortable on this chat," Diana had told Cecily, "Because everyone here is so lucky and I think that this poor young man… he's just a kid who's probably had bad luck. Had an unstable childhood; grown up without any hope of a good job, or of ever owning a house himself. You know? I just feel as if it could have been me, if I'd been born in only very slightly different circumstances. I mean, I'm working class; I didn't have it easy when I was growing up, either. My mum was a single mum. My dad was not much use to us. But my generation was so much luckier: I could get a job as soon as I left home at sixteen. I could afford to rent a flat on my salary. You know? I think it's much harder now. I feel sorry for young people today, I really do. I know it's wrong to steal, but…"

And Cecily had said, "I know! I just found the whole conversation kind of ugly. People were enjoying it too much."

"Yes! Exactly!" Diana had re-joined.

And that was what she liked about Cecily: on so many issues, they completely understood each other.

She sat up and looked out across the beach to where the waves came up, one behind the other, and rolled onto the sand. It reminded her of when she took Olivia to gymnastics sometimes, and she would wait on the side-lines, watching the line of little girls each, one after the other, come up, bounce on the little trampoline and leap over the horse.

And there was the whole issue of the class trip to the Hindu temple. That was when the girls were in Year 3, before the Brexit referendum. She had told Cecily about it, because Olivia and Julia were such close friends.

"I just want to tell you," Diana had said, "that Olivia is not going on the trip to the temple next Thursday because – I don't know if you know this, but I heard from the people that went last year that when they go into the temple, the girls all have to sit behind the boys."

Cecily had stared at her. "Oh!" she said, mystified, as if politely wondering what Diana's point was.

"Well, I don't know about you, but I am not having my daughter being degraded like that," Diana had said.

Cecily had looked a bit taken aback.

So Diana had explained, "I know that most people don't think this is a big deal. They say it's an educational experience and that they'll all discuss it in the class afterwards. But…well, just imagine if the rule in the temple was not that all the girls had to sit behind the boys, but that all the black children had to sit behind the white children. Would they want the children to go through that educational 'experience'? Of course they wouldn't! They would never allow the black children to *experience* having to sit behind the white ones. The parents would be up in arms! But somehow, it's okay to do that to girls?"

"Wow!" Cecily had looked quite amazed. "Did you tell the school?"

"Yep."

"What did they say?"

"That they're sorry to hear that Olivia isn't coming, as they think it's important to 'respect other religions.'"

"And what did you say?"

"I told them that it's more important to respect our laws, and that women and men in this country are meant to be equal."

"Wow!" said Cecily again, looking shocked.

But later that day, when they'd met at the school gates, she'd said, "I've been thinking about what you said. And you're right. It's not okay. Most of the main world religions are mired in misogyny and actually it's important not to respect that."

Julia didn't go on the trip to the temple either, after that. Both girls stayed at school all day. And Diana had been quite proud of herself for convincing Cecily. That was what she meant: when they talked, they understood each other. It was just that so many subjects nowadays were so taboo, especially among muddled liberals like Cecily, that you never even got to actually talk about them.

Eyes closed, she listened to the roar of the sea breaking on the pebbles. It was so restless, so relentless. It was hard to believe that it was not alive in some way; that there was not some intention in the way it hurled itself again and again and again against the land.

It gave her a funny feeling, with her eyes closed like that, listening to the sea beat against the shore. She could almost imagine she was a child again, back at Ramsgate, where she had spent so many girlhood summers staying in rooms with her mum and her nan. Pegwell Bay, near where they stayed, her mum used to tell her, was supposed to be the site of the early Saxon invasions into Celtic Britain. Diana's mum had known a lot about history: she'd become quite an amateur historian in later life. There were just a few Saxons in the first bunch that came over. They'd come as mercenaries, at the invitation of the King of the Britons. At least, that was how her mum had told it. And she would laugh. "God knows what the ordinary people thought about those warlike immigrants being invited in by the King!" But it was definitely a bad idea to let them in, because before you knew it, those Saxons were bringing over all their relations. And before long, they were fighting the Britons, and winning. One of them – Diana couldn't remember which, although her mum would have known – made himself the King of Kent.

She knew this story because her mother had told her, more than once, down on the beach at Pegwell Bay. She had picked up handfuls of the sand and let it sift through her fingers, as they sat there, looking out to sea. "Just think," she would say, "perhaps they pulled their boats up on this very sand, right here. Little did the poor Britons know, when their King invited the Angles and Saxons in to fight their wars, that he was sowing the seeds of their destruction. But before long Saxons had taken over the whole country. Soon there was hardly a trace of the indigenous people; the Celts that had occupied these islands since at least the Iron Age."

As a young child, Diana had found them awe-inspiring, her mum's bits and pieces about the olden days. But as a teenager she'd begun to realise that there was a framework, a modern political element to all of this interest. Not that she ever really articulated this dawning awareness, even to herself. It was more just that she developed an aversion to her mum's historical reflections and did her best to avoid them. Her mother, it began to seem to her by the time she reached her late teens, represented an outlook that was shameful, that was unacceptable, that was dirty, and that she didn't want to be part of. She had wanted then, in the '90s, to be part of the progressive world, to be successful, to be modern, to go with the flow.

In the years before she died, Diana's mother had actually moved out permanently from London to a flat in Ramsgate at the beginning of the millennium. That was because Greenwich, where she'd grown up in the 1930s and '40s (where she'd lived her entire life, in fact), had gradually over the years become alien to her. She'd left because everything she had known as a child had changed. First it was the Caribbeans and the Punjabis, she would say. And then the Gujaratis. Then the Pakistanis and Bangladeshis. And then, later, the Nigerians, the Lithuanians and the Poles. The pub had gone; they now had a mosque on the site instead.

If Cecily ever met her mother, she'd probably think her a racist, thought Diana now, squinting through half-closed eyes at the glittering waves. And that was basically what Diana herself had felt as a teenager. She knew very well, then, that some of the things her mum said could not be said. And because she'd so wanted to be accepted socially, she'd tried not to hear them. She'd done her best to discourage her mother from even expressing her worries and her feelings, and if she did, Diana tried not to hear them. Which was cruel, she realised now.

When Diana was a child they'd had social housing, and her mother *had* tried to get on with the new Caribbean neighbours, when they arrived in the early '70s. It wasn't that they were unfriendly; it was just that they partied loudly sometimes, and late at night. They played "their reggae music," her mother said. She'd gone round a few times to ask them to turn it down, but every time they just patted her on the shoulder and told her to live and let live. She could play her music as loud as she liked; they wouldn't mind, they'd say.

Sometimes she'd come back in good spirits, Diana remembered; the man who usually opened the door was very charming. Much more charming than the old drunk who lived on the other side, who was mostly quiet but used to go into the back garden and shout at his cabbages on Sunday mornings. Their Caribbean neighbour was so charismatic that, if he spoke to Diana (and a couple of times, he did address a few words to her as she stood on his doorstep, holding hands with her mum), it made her squirm and she found herself helplessly smiling and smiling and smiling. The pleasure was so intense that sometimes she covered her eyes and pretended that she wasn't there. It had actually tickled her mum's humour how entirely this man always failed to get her point about the noise. But the fact was that the issue was never resolved, and the parties went on. They didn't bother Diana. But her mother complained that she spent night after night sleeping with a pillow over her head.

It was a culture clash. And eventually Diana and her mum had moved up the street. But it wasn't easy, as around that time the Greater London Council changed their rules on council house allocation, so that there was no waiting list as previously; instead, the allocations were done based on need. And with all the Bangladeshi families now arriving, often with many children at their mothers' skirts, Diana's mum said, they, who already had a home, had no real case to make.

In later years, when Diana went back to see her, her mum complained that when she went to the shop she was intimidated by women in long black robes that looked to her alien and medieval, speaking in words she didn't understand. That was the thing: if she walked down the street, or got on a bus down the Old Kent Road, for example, she was more likely to hear Yoruba or Bengali or something, than English. And that was before the Poles and the Lithuanians started to arrive.

"All this on the Old Kent Road!" Diana's mum would marvel. "The Old Kent Road! Do you know, this was the very road that Chaucer's pilgrims walked along to Canterbury!"

Like everybody else, her mother wanted to feel that she belonged. And how could you really belong in a place when you didn't even understand what the people around you were saying? And so she had moved out in the late '90s, shortly after they closed the local pub.

Diana had never told anyone about any of this. If she did, people would say that her mum had moved away because she was racist. But it wasn't really that. Okay, maybe it was, partly. But not just that. Her mum wasn't young anymore, and she had found that her way of life, her assumptions, her culture, her sense of belonging, were gradually being eroded. Not only the pub, but the local pie and mash shop had disappeared. It was like the book Diana had been reading with her book club, about Nigerian culture being destroyed by the invading British. *Things Fall Apart*,[5] it was called, or something similar. Well, she'd not been able to say this at book group, for obvious reasons, but it seemed to her that in some ways her mother had experienced a kind of things-falling-apart here in the very capital of England.

"And do you know, they never asked us!" Diana's mum used to marvel bitterly. "It's supposed to be a democracy, but whether we wanted all these immigrants, they never asked us even once!"

Immigration had begun to increase dramatically after World War II. Her mother had looked it up. But recently it had gone completely crazy! In just the twenty years between the 1991 and 2011 censuses, her mother said, the foreign-born population had literally doubled.[6] According to her, there had never been immigration on this scale at any time in our history to date, including the gradual invasion of the Saxons! So no wonder people didn't like it! Nobody likes to watch their culture disappear before their eyes. In the Royal Borough of Greenwich, where Diana had grown up, her mother would tell her in an amazed voice, nowadays white British constituted only about half the population.[7]

And her mother was right, Diana had to admit. *Whether so much immigration is good or whether it's bad, it's just a fact that nobody – neither Labour nor Tories – ever asked us whether this was what we wanted. We were not asked; not really even warned, straight up. We were just told – after the event, patronisingly – that it was good for us. Well, that it was good for the economy, more precisely. And whatever's good for the economy, well, of course there's no alternative; if it's good for the economy then we all just have to suck it up.* It wasn't surprising that people felt they should have been asked, as they – the white British – were the indigenous people now. People mocked the idea that Western European states could have 'indigenous people'. Only people like the Amazonians or the Australian Aborigines were allowed to claim indigenous status nowadays. "None of us is indigenous in Europe; we all came from somewhere else!" people would say. But that was the same with all people everywhere, except maybe Botswana, which Diana had heard was where humans originated from. Even the Aborigines had come from somewhere else originally. And apparently *Homo sapiens* had even mated with the Neanderthals! So if no one anywhere was really indigenous, then why couldn't the British, who had occupied these islands for over a millennium, lay claim – nowadays – to be as indigenous as anyone else?

But people like Cecily could not understand this feeling of 'things falling apart'. Cecily couldn't understand because she personally had never experienced it: her own world had never been displaced. She had grown up in Blackheath Village, which was still predominantly white and middle class. She'd gone to Oxford University after school, not her local branch of Debenhams. Cecily would no doubt argue, the way educated people like her did, that it wasn't true that immigration displaced only the working classes; that there had always been loads of foreigners taking university places and graduate jobs. But it was not the same. The foreigners who came to universities and took graduate jobs dressed like British graduates, ate much like British graduates, and shared a certain international culture that comes with money and education and travel for pleasure. And they spoke perfect English. In the posh neighbourhood where Cecily grew up, she would never have found herself in a situation where, on entering her local shop, she could not understand what anyone was saying.

*

Cecily looked at her watch, as they got back to the house after the beach, and nudged Diana, saying, "Seven o'clock! Do you think that means it's okay to crack open the wine?"

"You read my mind!" Diana said, but then, seeing that the girls were about to race ahead through the hall, called out sharply, "Olivia! What are you thinking?"

Olivia stopped in the hall and turned around, saying, "What?"

Cecily watched in surprise as Diana, still on the threshold, reproved her daughter, in shocked tones, "Your shoes! They're full of sand and grit! You can't just go traipsing that all through the house!"

"Oh!" Olivia exclaimed, realisation dawning across her face. "Sorry, I just... er..." And she came back through the hall towards her mother, who was standing outside in the porch.

"Come back out here and shake out your shoes!" Diana commanded. And then she turned to Cecily, saying, "I'm so sorry!"

"Oh... well... you really don't need to..." Cecily began, but then stopped herself as she saw how Diana and Olivia stood on the threshold and began taking off their shoes, one by one, and shaking them out and brushing them off.

When Cecily was a child, her mother had always made a point of saying, when people came into her house, "Oh, for goodness' sake! There's no need to take your shoes off!" Her tone would be one of expansive liberality. But there was an undercurrent of impatience. And in fact, it now occurred to Cecily, liberality had very little to do with it. The reason her mother quite ostentatiously instructed guests not to take off their shoes was that she actually looked down on people who took their shoes off when they came into the house, in the same way that she looked down on women she considered overly house-proud. Cecily had always vaguely understood that this business about not taking shoes off related back, ultimately, to that same mystic code. Like the barrels and the water, it was part of some ancient Puritan inheritance. She had half-assumed, on some unconscious level, that the argument for not taking off your shoes in the house was that an exaggerated concern with hygiene and tidiness might reflect a shallow and un-Protestant prioritising of form over spirit. Later, she'd thought that perhaps her mother's scorn for housework was an expression of her feminism. It was only now, watching Diana, that she began to wonder whether it was something else: not inherited high-mindedness so much as inherited snobbery. Taking off shoes and worrying about dirty floors were, historically, concerns for the lower classes, it struck Cecily now. Taking off shoes was for the peasant men who worked the fields and couldn't come into the house with mud-clods on their boots. Concern for the floors was for the serving girls and common people who cleaned houses; it was not a matter for ladies.

Cecily could see Julia standing in the hall, also watching in surprise while Diana and Olivia balanced themselves by holding on to the wooden supports of the porch and shook the sand and earth from their shoes. And, feeling suddenly embarrassed, Cecily went back out into the porch herself and took off one of her own shoes, banging it against the side of the house.

"Actually," she said, "that's a good idea!" Mostly as an explanation to Julia, who was staring at her in amazement. Cecily avoided her daughter's eye.

"Well, yeah!" Diana was saying. "Of course! You don't want sand all over the house!"

They came into the sitting room to find Victoria literally about to open a bottle, which made them laugh.

"Great minds think alike!" Diana declared.

Victoria looked up, taking in the two of them, rosy-cheeked from the sun and the wind and laughing. "What?" she asked, intrigued.

"Oh, we were just saying it's time for a drink – and there you are with the bottle!" Diana cried.

Victoria smiled, saying, in her poised, throwaway way, "Oh, I know… I'm gasping!"

Victoria went to the dining room and brought out three glasses on the old tray with the Constable print of Salisbury Cathedral. Cecily was touched. She would never have expected Victoria to use that scratched-up old plastic tray from their childhood. It was the tray on which their grandmother had brought out garibaldi biscuits for their elevenses, when they were little. Their grandfather had called them "squashed-fly biscuits", which – for a while – they had found hilariously clever. Although their grandmother hadn't actually called it elevenses; she had called it "second breakfast", which was her German term. And, as Victoria popped open the bottle in this general merriment, it occurred to Cecily that anyone who peeped through the window now would think that they were all carefree and convivial here: friends and family; bubbles and laughter.

But in reality, over the five hours since they had arrived, really carefree moments had been sparse. There had been that fleeting instance of exuberance with Diana and the children when they ran down to the beach, and afterwards, when they took the photos. And then just now, when Diana said, "And here you are with the bottle!" when they were all swept up in that spontaneous second of comedy. But that was it. Those were the only moments in the whole of the afternoon. Which would make just about three minutes of joy, in all those hours since they'd arrived. The rest of the time, Cecily had been dodging her fraught and lonely way between shifting perceptions of reality which were forever threatening to subsume or overturn each other. Life! It was like being an indigent gold digger sifting anxiously, day after day, through a stream of mud and grit and water for those rare specks of gold.

It really was, moreover, just a second of unity that they had when they all laughed, then, because after that Victoria began filling the glasses. They were the old-fashioned champagne saucers on short stems, etched with frosty wild roses. They had been in the family, here in the house, since before the first world war. In an old cigar box in a drawer in the study there was a yellowing photo of some long-ago celebration, in which Cecily and Victoria's great-grandparents were standing around raising these glasses. And, as Victoria poured, Cecily noticed that what she was pouring was actual champagne. Real champagne, just like in the old photos. She experienced a little shock. Nothing dramatic; just a slight shock, followed by a vague sadness. It was not that Cecily really cared about money or power or status, or any such thing, of course. But still, seeing her sister uncork real champagne so casually was an uneasy reminder that, increasingly, Victoria and her husband moved in socio-economic spheres quite beyond Cecily's reach.

"Dan and Florian are just doing dinner, by the way," Victoria said in a managerial voice, looking from Cecily to Diana.

"Oh, of course! Dan's arrived! I'll go and say hello," Cecily said.

But at that point Zac came bounding in and, seeing the champagne glasses, asked mischievously, "Are you celebrating the prorogation?"

Cecily's heart thudded. But surely, even if they tried, the Queen wouldn't let it happen?

Victoria took a sip of champagne, looking indulgently ruffled, exasperated. "Oh, stop it, Zac! Goodness!" she chided. She turned towards Diana. "Everyone's making too much of this Brexit thing! I'm sick to death of it!"

Cecily turned away. Or rather, she swung away, pretending to wander aimlessly over to the fireplace. *Making too much of it?* Surely it was hardly possible to make too much of it? But she couldn't say anything, which in itself seemed like madness: a national crisis, and she couldn't speak about it even among her friends and family. But that was how it was. Brexit was at once too deep, too emotive and too complex to even begin to address. It tapped such profound cultural roots that every Brexit-related word was in itself a landmine of contention. 'Democracy', 'sovereignty', 'culture', 'freedom': each of the buzzwords could be used in so many ways that the number of possible diverging lexical and epistemological trails of understanding was exhausting even to contemplate. She moved over towards the fireplace, and rested her forearms on the back of one of the dusky pink bergère armchairs. The fact was, the prospect of Brexit felt like a violation of her whole self.

She contemplated the art nouveau tiles around the fireplace, with their pattern of climbing wild flowers in burnt orange and gooseberry green. These old French armchairs. The small, painted Black Forest weather house on the mantelpiece that had belonged to her grandmother. It had a little wooden woman in German folk costume who came out of the log cabin when it was sunny, and her little husband in lederhosen who came out when it rained. It had fascinated Cecily as a child, that weather house. As had, of course, the vases Victoria had taken, which should be standing here right now, on either side of the fireplace. Those two beautiful Italian vases, each as tall as a stool, with looping vines and flowers and foliage in orange, yellow and limpid turquoise, and strange, bearded yellow dragon-birds chasing each other around the vases' smooth, round bellies. Why on earth had Victoria hidden them?

And then she looked at the books. From where she stood, looking at just the shelves in the alcove to the right of the fire, she could see the King James' Bible, partly based on texts translated from the Greek by Tyndale and published in Germany back in the sixteenth century; she could see Plato's *Republic*, Dante's *La Vita Nuova*, Goethe's *Elective Affinities*, Simone de Beauvoir's *The Second Sex* – all of which, she knew, had contributed to who she was. For her, Englishness was all about being part of Europe; one branch of a shared European culture still traceable back more than two thousand years. And when she looked around at all this furniture; the doors on the old cupboard on the wall underneath the front window that some friend of her great-grandmother's had painted in what was meant to be Pre-Raphaelite style, she felt almost tearfully protective of this house and its memories; of its dignity as part of a European past; its sense of working quietly towards a kinder, fairer European future.

It was Winston Churchill, whom the Brexiters claimed as their hero, who had helped create the European Council and the European Convention on Human Rights and had even proposed a shared European army. In 1949, Churchill, who played an active part in founding the Council of Europe, said, "The dangers threatening us are great but great too is our strength, and there is no reason why we should not succeed in… establishing the structure of this united Europe whose moral concepts will be able to win the respect and recognition of mankind…"[8] But Brexiters ignored all this. From at least 2009, they had begun manufacturing a fictional history within which Churchill was some kind of proto-Brexiter. They pretended that the European Union, one of the world's most successful projects in peace, justice, prosperity and good government, was somehow an enemy. They denied the founding role that Britain had played in the EU's creation. They dismissed the fact that being an EU citizen was a central part of Cecily's identity.

She moved back over to the table and refilled her glass. Diana and Victoria were still complaining about how Brexit dominated the news cycle. And as she put the champagne bottle down, her eye fell once again on the old Constable tray. She had always liked it. The dreamy farmer with his cart and horses stopped in the water meadow, reflected in the water. The friendly fields edged with gently dilapidated fences. And in the background, the rising spire of Salisbury Cathedral. You had a sense that there was some safe principle here, expressed in that cathedral spire, investing everything below with quiet contentment.

Champagne in hand, Cecily wandered over to the

other side of the fireplace. Here were all those old books of hers, from her university days. *The Collected Complete Works of Daniel Defoe; A Vindication of the Rights of Men* by Mary Wollstonecraft; *Songs of Innocence and Experience* by William Blake. She sipped her champagne and moved further along the time-warped bookshelves, until she reached some of their grandparents' old books. Here she noticed the title of a book she'd never seen before: *The Spirit of England* by George William Erskine Russell. She turned the words over in her mind. *The Spirit of England*! Wasn't that also a piece of music by… was it Elgar? *The Spirit of England*. What exactly could that mean?

"Dinner's almost ready – five, ten minutes!" Dan, red-faced and bowing with a flourish, had appeared at the sitting-room door. He had a big butcher's apron tied around his portly stomach. Quite crass, Cecily had always found him, with his flashy cars and his showy wines and his blokey bonhomie. But now he awoke in her a mild but warm affection, as he stood there, alcohol-flushed and benignly beaming.

"Oh, Dan! I forgot to come and say hello to you!" she said.

Dan wiped his brow and waved her apologies away, joking, "It's okay, I'm only a lowly cook…"

"Oh, have you been cooking all this time?" asked Diana, hurriedly putting aside her champagne and getting to her feet from the old velvet sofa. "And none of us have been helping…"

From the arm of the sofa, where she was sat, Victoria raised a hand in a light, little 'stop' gesture, signalling to

Diana that her guilt was entirely superfluous. "It's okay, Dan just loves cooking!" she explained. She straightened her skirt, smoothing the creases. "It's what he does to relax! You know – on holiday. Dan, this is Diana, by the way!"

It irritated Cecily slightly, that Victoria was introducing Diana in what seemed to her a proprietorial way. Dan stood there smiling, affably twitching a tea towel in his broad, stubby hands. It wasn't the first time, either, thought Cecily, watching him, that she had experienced a swimming of warmth towards him like this. So strange, when she was at odds with some of his most basic attitudes. He had been so anxious to differentiate his son from everyone else's children, for example, that he had sent him to private school from the age of three. He wanted Zac, as he quite openly explained, to "get ahead". Whereas Cecily was convinced that fee-paying schools should be abolished altogether. So they were unaccountable, these subversive swirls of sympathy she sometimes felt rippling towards him. Perhaps they were just an oblique backwash from the undercurrent of fear, spite and antipathy she often felt for Victoria. Or perhaps it was simply that, even though she saw him as being, ideologically, on the opposing side, his unpretentious, breezy optimism sometimes disarmed her.

"Pleased to meet you!" Dan was saying to Diana. And then, addressing everyone again, rubbing his hands together, "Now, what I really want is for someone to come and lay the table, and someone else to go and bring in the kids from outside."

"I'll get the children!" Cecily offered. That was what she wanted, she realised now: an interlude outside, in the garden, away from everyone else. This insouciance about Brexit between Victoria and Diana had ruffled her up no end; especially since she had not been able to finish her own conversation about Brexit with Diana earlier.

"Oh, I'll help you with the table, then!" said Diana to Victoria, as Cecily headed into the dining room and towards the French windows. "I'll just pop to the loo first, if you don't mind! This champagne has gone straight through me!"

*

Victoria went into the kitchen and began rummaging around in the drawer for a tablecloth. She was feeling elated; triumphant, even. It was partly the champagne. But the alcohol had not supplied, only heightened, her jubilant sense that she had managed to get on top of things. It was alright.

She had felt uncertain, earlier on, when she and Diana had first met. More than uncertain, in fact. She'd felt the threat of a re-emergence, the clutching fingers reaching out, of that feeling of worthlessness or anger that had stalked her childhood and adolescence, then retreated for a while when she left school, only to return and engulf her in that period after university, after Matthew.

She didn't know herself, even now, what exactly it was that Matthew had set in motion. But after he'd ended it, for at least a year, everything she did and everyone she met was heavy and unreal, as if she were moving under water. Her inner and outer lives seemed to split; she thought about him constantly. She went over and over scenes in her head; she remembered things he'd said to her, or she'd said to him, that at the time were unimportant, but now throbbed with transcendent meaning. She spent whole evenings crying and drinking the cheap Australian wine she favoured at the time – the kind that was labelled 'crisp' or 'fresh' or 'light-hearted' – and wallowed for hours in a solo orgy of grief. Sometimes, during these orgies, she wrote down drunken messages to Matthew that occurred to her as wildly inspired, but which, in the morning, turned out be both banal and incoherent. And then she got in with a druggy crowd and spent a lot of time in nightclubs. She met one of Matthew's friends in the corridor at a club in Brixton; one of those 'industrial' clubs which were all pipes and cement and brick and damp, with manufactured graffiti on the walls. She'd said some truly embarrassing things, she was sure, although she couldn't remember much of the conversation; only that at one point she'd been laughing and clinging to his arm, and he'd been trying to get away. For days after she didn't sleep at all, writhing in humiliation, imagining excruciating versions of conversations that this friend might have about her with Matthew. And of these horror-fantasy conversations she imagined Mattew having with his friend about her were shot through with a searing humiliation and charged with crazy sexual energy.

But then she'd met Dan, and, gradually, she'd regained her self-esteem. She knew, now, how to ignore – how to reach over and around – that sinking feeling of worthlessness when it came. And, despite that wobble earlier today, she knew that these few days of holiday were going to be okay:

she had managed to find a way to be safely at the centre. Every time Brexit was touched upon, she could see, both Cecily and Diana floundered. And this offered her a way in; an entry point, where she could come in from the outside. Cecily and Diana were not necessarily at one, she realised, watching them, and she, Victoria, was not necessarily the 'other'. There was a space for her in the middle, between them.

Should she feel bad? She wondered fizzily. She would actually like to be one of those people who were open-hearted, who didn't need to enter into – didn't appear to even see – the power games that emerged whenever people formed groups. There weren't many people like that, but she had met a few in her life. She had actually made some effort to try to be like that herself at one point, when she was younger. And there had been contexts, brief periods, when being at the centre of things just happened to her; when she didn't even need to manufacture it. That had happened when she went travelling in South America after her A levels, for example, and fell in with a crowd of Australians. With them she'd felt relaxed, generous. But even that, she realised when she thought about it, had been because she had been going out with the most charismatic boy in the group, and through him had had a kind of instant status that she didn't have to create. But that period was an exception. In the main, she'd found that somehow, for her, being guileless never worked out. If you didn't learn to play the game, she'd discovered, then you automatically lost it.

The trouble was, really, that she was just too observant. She saw too clearly the social jostling for position that happened within *every* group of people literally *all* of the time. And what was she supposed to do? Just let other people elbow her out into the margins? Being on the sidelines in any group held a peculiar terror. On the sidelines was how she had always felt within her family. She'd spent too much of her childhood feeling like that to tolerate it as an adult. It was hard to pinpoint exactly how they had done it to her, her family. For them, every tiny aspect of life – from the way you dressed to the way you ate and even washed – was seen as evidence of your moral state, and could be used against you. Baths were time-honoured; showers were frivolous. Not eating the crusts on your bread was debauched. Books were good; TV was bad. Rah-rah skirts, which were all the rage for a year or so when Victoria was about eleven, had been for her mother – inexplicably – anathema. Victoria was not allowed to wear them, even when she was given one for her birthday by her best friend.

All the things she wanted, it seemed when she was a child, were things that one shouldn't want. Her very desires were evidence of her basic depravity. It wasn't even just her: Cecily had wanted some of them too. A Barbie doll, for example. They were not allowed Barbie dolls because her mother felt they objectified women. That term 'objectify women' had not even been coined in back in the 70s, but her mother had felt that something about Barbie was wrong, even if, as yet, she had no language with which to articulate it. Now, of course, aged forty-nine, Victoria could see what her mother had meant. But her mother could never see Victoria's point of view. Back then, Barbie had appeared to be free; miraculously free. She was not a baby that needed looking after, like other dolls; she was an adult and no one could tell her what to do. She was an autonomous, glamorous consumer; she could have whatever she wanted: a house, a horse, a car, an endless wardrobe. Even Cecily had wanted one; even Cecily was not entirely content to confine her imaginative play to being a mother to the traditional baby dolls their mother atavistically approved of.

They'd planned to buy one once. Victoria had 'found' the money on their mother's bedside table. She did know, really, when she found those two pound notes lying there, that it wasn't hers to take. But she also knew that, in claiming to have found the money, she wouldn't exactly be lying. More importantly, though, she had felt that the money was rightfully hers in some potent, urgent sense more cosmic and more compelling than any ordinary human argument. The money to buy a Barbie *must* be hers, this cosmic logic went, because she so desperately wanted one. Cecily, then aged four, was persuaded by this argument, especially since it was possible that Victoria hadn't actually told her *where* she had found the money. And they were both transported to an ecstasy of joy, contemplating those promising paper notes in Victoria's hand. They hadn't actually worked out *how* they were going to buy the Barbie, though. And long before they'd come up with a plan, their mother found the money in Victoria's underwear drawer and the whole thing went up in flames.

Cecily had burst into tears the moment their mother confronted them.

"Why did you take the money?" their mother demanded.

Of course, Victoria was not going to tell her. She kept

her lips shut tight and didn't say a word. But Cecily couldn't be trusted and blabbed it all straight away.

For the rest of her life, Victoria reflected now, that event had been referred to by the family as evidence of her faulty character. Jokingly, of course, in later years, when she had reached adulthood. But nevertheless, the message was there. And it was so unfair. Because was there really anything so terrible, at age seven, about desperately wanting a Barbie? After all, at least she had not lost her nerve and given the game away like Cecily. If anyone, it was Cecily, it seemed to her now, looking back, who should feel ashamed.

But now there was a busy-ness and excitement in the kitchen that fed into her elation after her drinks with Cecily and Diana. Dan's curry smelled wonderful! An evocative medley of cumin, ginger and lime. And for a moment Victoria felt like someone who led a fulfilling life; someone who really was the centre of this social situation, here in Dover, with her talented cook of a husband. She and Dan actually did quite a lot of entertaining. But somehow it never felt quite real; she never felt that she had entirely become that person she wanted to be. She didn't know why, but that imposter syndrome she'd read about, that many women apparently felt at work, was for her, actually, more how she felt in almost *every* situation.

Florian was shaking up one of his salads over by the sink, and in this state of elation Victoria felt almost sad that she had consistently run him and Cecily down in front of Dan. Always, she deprecated them, casting them as dowdy, earnest and exacting. But for a brief moment now, glancing at Florian, she regretted this. Suppose she had spent the thirteen years since Zac's birth building up family relations instead of feeding a grudge against Cecily?

Oh, but that was just silly. With Cecily it would never have worked. In fact, it was Cecily in particular who made Victoria behave badly. She couldn't help it. It was just this sense, instilled in her from childhood, that Cecily was the favourite. And not just their mother's favourite; it went beyond that. Somehow, Victoria had grown up believing that Cecily was even the favourite of God, or whatever power was the ultimate judge of the entire universe. And sometimes she felt she'd spent all her life so far, and would spend the rest of it, desperately trying to prove to this power (which, though invisible, was always watching her) that *she* was more important.

There were two tablecloths in the drawer. One had a stain towards the right-hand corner; she could see that without unfolding it. And when she shook the other out, it appeared to have been nibbled in places. Wincing in distaste (hopefully it was a moth, rather than a mouse, that had gnawed away at it), she shoved the tablecloth back into the drawer and tried to close it. But it was an old oak dresser and the worm-pocked drawers had no metal runners, just wooden grooves, so that they always got stuck when you tried to close them. She had to pull the drawer back out three times and wiggle it a lot before it would close again. That was the trouble with this house: everything was decrepit and to some extent dysfunctional.

She went to the airing cupboard to look for an acceptable tablecloth. And, looking at all the old linens piled up there, she realised with rising frustration, as she had so many times before, that sharing this house with Cecily was impossible. It was just *impossible*! It wasn't only that some of the linens had buttons missing, or were faded, or threadbare in the middle. This motley collection of duvets and sheets were all slightly different sizes, so that often you'd make a pile of what you thought you needed to make the beds and head upstairs with them, only to find that this sheet was ten centimetres too small to stretch over the mattress on that bed, or this duvet cover didn't actually fit that duvet. And then you'd have to fold them up again and take them back downstairs and try your luck with some other ones. If it were her house, she would chuck out these mouldering, ill-assorted old linens and buy nice, crisp new sheets and duvet covers, and duvets and mattresses, all in standard sizes, so that they would always fit. But if she ever did that, she knew that Cecily would object. "Oh, but I remember these ones from when we were little! Look at those crazy '70s flowers!" she would cry, all emotional, or "Oh, but these are the pillowcases that Mummy embroidered when she was at school!" And within those words there would be the implication that Victoria didn't know how to value what was valuable; that throwing out even moth-eaten napkins would be an act of disloyalty to their parents or grandparents, or a stain on their souls, or some such mawkish notion.

The airing cupboard also smelt slightly of damp (something to note, if they were going to buy out Cecily), but, after rummaging through the shelves, she found a half-decent tablecloth: linen with formal, mid-twentieth-century diagonals of stylised primroses. And when she came back, she found Diana in the kitchen, oohing and aahing over Dan's curry.

*

In the kitchen, Diana noticed as she and Victoria began to collect up cutlery and crockery, there were big, brass bells hanging on the wall. "What are *they*?" she asked.

"What?" Victoria followed her gaze. "Oh, God! They were for the servants!" she said with a little smirk, as if servants were something a bit racy.

Diana found herself imagining that she was in a dolls' house. Perhaps the champagne had gone to her head. A Victorian dolls' house! She hadn't had a Victorian dolls' house as a child; she'd had a Barbie Dreamhouse. But a girl in her class at school had had one; she'd seen it at her birthday party. All the little peg-doll servants in the kitchen, with tiny sacks labelled 'flour' and 'sugar' piled up in the corner, and big (too big, for the scale, she'd noticed) brass cooking pots on the miniature black iron stove. The family were made of porcelain and dressed in satin and lace, and sat stiffly upstairs on teeny, velvet sofas. Quite shocking, it seemed to Diana now, that while the peg dolls in the kitchen were assigned servant status, the porcelain family upstairs were mistresses and masters. Although it hadn't seemed in the least shocking to her as a child: back then, to her primitive, childish mind, it had seemed – she could still remember – quite right, appropriate, and satisfyingly in order.

Back when Cecily's family first moved in, Diana

pondered now, here in the kitchen there would have been only the servants. Sometimes, perhaps, the lady of the house would have floated in to order meals from the cook. But otherwise, they wouldn't have come in here, Cecily's ancestors. They would have just sat on sofas like those porcelain dolls, ringing bells and asking for… what? Tea, maybe? Cocktails? Just as if they lived permanently in a luxury hotel!

Reverting to real life, Diana noticed that the cutlery was silver-plated. Old, heavy, curvy, decorative silver. Some of it had bone handles; some of it had not. There were probably about three sets here, all mixed up; that was what happened, she supposed, when cutlery sets were passed down through generations. And all of it very tarnished.

"It's quite tarnished," Victoria said then.

Looking up, Diana saw that she had been watching her turning one of the forks over in her hand.

Victoria was grimacing, almost apologetically. "I'd get it sorted out if I could…"

"No, no, no!" Diana responded hurriedly. "Not at all! I was admiring the antique look. You know, the tarnish doesn't matter at all; I think it actually adds some shabby chic."

Victoria wrinkled her nose, and then laughed. "Shabby, anyway…" she said.

Funny, Diana thought, that back then, when those bells on the wall were in use, she and Cecily could never, ever have been friends. Cecily's grandfather had probably been a lawyer or something; her own grandad had worked on the docks, and her grandmother had worked as a maid before she married. In fact, if she'd lived in Dover, she might have been a maid in this very kitchen! Different worlds!

Diana's grandad, according to her mother, had been a bit of an activist in the Labour movement. He'd died quite young, of pneumonia or something, when Diana was very small. But her mum said he'd been briefly arrested during some kind of general strike when he was young, and had for the rest of his life been handicapped by a criminal record. He'd always voted Labour, as had Diana's mum, of course. She'd been brought up that way.

Much good it did her, that was what she used to say in later years, with a wry chuckle: "Much good it did me…" Diana could see her saying it, topping and tailing beans, her hands veiny and gnarled by then, in that little Formica kitchen at her flat in Ramsgate. She'd had her back to Diana, who was sitting at the table drinking tea, not helping, being lazy. Her mum always made her lazy: she was so energetic, so quick, that you couldn't help her with anything. She'd finish the task, whatever it might be, before you had a chance to offer help; or even if you did try to help, she'd get so impatient, because you didn't do it her way, that she'd shoo you off almost as soon as you had started. So Diana had been sitting at the table, drinking tea, when her mother said that, and her mum had been standing at the counter with her back to her. And then she'd turned around, in the cumbersome way in which old people turn, to look at Diana and say, "Much good it did me, voting Labour all my life." And she'd laughed that brisk, sceptical, but vivacious laugh of hers.

She stopped to clear her throat then, jerking her shoulder with an irritable twitch, as if she had an itch on her wing bone but couldn't scratch with her wet hands in the bowl of soaking beans. Then she looked round to check that Diana was listening, before continuing. But Diana already knew what was coming next.

"They turned away from us," her mother said. "The Labour Party was created to represent the English working classes, but from the sixties, they began to turn away. They began to think they were meant to speak not only for us, but for everyone who is oppressed throughout the world." She shook her head; knife in one hand, clutch of beans in the other. She never would use scissors to top and tail beans, even after Diana showed her how it was so much quicker.

Her mother had said the same thing a hundred times before. She'd said it back in 2010 when they'd sat watching Gordon Brown making an election speech. "Listen to that!" she said. "Does he talk about Thomas Paine? Does he even talk about Keir Hardie? No! He talks about apartheid in South Africa; he talks about Americans: Martin Luther King and Barack Obama.[9] Both heroes, we get it, but what's his point? He wants us to elect him to represent *us*, so why is he talking about the struggles for justice of people thousands of miles away? Why isn't he talking about *our* struggles? I mean, what have these people got to do with the working-class voters in the UK today?

"The Labour Party became, by the '80s and '90s, just another party wheeling and dealing with the establishment. Then they started wheeling and dealing with ethnic and religious groups as well, getting into all that identity politics." That was what Diana's mother said. She'd heard that Ken Livingstone, the Labour candidate for Mayor of London, had declared in the Finsbury Park Mosque that if elected he would make London a beacon of Islam.[10] And she was sure that such declarations didn't come for free. "And what use is that to *me*?" she would say. It wasn't as if the Tories weren't as bad. That was the thing: Tory or Labour, it made no difference! Party funding and self-advancement were all they cared about.

All those times, Diana had refused to really listen to her mum. She'd hated those conversations; hated the way her mother talked. She didn't want to hear, let alone understand; to understand might mean to become infected. It was taboo, among the middle classes, to question that immigration was a good thing for everyone in every way, and by then Diana was – if you looked at her income, her lifestyle and her friends – demonstrably middle class. She and her friends were on the 'right' side, the side with cultural hegemony, and that was where she had always wanted to be. Ever since she was a teenager, she had been trying to dissociate herself from the angry, bigoted losers like her mum and join the ranks of the happy, spending winners.

But in the years since her mother's death, she had undergone a change. It was as if, now her mother was gone and couldn't see and think about these things for herself, it was Diana's duty to see and think about them for her.

*

Cecily stepped out through the French windows onto the terrace, where there was a small wooden table and bench, so dry and cracked by weather now, they were crying out for attention. There was the lawn ahead, where her grandparents used to play croquet. It was overgrown now and threaded with daisies and love-in-a-mist; they'd have to dig out the lawnmower. There were the great, rustling trees encircling the garden. And there was the low, rambling ilex oak at the back by the entrance to the field; always so perfect for climbing, as it had as many trunks as branches. And beyond the field was the sea.

The children were sitting on the long, low branches of the ilex, just as she and Victoria used to. The sky was wide and pale with the imminence of dusk, and the branches were already almost silhouettes against that fading sky. There was that excitement in the air that she remembered from childhood summer twilights. Now she'd spotted the children, she was unwilling to interrupt them, somehow. So she stood at the edge of the lawn, from where she could just see their shapes in the tree, and hear the murmur of their childish voices.

And then Florian came out through the French windows, saying, "Did you find the children?"

She indicated them with her head, and he came over to where she was standing, and watched them as well.

"You know," he said, after a while, "I was thinking about what you said about Henry VIII's coup."

"Really? You were thinking about that?" she said, surprised. Often, nowadays, she had the impression that he hardly heard anything she said. She was touched, actually. He was looking tentative, shy, almost boyish: in the draining light, his cheeks looked soft. It was remarkable, rather than mundane, for a moment, that this man was actually *her* man.

"Yes – well, it made me think of Pinochet seizing control of the state in Chile and selling off all its assets to his cronies. Or Yeltsin and Putin flogging state assets to a mafia of retainers in post-communist Russia. You know? Basically, ideologically sanctioned handing out of public assets as patronage."

"Ha – I guess," said Cecily.

"And it's like… I don't know… so many people thought, in the '90s, that we'd reached the end of history. You know? Communism had been shown to be 'wrong' and the so-called 'free market' was 'right', and we all thought that there were no more battles to fight, no more problems to solve, because we'd finally found all the answers! Do you remember?"

"Yeah, yeah," Cecily said, "and I feel like such a fool. I was so completely taken in by it all at the time. Trickle-down theory and all of that."

"And now it's like the Gods are laughing at us, because of course we hadn't solved anything at all. Because human nature is still just human nature. We thought that we'd squared the circle; that growth could be eternally fuelled by debt, and we'd all get richer and richer happily ever after. But it turns out that nothing was new and nothing had changed. Not since the beginning of time. That neoliberal revolution we all cheered for in the '90s was just another con trick in the history of humankind, perpetrated by corporates who, behind the scenes, were doing what the power-hungry have always done: changing all the rules to channel all the wealth in their direction."

"Huh," she said. She was watching the children: their

shadowy shapes against the fading, fading sky. She was looking at them because Florian sounded just a little too excited, too Peter Panishly pleased with the cleverness of his thoughts. But at the same time, that occasional excitement of his – though she sometimes had an incomprehensible urge to knock it down – was also what she had fallen for.

"You know," he insisted, "it's always the same story. Whether it's ancient Greece or modern China; feudal France or communist Russia. Every new ideology just ends up being used to justify why those who want power should have it."

"Have you called the children?" Victoria shouted out through the French windows. The curtain blew in front of her face and she pulled it impatiently out of the way. "Have you?"

"Oh, not yet, sorry!" Cecily answered. She looked back at Florian, grimacing to show that this conversation could not be continued, and then turned and called out into the field, "Children! Supper's ready!"

*

"What's for supper?" Julia called into the kitchen, as they all came in from the terrace to the dining room. "Someone said it was lamb curry?" She looked anxious.

"Not for you," Florian told her. "Dan's done something with lentils."

Julia looked dismayed. "*Just* lentils?" she asked. She'd recently turned vegan, but that didn't mean she actually liked any vegan food.

"And rice!" her dad said, in an upbeat tone.

Zac was looking at her. "Do you not like lentils?" he asked.

She made a face.

"So why don't you just have the curry?"

"Ha, ha, very funny," Julia said.

"But *why*?" Zac insisted, laughing.

"Because I'm vegan; because killing animals is cruel and it's bad for the environment," she retorted impatiently. "Did you not even *know* that?" And she pushed past him.

Zac turned to Olivia, asking, in mocking tones, "Are you vegan too?"

"No, no," Olivia said, a little hurriedly, "I'm having the curry."

*

All of the plates here were different, Diana noticed, as she, Victoria and Cecily began to lay them out in front of the seated children, and all around the table. They looked like the kind of collection you might find in a junk shop, and many were chipped or the painting on the enamel somewhat faded. Not that that bothered Diana; not here. In fact, she felt, as they laid out the plates, as if she had a heightened perception, like you do when you are travelling.

"I just love all this old English china!" she exclaimed. She held a green scalloped plate, cherishing it lingeringly in her hands, before placing it down between a knife and a fork. Picking up the next one, she turned it over, reading the stamp on the bottom. "Royal Crown Derby! That sounds old-fashioned!"

Victoria laughed. "It's mostly a bit of a mishmash. Just whichever ones have survived the years without getting broken."

"Oh look at this one!" Diana held up a gold-rimmed plate with a design of delicate burgundy flowers with green and gold tendrils.

"I think that one's French, actually... it might be a Limoges!" Cecily said.

"Oh!" Diana said, putting the plate on the tab "Well, it's still lovely." She reached for another, with rural scenes painted on it in burnt orange, and turned it over to look at the stamp.

"That's French as well," Cecily said, watching her. "Most of it's not English, actually. A lot of it is Limoges; some is Czech, I think."

Diana turned the next plate over in her hands, and read, 'Royal Staffordshire Pottery. A. J. Wilkinson Ltd.' And, perhaps because Cecily had made her feel somehow stupid, she said, "Well, this one is English", and held it out to show her. *Weren't we once famous for pottery?* she wondered. She seemed to have a vague recollection of it. *In Staffordshire? And Stoke-on-Trent, wasn't it?*

"Yes, it is," Cecily agreed, and then laughed. "But it's imitation Dutch. You know, that blue and white. There's quite a lot of that as well."

"God, Cecily! You really are an expert!" Diana remarked. She laughed, and rolled her eyes jokily, but it came out in a voice that was different from what she had intended. And then hurriedly, so as to change the subject, she turned to Victoria and asked, "Does it matter who sits where?"

"Let's have the children at one end, shall we?" Victoria suggested authoritatively. "Olivia, darling, do you think you could move round two seats, and the rest of you move round after her?"

"Right – I'll go and start bringing in the food," Florian said.

As the children shuffled round obediently, Victoria went into the kitchen and came back carrying a box, saying, "You know what, Diana – there is one plate you'd probably really like to see!" She laid the box on the table, explaining, as she lifted the lid, "We keep it in here now, because it's very precious."

Diana looked into the box, and there, lying on a bed of tissue, was a soft grey-blue plate with a raised image of a man kneeling. Though the man was white, to match the border of the plate, you could see from his lips and his Afro hair that he was meant to represent a black man. He was in chains, and round his body were the words, in raised white letters, 'Am I not a man and a brother?' Diana felt a bit flustered with everyone watching her, waiting for her to comment on this. She didn't know quite what she was looking at, or what she was supposed to say.

"It's a Josiah Wedgwood plate made in protest against the slave trade," Victoria explained. "Back in... like... er..."

Diana noted with relief that she wasn't the only one here who didn't know all about plates.

"End of the eighteenth century," Cecily said. "I'll go and get the water jug."

"And we've had it in the family *forever*! You know, it could be three generations, or more, as far as anyone knows," Victoria continued.

"Wow, that's amazing!" Diana said, and she really did feel moved. "A real antique! And so significant!" *You see, Cecily!* she wanted to turn to Cecily and say, then: *there are reasons to be proud to be British. We renounced slavery! The first country ever to unilaterally do so, in the entire history of the planet!* But Cecily was in the kitchen, filling up the water jug. And anyway, it was not the kind of thing you could say.

"Slavery was actually in Africa long before the Europeans arrived, though," Zac said, surprising everyone. He looked delighted at their discomfort. "It was! We learnt about it in school!" He cried, as if one of them had contradicted him, though no-one had said anything. "Slavery was completely normal in loads of African countries. There was this King or something in, like, Benin in the nineteenth century, who said..." He put on an important, kingly voice with a ridiculous accent. "The slave trade has been the glory of my people... or something like that." He began to giggle at the voice he had put on, but then pulled himself together and continued in the same voice, "It is the fountain of all our riches."[11]

Diana didn't know what to think or where to look. Was this true? Through the kitchen door, she could see Dan tasting his curry, and Florian sprinkling coriander over a great tureen of steaming rice. Cecily came back with the water jug and placed it on the table.

"And it wasn't even banned in Ethiopia until, like, the

Second World War or something! There was still slavery in… I think… Nigeria then, too," Zac insisted.

Cecily shrugged irritably. "There's people trafficking and slavery in Britain today," she told him.

Diana applied her attention to the table: she began turning knives around so that their blades all faced the right way.

"Zac, can you see if Daddy needs any help bringing anything in from the kitchen?" Victoria said.

But at that moment Dan came through the doorway with a large, steaming, fragrant dish and placed it triumphantly on the table. After him came Florian with the rice.

"Oh, my goodness! That looks wonderful!" Diana said quickly.

Dan was rosy, his cheeks dimpling with pleasure. He placed the steaming dish on the table and stepped back, looking around at everyone. "Oh, that plate!" he exclaimed, his eye falling on the plate in its box. "Quite amazing, huh? A plate like that is worth about three hundred quid on eBay!" From the kitchen, he hadn't heard what Zac had been saying, Diana realised, because he stood there looking from her to the children, surprised that they were not more responsive, and repeated insistently, "Three hundred quid for a single plate!", shaking his head at the madness of the world, and chuckling.

"That *is* a lot for one plate," Diana agreed eventually, as the silence was becoming awkward. "And that curry smells truly wonderful!"

*

She would really have to have words with Zac, thought Victoria as the meal began. He was going to have to learn that some things just could not be said in certain milieux. It didn't matter with people like his school friends and all that world, because they knew what you meant and wouldn't take what you said the wrong way. It wasn't even Cecily and Florian so much, although they had their lefty opinions. But with people you didn't know, like Diana, you had to be very careful. Everyone was so touchy nowadays, so politically correct, that they could take things all wrong, or attach the wrong importance to them. And then suddenly, anything you said sounded sexist or racist or elitist or selfish, or something else that you hadn't meant at all.

She was feeling irritable again. Not so much with Zac, because he was only a child, after all. How was he supposed to know what was okay to say and what wasn't? Especially when what he'd said was only the truth; presumably it was what he had been taught in school. It was more that she felt annoyed with Cecily for putting them in this situation. She always managed to do this to Victoria: put her and her family on the moral low ground and make them look like oiks. Who knew – it could be that, because of that whole stupid conversation about plates, Diana now thought Zac was some kind of racist! And it would just never happen with the people Victoria knew; with the friends she and Dan had made at work over the years, or the friends from Zac's old prep school. No-one policed anyone's political views there, and no one thought anyone else was the Devil incarnate just because they might vote Conservative, or make a joke that wasn't completely 'woke'.

Cecily was always boasting about how, unlike most people, she had moved further to the left as she got older. She clearly thought that this demonstrated something noble or virtuous about her. But it didn't demonstrate anything of the sort, in Victoria's opinion. What she noticed was that with every year that passed, she got richer and Cecily got poorer. And of course, it was always the poor who were left wing. The poor always thought that the rich ought to share their money, although once they became rich themselves, they rapidly changed their minds.

Victoria had once said as much to Dan – "She wouldn't be so lefty if she had more money!" – when she was annoyed with Cecily.

And he had almost spurted out his beer with laughter. "You know what – you're right on!" he'd said.

And sharing everything out equally was never going to happen. It was just a nice idea, like heaven; but, like heaven, equality was impossible even to imagine once you got down to the nitty-gritty detail. It just wasn't the way of the world! Think about their very own ancestors, who had bought a house built by the famous Voysey! It wouldn't have come cheap, would it? And the only reason they had that money was because they'd played the capitalist game. Their great-great-grandfather had been an arms dealer, if Victoria remembered rightly, or maybe a banker. Something like that, anyway, that Cecily would disapprove of. But the reality was that it was only thanks to people like him that the artists and intellectuals that Cecily admired had got anyone to commission their work. Who had funded Cecily's beloved Renaissance? It wasn't St Francis of

Assisi, was it? It was the corrupt Popes who were dripping with gold, and the Medici bankers! And besides, for all her talk about how the rich should pay more tax, what good was Cecily actually doing in the world? Victoria herself had given several hundred to charity this year, which was probably a lot more than Cecily.

"This is delicious," Diana was saying. "It tastes so authentic!"

Dan beamed. "It's all in the marinade," he said. "A *load* of spices. And in fact, I only had a couple of hours to marinate the lamb today. It's even better if you marinate it overnight." He noticed then that Julia had not eaten much, and laughed. "Hey, Julia," he teased, "how are the lentils?" Dan found vegetarians and vegans vaguely ridiculous.

As a child, Victoria remembered, Cecily would always eat the food on her plate that she *didn't* like first – the vegetables and stuff – and keep her favourite bits till last. She was praised for this, which meant that then she did it more ostentatiously.

"She'll go far in life!" their grandfather had once commented, absurdly, as the whole family admired Cecily's attitude to her plate of food.

This had rankled with Victoria, who liked to eat the best bits first. And, out of defiance, she had continued doing that, even though she knew that this would cast her, in the eyes of her tedious family, as profligate. *Sucks to them, though*, was what she thought now. Because things had changed and their ridiculous moral codes were now outdated. Victoria and Cecily had come of age not in some grim, parsimonious nineteenth-century era where you had to scrimp your pennies in order for the pounds to look after themselves, but in the naughty '90s, and by then. 'Material Girl' Madonna taught the world that you had to spend money to make money. And who was it, after all, who had gone further? Was it Cecily or was it Victoria?

*

Cecily didn't sleep well that night. She kept waking up, with a heavy sense that everything was at odds. At about four in the morning, she woke for the last time, and lay in bed, staring at the ceiling. She felt harried by worries, but when she tried to identify them, they merged or slipped momentarily out of her mental vision.

There was Brexit. All the time, ever since June 2016, Brexit had been stalking her peace of mind. It hardly felt real: it felt like being in a distopian bad dream. She rolled over and, reaching for a glass of water, noticed within the pile of books on her bedside table *Areopagitica* by John Milton, and a book about the English Civil War. She'd scooped them off the shelf just before she went to bed, imagining she might look into them over the next few days. *Areopagitica* she dimly remembered from her university days; it was written during the English Civil War. Milton had been on the winning side of that war, it had occurred to her when she took the book off the shelf, whereas she was on the losing side of this one. Was this awful loss and grievance that she felt over Brexit, she wondered now, how it had felt to be a Cavalier on the losing side of the civil war of the seventeenth century? And would she, Cecily, even have been on the losing side back then? Would she have been a Cavalier, or would she have been a Roundhead?

It was impossible to know, so she dropped that yarn of thought and rolled back onto the pillow. What mattered now was the urgency of the present. What mattered now was that half a nation had been tricked into blaming the EU for the neoliberal ideology that had been siphoning wealth from the poor to the rich in the Anglo-Saxon world for the past forty years, while simultaneously shrinking public services and dismantling labour unions. It was not the EU: it was Britain and America who had created this new paradigm within which inequality grew daily. It was Margaret Thatcher and Ronald Reagan and their disciples, cheered on by the billionaire press owners in their tax havens, who had led the way in selling our public services into private hands and dismantling the laws and regulations that protected us from the greed of predatory corporations, to the point where all we in Britain had left were those rights which the EU guaranteed us: social and human rights, food standards, and health and safety legislation. These were the last protections we had, after forty years of rapacious neo-liberalism, and they were what the billionaires who had funded Brexit wanted to finally sweep away. That was the worry of Brexit.

But there was also the house. The dripping roof, the failing sewage system, the insidious damp. All these represented worrying expense that was beyond their means, hers and Florian's, but was perhaps trivial for Victoria and Dan. And this very difference made the whole issue uncomfortable to broach.

And then there was Victoria swiping the vases. It seemed an act of such outright hostility that Cecily couldn't even begin to understand it.

And on top of *that* there was Diana. Cecily had this terrible foreboding that somehow Victoria was going to win Diana over to her side. It sounded ridiculous when she tried to articulate this foreboding in actual words; ridiculous and utterly infantile. But that was how she felt. She had a churning sense that *that thing*, that thing that had happened so many times in her childhood, was beginning again. That Victoria had once more cast her charmed nets over the sea. Always, when they were together in social situations, it seemed that Victoria gradually collected all the strings, until everyone became puppets in her hands. And she even had Cecily under a spell, so that, although she inwardly protested, she too actually *behaved* like a puppet. She said and did things that she didn't want to say and do; that only Victoria wanted her to say and do. Like now, with Diana – when Victoria was there, Cecily became awkward and everything she said or did was wrong and offensive.

That moment on the cliff, when she had felt that she might come to understand how Diana thought, how she saw this political and cultural crossroads at which they now found themselves, already seemed – after drinks and dinner – like something from another time. Because by the evening, things had been different. There had been that edge of impatience in Diana's voice, when they were looking at the plates. "You really are an expert!" she had said, and there was a sneer to it, almost. Unless, of course, Cecily had imagined it. Victoria's presence always caused her to move

118

into nervous, defensive mode, so that sometimes she started to sense threats and ill will where perhaps there weren't any. Possibly, Diana had meant nothing at all by it. Or, even if she *was* irritable when she said that, perhaps she had just been hungry? And this was the trouble with other people: the awful fact that, most of the time, you never knew – except in those brief, rare moments – whether what you thought they might be thinking or feeling was what they were *actually* thinking or feeling.

All in all, there was just a general sense of multiple, convoluted threat. But it troubled her, that word 'expert'. The Brexiters had said it. Hadn't the Lord Chancellor, Michael Gove, smirked on TV just before the 2016 referendum, saying, "The people in this country have had enough of experts"?[12] And on Diana's face tonight, there had been something of that same smirk. Or had she been imagining it?

When she was young, Cecily suddenly remembered, and studying the history of art, an Italian boy she knew had started telling her how to make a puttanesca sauce. She'd already made a puttanesca sauce several times, in fact, but when she told him this, he told her that she still needed to learn the 'correct' way. She had laughed at the time. She had found it absurd that anyone could imagine that there was one 'correct' way to make anything. The boy had seemed fussy, narrow-minded, and she had felt, though she was ashamed to admit it now, superior. Looking back, that feeling seemed to her a classic kind of English boorishness; an aggressive aversion to prescription, to theory, to authority… to expertise.

Unable to sleep, she sat up and placed her feet on the carpet by the bed. It was stringy, threadbare, under her feet. She picked up her 'phone and her cardigan from her chair and slipped out of the room. Holding her nose, she hurried past the faint, sickly smell wafting from the bathroom, until she was down the corridor and down the stairs. She tiptoed across the tiled floor of the kitchen, so as not to expose too much of her feet to the cold, and made herself a cup of hot milk, not closing the microwave door afterwards, for fear that the ping of the closing door would wake somebody up. She was just about to leave the kitchen when she heard a scrabbling in the wall behind the fridge. She took a few steps nearer, but it stopped. And though she waited, unmoving, for nearly a minute, she heard nothing more.

She tiptoed out into the sitting room, with the hot mug cupped in her hands, and curled up in one of the faded pink velvet armchairs. Then she turned on the standard lamp and looked about. The girls' midnight feast must be over, because here were more of the old books, and a few sweet wrappers strewn about the floor. She leaned forward to read the title of the nearest book: John Foxe's *Book of Martyrs.*

Picking it up, she turned it over in her hands. The dust jacket had an illustration, probably after one of the original woodcut impressions in one of the sixteenth-century editions, of a woman burning at the stake. The book, she knew from a university history course long ago, was a kind of hagiography of the early English Protestants who were persecuted and put to death for their beliefs. She thumbed through it, and then, curious, she consulted her phone. According to Wikipedia,[13] this book had been so popular that it went through four editions before Foxe's death in 1587. And in 1571 a convocation of Canterbury ordered that the latest (second) edition be available for perusal in churches.

After that, posthumous editions added content to Foxe's original. A 1632 edition covered what it called 'persecutions in these later times', including the Spanish invasion in 1588 and the Gunpowder Plot of 1605. Wikipedia[14] asserted that a certain John Milner, author of *The History Civil and Ecclesiastical and Survey of the Antiquities of Winchester* had noted in the 1790's that copies of Foxe's book, with its gruesome woodcuts, could still be found 'chained to the desks of many county churches'. Even into the nineteenth century, new editions and abridgements were being issued. The extent of this book's influence on the mentality of the English appeared to be enormous.

Having skimmed the introduction, she flicked through the book until she came across Foxe's first 'modern' martyr: John Wycliffe, a fourteenth-century critic of the Catholic Church 'whom the Lord raised up here in England, to detect more fully and amply the poison of the Pope's doctrine and false religion'.[15] Wycliffe, Foxe continued, lived at a time when 'the simple and unlearned people' were kept 'far from all knowledge of the Holy Scripture' and taught 'nothing else but such things as came forth of the court of Rome.'

Wycliffe, Foxe continued, 'perceiving the true doctrine of Christ's Gospel to be adulterated and defiled with so many filthy inventions and dark errors of bishops and monks', resolved to 'call back the Church from her idolatry'. "'I defy the Pope, and all his laws!'" Foxe had him cry.

Further on, in Foxe's hagiography, came William Tyndale, author of the first English translation from the Bible based on Greek and Latin texts. The full edition of his New Testament was published in Worms in 1526. Tyndale was, Foxe said, 'a special organ of the Lord appointed… to shake the inward roots and foundation of the Pope's proud prelacy'. Tyndale's translation was condemned by the (at that time still Catholic) Church authorities under Henry VIII, 'to the intent (as Tyndale saith) that the world being kept still in darkness, they might sit in the consciences of the people through vain superstition and false doctrine, to satisfy their ambition, and insatiable covetousness,' Foxe wrote. While in Antwerp, Tyndale was betrayed to the Holy Roman Emperor at the court of Brussels by a fellow Englishman, and subsequently arrested, convicted and executed for heresy in 1536.

Cecily found herself gripped as she read. The passion and hatred seething within Foxe's words was almost biblical in its virulence. And the text was so strangely direct, lively and readable that it was curiously persuasive.

Foxe now proceeded to the roller coaster of revolutions and counter-revolutions that characterised the end of the sixteenth century. The state, which had remained Protestant under Henry VIII's short-lived son Edward VI, swung abruptly back to Catholicism under Mary I, and then back again to Protestantism under Elizabeth I. Describing the Marian return to Catholicism, Foxe wrote, 'The papists violently overthrew the true doctrine of the Gospel, and persecuted with sword and fire all those that would not agree to receive again the Roman Bishop as supreme head of the universal Church, and allow all the errors, superstitions and idolatries, that before by God's Word were disproved and justly condemned.'

She put the book down again. She had the strangest sense that it was alive. Even though she'd put it down, and looked out at the gradations of dark outside, beyond the lead-paned imitation Tudor window, it was as if she could still hear the book all around her; not so much as voices, but as a kind of rhythm. There seemed to be some pulse, some arrangement of thoughts into rhythmic groups and clusters, so that they raised emotion: a rousing sense of longed-for coherence that seemed – tantalisingly – just within reach. What was stranger still, as she sat there, thinking about it, was that there were thought patterns within this work of Foxe's that seemed uncannily modern and familiar; somehow connected with the drumbeats of the Brexiters.

Each of Foxe's martyrs, at some point in their story, had been condemned by the Catholic Church authorities in England. Wycliffe was summoned to St Paul's to be examined by the the church authorities, whom Foxe, Cecily noted, described as Pharisees. 'Then,' he wrote, 'began the Pharisees to swarm together striving against the light of the Gospel, which began to shine abroad; neither was the Pope himself behind with his part, for he never ceased with his bulls and his letters to stir up them who otherwise, of their own accord, were but too furious and mad.' The original Pharisees were the Jewish religious authorities who, according to Gospel, examined Jesus and attempted to trip him up with his own arguments, and ultimately cooperated with the Romans to have him condemned and executed. So this reference to the Catholic church hierarchy as 'Pharisees' appeared to draw a parallel between Wycliffe and Jesus. The suggestion seemed to be that Wycliffe was condemned by the tendentious reasoning of theological 'experts' of his day, much as Jesus had been condemned by the tendentious reasoning of the Pharisees – the theological 'experts' of his own time.

Was this an ancient drumbeat that Gove had echoed with his disparaging of 'experts', Cecily wondered? His disparaging of all those economic experts who warned repeatedly that Brexit was a terrible idea? Within a world view where salvation by God was the ultimate goal, and God's favour or displeasure the ultimate arbiter of success or failure in reaching that goal, Church authorities, those who claimed to be able to divine and predict the mind of God, were the ultimate experts. Now, by contrast, we lived in a market economy in which the ultimate measure of success was generally considered to be prosperity and well-being in this life. Consequently, the invisible hand of God, giving or taking away prosperity, was commonly perceived to work through the economy, and so the 'experts' of our day could be said to be those able to divine and predict the workings of the economy.

"I'm asking the British public to take back control of our destiny from those organisations which are distant, unaccountable and elitist," The Brexiteer Gove had said in an interview on Sky News with Faisal Islam, if she remembered rightly. "The people in this country have had enough of experts from organisations with acronyms saying that they know what is best and getting it consistently wrong."

Gove had said, "I think the people in this country have had enough of experts", it seemed to Cecily now, just as Henry VIII's crony Cromwell might, four hundred years ago, have said, "The people in this country have had enough of prelates!" It was as if, it occurred to her now, he was playing tunes we half-remembered from way back in in our national psyche. As if his words were like a dog whistle to our atavistic prejudices. This *Book of Martyrs*, with its virulent hatred of continental Roman impositions, with its militant willingness to glorify a rapacious cynic like Henry VIII as a great, godly Prince, even as he murdered and plundered, simply because he was the key to realising their ideological ends, seemed to uncannily prefigure the Brexit spirit. She put it down.

Instead, she picked up the Shakespeare. *Henry VI, Part Two*. It lay open, still with a sprinkling of pink sugar across the centre fold. She read, as Julia had earlier, 'Ignorance is the curse of God; knowledge is the wing wherewith we fly to heaven…' and found herself puzzled. There she had been, spinning theories about how our English distrust of theories and experts originated in the sixteenth-century rejection of the Catholic Church. But this book seemed to sing quite a different tune: here in *Henry VI, Part Two*, written around 1591, right in between the fourth and fifth editions of Foxe's *Book of Martyrs*, Shakespeare was singing the praises of knowledge.

She sat sipping her hot milk for a while, feeling confused. But then she remembered that, in English Protestant tradition, it was the Catholics in Europe and Ireland who lived in superstitious ignorance, slavishly dependent on the rituals and interpretations of corrupt, power-hoarding priests. By contrast, the Anglican English, whose monarchs allowed them to read the Bible, had access to the only genuine 'knowledge': that is, to God's revealed truth which, thanks to the priesthood of all believers, was available to all.

Gove's words, it seemed to her now, revived rhythms of English Protestant tradition and made it appear that the truth about Brexit, just like biblical revelation, supposedly needed no interpretation – was self-evident to the simple, pure and honest Brit, while those 'experts' who tried to deny this truth by claiming special understanding and confusing us with bogus economic theories, were cast in the role of Foxe's manipulative, erstwhile priests. "I'm not asking the public to trust me. I'm asking the public to trust themselves," Gove had told Faisal Islam in that interview. "I'm asking the British public to take back control of our destiny from those organisations which are distant, unaccountable and elitist."

And what was so pernicious in all of this, Cecily thought, was that, of course, people in the UK really did feel abandoned and unrepresented by the institutions that were supposed to defend their interests. But it was the hegemony of Anglo-Saxon neoliberalism within those institutions, growing since the 1980s, that had oppressed them; the lie that GDP was a substitute for health and happiness. The irony was that the neoliberalism that was against our interests was the ideology of the Brexiters themselves, while it was social-democratic Europe, if anyone, that stood between us and the ravages of the class war that the neoliberal, transatlantic rich wanted to wage against us. It was the Brexiters that were the villains in this story, and yet they had snake-charmed half the population into thinking they were our saviours.

She became aware that she was sleepy, then, and decided to make her way back to bed. But just as she was drifting off, in that liminal period between sleep and waking, she was startled by words that appeared unaccountably in her mind:

With a rowley, powley, gammon and spinach,
Heigh-ho! says Anthony Rowley...

They were words from some folk song half-remembered from her '70s childhood. She didn't even know, now, where they came from. But here they were, emerging inexplicably from her subconscious forty years later, and the atmosphere they evoked was powerful. Coming back straight from childhood, it was an atmosphere of the macabre; of menace.

DAY 2

Tuesday 27ᵗʰ August 2019

The feather duvet had such a soft, cloudy weight about it, and the pillows too, that, even though there was the slightest dampness about the pillows, Diana had the sense of living in some special, old-fashioned kind of comfort. This was the first thing she became aware of when she woke. The next was the sun: it was a beautiful morning. She could tell that as, even though the ticking curtains were drawn, the brightness of the sun behind seemed to almost fill them, like the wind in a sail, and a warm, golden fuzz of light blazed along their edges. She stretched voluptuously in the bed and then sat up and looked around.

As well as the mixed pile of books, on the bedside table was an old jug with folk designs on it: colourful dancing ladies in wide skirts and little sleeveless waistcoats. It made her think of Hansel and Gretel or something: fairy tales. Next to the jug was a heavy-bottomed glass. There was also an old, oriental-looking coffee pot which couldn't serve any purpose there at all. It looked as if it had simply been put down there by mistake one day, and never moved again. Which seemed to her – suddenly – a wonderful thing. It had a broken spout and a handle that had been cracked into pieces, it seemed, and then painstakingly mended. One tiny triangle of pottery, the size, perhaps, of a sesame seed, had never been recovered, but its memory remained as a teeny triangular gap.

She was uplifted by a wonderfully buoyant, holiday hope and newness; a feeling she remembered from childhood mornings on summer days when there was no school. The sea and the sun and the wet, green grass called to her, so she swung her feet out of the bed onto the old rug, and then pattered over the cool terracotta tiles to find some clothes.

The girls and Zac were all asleep, she saw, peeping into their room on her way into the sitting room. She'd heard them faintly last night, giggling over their midnight feast. She didn't quite dare go into the kitchen to make herself a cup of tea: it seemed presumptuous (what if Victoria walked in and found her just helping herself?) And so she just opened the old French windows in the dining room and went straight out into the garden.

It was a heavenly morning! The sun warmed the dewy grass and shimmered off the leaves of the gracious old trees that stood, like druidic guards, about the outskirts of the lawn. She couldn't see the sea from where she was, but she could hear its primeval roar. She wandered round the garden and round the side, she found a wide, stone bench, from where she could look out over the limestone cliff road, and the fields which sloped down dramatically to the sea. It was cold, that stone, and mostly in the shade, but she sat on the one corner that the sun could reach, and the view was just fantastic. She could just make out, over in the distance, that the Dover lighthouse that she'd noticed as they were arriving in the car yesterday was flying a Union Jack, which reminded her of some of the conversations that had come up yesterday. Somehow, so many topics had taken on a political significance which had been uncomfortable, since Brexit always managed to cast her and Cecily – against their wills – onto opposing teams.

Much as she liked Cecily, there were occasions when she found her tedious. It was those times when, instead of being the thoughtful, receptive person Diana admired, she became just a mass-produced mind; a predictable product of her class, upbringing and education. She seemed to sort of assume that because of that upbringing, she knew better than Diana about everything; that she represented 'right opinion' more than Diana did. But just because Cecily had gone to university and Diana hadn't, that didn't mean that Diana didn't understand what was going on in this country. In fact, almost the opposite was true: it was precisely *because* her family had always been wealthy and their interests had always been represented by the political classes, that Cecily couldn't really understand what was going on, or how, over the past few decades, those liberal values that so buoyed up families like hers had left many people like Diana's family floundering.

Diana's Great-Aunt Jan, a school dinner lady back in the '80s, had been sacked from her job for using the n-word. It sounded terrible when you said it like that. And it was terrible, but not quite in the way that it sounded. What had happened was that, as Auntie Jan was crossing the busy playground on her way home towards the end of lunchtime one day, a little black girl, who was running, had fallen over. Diana's aunt, a big, round, kindly lady, had hurried over to pick her up, and had taken her to the nurse's office (schools used to have them, then). And, since the nurse was busy with some older children, Aunt Jan herself had cleaned the graze with Savlon (which you were allowed to do in those days) and gone to the shelf and taken down the box of plasters. She thought the little girl might cheer up a bit if she was allowed to choose a plaster from the box. But the girl was so shy that she didn't quite dare, so Diana's aunt tried to encourage her.

"Shall we do 'Eeny, Meeny, Miny, Mo' to pick one?" she suggested.

And then Aunt Jan tried to jolly the child along by reciting the rhyme. "*Eeny, meeny, miny, mo, catch a ****** by the toe...*" She chanted, and then laughingly lifted up the plaster that her finger had landed on.

The little girl smiled, then, and they put the plaster on. And Auntie Jan thought nothing of it, other than being quite chuffed with herself for managing to make the shy girl smile, until she was informed, two days later, that one of the teachers, who had happened to come to the nurse's office at that moment, had made a complaint.

And so, before she knew it, Aunt Jan had been sacked as a racist, even though she'd really just been mindlessly repeating a counting rhyme she'd known since she was a child and, because she'd learnt it as a child, had simply never thought about the meaning of the words. Who does? There were so many of those nonsense rhymes. Great Aunt Jan was born in 1934 and had never been abroad. As a child, everyone she knew was white British and had assumptions that were what you would now call white supremacist, although that expression had not yet been coined because those assumptions had not yet been questioned.

"There are lots of racist words we use that you'd never know were racist!" Jan would tell people earnestly, latterly. She'd taken it very hard, what happened to her: she never got over the social humiliation. For the rest of her life, she would tell people in an insistent voice, "There are lots of racist words that we all use even today without thinking!" She became an expert on these things; she began to talk like a dictionary. "There's 'nitty-gritty'. Do you know what that really means? It comes from the days of the slave trade; it used to be used to describe the human waste and debris left in ships when slaves were marched out onto land after a journey. Then it was applied so as to include the slaves themselves. It's banned in the police force! Did you know that? Then there's 'hip hip hooray' – that comes from the rallying cry '*hep hep*' used in Jewish pogroms. And of course, 'long time no see' was originally a way of mocking the way Native Americans spoke English?"

But Diana had an inkling of how it had felt for Auntie Jan when that incident had happened. The shock. She herself had once told a joke to a group at a school friend's birthday party, in her first year of secondary school. It was a joke she'd heard her mum's boyfriend tell, about an Englishman, an Irishman and a Scotsman. She couldn't remember how it went now, of course, but the punchline was, as it always was in those jokes, about how stupid the Irishman was. And just before she got to that punchline, one of the girls had put up her hand, sarcastically, like you put up your hand in class, except that this was a party, not a classroom. And once she'd got everyone's attention she said, in a meaningful voice, "By the way, I'm Irish."

It was like Diana could feel the goodwill around her vanish.

"Yeah, actually, my grandmother was Irish," another girl said.

And Diana was left high and dry. She never finished the joke. In that moment, she went from the popular centre to the shunned outside of the group. She'd never experienced shame quite like that, before or since. It was to her amazing, as she lay in bed that night, that only that morning, it had never occurred to her that there was anything wrong with the joke. What a monster that-morning-Diana must have been! Because as she lay in bed after the party, it was perfectly obvious that those jokes were awful; that they slandered an entire nationality. And how was it possible that until today she'd just never seen that?

The wind whipped up in the trees, and she did her cardigan up. But the problem with immigration, it seemed to Diana, wasn't so much race. It was culture. It just wasn't true that you could accept limitless numbers of migrants, from different places with different cultures, and not see your habits and customs challenged, and perhaps overruled. She'd be the first to admit that nowadays, after seventy years – perhaps three generations – of post-war immigration, there were many English people of various shades of brown whose recent ancestors came from somewhere else, but they themselves were no less English than she was. Those Poles who had arrived in the past ten years or so were obviously much more foreign now than anyone whose parents or grandparents had arrived here from the Caribbean or the Punjab in the '50s or '60s. It wasn't about skin colour; it was about culture.

Most of her friends – her middle-class, mixed-ethnic circle of friends – saw multiculturalism largely as a question of cuisine. They thought it was lovely that nowadays, in London, if you wanted to go out for a meal with your friends, you could choose from The Tower Tandoori, The Pomegranate (Syrian Kurdistan), The Thai Tiger, Izakaya (Japanese) U Sławka (Polish), and many more. Diana loved it too. She also loved that, as well as Tesco's and Sainsbury's, she could shop at the Chittagong Grocers or the Glory Afro-Caribbean Supermarket or the Fenhua Liu Superstore.

But her problem with immigration was that – well, like her mother used to say – recently the culture she thought of as hers was being overwhelmed. She'd read in the paper, a few years ago, that nowadays half of inner London's schoolchildren didn't even have English as their first language. And the fact was that you couldn't confine cultural influence to the kitchen. The things we were allowed to think and say were also being slowly transformed. Last summer, Diana had been sitting on the Tube when a woman boarded the train, swaddled in black. She was with her husband, and so handicapped by her outfit that he actually had to help her find her way to a seat. There was a heatwave, and Diana remembered looking from that woman to her husband. The woman was blanketed from head to toe in sun-attracting black in over thirty-degree heat; her husband was manspreading freely on the seat beside her, in jeans and a T-shirt, cool and airy as you please. It had upset her. Just think of the suffragettes, and the women who braved social ostracism to escape the handicap of gloves and corsets and long, inhibiting skirts! What on earth would they make of it all?

Of course, other cultures also socially conditioned women into handicapping themselves. In fact, patriarchies the world over got a kick out of debilitating their women. There were the Chinese women who'd famously deformed their feet by breaking and then binding them; and there was somewhere in Africa where the women wore those elongating neck rings. And there was modern Western culture. Diana had seen girls shivering half naked at bus stops on a winter night out, socially groomed into exposing the maximum amount of skin, while the boys were dressed warmly. On that same summer Tube ride, in fact, when she looked around, she could see several women teetering in crippling high heels. But at least – and that was the thing – there was only a very weak social taboo against pointing out that high heels were a feminist issue. Whereas you weren't allowed to even mention niqabs or burqas, except in tones of respect.

About ten years ago, her mother had phoned to tell her that the Archbishop of Canterbury had made a speech in which he said that it was unavoidable that elements of Islamic law would be adopted in Britain to help Muslims integrate.

What the hell? Olivia was a tiny baby at the time, and Diana had looked down at her daughter and felt fury rising.

As Cecily said, all the major world religions were inherently misogynistic. The Anglican Church had come some distance from its patriarchal roots, in that respect. But now it looked like it wouldn't take much encouragement for it to abandon its pretence of respecting women's rights, and slip back into its bad old ways. Our laws could all change; they could go backwards as well as forwards. And the Muslims weren't the only threat. If Catholic Poles kept on pouring in the way they were now, who knew? Perhaps the Archbishop of Canterbury would suggest that Polish priests should be able to keep their congregations from seeking abortions.

It could happen. In fact, her mother told her back then, sharia councils were already operating in Britain, even as the Archbishop spoke. Her mother had heard that there were women here in England who had been through Muslim marriage ceremonies, but never had their marriage registered in the civil courts. Under sharia law, she said, a man could divorce his wife unilaterally, although for women it was not so easy. And if a woman's marriage wasn't registered in the civil courts and her husband decided to divorce her, she would have no legal right to financial support. Diana's mother had heard that sharia councils let men have multiple wives, and that they permitted inheritance laws which discriminated against women. All this, here in England! And they approved wife-beating. Here in England! And the worst thing about it was that the state failed to help women in these situations. Diana's mum had read in the news that the police and other authorities just avoided getting involved for fear of offending powerful people in those communities.

And most terrible of all was the way the police failed women over so-called 'honour' killings. There was that girl who was murdered by her own father and uncle, for leaving an abusive husband who wouldn't let her have a bank account. Her father had threatened her several times before he murdered her, and the poor girl had tried to get police help, but they had dismissed her as 'hysterical and scheming'. Two weeks later, she was dead; her father and uncle had pushed her off a cliff.

This fear people had of being accused of racism, or of offending religious sensibilities, meant that women's rights were being eroded before our eyes. And who was going to protect women if the government and the supposed enforcers of the law didn't? Who was going to protect Diana and her daughter?

"Good morning!"

A pleasant, BBC-breakfast-time voice startled her out of her thoughts, and she looked round to see Victoria standing there, a blanket over her arm and a tea tray in her hands. She had already done her hair and make-up, Diana noticed, suddenly feeling scruffy.

"I thought you might like a cup of tea," Victoria said.

*

She'd spotted Diana from her bedroom window, sitting on the bench and gazing out to sea. As she'd watched, Diana shifted her position and kind of hunched, as if she was cold, stirring a surprising response in Victoria. She looked… humble, sitting out there on the stone bench; alone and small with the trees and the sea and the sky stretching out around her. It irked Victoria to see her looking so powerless. But at the same time, she also felt sort of touched and protective.

When she went downstairs, she found that Cecily wasn't up yet; it was a golden opportunity to build up some rapport with Diana. Since they were all going to be there for several days (well, at least until Victoria made up her mind as to whether to speak to Cecily about the house), she couldn't bear to be there just as a hanger-on to this bizarre new performative friendship of Cecily's. It was similar to the feeling she got when she was walking down the street and there was someone right in front of her. She couldn't bear it – she just felt constrained, uncomfortable; she had to take a different route, or overtake. And similarly, the only way for her to feel free and autonomous in this situation was to get herself out of the cramped side-lines and into the space of the centre. It felt sneaky, as if she was acting against Cecily in some way – which she supposed she was: she was trying to oust Cecily from the role of most central person within this group of three in which they found themselves. But strangest of all was that, though part of Victoria felt ashamed, as if what she wanted to do were shabby, another part of her felt positively thrilled by the dangerous spite; by the sheer energy of her egoism. And that was it: no matter what was right and what was wrong, she was usually driven not by either, but by some other inner imperative which just afforded her no choice.

That stone bench where Diana was sitting was always cold, Victoria knew, and so she fetched her own blanket from her room: the nice, soft fleece blanket that she brought with her when she came here. She brought it because it was nice to curl up on the big, green sofa with a blanket in the evenings, and she couldn't bear the itchy, old, woollen blankets that had lurked in the airing cupboard here forever and which – she'd always imagined, even when she was a child – were full of lice or fleas. She couldn't wait to get rid of them, which was one reason why she'd wrapped them around the vases. Once she got the vases home, she would throw the blankets away.

She found and washed the tea tray again, even though she'd scrubbed it only yesterday (why was everything in this house always slightly grimy?). And as she dried it with the tea towel, she noticed that on the back was the inscription 'John Constable, *Salisbury Cathedral from the Meadows*'. Then she made two big mugs of tea to put on it. She'd always liked the picture on that tray. It was soft and peaceful, with the lovely old church and the rainbow. She remembered it from when she was a child. Once, when she was very little, before Cecily was old enough to come as well, Victoria had come to stay here all by herself. Granny had made her a dolls' tea party, with Iced Gems for biscuits, tiny cucumber sandwiches, and sweet, milky tea in a little china children's teapot with a yellow rabbit on it and tiny yellow rabbit teacups. They'd taken it all out to the garden on this tray, and they'd arranged the dolls around it and fed them all the food. It was sad to say, but looking back it seemed to Victoria that those first three and a half years before Cecily was born were the brightest, lightest and most blessed days of her life. She couldn't remember much about them; only that feeling of abundant light. If she had been an only child, she would have been a thousand times happier. She would have had so much more room to just *be*.

It was a shame the tray was so scratched and marked now: it had some funny brown stains on it, and some scribbles in biro by some child.

She saw, when she opened the fridge to get the milk, that – as usual – Cecily and Florian had brought all their leftovers from home. They'd brought a carton of milk, already opened; the remains of a chunk of Cheddar, dry and cracked about the edges; an open pot of Greek yoghurt; and some kind of lentil pie, a third of it already eaten. Jesus! They'd even brought a half-drunk bottle of Prosecco! Half a bottle of Prosecco and they'd brought it in the car all the way from London? Surely by now it would be flat. In her stomach, Victoria developed a knot of anger on seeing all this; an urge to fling some of it, all of it, any of it, into the bin. Realising this, she marvelled at herself. Why on earth should it bother her what Cecily chose to put in the fridge?

And that was the most maddening thing: that she was never able to separate herself from Cecily; to be unaffected by her. Always Cecily managed to make her feel those childhood emotions: ugly, humiliating emotions that she never wanted to feel ever again. Witnessing this penny-pinching within their shared fridge evoked for Victoria an awful itching, biting, scratching helplessness. It reminded her of everything she had managed to escape from her dowdy '70s childhood of fish-paste sandwiches at chilly picnics, served from scratched and clouded old plastic Tupperware boxes which were always haunted, somehow, by a smell of bleach and mouldy bread. That parsimonious English childhood in which everyone, from her parents to her grandparents, saw the using up of leftovers as a high-flying virtue; in which failing to eat your crusts (as Victoria had once tried to do, cutting them off in the casual way that she had seen her friend Katy do) was regarded as evidence of a weak character. How she had longed, as a child, to be free of them all and to lead a glamorous life like Katy! Katy's family had been to New York; she had a shower in her bathroom and choc ices in her freezer. If you went to her house after school, you got Maryland cookies and Jaffa Cakes. And she was allowed to drink fizzy drinks at the weekend, and paint her nails. Victoria's mother had believed that chocolate biscuits were somehow debauched; so when Katy came round to their house after school, Victoria was mortified by the plain digestives on offer. She could still remember Katy's face when her mother held out the plate.

In her childhood struggle against dowdiness and sniffy thrift, Cecily had never been any kind of ally. Victoria had always, always been alone in her rebellion; in her desperate yearning for a more glamorous life. There was the week their cat died, and she and Cecily were both so upset that, when they passed the cat food in the supermarket, they began to cry. Seeing how upset they were, their mother – for the first and only time that Victoria could remember – had abandoned a lifetime of wholesomeness to suggest, wildly, "How about we buy a SodaStream?"

And Victoria, aged twelve, couldn't quite believe her

luck; that such a day could ever have dawned. SodaStreams, at that time, were all the rage. And at first Cecily was equally elated, as they rushed, on their mother's whim, to the appliances section. But then, once they had chosen the machine they wanted and Victoria actually held the box in her arms, imagining how she could show it off to Katy, just as they began heading for the tills, Cecily suddenly stopped, stricken, halfway down the hairdryer section, and cried, "Oh, we can't! We can't do it! It's just too awful: supposing Tabby looks down from heaven and sees that we've replaced her with a SodaStream?!" Who needed a sister like that?

"Oh, you're right!" their mother had immediately agreed, and they were so puffed up, the two of them, with their own higher values, that no one had even thought to ask Victoria what she thought. Back went the SodaStream onto the shelf; Cecily glowing with virtue and their mother glowing with pride in her younger daughter. They were positively transported by this act of relinquence. Only Victoria had been left feeling alone and furious; her chance snatched away in the very same moment it had come within her reach.

She put the blanket over her arm, poured milk into each mug and then picked up the tray and went outside. She'd thought that Diana would probably notice her as she came into sight from around the side of the house, but she was lost in thought, staring out to sea, and so Victoria called out to her, "Good morning! I thought you might like a cup of tea!"

"Ooh, lovely! How thoughtful!" cooed Diana, in that slightly daft way she had. Slightly daft, but not unattractive,

Victoria thought. "I like the picture!" Diana commented, looking at the tray.

"Yes," Victoria said, "it's Constable. Salisbury Cathedral."

"Oh," said Diana, and then she grimaced, picking up one of the mugs, and smiled. "I don't know anything about art. I'm sorry."

"Don't be silly! You know what you like, I'm sure, and that's all that matters!" Victoria told her, putting down the tray and lifting the other mug.

"Oh!" Diana looked quite touched. "That's a lovely way of looking at it!"

Victoria had a pleasant feeling, as she sat down on the bench, that Diana thought she was admirably erudite. It was not a feeling that she thought she really deserved: Cecily was the one who knew stuff. But that only made it more pleasant. Throughout their childhood, Cecily had always known better, which was particularly galling, given that she was three years younger. Victoria still remembered the time when Cecily had insisted that South Africa was a country, when Victoria had been sure that it was just a region. She had been absolutely certain – well, it made sense. South America, Southern Europe: 'South Something' was always a region. She'd been so sure that she'd thought that, for once, she could be the one to humiliate Cecily rather than the other way round, and so she'd asked their mother at supper, "Isn't it true that South Africa is not actually a country?" But of course, it turned out that Cecily was right again and she was wrong. And that was only one of the many disputes they'd had. To list only the points of contention that she could still remember, they'd argued about whether

Jesus came from England; whether there were penguins in the Arctic; whether you have to write backwards in order to be able to read the words in a mirror. And every time, whatever the question, it was always Cecily who was right.

Worst of all, though, was not that Cecily knew facts; it was the way she always managed to outshine Victoria when it came to 'values'. Their parents didn't go to church, being conscientious atheists, but when they went to stay with their grandparents at half-term or in the Easter holidays, their grandmother sometimes took them to Sunday school.

"Should an all-knowing God have been able to see what would happen when he preferred Cain's sacrifice over Abel's?" Their Sunday-school teacher had once asked. Victoria couldn't have cared less. She spent most of those sessions drawing Princesses and their pets, or plaiting her hair into hundreds of tiny, tiny plaits. But of course, Cecily had piped up with some goody-goody answer that made their teacher go all smiles. And afterwards, the teacher had told their granny – in front of Victoria – what a mature understanding Cecily had of spiritual things, and how she might really grow in the faith. And their grandmother – Victoria's own grandmother – had reached out and put an arm round Cecily, hugging her proudly close, while Victoria stood there shifting from foot to foot, apparently invisible.

"Have you got any plans for today?" she asked Diana.

"What?" Diana looked surprised. "No… I just thought… well, is there anything in Dover that we should see?"

*

By the time Cecily woke, the children were all up and eating breakfast.

"Is it true we're going to Dover Castle today?" asked Julia when Cecily came into the dining room.

"Dover Castle? What?"

"Aunt Victoria said we're all going to Dover Castle after breakfast!" Julia explained.

Diana came in from the kitchen at that point, saying, hurriedly, "Oh, yes! Victoria suggested we all go as it's a real landmark." Then she added apologetically, "What do you think?"

It was not only childish; it was positively churlish for Cecily to mind that her sister and her friend had made plans when she wasn't there. Of course, she pretended she wasn't bothered in the least. "Okay, why not?" she said, trying to sound positive, light-hearted and open-minded. But Victoria always did this. And once again, Cecily had a rising feeling of anger and turbulence which meant it was better if she left the room before anyone saw it on her face. "I'm just going to the loo," she said.

She went upstairs. And then, because she'd said she was going to the loo, she actually did go to the bathroom near Victoria's room, so as to avoid the awful smell in the other bathroom. And on the way, passing Diana's bedroom door, she remembered the vases. She pictured herself rushing in, grabbing a vase and bolting with it to her own bedroom. Diana and Victoria were down in the kitchen. She could easily do it. Somewhat excited by this thought, she decided to go to the loo first, and consider it there. Where could she put the vases, though? Under her bed! And would she have time to get the first vase and then bolt back for the second? Or should she leave the second one there for Victoria? There was an argument for doing that: it would be fairer, after all. On the other hand, if a vase remained, that might make it easier for Victoria to ask about the other. And there would be so much more satisfaction in removing them both! How funny it would be to beat Victoria at her own game, because could she possibly object, since she had moved them in the first place?

She came out of the bathroom and halted again outside Diana's open door. Could she really do it? What would Florian say? Wait – but what might be the long-term consequences of something like that?

And then Zac came around the corner, and in an instant, the whole mad plan was gone. Shocked at herself, Cecily went to her room, sat on her bed, and took a deep breath.

When she was small, she would have done almost anything for Victoria. For a long time, she had just adored her, as younger sisters do. But Victoria had hurt her too many times since then, and that feeling (which she could still, funnily enough, remember; that even to this day came back sometimes), that warm, sunny feeling of love and admiration, had mostly turned into something else.

Those vases belonged, by rights, to Cecily. They came from Italy, home of the Renaissance, and who was it, she or Victoria, who cared about the Renaissance? It was Cecily, not Victoria, who had gone to Florence to spend two years studying Marsilio Ficino. And it was Cecily, not Victoria, who had found and bought a candlestick that matched the vases, and brought it home as a gift for their mother. How she felt about the vases reminded her of some quote from Milton's Areopagitica which she remembered vaguely from her university days. How did it go? Something about books carrying a spirit within them. And then she remembered that Areopagitica was actually right there on her bedside table, so she picked it up and began to flick through the pages, looking for that quote. There it was!

> *For books are not absolutely dead things, but do contain a potency of life in them to be as active as that soul was whose progeny they are; nay, they do preserve as in a vial the purest efficacy and extraction of that living intellect that bred them.*[16]

It seemed to Cecily that artefacts carried a spirit within them too, and so those vases carried something of that wonderfully clear analysis of humanity that had so attracted her to Renaissance Florence. The churches that – on every square – managed to reflect, in heavy stone, the longed-for symmetry of ethereal heaven. Those perfect domes that rose like miracles; tributes to an unseen, divine perfection. All that was secretly invested in the curves of those graceful Florentine vases. How could Victoria have just pinched them?

Florian came in then. "Have you had a chance to talk to Victoria yet?" he asked.

He stood there, all masculine and purposeful with his loose shirt hanging off his wide, spare shoulders, and a sort of readiness about him: alert, as if he could spring in any direction at any moment. She could feel his impatience vibrating across the room towards her; see it in a twitching muscle in his thigh. And now she had to tell him that, incredibly, there had not seemed to be a suitable occasion in all of yesterday to raise the matter of the bathroom with Victoria.

"Oh, God! No, I haven't!" she confessed.

Florian barely paused, only gritting his teeth and drawing breath through them – briefly, briskly – to show that he had expected as much, before continuing, "Well, you could ask her now. I think she might have gone into the study. I heard her calling Zac in there as I was coming upstairs."

She found Victoria at her computer in what had – throughout their childhood, when their grandparents still lived here – been referred to as their grandfather's study. Of course, back then, no one had ever thought that their grandmother might need a study, even though they were both retired and it was she, not Grandad, who was the one with a degree. The study was a tiny wood-panelled room with a solid oak door with those black-iron latches so beloved of the Arts and Crafts movement, and in Cecily's childhood it had always smelled of pipe tobacco. Even now, thirty years after Grandad's death, it was little changed. He had been a fearsome figure, with his severe, skull-like face and his wild white facial hair, so that even now, years after his death, the room retained, hovering within its tobaccoey smell, an aura of fear. It had the same massive, dark oak desk topped with green baize; the same china dish full of paper clips; the same huge, ancient hole punch. The only difference was that now, sitting in Grandad's crimson leather chair, so decrepit that it was acned with little marks all over, was not Grandad, but Victoria. She had unpacked her computer and spread almost the entire desk with papers.

"Oh, have you moved in here?" Cecily had said before she meant to. She knew how effortlessly Victoria could read between her lines.

And of course, Victoria did. "No, no, don't worry! I haven't appropriated Grandad's study, if that's what you mean!" she said immediately, but laughing, as if they were both joking. "It's just that Zac has a mammoth project to complete before the end of the summer, you know, and I really, *really* want him to be somewhere where no one will disturb him. You know, it's maddening, as his teachers all say that he could do so well, but he's just *so* easily distracted... and he really, *really* needs to prepare for this year!"

In other words, thought Cecily, yes, Victoria *had* appropriated the study. And was not only for her 'genius' son. Zac's schoolbooks were only at one end of the desk. "Oh," she said, glancing pointedly at Victoria's papers and computer.

Reading this, Victoria continued, with a little laugh, her eyes all faux-communicative and her expression overly animated, "Oh, and so I've had to come and set up here too, to make sure no one comes in and disturbs him. I hope you don't mind; it's just..." She took a deep breath and then blew it out. "He's just so *easily* distracted, I have to watch him like a *hawk!*"

That was the thing about Victoria. She always managed to frame things so that you felt bad if you didn't arrange yourself around her. It was simply not fair. Cecily had work to do too (although she hadn't expected to get much done here), and so did Florian. Both of them could have done with a quiet place like this over the next few days. And Victoria had not even asked! Cecily half-considered saying this, but there was no point in even trying to set herself against Victoria. Victoria had somehow managed, even in adulthood, to retain that mysteriously incontrovertible childhood authority that she'd always had as the older sister. This power that Victoria had over her made Cecily conflict averse: look at how she could not even imagine a way to mention the vases! But standing there in front of Victoria, she felt a sense of foreboding. There were so many mines buried under the road that stretched into the future. This was exactly what she had been afraid of: that they would not know how to share the house after their mother had gone. How were they ever going to navigate their way forward as sisters without their mother to adjudicate? They would not be able to either avoid or address their ancient conflicts.

"No, it's fine – you and Zac can work here," she found herself saying.

But Victoria was looking at her sceptically, as if she could read Cecily's mind; as if she knew that Cecily was secretly bridling at having to give precedence to Victoria in this way. And because Victoria could read her emotions like this – absurdity of absurdities! – she actually felt compelled to elaborate, to attempt to convince her that she and Florian really *didn't* need the study at all.

"It's completely fine!" she heard herself going on. "The girls haven't got any homework over the summer anyway, and

I can do mine in… well, it's fine, really!" And then she hated herself for being so cowardly, for always placating Victoria. But she hated Victoria even more for having the power to make her. She changed the subject quickly. "What I actually came in to ask was… have you been into the bathroom?"

"Have I been to the bathroom?" Victoria repeated in perplexed tones. She began to laugh.

And for an entirely unexpected instant, seeing Victoria's humour tickled, Cecily experienced a rush of childish elation. For an instant she was back in one of those happy childhood interludes when they were together, her and Victoria, possessed by a fit of giggles, perhaps, or jumping imaginary ponies all the way down the path to the beach. Briefly, only briefly – but oh, so happily! – she was once again the adoring little sister.

It passed within seconds. "I mean, there's a funny smell in our one," she continued. "We're afraid maybe the pipe to the sewer has burst behind the wall or something."

Victoria winced. "Euw!" she exclaimed in a demonstration of fastidious disgust, and opened out exasperated palms. "What did you *do*?"

Cecily was taken aback, "What did *I* do?" she repeated, indignance flaring. "What did *I* do? Nothing! I've only just arrived!"

But Victoria ignored this, and continued to look at her expectantly, as if waiting for a more convincing explanation.

Cecily stood glaring at her to communicate her outrage. But then the spreading silence began to threaten a rupture so unthinkable that she felt compelled to put things right. "Florian is phoning around to find a plumber," she said.

Victoria turned away and reached over the desk for a pile of papers, and then sat down with them. She glanced at Cecily only briefly, and nodded. "Okay, great," she said. She looked at Cecily as if she now expected her to leave, and when Cecily didn't leave, she waved the papers. "Got to get through these before next Monday." She was a PR representative for an American medical company.

Cecily understood that the subject of the bathroom was closed, for now. But she had to show Victoria that this was not the end of the matter. "But have you seen the stain on the spare-room ceiling?" she said. "I'm afraid there's a leak in the roof somewhere…"

"Are you sure?" Without looking at Cecily, still leafing through her papers, Victoria frowned.

"It looks kind of puffy, and I'm sure it's worse than before," Cecily said.

"Oh, well… it's an old house," said Victoria briskly, placing her papers flat on the desk. She turned on her computer. "Sorry; better get on with these. Shall we talk about it later?"

It seemed that Victoria was trying to dismiss the subject, which puzzled Cecily, so that somehow, she just couldn't leave. "I'm just a bit worried about how much time it's all going to take, and how much it's going to cost. What with Brexit taking away our right to free movement, it looks as Florian might have to apply to become a British citizen, which is not only very time-consuming, but cripplingly expensive. It's a racket nowadays, you know."

Victoria sighed, looking at her screen. She looked down at one of her papers, and then back at the screen.

But, annoyed now at Victoria's lack of concern about her family, Cecily continued, "And the government keeps threatening to remove other rights as well, like the right to free healthcare. They're saying that, as an EU citizen, Florian might end up being forced to pay extra for healthcare, even though he already pays for the NHS, like we all do, through his social security payments."

"Well," Victoria said, part soothing, part dismissive, as if assuming the voice of the grown-up, "I don't think we should assume the worst. I can't imagine the *British* government, the oldest democracy in the world, is really going to start taking away people's rights."

When Cecily opened her mouth, Victoria was already holding up a palm in front of her face.

"Don't start!" she said.

But Cecily had already started. She was so riled that she couldn't help it. "You're joking, right? Because first of all, we're not much of a democracy if a referendum can be illegally bought with literally no consequences. And secondly, a plan to take away people's rights is *exactly* what Brexit is!" She was spluttering slightly.

Victoria consulted the ceiling in a show of patience and forbearance, and then said, "Sorry, I really haven't got time for this."

"It's a plan to successively remove our rights: first free movement, then the human rights guaranteed by the EU, then our employment rights, our rights to health and safety, our rights to food standards and environmental standards. That's precisely the whole point of it!"

Sitting at the desk, Victoria winced in distaste while

Cecily stood there breathing heatedly. "Oh, grow up, Cecily!" she retorted, shaking back her hair. "I know you're very worked up about it, but the fact remains that, although you may have time for crusading, I've got to get these emails sent."

Moving forward, Cecily glanced over Victoria's shoulder at the email she was writing. There was the logo of her company in thick orange letters heading the page. Well, of course her corporation wouldn't see things in these terms: they'd been trying to get leverage over the NHS for years, and a UK cut loose from the EU would be more vulnerable. "Well of course, for US medical companies, Brexit is probably great news," she remarked sourly.

Victoria put both palms flat on the desk and turned to look at her, feigning righteous indignation. "Are you *actually* reading my personal correspondence?"

"I'm sure they see the severing of our ties with the EU and making us a vassal of a barbaric, capitalist America as a great opportunity to make money! They're probably cheering it on!"

Victoria shook her head, once again acting the grown-up. "You should listen to yourself, Cecily, because you're really starting to sound like a conspiracy theorist! It may come as a surprise to you, but funnily enough, not everyone sees the world as a Doomsday battle between the wicked and the righteous! Can you just let me get on with this?"

"Well, it's—" Cecily began.

But Victoria interrupted her, raising a hand again and saying, in a snooty voice, "No, really, can you just let me get my emails done?"

Sulkily, Cecily went out of the study and down the corridor to the sitting room, possessed by a childish feeling of defiance and helplessness. Again, somehow, as always, Victoria had won.

And then she remembered Diana in the dining room with the children. How loudly had she said all that about Brexit and stuff? Could Diana have heard? She must get a grip. The last thing she wanted was for Diana to feel uncomfortable staying in their house.

*

"Dover Priory was up there on the left," Cecily said, as they drove to the castle.

She glanced over her shoulder at Diana, who was in the back with the girls again, but Diana was looking out of the other window.

"Dover what?" Diana said, turning.

"Dover Priory, you know? The medieval monastery. Do you remember? In your room there's that print of an eighteenth-century drawing of the ruin?"

"Oh, yes! What, so it's round here?" Diana said, looking about her with an excessive eagerness that dismayed Cecily, as she realised she was affecting it just to please her.

"Well, no – it was ransacked and then mostly left to become a ruin. But what's left of the buildings have become part of a private school," Cecily said.

"Oh!" Diana responded slowly. And then, as if she were trying to think of the appropriate thing to say, "Well, that's so interesting!"

There was, Cecily thought, watching Diana's gaze drift back to the window on her right, an inexplicable distance between them this morning.

Cecily thought of all those monks who'd had their world turned upside down. They'd been turned out of their home, a priory that had stood since the twelfth century, and then watched it being asset-stripped by the upstart new Protestant elite. It was Cranmer himself – Henry VIII's right-hand man, if she remembered rightly – who got the priory lands. She'd heard somewhere that for decades after the priory ceased to function as a charitable institution, the homeless continued to seek refuge in its abandoned barn. Apparently, the town had records on this because under the Tudor Poor Laws of the later sixteenth century, town officials were required to round up and expel vagrants from the town. And how must it have felt for the poor and homeless who had depended on monastic charity when that world, in which monks had a duty, under Catholic social theory, to help them, just vanished from one day to the next? How, she wondered, did the Crown's destruction of the monasteries affect that medieval Catholic notion of society as an organic whole, a body of mutually supporting parts?

There were more and more vagrants as the sixteenth century went on; not only because of the multitudes of homeless cenobites, but because of 'enclosures'. Enclosure was one of the running themes, she remembered from her university days, of late medieval and early modern English history. From the thirteenth century when the European wool trade began to flourish, local potentates, in order to raise sheep, began to claim private legal rights to land which had until then been owned and farmed in common according to unwritten ancient tradition. The numbers of dispossessed rural families increased throughout the early modern period, drifting to cities and – by the end of the eighteenth century – providing labour for the burgeoning Industrial Revolution.

"Here we are," said Florian, interrupting her thoughts. "This is Dover Castle!"

*

The castle rose up on the bleak hillside in front of them like a primitive spaceship from a harsher world. A grim, grey hulk, its cuboid structures massed together, so that you could hardly tell the great, thick walls of outer wall from the those of the battlements or indeed, the castle itself.

"God!" Diana exclaimed, when they had all got out of their respective cars and stood in the car park. "It's not exactly beautiful!"

Cecily laughed, and Diana was relieved to see that she didn't seem tense, the way she had earlier this morning when Diana and Victoria first talked about coming here. But now she noticed that Victoria looked taken aback at her reaction to the castle, and was suddenly worried that perhaps she had offended her. Perhaps a good guest ought to be a bit more positive?

"Well, I suppose it *is* a fortress," Cecily said. "I mean, it wasn't meant to be beautiful; more like... functional. Maybe even scary-looking."

"The foyer is down here!" Victoria called. She had walked on, leading the way with Zac. Dan had stayed back home because he had some business to catch up with.

They all followed, and then Zac turned round, walking backwards in front of Cecily and Diana so that he could say, "Yeah, it was a military investment. To protect the country against invasion."

"And also probably to prevent the vanquished Saxon nobility from trying to overthrow the Norman conquerors and regain their confiscated lands," Cecily added.

Zac said, in conversational terms, to Diana, "Do you know that they had soldiers garrisoned here continuously, right up until the 1950s?"

Diana was tickled that this could be a thirteen-year-old's way of making conversation. "No, I didn't! And why did they stop then?"

She glanced round to see where the girls were, and saw that they were lagging behind. They had gone off the path and down the grassy slope that ran down from the car park, to where there was a challengingly thin wall to walk along. Of course, they were a couple of years younger than Zac, but still, it was amazing, the difference between them and him, Diana thought. Zac seemed completely comfortable talking to adults on an equal basis, and to find it natural to be interested in adult stuff like history and war and politics. You'd never get Julia and Olivia discussing Brexit or who built Dover Castle and why – they wouldn't give two hoots! They were far too busy trying to place one foot in front of the other on the flinty wall without falling off. Maybe it was something about their schooling? They went to state school, after all: should she have sent Olivia to private school? Or was it because they were girls? Was it that they could see that, for time immemorial, all this business of ruling and fighting had been the exclusive preserve of men? Were they naturally uninterested, or were they socially conditioned to concern themselves with other things?

"Over here!" called Victoria, as she and Zac went into the foyer. She was over at a counter.

It was refreshingly empty here, thought Diana, looking around the spacious foyer. Not like the jam-packed museums in London. And in London the hordes were from all over the world, whereas here there were only a few pale, Anglo-Saxon-looking families, much like them. Well, Florian and Julia excepted, of course.

She'd met up with Cecily at the National Gallery a couple of months ago, because Cecily had wanted to show her the Leonardos, and it was so crowded there, it was horrendous. First of all, they couldn't go up the grand stone steps to the main entrance, because that entrance had been closed.. Diana was more disappointed at this than she would ever have expected. Not to be able to walk up those lovely steps which look out onto Trafalgar Square? It had seemed almost a violation of her rights. And in fact, she was so annoyed that when she saw a museum worker at the top of the steps, she called out to him, "Why aren't we allowed in at the front entrance?"

"It's because of safety procedures. You know, bombs and stuff!" he called back.

Because of terrorism, in short. *Jesus Christ!* she'd thought angrily. *What have we come to? And what kind of person wants to bomb people entering a free, national art gallery in the first place? They should be celebrating that such things exist!*

So instead they had to queue outside the little Sainsbury Wing, and allow themselves to be searched and their handbags looked into. What a world away from how it used to be, when she came here on a school trip once as a teenager. Back then they had just waltzed up the steps and into the foyer, easy as anything. No X-rays, no bag checks, no officials, no nothing. No queueing, either. For God's sake! It wasn't even a weekend; it was a Thursday afternoon within office hours! And yet the queue was thick with groups and stretched at least five metres into the street. People of every shape and size and nationality; less than half of them speaking English.

Should be called the International Gallery! she had thought of saying. But instead she said, "God! So many people!"

And Cecily grimaced wanly in agreement.

Later, though, when they were out of the queue, Diana said, "I know it maybe sounds mean. But it just makes me sad that nowadays you have to queue to get into the National Gallery even on a weekday in office hours."

"Yeah, I know," Cecily agreed. "Have you ever been to the Uffizi in Florence? I've often wondered what it would feel like to be a Florentine wanting to see *The Birth of Venus* or something. You know, because of all the tourists you have to buy tickets days or even weeks before! And even then, you have to queue when you get there."

Diana had never been to Florence. But she could

sympathise with the Florentines. And that was the thing: she would have no problem with somewhere like Florence closing the Uffizi to foreign visitors for periods of time, if that was what the Florentines wanted. She would find it totally understandable.

They joined Victoria at the counter, where she was asking the ticket man, "Do you still do those little tours of the castle?"

"Yep! We certainly do!" said the ticket man, in a jolly, old-fashioned policeman type of voice. He looked past fifty, with jowly cheeks; droopy eyes; and a soft, pale blue lambswool jumper smoothed over an ample paunch. Despite his aging physique, he had a naive expression, and stood almost like a toddler, unselfconscious, stomach sticking out. "But there's none now till four o'clock, so I don't know if you'd want to wait?"

It was only eleven.

"Not until *four*?" echoed Victoria in disbelief, shaking back her hair. Her manicured hand flopped with a little smack onto the counter. "Not until four o'clock in the afternoon? *Really*? Are you *sure*?" She turned to the others, grimacing her amazement and dismay, and then back to him.

"I'm afraid so," he said regretfully. After a respectful pause he added, in a comfortable Estuary accent, unnaturally accentuating certain words, like a newsreader, "But we *do* actually have quite a few guides *around* the castle. You can spot them because they're all got up in twelfth-century garb. And they're happy to *answer* any questions you have."

As 'white British' as they come, was this ticket seller,

Diana thought, with his watery blue eyes and his pink cheeks and his nasal voice. His contented, middle-aged dowdiness and his Estuary accent were a relief to her, to be honest. She could picture him at home, sitting on the sofa with his wife, sharing a cup of tea and watching the *Antiques Roadshow*. It warmed her heart. At the National Gallery, every single attendant they had spoken to (and there were many, because they'd kept on getting lost) was under twenty-five and had a foreign accent. So much so that Cecily, who loved accents, got quite excited and kept trying to guess where everyone was from. ("Was that a Spanish accent? Or Italian? Damn it! I should have listened out for the 's's!") But Diana was thinking, *What is wrong with this country that our National Gallery can't or won't pay enough to employ people who were born here?* Now, to her horror, she suddenly realised that while she had been daydreaming, Victoria was paying.

"Wait, wait! I want to get the tickets!" Diana cried, trying to push in next to her, but it was too late: Victoria was already turning away from the counter, waving pieces of paper. "You haven't bought them all? Oh no!" Diana began to fumble in her handbag. If there was one thing that made her really uncomfortable, it was being in someone's debt. "How much do I owe you?"

But Victoria just smiled a well-defined lipstick smile. "It's fine, don't be silly!" she said, and began to hand the tickets out.

As she was doing so, Florian got a phone call and mimed to Victoria to give him his ticket, mouthing 'plumber' before making his way to the back of the foyer, so that he could talk. They didn't know whether to wait for him or not, but, seeing that they were hesitating, he waved at them to go ahead, so they went up some crude, narrow stone steps up the inside of the castle wall, coming out onto a stone landing. A doorway on one side led off to what was almost a sort of cave, which echoed when the children ran into it. The adults followed.

"What's that?" Olivia asked Julia, looking out over a low wall at the end of the cave.

"It's a—" Julia began.

But Zac shouted over her, "It's a well! What did you think it was? A toilet?", and then laughed excitedly.

"Euww!" Olivia grimaced., taking feigned, flirtatious offence, and jabbed him with her elbow, which made him roar with delight.

"A well?" Diana moved forward curiously. And there it was: a great, round hole, falling away down, down the side of the castle wall, and deep into the ground. "A well *inside* the castle?" she marvelled.

"It's the medieval version of running water!" Victoria said.

"Are you supposed to make a wish?" Diana asked, reaching for her purse. "Shall we drop a penny down it?"

After the children had all dropped pennies down the well, they walked through Henry II's kitchen, dining hall, and several other large, crude, chilly stone rooms. When they were in Henry's bedchamber, Florian reappeared, walking in with that observant, careful manner of his. He looked confident as he walked into a room, but – on some level – wary. He was the type of person, Diana thought, who was never absent-minded, never clumsy. She couldn't imagine him ever knocking a glass over, or tripping up. Seeing Florian come in like that and raise one hand in an understated wave when he saw them spot him, she wished once again that Steve, her husband, could have come. Steve was quite unlike Florian: he was rather overweight nowadays, and absent-minded when it came to almost anything except his shops. But even so, seeing Florian turn up like that, a solid, husbandly figure, made her feel suddenly a little homesick. It would have been nice, among these people whose ways were not entirely familiar, to have had old Steve here at her side.

"I'm sure I remember reading once that Aliénor of Aquitaine found the conditions terribly primitive when she was in England," Cecily said. "You know, she came from the musical and literary court of Provence."

"Who's Aliénor of… I mean, what did you say?" Diana asked.

"She married Henry II, who built this castle as it is now," Cecily said. And then to Florian, as he approached, "Any luck?"

"Nope, he was busy too," Florian said. "Seems like they're short of plumbers down here as well."

They climbed to the top of the crude, massive stone stairs and then went outside onto the keep, from where you could look down over battlements at Dover, and on further out to sea.

"That's the Roman lighthouse!" Zac told Diana, pointing to a small, knobbly, cylindrical stone building.

It had been so battered by the elements that it looked, Diana thought, like not much more than a knobbly stump of stone – almost like a half-melted stone snowman. But *Roman*! How incredible! A *Roman* lighthouse, still looking out to sea all these centuries later! Consulting the leaflet she had picked up in the foyer, she read that the lighthouse was perhaps the oldest surviving building in Britain. And then she looked at it again, and tried to fully invest the sight with the marvel of this knowledge. The oldest surviving building in Britain! According to the leaflet, the castle itself was also pretty ancient: first built by William the Conqueror, and then rebuilt at the end of the twelfth century. And from then, just as Zac said, it had been continuously garrisoned, right up until 1958!

She looked out at the stony outer-curtain walls snaking down below, with flanking towers every hundred metres or so, all along the contours of the grassy hillside. Garrisoned continually from the time of William the Conqueror till 1958! Just think of all those centuries rolling by, and yet the view that the soldiers saw from the battlements would have been the same: this same green hill; the same glittering sea. This fact stirred something in her. It gave her a tremendous sense of stability, of belonging, of significance.

"But it's *amazing*," she said, "to think that it was garrisoned from the time of William the Conqueror till 1958! Just to think that this same Dover, this same England, has been here all this time!" She felt roused, emotional; almost as if there were some grand hymn welling up inside her. And in fact, there *was* a hymn, wasn't there? One that gave her that same magnificent, rousing feeling. How did it go? *And did those feet…*[17]

Cecily was looking at her in a funny way. She said

nothing, but followed Diana's gaze out over the ramparts. There was something on her mind; Diana could tell by the way she kept taking little breaths, as if she were about to speak, and then closing her mouth. And then she said it: "Although, well, you know, when they first built this castle, it was for the Norman French who had just conquered us."

The girls went off and began practising cartwheels on the grassy bit in the middle of the keep.

"Well, sort of French," Cecily continued musingly. "Because they were originally Vikings, that were bought off."

"Really? They were Vikings?" Zac asked.

"Yeah," Cecily said, turning to him. "Norsemen. You know, the King gave them land in France as a bribe so they wouldn't raid the French coast anymore."

But Diana could feel the panic of being left behind. "Wait... sorry to be stupid. But who are we talking about? Who built this castle?" She looked down at the leaflet again, but couldn't find the bit where it said.

"Henry II. William the Conqueror's great-grandson. He built the castle as it stands now. But William had also built it before," Zac said.

Diana became aware that she was once again being instructed by a thirteen-year-old, and that this felt quite natural to both her and Zac. There was something about his air of easy authority which meant that both of them were comfortable with him taking on the teaching role. Why was that? "And he was a Viking?" she asked, playing up her confusion slightly, as she had a hunch that he would find that funny.

"No!" Zac said, laughing. "He was French!"

"So what… wait! Now I'm completely confused! I thought the Normans were French. What was that about the Vikings?" Diana demanded, laughing, really camping up her bewilderment.

"Wait a sec, I'll explain!" said Zac, whipping out his phone. "Ah!" And then he began to quote, "'The Normans were Vikings who settled in north-western France in the tenth and eleventh centuries and their descendants. These people gave their name to the duchy of Normandy…'"[18]

"God! Isn't it complicated?!" Diana said. She looked round to see where the girls were: still practising cartwheels.

"So William the Conqueror was Norman French. And he was married to Aliénor of Aquitaine – also French, but from right down in the south," Zac said.

"When Aliénor and Henry married," Cecily said, "between them they already owned most of France, and then they also got England, which Henry inherited through his mother. It wasn't until they lost their lands in France, in 1453, that our monarchs really became monarchs of just England."

Diana experienced a surge of irritation; there was something about Cecily's insistent tone; a sense that there was some secret message in what she said, beyond the actual words.

"In fact," Cecily went on, "our royal family didn't even speak English until like, the thirteenth century."

And then Diana knew. She knew what Cecily was up to. She was trying to teach Diana that we were a part of Europe, that we had always been a part of Europe, and she felt cross. Did super-middle-class, super-educated Cecily really think she was an idiot? That she had no idea that we'd been invaded by the Saxons, or that we'd been conquered by the Normans long ago?

"God! These medieval dynastic marriages are like international corporate mergers!" Florian remarked. "They even have their logos – you know, their coats of arms. A marriage is performed, and suddenly whole swathes of land and peasants are working for a Prince with a different title, just like nowadays swathes of employees find that they are no longer working for Kraft Foods, for example, but for Unilever!"

Diana was impressed. "Wow!" she said. "I've never thought of it like that!" Although really it was more than that. It wasn't just that she had never thought of it like that. She didn't have the kind of knowledge in the first place, that she might be able to rearrange into thoughts like that. She'd had no idea how medieval society worked, and it had never occurred to her that it could be within her remit to think about the nature of corporate mergers either.

"And actually," Florian went on, "that analogy may be more sinister than it seems. Because if you look at who decides elections in corporate America today, it's maybe a few hundred owners of corporations. It's funding that wins elections and party donations that determine policy. It's as if the corporates really have reverted to the role of medieval nobles with their households of retainers. They are the new over-mighty barons, who make the Kings and control the lawmakers."

"It's basically become a plutocracy, now, America," Cecily agreed. "And the UK is not far behind!"

Diana literally couldn't follow. It was as if they were speaking in some code she'd never learnt! And then she happened to glance at Victoria, who smiled and then rolled her eyes.

"What?" said Zac. "I thought America was a democracy?"

"Just look at those girls doing their cartwheels!" Victoria exclaimed.

"Not really," Florian told him. "It's been corrupted by money. Political parties are in the pockets of big money."

Victoria moved over to Diana and said, nodding in the direction of Julia and Olivia, "Aren't they sweet? Shall we go and take some pictures?"

They crossed over the battlements to where the girls were. Diana was relieved to get away. It was depressing, this world view inhabited by Cecily and her husband. Though she'd been friends with Cecily for two or three years now, she'd only known a small part, it was beginning to seem, of how Cecily saw the world.

"She's so pretty, your daughter!" Victoria said. "That gorgeous hair! Did you used to have yours long like that? Because it's that same auburn…"

"I did, actually," Diana told her, flattered. "I used to be able to sit on it when I was a girl!"

Victoria took a run of pictures, and Diana fumbled half-heartedly for her phone in order to join in. The truth was, she felt confusedly disappointed. Just a moment ago she had had that wonderful, deep, rich, vibrant feeling – an enormous sense of stability and significance – that she would have liked to share with Cecily. In fact, she felt sure that had they been by themselves, Cecily would have understood. But with Florian there talking his knowing talk, and everyone else, Cecily became a different person: all doom and gloom and long words and inaccessible.

"Does Olivia do competitions and stuff?" asked Victoria, lowering her camera. "I used to be pretty good at gymnastics myself, when I was at school."

"Did you?"

"Yeah, yeah. My coach said that I should consider aiming for nationals, and maybe even Olympics and stuff."

"No way! Really? And did you?"

Victoria laughed, waving the subject away. "No, no. My parents weren't really into it." She turned and looked directly at Diana, adding meaningfully, "Gymnastics wasn't the kind of thing they valued."

"Oh no!" Diana felt awfully sorry. She knew that teenage experience of wanting things that the people around you didn't recognise as desirable. But at the same time, she felt that Victoria was trying to put over a bit of a sob story.

"Yeah." Victoria smiled sadly, and then, changing the subject briskly, as if tearing herself away from the tragedies of the past, "Shall we get fish and chips for lunch? There's a nice place where they do takeaway – really classic; not greasy or anything. What do you think?"

She turned to Diana, and for a moment she looked just like Cecily: she had those same creamy cheeks, and that round, heart-shaped face. But it wasn't that, so much as her expression: a particular engagement; a curiosity in her eyes. Diana felt an unexpected uprush of warmth towards her.

It was as they were heading back to the cars that Zac let

out a joyful "Hmmph!" The three women turned to look at him. He was staring at his phone, and then he looked up at them all, his face shining with excitement.

"Looks like it's really going to happen: more and more voices are backing prorogation!"

Florian, who was up ahead, had already opened the driver's door, but now he turned around. "Seriously?"

And Cecily cried, "No, come on! Surely this can't be?"

Zac glanced back at his phone, and then at Cecily. He was laughing.

He looked jubilant, Diana thought. Watching him, she almost felt elated herself. Although she didn't know quite what the fuss was, with all this prorogation stuff. In fact, in the past few days she'd almost preferred *not* to know. Since the referendum, she'd tried to switch off from all the arguing about ways and means; all those legal cases and that. She had always known, after all, that there would be a huge backlash of outrage from the liberal establishment, the ones with a stake in all of this globalisation, who flattered themselves with half-baked ideas about world harmony and post-imperial guilt. The ones who were privileged and well-educated enough not to understand how some people felt threatened by the never-ending hordes of immigrants. She'd expected that, and so all this fuss about proroguing Parliament had not interested her, really. It just seemed like concocted outrage, because in fact, from what she'd heard, Parliament was being prorogued all the time. And to be honest, it did seem that some groups within it had been deliberately making things difficult.

Cecily turned away and climbed into her car. And,

catching sight of her face, just before she shut the door, Diana felt a pang of sympathy. Poor Cecily looked really grim. If only Diana could explain to her that none of this was really bad. That it just had to happen, and it would be for the best in the end. We couldn't go on accepting more and more people into the country: we were already just about bursting at the seams. But, of course, she could never say any of that to Cecily, or to anyone else, in fact. Not among their circle of friends, at least. Among the middle classes in London these subjects were completely taboo. You simply couldn't raise them!

Julia and Olivia climbed into the car after Cecily, and Victoria began fumbling in her bag for her car keys, and then looked at Diana.

"Do you want to come with us?"

Diana hesitated. Here was Victoria looking all friendly and inviting, but there was poor Cecily sitting gloomily in her car, staring ahead.

"It's quite crowded in that car. I can't imagine how you all five drove all the way down to Dover in it!" Victoria said.

"Yeah…" Victoria was right: it would be a bit silly to have five people in Cecily's little car, and just two in Victoria's seven-seater. And surely Cecily couldn't be so childish as to be offended? "Oh yes, thanks, I'll come with you, shall I? That would be lovely!" Diana said.

*

M ilton's *Areopagitica* was published, Cecily knew, in November 1644, at the height of the English Civil War. When they'd got back after lunch, she'd fetched it from her room and taken it into the sitting room. She'd wanted to reread it because – having been reminded, since arriving here, of its existence – she had a feeling that there was something in it, something she could half-remember, that might give her some insight into all of this madness that was going on today. She picked it up for that reason, but also because the past seemed to offer an escape from this awful present in which that ominous prorogation was, incredible though it seemed, looking ever more likely.

It was incredible because the principle that Parliament should be sovereign over the executive was one of the defining principles of modern English history. Parliamentary sovereignty was one of the issues two hundred thousand people had died for in the civil war that had led to the execution of Charles I; that had justified the 'Glorious Revolution' and the deposition of James II in 1688. It had been the pride of the English, ever since, that we were not ruled – like other nations – by tyrants with absolute powers: our executive was restrained by Parliament; by the representatives of the people. Or at least some of them.

The entire Brexit campaign had been fought in the name of this parliamentary sovereignty, which they said meant that British matters would be decided not in Brussels but by our elected representatives at Westminster. And yet now they wanted to prorogue Parliament, to gag our elected, 'sovereign' Parliament, in order to get Brexit through. It was bonkers. And yet no one – not the press, not the Opposition, not *anyone* – was really calling them out on this.

She opened the book. The pages had a slight sheen to them, like the pages of a textbook. They felt dusty and two of the middle ones were loose. She'd better try to find some Sellotape to stick them back in before they got lost, she thought, straightening and smoothing them with her hands.

'This project of licensing crept out of the Inquisition,'[19] Milton had written. Though he was an evangelical Protestant, and on the parliamentary side, *Areopagitica* was a polemic against a parliamentary law 'licensing' (i.e. censoring the output) of printers. Such laws, Milton said, attempted to control access to truth, and imitated the practices of the very Catholic Church from which the English had liberated themselves. Censorship was also unnecessary, he seemed to say, because there was no need to police God's Truth, as Truth was just so innately powerful that it would triumph in a fair fight. 'Let her and Falsehood grapple; who ever knew Truth put to the worse, in a free and open encounter?' Milton asked.

Besides, he said, censorship would not even achieve the ends it set out to achieve. For the disciple of God's Truth, encounters with Falsehood could actually be *helpful*, in order to test the true disciple's mettle and to understand the value of truth: 'He that can apprehend and consider vice with all her baits and seeming pleasures, and yet abstain, and yet distinguish, and yet prefer that which is truly better, he is the true warfaring Christian.' Censorship could, in fact, function as a kind of debilitating mollycoddling which prevented a would-be pilgrim from building up their religious muscle and stamina.

'I cannot praise a fugitive and cloister'd vertue, unexercis'd & unbreath'd, that never sallies out and sees her adversary, but slinks out of the race...' Milton went on.

*

Victoria went to look for Dan when they got back. He was out in the garden, just as she had expected. He'd put the hammock up between the house wall and the walnut tree to the left of the terrace, and he was lying there with a beer and a recipe book, wearing just a pair of shorts. Seeing her coming, he dropped his hand, still holding the book, so that his arm dangled down the side of the hammock, and pushed his reading glasses back onto his head, as he watched her approach.

"You look very flushed!" she remarked, when she came within the horizon of his hearing. "Is that beer or sun?"

She stopped in front of him, taking in his soft, flabby, hairy paunch and the white flesh of his thighs squashing against the hammock. It made her feel ashamed, repulsed, and triumphant all at once. If she were more secure, she thought sadly, there wouldn't be this part of her that found comfort in her middle-aged husband's deteriorating physique.

He rubbed his forehead with the back of his arm, laughing good-naturedly. "Bit of both, I expect."

They were not exactly smiling, but the mood was like smiling; both a little awkward and kind of happy.

"So how was the castle?" Dan said, gesturing vaguely with his book towards the deckchairs now set up next to the old table and bench on the terrace.

They both half-laughed, because although they had been married for fifteen years, the amount of time they had together alone in the garden was so indeterminate, and its purpose so unclear, that they didn't know quite what to say: it felt as if they were acquaintances who had been thrown together by chance at the bus stop or something, and were making small talk.

She dragged one of the deckchairs nearer and sat down. "Same as ever. We got fish and chips for lunch."

"Ah!" He stirred with interest, trying to raise himself up on one elbow, which in the hammock was not such an easy feat. "It's quite good, that place, as far as I remember. Haddock or cod?"

Victoria shook her head, indulgently disparaging. He was such a greedy man! "Cod, I think."

Dan nodded thoughtfully. And then he swung his legs down to the ground and picked up his beer from the grass. He took a swig and scratched his shoulder. His stomach folded into two large rolls, and she could see, as he scratched, that the mass of hair in his armpits had formed tails beaded with sweat. As she watched one drop dangle, dangle and then splat onto his bulging thigh, it occurred to her that her entire life had become pointless. The pointlessness was contained, expressed, encapsulated in those wet tails of hair in his armpits, above his flabby paunch. This was all she had: a slightly revolting physicality that was empty, empty.

"Did you get a chance to speak to Cecily about the house?" he asked.

Struggling with this unexpected meaninglessness, it took a moment for Victoria to process his words. "No, I haven't," she said. "Not yet because… it's quite difficult with Diana around…" But she hardly knew what she was saying.

The meaninglessness of everything had drained all sense even from her own words.

"Yeah, because we'd really like to have a holiday place of our own, right? I mean, we'd like to have this house, but if she'd prefer to buy us out that's fine. We can always look somewhere else instead. Maybe even France?"

"With Brexit?" she asked, mechanically.

"Well, will it really make any difference?"

There was a brief silence, in which you could hear the sea hurling itself against the bottom of the cliff; and then the wind tugging and buffeting seagull shrieks across the sky. And in an instance of clarity, Victoria realised that she didn't want any other place. She couldn't imagine this place not being hers, and she didn't want it to belong to anyone else.

The house. The house – the word was meaningless at first, but then it suddenly flooded with meaning. *The house!* Within perhaps a fraction of a second, there crossed her mind an image of her grandparents, and then her mother, in the sitting room. And almost simultaneously she saw the bathrooms how she wanted to redo them, the swimming pool she envisaged, the pizza oven – so many complex emotions forming images in the blink of an eye! And with these images came an uprush of joy and purpose – she felt alive again!

Of course! She was going to talk to Cecily about the house. And for the first time, she felt absolutely certain that, yes, she was going to do it. She *was* going to talk to Cecily. She was going to take the house and make it wonderful; link its story back to the past and send it on, curving resplendent, into the future: an expression of her lifelong desire. And Zac and his children would live in it for generations!

"I'll talk to Cecily," she said decisively, "before we leave!"

Dan was watching her, nodding. They neither of them said anything for a moment, but the wind rushed, rustling high up in the summer trees, and shook armfuls of bushy branches. She looked at him again, sitting there in the hammock, with his beer and his comfortable smile, and his hairy feet planted in sliders on the ground, and for a moment she thought she loved him. Not *that* love; not that frightening, incomprehensible love. Not Matthew. But he could be something else. He'd rescued her, after all. He was comfortable in the real world, Dan. And it was such a relief; to escape the crazed, judgemental spirits of her childhood, who praised or punished you on the basis of strange rules which were always secret, unwritten and unnatural.

She leaned her head back and looked up at the sky. Three seagulls were circling up there, the wind sweeping them off to one side as they flew, so that they looked almost as if they were swimming, swimming, swimming against the current.

What amazed her most was that, until they split up, she had had no inkling that Matthew was going to be such a monumental figure in her life. While he was still there, it was just *unremarkable* that he was her boyfriend. It was only when he was gone that he became so horrifically significant. She began seeing him everywhere: that lean figure; that slightly careful, slightly arrogant way that he moved. She'd see him just ahead on the street turning into a shop, or standing across the road at a bus stop. At work she glimpsed him in the corridor, when there literally no way he could have been there. She even imagined she'd seen him here at Dover, once, walking into the sea. But if she actually *had* met him in the street, in those days when she thought she saw him everywhere, she would have hardly been able to cope. He had so blown her confidence that she would have stammered and stuttered; her legs would simply have given way in the blinding terror of his presence.

Even when she began going out with Dan, she was still obsessed with Matthew. She actually took Dan to Brighton, where she and Matthew had attended university; and not just once, but several times, on the pretext that she was nostalgic about her university days. She took him to places where she'd been with Matthew, in the insane hope that Matthew might magically turn up, see her, and be so wildly jealous that he came back to her, even though Matthew didn't even live in Brighton any more. She took Dan to the café in The Lanes where she and Matthew used to go for pain aux raisins, and a restaurant on Ship Street where she and Matthew went for their first date. But then of course, gradually, gradually, as the months went by, she thought about Matthew less and less.

*

'I cannot praise a fugitive and cloister'd vertue, unexercis'd & unbreath'd, that never sallies out and sees her adversary, but slinks out of the race...' read Cecily, lying on the green velvet sofa.

There was something she remembered now, reading the

word 'race', from her childhood visits to the church here at Dover with her grandparents. One of those Sunday-school sessions, sitting on creaky chairs in the 1930s parish hall, whose windows were too high to see out of. Sunday school there was run by a Mrs Spooner, a tall, vivacious woman with sparky eyes and a suppressed impatience that would come out, sometimes, in exaggerated movements, or an excessively loud laugh. It was one of those letters from St Paul to an enclave of Christians somewhere in Greece – the Corinthians or the Thessalonians or something – that she was thinking of. A letter in which Paul had compared the patience, stamina and determination required of a practising Christian to the patience, stamina and determination required to run a race. She remembered that Sunday-school session because, at the age of ten or eleven, or whenever they'd read that passage, she'd found it baffling. Her experience of running, in primary school, was limited to glorious hundred-metre bursts. She was the third fastest in her class, and she couldn't imagine, sitting on that creaky chair in that parish hall, what running races had to do with patience. Now, of course, she realised that St Paul was not talking about sprinting. The race he had in mind must have been something like a marathon.

But her mind was wondering. She reapplied herself to the book and read again: 'I cannot praise a fugitive and cloister'd vertue, unexercis'd & unbreath'd, that never sallies out and sees her adversary, but slinks out of the race...' Perhaps this race mentioned by St Paul was also the race that Milton had had in mind when he wrote those words?

And then she remembered her great-grandfather's cold baths. Perhaps there really had been a spiritual secret within those daily press-ups and those cold baths, and behind her parents' mysterious requirement that she bathe in the freezing July sea, and that she go to school whether or not she had a cough and a sore throat. Perhaps it harked back to a school of thought, developed by early Protestant readers of their new English Bibles, wherein both body and soul had to be constantly tested and exercised and exposed to adversity in order to develop virtue. Perhaps it was part of a tradition traceable all the way back through the centuries to St Paul. Or even further back? To the Greeks?

For an instant, she felt as she had long ago when she was a child on the beach: that she was once again in the presence of something profound, something momentous, something clean and beautiful and earthy and eternal. But then, at the same time, there was something else mixed up with this moral philosophy; something far less clean. It wasn't just Milton's tone, which sounded pompous to her twenty-first-century ears. It was something else. Well, here again she could sense the same crazy webs of consciousness that were so evident in Foxe's rabid propaganda. It seemed to her that, in Milton's mind, the ideas of bravery, virtue and freedom were clustered together with Protestantism, and that there was an opposing mass in which were bundled Catholicism, jealousy, fear, bondage, authoritarianism and corruption.

She turned back to the book. 'I cannot praise a fugitive and cloister'd vertue, unexercis'd & unbreath'd, that never sallies out and sees her adversary, but slinks out of the race…'

'Cloistered'. It was an arresting choice of word.

"Mum!" Julia called from the hall. "Can we go to the beach?"

"Wait a sec!" Cecily called back, because she was considering the word 'cloistered' and didn't want to lose her train of thought. She was picturing the cloister of a small German monastery she had once visited, on the banks of Lake Constance, with its Italianate paved courtyards and stone galleries seeming to reference a whole cultural world far away in the sunny south. A 'cloistered' virtue, Milton said.

She lowered the book and looked across the room to the windows at the other end, where the afternoon light slanted in, beatifying that chosen corner of the table. It was only Catholicism that had cloisters: Henry VIII had looted and abolished them. Couldn't you sense it, there again in these almost unconscious references: that same ubiquitous, underlying hostility to the Church of Rome? It was hardly surprising. After all, the civil war parliamentarians really *had* mostly been possessed with rabid Foxean hatred for Catholicism. The Westminster Confession of 1646, an official text, for example, stated that the Pope was the Antichrist. But what interested her most was the way in which this tangled knot of anti-Catholic associations appeared so ingrained in Milton's mind that he could attribute the Puritan Parliament's desire to use censorship to a kind of unconscious Catholicism. Catholicism seemed in his mind to represent not a religious organisation, but a clustered caricature of vicious habits and attitudes.

Outside, audible through the open front window, a gust of wind swept, sighing, through the trees, shaking bushels of glossy green against the bright blue sky. Not long after it subsided, leaving the branches still dipping and bobbing slightly, another rush of wind came moaning up from the coast and hassled and rustled its way through the trees again. And in fact, Cecily thought, our entire national history after Foxe's death had been understood within the paradigm he had set up in his *Book of Martyrs*. History, from Foxe on, was the endless battle of virtuous English Protestants to free themselves from successive 'Catholic' plots to bring down, take over, and tyrannise he country.

"Mum! Mummy!" came Julia's voice again. "Can we go to the beach?"

*

Cecily didn't go to the beach with Diana and the children. After the news about the seemingly impending prorogation, she really could do with a break from socialising for a while. And since she and Florian needed to do their bit with the shopping at some point, it seemed a good idea to go now, since they would need some milk for teatime anyway, and get away by themselves.

But when she'd told this plan to Julia, she thought she'd detected something – just a slight shadow of dismay – cross her face. She'd gone down to the hall to find the children keen to go to the beach, and said that she really had to go to the shop, so maybe they could go without her? Julia had looked up sharply, and Cecily had thought she saw that shadow flit across her face. Although she also wondered, even at the time, if she'd imagined it.

It took them a while to get ready, and, thinking about Julia's face, Cecily hung about with them, wondering whether she ought to go to the beach with them after all. And when, just as they were going out of the door, Olivia went running back into the house to get a towel, she saw an opportunity and drew Julia over to the lavender bushes, away from the others.

"Will you be all right if I don't come?" she asked hurriedly, a little breathless.

Julia then seemed fully absorbed in blowing off a ladybird that had landed on her arm; Cecily didn't know whether it was a cover for some kind of discomfort or not. But then, looking up, Julia said, "Yes! Of course!" so breezily that Cecily wondered if she could have misread that earlier look.

"Are you sure?" she persisted, just in case, although she also didn't want to be all on top of Julia, giving her no space.

"Yeah, yeah, it's just…" Julia began, and then shrugged. "No, it's fine!"

"It's just *what*?"

There was the slightest hesitancy, and then Julia said, "It's nothing. It's just, Zac's being annoying, as usual."

"Oh, really? How?"

"Oh, you know – just showing off *all the time*!" Julia shook her head, frowning, and then added, "And Olivia *likes* it!"

"Oh…" Cecily said, and they shared a helpless grimace. "Do you want me to come too?"

But now Olivia was back with her towel and the others were calling, "Come on!" and there was no time to talk further.

184

"No, it's fine. It's fine," Julia said, and, quickly hugging her mother, she turned back to join the others.

*

"Have you got the list?" Florian said, as they turned out onto the cliff road. Victoria had texted a list of things to buy.

"Yeah, yeah, it's on my phone," Cecily assured him. She didn't feel like checking it just yet, though. Not with the sea stretched out and glittering down below. When she opened her window, she could hear the surf gathering itself up and hurling itself against the rocks, and then falling back and hurling itself all over again. It was at the same time naggingly restless and transcendently peaceful.

The Brexiters had picked up the cadences, the same notional-emotional clusters, as the seventeenth-century parliamentarians, she thought, looking out over the water as they drove along. They had revived Foxe's drumbeat, and roused the same old paranoia. In the Brexiters' claims that our 'sovereign' Parliament needed to be free from the 'undemocratic dictates' of the EU, she could hear, in the background, old John Foxe fuming about 'papist tyranny'. In the Brexiters' demands that we needed to – as she remembered a *Telegraph* article had put it[20] – 'Cut the EU red tape choking Britain after Brexit to set the country free from the shackles of Brussels', she could hear 17th century parliamentarians crying out against 'papist' slavery. The Brexiters said that we needed a 'bonfire' of EU regulations, quotas, licences and restrictions, and now in those words

Cecily heard oblique references to Guy Fawkes, and the fires that had celebrated his barbaric execution and the foiling of his desperate 'papist plot'.

She held her blowing hair back from her face with one hand. Driving along the cliff road, you couldn't always actually see the beach directly below you, as it was obscured by the grassy verge between the road and the cliff edge.

It seemed to her that there was something more, something further in those lines from *Areopagitica* that she hadn't yet identified. Another underlying rhythm of thought that she recognised and which disturbed her. Those arguments against censorship. Those rousing ideas of liberty and choice and freedom; the fervent insistence that they must not be trammelled, hindered or confined… where else had she heard that tune?

"What are you looking at?" Florian said.

She turned back to him. "Oh, I wasn't, really. I was just thinking."

He glanced at her. "About…?" he said.

"Well, I just… this Milton that I was looking at earlier."

He winced humorously. "Milton?" he said. "That's some early modern poet, right?" Although his knowledge of English literature was extraordinarily good, considering that he was German, he had, understandably, certain gaps and uncertainties.

"Yeah!" she said. "But what I was thinking about was… well, he said this thing: 'Let her and Falsehood grapple; who ever knew Truth put to the worse, in a free and open encounter?'"

He glanced at her again and then at the road ahead, and back then at her again. "What?" he said.

"Well, he was talking about press censorship. And he said, 'Let her and Falsehood grapple; who ever knew Truth put to the worse, in a free and open encounter?'"

Florian frowned and gave a shrug, keeping his eyes on the road this time. "What about it?"

"Well... I don't know. It reminds me of something, but I can't quite think what. What does it make you think of?"

"Oh!" he said, and then rearranged himself on his seat. "Say it again," he said.

"'Let her and Falsehood grapple; who ever knew Truth put to the worse, in a free and open encounter?'"

Florian thought for a minute. And then he laughed. "What does it make me think of?" he repeated, and then shrugged. "To be honest, my first association is actually another Milton: Milton Friedman! Or some other one of those 'free-market' types. I mean, they're the ones that usually go around spouting pseudo-aphorisms of that kind."

"Really?" she said. "It makes you think of them?" It was one of his hobby horses: the fallacies of the neoliberal tradition.

"Oh, God – you know. Well, there's Friedman, who is supposed to have said, 'Underlying most arguments against the free market is a lack of belief in freedom itself[21].' Or there was his mentor, Friedrich Hayek, who I think said, 'Our faith in freedom does not rest on the foreseeable results in particular circumstances but on the belief that it will, on balance, release more forces for the good than for the bad.'"[22] He shrugged again. "You know. Those kinds of types."

Cecily grimaced.

"Or there was Enron chairman Kenneth Lay," Florian went on, "who apparently told *The San Diego Union-Tribune*, 'I believe in God and I believe in free markets.[23]'" He glanced at her, and then added, "Shortly before his company collapsed in an ignominious scandal of fraud and corruption."

Cecily laughed. "But what was that middle one again? The Hayek one?"

"'Our faith in freedom does not rest on the foreseeable results in particular circumstances but on the belief that it will, on balance, release more forces for the good than for the bad,'" Florian repeated.

"My God!" Cecily said. "To me that sounds almost religious, you know. It's like saying, 'God works in mysterious ways.'"

Florian looked at her. "Well, yeah," he said, "it is like that. For them. The market is like the most dominant God in their pantheon."

She knew from the sudden earnestness in his tone that there was more he wanted to say. She looked back at him expectantly.

"People think a God is something that people consciously choose to believe in. People say, 'I believe in God' or 'I don't believe in God.' But it's not like that. Your Gods are just the powers you put most trust in. That's what Gods are."

"Okay," Cecily said. She could feel him getting excited by his own train of thought again; once again she experienced an uncomfortable mix of irritation and admiration.

"My point," Florian went on, "is that although we in the

West kid ourselves that we have no official Gods any more, that's only because we don't know ourselves. Mammon – the worship of money or power – is now the de facto mainstream religion. Money now has all the characteristics of a dominant God. Over the past few hundred years, the value of everything has been monetised – it's been brought under the power of the market (i.e. money). The value of anything and everything is now what the market says it is; there is no higher authority. That's one indication of the primacy of money in our conceptual world. The other is that it's now orthodox belief that the market must be submitted to unquestioningly. The market must be appeased with sacrifices; another characteristic of a God."

Cecily laughed, although she knew he was very serious. "Sacrifices?"

"The market demands that we sacrifice the environment so that the market can 'grow'. And so we sacrifice it. The market demands that we sacrifice large numbers of people, and so we sacrifice them too. To please the market, those people must be allowed to become poor or even homeless."

"Wow!" said Cecily.

"Yep," said Florian, "it's Mammon."

But there was still something needling her in those words of Milton's. "But do you think that Truth and Falsehood ever really *do* fight in a fair contest? Like, for example, in England now?" she asked him.

Florian said nothing immediately. But then he snorted. "Well, when you look at who owns the media here, it looks like nearly all of it belongs to magnates who support the Tory agenda in return for not paying taxes," he said.

"And then there's the BBC, which now also seems to be controlled by Tory supporters. And there are the American libertarians, and the Russians. I'm constantly hearing new horror stories about the dark money being poured into right-wing think tanks and publications and research centres and social media." He glanced in the car mirror. "It's not an even playing field," he said, steering the car into the left lane. "Don't know if there ever was one."

"Yes!" she exclaimed. "Yes! I knew there was something that bothered me about that quote!"

"It's those who control the media – that is, those with access to capital – that set the agenda," Florian said. "What *was* that quote again?"

"'Let her and Falsehood grapple; who ever knew Truth put to the worse, in a free and open encounter?'"

"Well, yeah," Florian said, "so it just makes me think of those dynastic libertarians who talked of 'free enterprise' and 'open competition', while failing to see that no such thing has ever existed. A market free from political control has literally never, ever – anywhere in the world – existed. And now it's lobbying by the powerful that shapes the rules of the market so as to favour them. And it shapes the 'news' we hear. And the values we form…"

He stopped talking and drove on for a bit, chewing his lip slightly. His boyish excitement had gone; he now appeared a little morose. Cecily didn't mind that. In fact, she wasn't sure how much she liked the way that Florian always aimed to be equanimous; to maintain a state wherein it was as if nothing really affected him emotionally; as if he'd begun, long ago, to try to learn the art of removing himself from the here-and-now grubbiness of real life. When he succumbed to moodiness, like now, it was almost a relief.

And then she began thinking about Victoria and the conversation they had had that morning. Why had she been so… *uninterested* in the state of the house? Victoria normally liked to have things perfect. Before their mother died, for example, she had terrified Cecily by suggesting that they all chip in to renovate the kitchen; to redo the bathrooms; to replace the old French windows that led out from the dining room onto the lawn with a huge, sliding glass wall.

It was only belatedly that she noticed that Florian had pulled up the handbrake and they'd reached the supermarket car park.

"Damn it!" she said. "I forgot to bring any bags!"

Florian looked at her: half disapproving; half affectionate. It was one of the little rituals of their relationship that they acted out… well, several times a day, probably. She couldn't remember now when they had first slipped into these roles: she the impractical scatterbrain; he the slightly exasperated ground control.

They made their way through the systematic concrete-and-tarmac car park, and as they approached the great block of glass and concrete that was the supermarket, Cecily felt a wave of boredom, almost fatigue, sweep over her. It had crept up on her gradually, over the years, this aversion to any kind of shopping.

Luckily, Florian was engaged and ready for action. "So what's on the list?" he asked, as they collected a trolley in the foyer. It was fairly crowded with people going in and coming out, and standing there, he looked suddenly out of place, although she couldn't work out why.

She checked the list. "'Coffee – Lavazza or Peet's. Buffalo mozzarella (for the pesto chicken). Champagne – preferably Moët or Dom Pérignon—'"

"Jesus!" Florian commented shaking his head. "Is she serious? Moët or Dom Pérignon?"

"It's like she's doing it on purpose!" Cecily stared indignantly at the list. "Lavazza? What the hell? She must *know* that we just buy Lidl's own brand."

"Well, I can handle the Lavazza," Florian said, "but Moët or Dom Pérignon?"

They moved forward into the shop, and it was then that she put her finger on it: what was incongruous about him. Here, at this supermarket, he was the only black man within sight.

"So what shall we do?" she said, dismayed. If it were just her and Victoria, she wouldn't care. She'd just buy the own brands. In front of Victoria she wasn't ashamed of being poor – well, relatively poor, because in the great scheme of things, thanks to family money, she really wasn't poor. But in front of Diana? What would Diana think if Victoria let it be known that when she asked for Lavazza, they'd just come back with the supermarket's own brand?

Florian spun the trolley around decisively. "Don't worry about it; we'll just get a nice Prosecco. There's no way we're going to get bounced into buying Dom Pérignon."

"Okay..." she said.

At that moment, an old man came up behind Florian, pushing a trolley. The angle at which Florian had just spun their own trolley meant that it was momentarily difficult for the man to pass, but because Florian was facing Cecily, he didn't see the man behind him. The old man said, "Excuse me!" in a loud, meaningful tone, glaring at Florian's back.

Florian looked round. "Oh, I'm sorry!" he said, and pulled the trolley back to make room.

The old man widened his eyes and nodded sharply, before passing on. Both Cecily and Florian gazed after the man, who was now proceeding with his trolley down the aisle. You couldn't tell, of course, whether the old man would have been quite as rude if Florian were white.

"Just ignore what she wrote – seriously, we'll just get a nice Prosecco," Florian said.

Florian had grown up with racism all around him. Back in 1946, his wealthy, white great-grandparents had all but rejected his grandmother when they discovered that she was pregnant by a black American army officer. It wasn't until after Florian's mother was born that they had reluctantly agreed to recognise their illegitimate granddaughter as their own. And even that was an exceptionally progressive and liberal approach in those days. A lot of the other babies fathered by 'coloured' American soldiers were born in secrecy and shunted off quietly to orphanages. But luckily, Florian's white family were wealthy and highly educated, and thanks to their social standing, his mother had had some protection from the racism that was fairly ubiquitous in those days. Even so, she had never felt accepted in German society when she was young. She had married a clever student, sent to Germany by his own wealthy family in Togo, and his later work for the United Nations had taken them abroad for several years. It was not really until the 1980s, Florian said, that attitudes began to change.

At Oxford in the '90s, when Cecily and Florian had met, he had been one of only a handful of black students. He was the only black student in her college, in fact. And he was a Rhodes scholar. When she'd googled him recently, Cecily had found that Cecil Rhodes had said, "I contend that we are the first race in the world, and that the more of the world we inhabit the better it is for the human race "[24] But back in their student days, no one they knew, not even Florian himself, had ever remarked on the irony of Florian being a Rhodes scholar when Rhodes had been a white supremacist. It was as if – and this seemed strange to her now – they didn't really think about it. Perhaps that was because in the '90s the fact that Europeans were white supremacist in the imperial days was knowledge axiomatic that it would have seemed strange to suddenly point it out. It would have seemed unnecessary to point out to Florian that Rhodes was a racist, in the way that it would have seemed strange to point out to Cecily the obvious fact that in the first nine hundred years of Oxford University's history, women were not allowed to take degrees there.

Or perhaps, conversely, no-one talked about it then, because back then we hadn't yet begun to really shine a light on how our ideological human pecking orders contorted our assumptions.

But we still had such a way to go. That was one of the things that this awful Brexit was showing us, it occurred to her. Our Protestant imperialist tradition was not simply white male supremacist; it was specifically *English* supremacist.

Look at the way we talked about our fellow Europeans; look at the way we treated the Scottish and the Northern Irish, who'd voted to stay in the EU. In our subconscious hierarchy of peoples, there were only Englishmen, gloriously isolated, at the top. From their deluded height, Englishmen looked down on absolutely everyone. Not just women, not just brown people, but also the French, the Italians, the Spanish and the other Europeans. The Scots, the Welsh and the Irish, too.

We were only just becoming aware of this inherited superiority complex we had. It made you wonder what other assumptions we'd hardly even begun to question; what terrible injustices we were now – all of us, this very second – perpetrating unquestioningly, in a way that would disgust and horrify later generations. There was, for example, as Julia was beginning to point out, the awful way we treated animals: raising them in metal cages; feeding them with hormones. Future generations would perhaps find it hard to believe that we could just let it happen…

"What else?" Florian was asking.

She looked at her list. "'Six avocados – preferably organic," she read. "And 'a kilo of chuck steak for boeuf bourguignon."

*

"Here's another quote for you," Florian said, as they were driving back.

"Oh yeah?" she said.

"'Nobody talks more of free enterprise and competition

and of the best man winning than the man who inherited his father's store or farm.'" [25]

"Oh, yeah. I've heard that, I think."

She felt a pang of discomfort. Most of what she had herself – their three-room red-brick house in South London, and this house here in Dover – she'd actually inherited. She couldn't say she'd ever earned much money in all her life. Florian also had family money in Germany to thank for his distinguished education, and he had never made much either: not from his stint in academia, and not from his succession of research jobs after that.

And then, as the sea came into view again, she wondered if Diana and the children were still at the beach, and if Julia was okay. You couldn't get too involved with squabbles and rivalries between children. You shouldn't weigh in, as on the whole, she thought, they were best left to deal with it themselves. But still she wondered what, precisely, was going on.

"Freedom! Always so much talk of freedom!" Florian went on. "And what does it even mean? It just means freedom for the rich to get richer at the expense of the poor. Freedom from trade unions and collective bargaining means the freedom to suppress wages. Freedom from regulation means the freedom to poison rivers, to endanger workers, to trample on human rights…"

"Yeah, yeah." She sighed.

And, glancing at her, he stopped and then shook his head and sighed as well, realising that it was too depressing to go on; they'd been through this so many times before. They drove on a while in silence.

*

"Hurry up!" she said to Florian, as they were unpacking the shopping when they got back. He was faffing around, tidying up the bottles in the larder. "Let's just get it unpacked before Victoria comes in."

Florian turned around and looked at her – half curious; half entertained – as if what she was saying made no sense. And then he turned calmly back to what he was doing.

"You don't have to tidy everything. Let's just put it away and go!" she pressed.

But he wouldn't be hurried. He moved no faster, placing the tins on the shelf with fastidious care, one by one. Florian always seemed to other people calm, unruffled, level-headed. But he had habits of intense orderliness in which Cecily sensed something quite the opposite: a very private kind of distress. It was one of the things that had attracted her to him in the first place: that stubborn, resistant orderliness of his. He constructed it about him like a barricade. He made their bed every morning. He rolled and bound and labelled all the cables to all his devices in his 'cable drawer'. He would never begin work unless his desk was completely tidy: the papers straight; the angles of the stapler and hole punch and Post-it Notes aligned. He never sat down to breakfast – a German breakfast, with bread and cheese and cucumber and tomatoes – until everything he needed was already sliced and set out neatly.

"Why? Are you afraid Victoria's going to tell you off for not buying her favourite brands?" he teased her now, carefully stacking tuna tins on top of each other.

She was. But of course, it sounded ridiculous when he put it like that. And annoyingly, he now seemed to be moving even more slowly. He had now begun re-organising the tins of tomatoes already on the shelf, before putting away the new ones. Right now, it didn't seem a tender indication of inner vulnerability, this fastidiousness of his. It was just annoying and, actually, pathetic.

"Of course not!" she retorted, untruthfully. But then, seeing his teasing face, "I just don't want her getting at me!" she justified tetchily.

Florian laughed. "Oh, come on!" he said.

She knew the anxiety she was exhibiting seemed childish to him. But that was the thing: he didn't understand about her and Victoria. She shoved the last fridge items into the fridge and left – slightly flounced out of – the kitchen. And then, almost as soon as she was hovering about the books in the sitting room, she experienced a feeling quite opposite – of gratitude, almost – towards Florian. Thank goodness he was not afraid of Victoria, the way she was! The knowledge that he was there, stacking tuna tins, uninvolved in – quite unmoved by! – their intimate furies, gave her a wider perspective, an escape.

In fact, Victoria didn't appear for ages after they got back from the shop. She was working in the study. And, since Diana was also still absent down on the beach with the children, Cecily picked another book off the shelf: a biography of Oliver Cromwell published in the early '90s, with a dog-eared but still shiny cover bearing a picture of the Lord Protector himself posed against a stormy sky, his wispy brown hair frazzled; his expression – above his high white collar – stern.

She felt a little unsound, digging around in these old books from her student years. She hadn't looked at any of them since her first-year exams, now more than twenty-five years ago; some, to be honest, she might have never opened. She wasn't even quite sure what she was now looking for, but still she began thumbing through the biography. And when she alighted on a letter Cromwell had sent to his brother-in-law, Colonel Valentine Walton, on the 5th or 6th September 1644, she experienced a buzz of excitement. How incredible that, in 2019, she should be able to read the very words that Cromwell had written to his comrade-in-arms in the thick of a civil war in the seventeenth century! She imagined him seated at some grainy, wooden desk by a window in an black-beamed house. He would be wearing high, brown boots like those he wore in one of the colour prints in the centrefold of the book; a black, woollen shirt, perhaps, with a white collar; and some thick, brown-suede waistcoat on top. The pearly, English light would fall on his page as he wrote on thick, fibrous paper with a scratchy quill. And from time to time, between sentences, he would look up and seek counsel from the receding view outside the window.

In early September there would be an overcast sky, perhaps; the leaves beginning to curl with yellow. The autumn sun, if the clouds should briefly part, would slant low and linger long, nostalgic for summer, over the fields and hedgerows. Or perhaps it was raining – a light, wet mist of drizzle, the falling water dulling all other sounds apart from those of the thoughts in Cromwell's head. In 1644, the civil war was only two years in, and the future still entirely unknown.

'We study the glory of God, and the honour and liberty of Parliament, for which we unanimously fight, without seeking our own interests…'[26] Cromwell wrote. '…I profess I could never satisfy myself on the justness of this war, but from the authority of the Parliament to maintain itself in its rights…'

Intrigued, Cecily took the book, and went and sat on the sofa. Out through the window, here and now in Dover, the August sun continued to shine. But it was gusty: she could see the trees that bordered the sloping fields swaying from side to side and rattling their leaves in the blustering winds from the sea. She wondered what it must be like for Diana and the children down on the beach. Choppy, perhaps. Not that they would really be swimming anyway. With the window closed, she couldn't hear a thing, which made the passionate writhing of the trees in the onslaught of headwind almost like some drama with the sound turned off. They looked like giant protagonists enacting the horrors and suffering of the ages, casting their branches from side to side like that. And then she raised the book and read those lines again: 'We study the glory of God, and the honour and liberty of Parliament, for which we unanimously fight, without seeking our own interests…'

It was a long time ago that she had learnt about the civil war. But she seemed to remember that not so long after Cromwell had written this, the famous Putney Debates were held to discuss the constitution and organisation of the state when peace came. At the debates, rank-and-file soldiers known as 'Levellers' had called for voting rights to be extended; for universal manhood suffrage, in fact.

But Cromwell and other landowners had countered the Levellers' arguments, maintaining that only those who owned substantial property should have a right to vote.

It was the landowners who prevailed; the Levellers were soon marginalised. And by 1690, if she remembered rightly, John Locke was writing, as if this were axiomatic, 'Government has no other end but the preservation of property.'[27] Meanwhile, seventeenth-century Parliaments had begun to pass legislation upholding the written legal right of local magnates to enclose common property over unwritten claims to common ownership of such land according to ancient custom. Until then, Parliaments had fairly consistently – if ineffectively – opposed it.

Her gaze fell on the gimp braid which edged the sofa in a darker green than the main upholstery. This, like the border on the chair in the master bedroom, was loose and loopy in patches, she noticed. Someone really needed to sew it back on.

Although she had studied this period in her first year at university, she could not really have been paying attention, it seemed to her now. None of what she had read had ever really shaken the unconscious assumptions she had begun learning back in infant school, writing firework poems for Guy Fawkes Night. She had been raised and educated, she realised only now, in a tradition that saw the parliamentarians who had won the English Civil War as heroes: humourless, puritanical, not much fun, perhaps, but still heroes. With their understanding of the way that power breeds desire for more power; of the need for legal constraints on the executive; their insistence that no one

– not even the King – should be above the law, they had seemed like prophets way ahead of their times, shining in their wisdom like divinely inspired harbingers of an enlightened modern era.

But now it all looked different. It was just not true that Cromwell and his colleagues didn't seek their own interests in the civil war and its aftermath. Parliamentarians had led landless commoners to war against the King with high-flown language of parliamentary sovereignty; of Protestant liberty versus papist tyranny. But all this talk just looked now like a sublimation of their own politico-economic interests into some noble-sounding political theory.

She looked up at the window again. The trees were still hurling their branches about in the wild winds. They looked vaguely ridiculous. Because when it came to the Interregnum, Cromwell's party excluded all but their own class – and their own group within their own class – from power. Basically, all Cromwell and his allies really achieved, via the civil war, was to get rid of the royal favourites who had occupied all the most lucrative monopolies and opportunities for patronage under Charles I. They had got rid of that existing 'in-crowd' and then, basically, just supplanted them.

She could faintly hear Victoria taking a call over the hall in the study. That warm, bubbly, TV presenter voice that she put on in social situations. Even from here, when she could hardly hear more than a thread of rhythm and intonation, it riled Cecily. And yet, at the same time, there was a part of her that found it almost endearing. Puzzlingly, it was almost loveable, the way Victoria needed to impress, to control, to dominate. Almost as if she'd never quite grown up; as if she were still a child play-acting, the way they used to when they were aged seven and nine, or thereabouts, and they filled sherry glasses with tonic water, sugar and lemon juice and sat in the sitting room, pretending to be grown-up.

She looked about the room at all the books and the carpets and the little tables acquired by her ancestors. And at the place, on either side of the fireplace, where the vases should be.

Those attitudes she had grown up with – those fetishes around barrels and cold water and eating crusts and wearing shoes in the house – it occurred to her now, began to seem less the outward manifestations of the universe's secret moral core, and more like a car-boot jumble of an inheritance from more-or-less hypocritical ancestors: part of one crockery set and part of another; half a pair of silver candlesticks; a drawer full of mismatched cutlery. Her family mores were perhaps just the random remaining bits and pieces of what might once have been complete sets of Protestant and classical, romantic, or even class-based beliefs. And all it really added up to was little more than a vague sense that one ought to cultivate a Spartan scorn for discomfort; a Lutheran exaltation of spirit over form; a Calvinist rejection of vanity – but then again, one should also, like Catullus, seize the day. And she couldn't actually explain, so many garbled generations later, quite why one should do any of those things.

*

Victoria closed the document and sat up straight, stretching her spine. In front of her on the desk sat her grandfather's old hole punch. Astoundingly heavy, it was, made of some cold, weighty metal in a milky shade of khaki. It had curves like a 1950s car, and the bottom was lined, like a snooker table, with rich green baize.

She looked around the study. It seemed so different now, this room, to how it had seemed when she was a child and her grandfather was alive. Back then he had occupied this room almost constantly, dominating the space, emanating his particular musty, dusty aura of repression, impatience and dissatisfaction. He didn't much like children. He didn't much like anything, it seemed, other than talking about hardship. She had not found him impressive, although the received family opinion was that he was impressive. Her grandmother had tiptoed around him, and often explained to them, in an admiring tone that didn't quite ring true, "Your grandfather is a good man but he does hate screeching. Your grandfather doesn't mean to be bad-tempered, but he doesn't like mess. Your grandfather is very respected in blah-blah-blah; would never stoop to blah-blah-blah; knows a lot about blah-blah-blah…" Victoria never really listened, or had any notion why her grandmother talked like this. Not that she wondered about it much: it was just one more of the inscrutable ways in which adults behaved.

It was her grandmother she had loved. Her grandmother had a big, warm laugh and a soft, expansive bosom that smelt – exotically – of talcum powder. They used to make apple cake, and Granny would peel apples and toss the spirals of peel into the air to see what letter they formed when they landed on the floor. That would be the first initial of Victoria's future husband's name, she'd tell her.

Granny doted on Victoria in those earliest days of her childhood, before Cecily became a person to be reckoned with. At least, that was how Victoria remembered it: just the two of them in a warm glow of bosoms and cuddles and dopamine.

And now that she had begun thinking about these things, she couldn't concentrate on work any more. She looked at her watch: she'd been here a good three hours, which was more than enough when she was actually meant to be taking a few days' holiday. She shook her head from side to side, to loosen the muscles in her neck, and then arched her back, to stretch it. Time for a run. But the prospect evoked mixed feelings: her anticipation of her exhilaration at the end of the run battled against her dread of the beginning. She looked up out of the window: it looked blowy outside, which raised her spirits. She liked to run when it was turbulent like this; the trees shaking their leaves like demented cheerleaders. It was cathartic. She stood up.

As she did so, someone knocked on the door, and almost simultaneously pushed it open: Florian.

"Oh, hi," she said.

"Hi." He smiled, in that slightly formal, but unhurried way of his. "Um…" he said, and kind of shook his index finger loosely in the air, as if trying to remember what he had come in for. He had such long, loose limbs.

For an instant, a wild, crazy instant, she felt as if he was Matthew. Not that he reminded her of Matthew exactly;

they could hardly be more different. Yet still there was that momentous way he made her feel; that sense, when he came into the room, that she was finally alive.

"Have you got a moment?" he said.

She felt strangely conscious of the trees outside the window, sighing and swaying in the high wind. And while she knew perfectly well that he would be here for some utterly mundane reason, she could imagine an alternative universe in which he'd come here compelled only by that momentousness that was between them. "Yes! What is it?" she asked.

"It's just… er… that I wondered if we could talk a bit about the house and some of the repairs that probably need doing…"

The alternative universe disintegrated rapidly, leaving her with a sense – a quite breath-taking sense – of humiliation. How absurd that she could have imagined…! And most absurd of all was that she didn't even like him all that much, as a person. She wouldn't want to live with him; to talk to him, particularly, about the things she usually heard him talk about. There was just that tremendous sense of significance, in his presence, that came from nowhere. It seemed to have absolutely nothing to do with her real and conscious self.

And she didn't want to talk to him about the house.

"Oh! Do you know what? I was just about to go for a run. Literally, *just* about to! Can we talk later?"

He looked at her. And for that second she felt as if he knew everything – *everything*; every single thing – that she had felt since he'd come into the room. As if he didn't want to talk about the house either, and had come in just to make a fool of her.

And then he was backing out of the door, saying, "Sure, yeah, of course. No problem." And, as she walked past him into the hall towards the stairs, "Enjoy your run!"

She went upstairs and got changed. She couldn't find her running shoes, and this made her feel turbulent in some way, as if the whole world were conspiring to frustrate her. She flung her other shoes aside, in the bottom of the wardrobe, with an anger that surprised her. And then she found the running shoes under her bed instead, and put them on.

Two mornings after Matthew had ended it, she'd phoned him. She couldn't help herself. There were no mobile phones then, but she'd phoned his university house, where he lived with two friends. His friend Dominic had picked up the phone and, when she asked for Matthew, said, "I don't think he's here. Wait a sec…" Curling her finger in the spiralling lead for the ancient phone that sat in the kitchen of the flat she rented, she then heard him ask someone else in the room, "Do you know where Matthew is?" She couldn't hear what the other person said, but she did hear Dominic reply, "No, it's *Vicky*. You know – his girlfriend."

Matthew wasn't there and they didn't know where he was, Dominic said when he came back on the line, but by then that hardly mattered anymore. Because the elation, the sheer elation of hearing herself described as Matthew's girlfriend had blown away everything else. She'd put the phone down, and for a moment, everything was fine. Not just fine, but wonderful. She'd imagined that if Dominic thought that she was still Matthew's girlfriend, then she really was still his girlfriend, and everything was okay, and none of the nightmare of the past two days was true.

It seemed incredible, now, the unbalanced state she'd been in.

*

She remembered later, as she ran along the cliff path, the very first time she'd met Florian. It was shortly after she herself had got engaged to Dan.

Because, in fact, that feeling had been there from the very first. That great, bounding, huge-sky, Matthew feeling. Not to do with anything Florian said; just his presence. Incredibly, he spoke English almost entirely without an accent. It was like the universe was trying to tell her something: that Cecily had this man. And immediately Victoria wondered, in those early days: did he make Cecily feel the way he made her feel? She was sure that he did, and had wanted to tell Cecily, *It's not just you; he makes me feel like that too. Don't imagine it's something special just for you.* Whereas Dan was... well...

She kept on running, around the bend in the cliff and down the cliff path, until she came to the point where she could see the beach. Looking out of the bay, she could make out Zac down there, with the girls and that Diana. The girls were doing gymnastics up by the embankment, and Zac was on the beach, near Diana and the water. Victoria couldn't see his face that well, but she could see him turning and swinging his arm, almost as if he were batting in cricket.

What was he doing? Oh, yes – he was skimming pebbles into the sea. She stopped, watching the girls. Olivia could easily perform flips and walkovers, even across the pebbles. But Julia was struggling even to kick all the way up into a handstand against the embankment wall.

Watching them, Victoria felt comfortably superior; gently scornful. She could have been a gymnast if her mother had been more supportive. Maybe not an Olympic gymnast, but who knew? Her mother had not been prepared to spend her weekends driving Victoria to competitions. "Besides," she'd added, "it's not just you: there's Cecily to think about! How is it fair on her if we spend all of every Saturday travelling halfway across the country and back to competitions?"

It occurred to Victoria then: why not visit them down on the beach as she went? Perhaps she could buy them ice creams; build some more rapport with Diana while Cecily wasn't there. She turned off the path and headed down the steps to the embankment. She could see Zac much better now. Down on the beach, he had stopped and turned towards Diana, and Victoria could see the smile he had learnt; the rumpling of his hair. Pride upsurged, quite suddenly, in her heart. It was competitive, socially, at his boarding school. But Zac was fine: he had taken to it like a duck to water. That pride she felt in him, when he came home for the holidays in his school uniform: a little slapdash, ironic, arrogant, like all the public schoolboys she had ever known. It was almost miraculous, the way he had picked it up: that way of walking, that way of talking, that worldly assurance most of all. He could talk to anyone: adults, children; he never felt inferior. And that was what she had wanted. She had wanted him to feel 'entitled', as they liked to say nowadays, to be confident; she had wanted him to be sure of his own worth, to be at home in *this* world in the way her own family had actively tried to prevent her from being, with their constant references to some imaginary other world, some imaginary other value system that didn't really exist. This constant call that she be separate from everyone else, that she set herself apart.

It was like at that Sunday school, here in Dover, where she remembered that lady had once read, "'Therefore, come out from among unbelievers, and separate yourselves from them, says the LORD. Don't touch their filthy things, and I will welcome you.'" Even as a child, aged eleven or twelve or whatever she was, Victoria had been sceptical about that. What 'filthy things' did they mean? Hot showers? Barbies? Soda Streams? What she wanted most for her own child, now that she had one, was that he should *not* feel set apart, dragged away, the way she always had. She wanted Zac to feel that he *belonged*, that he was *at home* in the world. Like Dan but more – well, classy. That debonair assurance, that *entitlement* was exactly what she most wanted him to acquire. She decided to go to the coffee bar and get those ice creams to surprise them all.

It was Julia who saw her first, from upside down, as she came down the steps from the embankment onto the beach. Julia looked surprised and quickly righted herself as Victoria called, "Hi, Julia!"

Diana and Zac saw her then, and moved back over the beach towards her, smiling.

"I've brought ice creams!" Victoria announced.

"What flavour?" asked Zac.

"What do you think?" she replied archly. She'd got his favourite: raspberry ripple with chocolate and nuts on.

But Julia looked embarrassed and wouldn't take hers.

"What's wrong?" Victoria asked.

Julia looked at her, so intensely that it was as if she were trying to convey a message with just her eyes. It reminded Victoria of Cecily.

"What?" she said again, not meaning to sound irritable.

Julia drew breath as if to say something, but then pressed her lips against each other in a straight line, as if to actually *prevent* words from escaping from between them, before letting them go again with a sudden outlet of breath. "Well, I'm a vegan," she said, her words tumbling out, embarrassed. "Sorry."

Of course she was! Of course she would be! Just like her mother: always trying to make herself superior; to set herself apart.

*

"To be honest, I'll be relieved when we're out of the EU and all this endless Brexit talk is over," said Victoria that evening, as they congregated for pre-dinner drinks. She was half laughing, half disapproving. "You know? And people can just get on with their lives again."

But Diana widened her eyes and nodded enthusiastically. "Oh, I know!" she said, sipping her champagne. "That's exactly how I feel!"

Cecily ran her hand over the slightly rough, threadbare

velvet along the curve of the bergère armchair and thought of Florian, who'd recently had to apply for 'settled status' in order to legally remain in the UK after Brexit. He'd been living in Britain for twenty-four years now, ever since he'd arrived as a student. When they'd decided to buy a house and have a child here, he'd never imagined that his right as an EU citizen to live here could ever be repealed. It was unimaginable: responsible states just didn't go repealing people's basic rights which were guaranteed by international treaties. He'd had to fill out forms and send bank statements and God knows what other proof that he genuinely lived here. He'd had to grub around and fill out forms just to stay in his own home with his own wife and daughter, and it had all been done accompanied by such a horrible feeling of humiliation and insecurity. And having to explain to Julia. How did you explain to your child that your own government was – with the support of half the country – suddenly stripping her father of rights that it had recognised for years and years and years?

"I'm not sure we'll just be able to get on with our lives, though. I mean, Florian, for example, is German, remember. He'll no longer have a right to be here the way he used to," Cecily said, trying to sound casual, matter-of-fact, because if you spoke a heartfelt word against Brexit in England now, it made everyone recoil; only flippant comments were socially acceptable.

Even so, Victoria and Diana both sort of became still and tried not to look at each other, as if what she had said was offensive in some way. Victoria was sat on the sofa, and when Cecily spoke, she stretched out her fingers and looked at her nails; Diana was perched on the other pink velvet armchair, champagne glass in hand, and she lowered her chin and looked into her glass.

And then Victoria turned, quite energetically, to face Cecily and said tartly, "But they can have settled status, can't they?" And then – "Oh!" – her eyebrows arched, her eyes grew wide, and her fingers fluttered to her neck in a gesture of concerned disapproval, "I hope Florian has remembered to fill in the paperwork?"

How would Diana and Victoria like it, Cecily thought with an uprush of anger? How would they like it if the government suddenly brought in new laws which demanded that they prove their right to live in their own home with the rest of their family? "Yes, he has, but there's no document given out to prove 'settled status'," she said. "You don't get any proof. You get an email from the Home Office; that's all you get."

She looked at Victoria, but Victoria wouldn't look at her; she was pretending to look into her wine glass. How could Victoria just not care about Florian?

She looked at Diana. There was a panicky need for support, for affirmation rising up inside Cecily: surely they could understand how awful this was for her family? But Diana just blinked.

"And as we've seen from the horrors of the Windrush scandal," Cecily continued, trying to keep the fury out of her voice, "Home Office statements are worth nothing if the political climate changes. And just look at how the government is whipping up hostility against other Europeans by claiming that EU citizens, who have every right to work here (that's the whole point of free movement) are 'jumping the queue', or by suggesting that EU citizens ought to pay double for healthcare after Brexit."

"Oh, but that's just talk, so as to strengthen their hand in the negotiations with the Commission," Victoria said with a dismissive wave of her hand.

Tell that, Cecily thought, *to the thousands of descendants of Caribbean immigrants who, although they were guaranteed British citizenship when they arrived here as children in the '50s and '60s, were not given any documentation to prove that. Now, fifty, sixty years later, some of them had recently been deported because they couldn't show documentation proving their citizenship.!* "Well, is it? What about the Windrush children?" she said.

"What's that?" asked Victoria in a bored, patronising voice, squinting as if Cecily spoke unclearly and she couldn't hear.

"The Windrush generation. Now the government is demanding they show documentation that the government never even issued."

"Oh, I know, that's just awful. But *Julia* will be all right, won't she, Cecily?" Diana intervened soothingly. "I mean, she's got a British passport, hasn't she?"

Cecily had never realised that Diana could be quite so maddening. "Well, yes. But not *everyone's* children will be! Besides, Florian won't!"

"Oh, come on, he'll be fine!" Victoria said, tossing her hair briskly and smiling. "Believe me, Cecily, no one has any interest in taking away Florian's rights." And then she turned towards Diana, smiling. "Can I fill you up? We *are* on holiday, after all!"

Diana smiled and held out her glass. But she looked back at Cecily, saying warmly, "I'm really sorry you're worried, Cecily. But I'm sure it will be okay."

"Of course it will!" said Victoria breezily, and she stepped forward to fill Diana's glass.

And that was that. Amazingly, Cecily noticed, both Diana and Victoria seemed now to feel that the subject was over. Because even as Victoria filled her glass, Diana was already gushing, "This is incredible – I mean, I almost never have real champagne!" in that role of 'admiring poor person' that she had taken on ever since Victoria had arrived. It was the last bottle; Cecily wondered if Victoria had noticed that from now on, there was only prosecco to drink.

And seeing that they had closed the subject, Cecily felt, childishly, like crying. She felt like chanting Martin Niemöller at them both:

First they came for the socialists, and I did not speak out – because I was not a socialist.
Then they came for the trade unionists, and I did not speak out – because I was not a trade unionist.
Then they came for the Jews, and I did not speak out – because I was not a Jew.
Then they came for me – and there was no one left to speak for me.

But of course, they would tell her that she was being ridiculous. We won the war against the fascists, remember? We were *literally* the anti-fascists, so nothing like that could ever happen here! That's what they would say.

She didn't quote Niemöller; she said, "I'll just go and check on the lasagne."

"Oh! Do you want some help?" Diana asked immediately.

"No, no!" Cecily answered her so quickly that perhaps it was almost rude. But she didn't think she could bear to even look at – let alone talk to – Diana right now. "There's really nothing else to do! It's nearly ready," she added.

In fact, she knew that the lasagne needed at least another ten minutes, so she took her glass and sneaked out through the dining-room French windows.

Stepping outside onto the lawn, Cecily felt that expansion of perspective again. The open sky, rolling hills and fresh breeze confronted her with such a dramatic widening of context that Victoria and Diana, Brexit, and all her other worries were for am instant like matters of only vague and local interest. Here it was! All the *real* world! The enigmatic sky! The worrying wind from early in the day had subsided; all was quiet. And way up high, daydreaming across the sky, were piles of self-absorbed clouds. They just hung there, Cecily marvelled, suspended; preoccupied with their timeless philosophy. The air felt wet; you could feel that night was on its way. It was not yet dusk, but already there was an absence of colour in the landscape. The sky was a washed-out white, the lawn was greyish, and the shrubs around the lawn had become undefined. The trees looked long-suffering, standing in the garden while the light drained gradually away. And as they stood, their twigs and leaves swayed, stirring ever so gently, ever so patiently in the evening breeze.

She remembered that from when she was a child: the way these trees were always waiting for something. If you came out here alone and stood among them, at any time of day, you got this strong sense that they were waiting for something; that they'd be waiting there patiently all day and all night long. As a child it seemed that the trees, too, were quietly part of that gnostic knowledge to which her mother, grandfather and great-grandfather were privy; that esoteric code to which were also mysteriously connected the eating of crusts on a slice of bread, getting up early, and swimming in a freezing sea. And even now, as an adult, though she had that very afternoon reached the conclusion that her mother had never actually been privy to the full gnostic code; that she had only, like Cecily herself, inherited a jumble of ill-assorted bits and pieces, she could still feel that holy awe that she had felt here as a child. There was still that feeling that somehow, somewhere, there really *was* a code, and if you could only find it, revelation would be yours.

The children were up by the stile at the end of the field, the two girls on the fence, while Zac stood facing them, his back to Cecily. They were all intent on something he was saying, or perhaps on something he had in his hand; she couldn't tell. They looked, from where Cecily stood, complicit; conspiring in one of those mysterious schemes of childhood. Remembering again how Julia had complained about Zac earlier, Cecily stood watching intently, trying to see if she could glean any clues about their current relations from the children's body language.

"Oh, here you are!" Florian came out behind her, holding a glass of wine, and stood beside her, following her gaze out across the lawn towards the three little figures. "I've finally got hold of a plumber," he said.

217

Thank goodness she had married a man who enjoyed solving household maintenance problems! Maybe it was actually not because of that other thing, but because of this, that she had chosen him? "Oh, fantastic! Thank you! How many did you have to ring?"

"I must have phoned about eight. But I've finally got someone who says he can come tomorrow."

"Thanks for doing that," she said again.

Florian sipped his wine. "Did you talk to Victoria?" he asked, after a while.

"Well, I did… But it's weird: she sort of didn't seem interested."

"Hmm." Florian looked down at his glass, and then into the distance. "I don't know how much it's going to cost…"

"Yeah, I'll talk to her again."

"Yeah, you'd better. I tried today as well, but she was going for a run." He took another sip of his wine and looked out across the field, adding, "But anyway, I think it really ought to come from you."

She glanced at him. Something about his way of pointing out that the house was hers, not his, was fleetingly erotic. Or maybe it was *that* – his self-abnegating sense of order – she had fallen for. That was an attraction too, like that of a man in uniform.

"And, well, you know that damp corner of the hall?" Florian continued.

"No? What?" she said, alerted by a change in his tone.

"The wall's literally starting to bulge."

She already knew this, she realised now, but she had been trying not to know it. Trust Florian to point it out.

"So we'll have to get someone in to sort that out as well," Florian continued, "Also, have you noticed how rotten the French windows are?"

"No... Christ!" She knew he was right to address these things, and yet all she wanted, somehow, was for him to stop. She had worries enough as it was. "Okay," she said, in what she hoped was a finalising tone, "well, I guess we'll have to pay half, somehow. Let's try and have a meeting with Victoria and Dan tomorrow at some point."

Florian took a sip of wine. That fleeting arousal had gone; Cecily no longer felt it on her skin or in her head or anywhere around. He was once again just her own, day-to-day-business, prosaic Florian.

He winced. "You know, I was on a website today," he said, "about Honduras. It said that there are these large areas of land there that for centuries have been cultivated by a people called the Garifuna, who owned and worked them in common so no one had proper legal titles to them. But a lot of these tracts are along the coast, and so in recent years the tourist industry has set its sights on them, and now it seems the government has let corporations take over large chunks of this land. They are intimidating the Garifuna and—"

She felt almost as if a bulb had switched on inside her head, like a cartoon character. "Oh my God! It's enclosure!" she interrupted.

"What?" Florian said.

"You know – how, in medieval England, the powerful started claiming legal rights to common land!" Cecily said. "So who are these corporations?"

"Well, there are loads of people involved, and also the government. They are creating these autonomous economic zones, called ZEDEs, which are a bit like charter cities or free cities. Don't know if you've heard about those? But anyway, what I really wanted to tell you was that it seems, from what I've been reading, that some of the big names connected with these initiatives are the same as the big names I've heard connected with Brexit."

Dan came out then, with a glass and a beer, which he snapped open with a sigh of contentment. "Just a quick breath of fresh air before dinner!" he said. He emptied the can into his glass, before placing it carefully onto the arm of the wooden garden bench on the terrace, "Cheers!" He raised the glass.

They clinked glasses and there was a moment of silence, during which Dan took a draught of beer. Watching him, Cecily knew that as he was savouring that gulp, he was deciding what to say next. And when she saw the dimples forming in his cheeks, she knew that he was going to try to tease her.

"So, Cecily," he said, in a jolly tone, "how do you like our new Prime Minister?" He was baiting her, as he always did.

"Why, what do *you* think of our new Prime Minister?" she retorted archly. She had an odd sense, suddenly, of being in a Jane Austen novel; some chilly, Regency English social situation in which everybody stood around in gardens being witty and polite and careful not to actually say anything. Transposed into that context, she would be – with her passionate opposition to Brexit – like one of those religious 'enthusiasts' the corrupt political elites of the eighteenth century had despised. In fact, it occurred to her, the raw passions of Brexit had had the effect of reviving, in much of the electorate, that old English distaste for 'enthusiasts': those Nonconformists, the earnest Methodists and Quakers, who spoke out against the slave trade. And something similar was happening in Brexit Britain in 2019. Nobody wanted to seriously address the corrupt dishonesty that was Brexit. They only wanted to joke about it.

Dan took another gulp of his beer and chuckled, and then, shifting his feet, looked benignly from her to Florian and back. "Well, you know," he said, and began to chuckle, "whatever you say about Boris, at least he's not boring..." When he pronounced the second 'b', a little flurry of spit globules flew out of his mouth.

Florian moved his wine glass to his left hand and then discreetly wiped a drop of spit from the back of his right hand. Raising his eyebrows, said, "Well, I think I might prefer *boring*."

But Cecily was finally baited. "Oh no, Dan, believe me, I met so many overconfident public-school thugs like him at university, all of them always seeking attention and trying to be the alpha male. I can't describe how utterly tedious they were. Each more tedious than the last."

Dan chuckled. "Unfortunately, the rest of the country doesn't seem to agree with you. He's very popular, apparently..."

She grimaced sulkily, muttering, "Thanks to the sycophantic media..."

But Dan was now turning to Florian, asking, "And what

do *you* think about Brexit, Florian? Do you think it'll go ahead this October?"

How could Dan talk so unashamedly to Florian about Brexit, Cecily marvelled, when Brexit deprived Florian of a whole raft of basic rights?

Dan raised his eyebrows while drawing on his beer, and then wiped his mouth hurriedly to add, "I mean, personally, I try not to think about it at all! Brexit, Brexit, Brexit! Nothing but Brexit. It does my head in. But still, what do you think?"

Florian smiled and shrugged. "I don't know," he said. "It's hard for a German like me to understand."

He was being ironic; Cecily looked to see if Dan had noticed.

Still holding his beer, Dan opened out both arms in a gesture of generous helplessness. "Do you know what? It's fucking hard for us Brits to understand too, to be honest!" He took another swig. "I just hope they know what they're doing, that's all!"

Dan took a sip of beer, and swallowing it, looked out across the field towards the children.

And following his gaze, the other two also looked over at the children, still lost in their game up by the stile, in the dimming light.

"I think the lasagne's probably just about ready," Florian said then. "Should we call the children?"

Dan put two fingers in his mouth and whistled heartily. And then he waved, also heartily, calling, "Dinner!"

Seeming in some way further away than they really were, the children turned their heads slowly to look at him. Almost unwillingly, the girls peeled themselves off the mossy fence, jumping down and wiping their hands on their jeans. And then the whole gang came walking slowly across the dewy grass towards the house, still talking, still absorbed by whatever it was they had been engrossed in.

*

"Did you go away anywhere else this summer?" Diana asked Victoria and Dan, as she picked up her knife and fork.

"Only for a couple of weeks," Victoria told her. "We went to Mauritius."

"Fantastic!" Diana said. She looked down at her plate and pushed lasagne onto her fork, wondering where Mauritius was. It was a name she'd heard before. Why had she never even thought of looking up where Mauritius actually was?

They had put the lights on, as the dusk was deepening, with the effect that the garden outside seemed to recede almost into non-existence and all significance seemed focused on the table and the people sat around it. She noticed that here they served table salt in an old-fashioned, bashed-up silver shaker, rather than grinding it straight from chunky crystals, as her friends in London did nowadays. Julia was shaking salt over her plate; vegans did that, Diana had noticed.

"How was that?" she asked Victoria.

"Good food – would recommend it!" Dan said. He was

holding his knife and fork pointing upwards, like the giant in the *Jack and the Beanstalk* book Diana used to read to Olivia. Or was it one of the *Mr. Men* books? That would have been before they it began to annoy her that there were no *Ms. Women* books; only the *Little Miss* titles, which blatantly defined all their protagonists as small (undeveloped?) and still maritally (sexually?) available.

Victoria rolled her eyes theatrically and tossed back her hair, apologising, "It's all about food with him!" and as Dan beamed – bashful, but basically unashamed – they all laughed.

"But it was *really good food*," he said again. "Amazing seafood, African food, Indian food, European – anything you like. There's a real French influence. So much better than Croatia, I have to say, which is where we went two years ago. The food there was pretty terrible. And the service."

"And it was also much, much better than France," Zac put in, "where we went at Easter. Like, literally *no one* spoke any English!"

Florian laughed at this, and leaned forward to address Zac down the table. "And how's your French?"

He asked it teasingly, but still he caused a hiatus of discomfort, which Dan fortuitously covered by grinning and pointing his knife at Zac. "Touché!"

Which made them all laugh again; Zac positively hooted.

"No, my French is not that good," Zac admitted, "but I'm going to drop it anyway. I'm going to do German, Florian, you'll be pleased to hear!"

Again Florian leaned forward to address Zac, commenting, in a kindly, encouraging way, "*Ach so!*"

Diana gathered that that was German.

"Yeah, no," Dan continued. "But Mauritius was gorgeous; I'd definitely recommend it. The hotel pool was massive, and the beach was really clean."

It sounded lovely, Diana thought. Maybe she and Steve would try it next year, if they decided to go for a sun-and-sand holiday again.

"What about you – where did you go?" Victoria asked politely.

And Diana found suddenly that she didn't quite want to tell them. It felt almost private. But of course, that was silly: it wasn't private; it was just where she'd been. "We went to Poland, actually," she said. "Just a weekend trip to Cracow." Poland might be the first place she'd been not just because somebody she liked had been there on holiday. They'd gone because she'd met a real Polish woman. That, and the fact that they'd come across a cheap short-break package deal.

"Oh!" Victoria exclaimed. "Eastern Europe! How was that?"

Magda was her name. Her daughter went to Olivia's gymnastics club. Diana and Magda sometimes sat and chatted when they took the girls to competitions; on occasion for hours and hours at a time, as those competitions could take all day. And then one day, Magda had brought some doughnuts with her. She said that in Poland they had doughnuts instead of pancakes for Pancake Day, which in Poland happened on a Thursday instead of a Tuesday.

"There are massive queues!" she had told Diana. She was a big, solid, comfortable woman with curly brown hair; when she laughed, the curls bounced about her face. "In my home town, where I come from, the doughnut queue goes all the way round the corner of the building."

In my home town, she'd said. And Diana had felt wistful; almost jealous. It was a lovely London community she lived in now, all basically revolving around Olivia's school. But she couldn't say she really *came* from anywhere, or ever had. Although perhaps North Greenwich had once, long ago, been like that for her mum.

Magda had made the doughnuts herself, because the ones here were not like the ones in Poland, she said. And they were delicious, if rather dry. But she said that was the thing with doughnuts: you should eat them straight away, as they did dry out, and she'd fried these ones early that morning – several hours ago. It had inspired Diana to make doughnuts herself, although they were not a success.

But getting to know Magda had made her curious about Poland. That and the fact that there were just so many Poles in London now, which was amazing when, twenty years ago, she'd never met anyone from Poland in her life. She'd hardly even known back then, if she was honest, that Poland existed. Neither it nor any of the other countries in what was then called 'the Soviet Bloc' had really figured in her education. You didn't learn about them in history; you didn't learn about them in geography…

"Quite pretty," Diana said. "Like, pretty, old buildings and paved streets. There's a nice square in the middle, with lots of bars and restaurants and stuff. Kind of medievally feeling, you know? A lot of green and copper-coloured houses, and…"

But when she looked up, it seemed that she was losing

Victoria's interest. There was just something about the way in which, as Diana talked, Victoria glanced surreptitiously down at her plate and unhurriedly prepared another mouthful of lasagne with her knife and fork, before returning her eyes, with a bright and attentive expression, to Diana's face. And Cecily, of course, Cecily had heard about her impressions of Poland – several times, in fact – last week. So Diana changed tack and tried to think of a subject that would interest them.

"...and really good food, actually, Dan," she said, turning to him. "Which surprised me, because for some reason I had thought it would all be, like, boiled cabbage and stodgy dumplings."

Cecily was surprised when she'd told her about Poland last week. Not that she had said so. But Diana suspected that Cecily had thought that she was uninterested in Eastern Europeans and their countries. But she wasn't – of course she wasn't! And she liked Magda. Besides, ironically, Magda actually understood – much better than Cecily, in fact – how immigrants could be a threat to your culture, and how the EU was unfair.

"Do you know how a Polish builder works in England?" she had said. "They come here and they rent a room which they share with other Polish men. And while they are here, they do nothing but work and work and work. But they earn maybe four times more than they could earn back in Poland, and also, if they have children back home, they can claim child benefit. There's no child benefit in Poland, but they can claim it here and send it there. And there, you know, it buys four times as much!" She had sat back and pulled the picnic thermos bag from the seat next to her onto her lap. It was full of carefully wrapped sandwiches and Tupperware pots of cut-up fruit. Magda always came to competition days with a feast prepared, and urged her daughter to eat during every break. "To be honest," she continued, "if I was English, I would have voted Brexit." And then she began reorganising all the sandwiches in the bag.

Magda was right. Of course no English builder with a wife and family to support could compete on price with a man whose house and family were in a country where the cost of living was a quarter of what it was here! This freedom of movement was putting our English workmen at a disadvantage, because it simply wasn't a level playing field.

Magda was different: she had married a second-generation Cypriot immigrant and settled down here. They ran a café. But that wasn't even the point: Diana had nothing, personally, against economic immigrants of any kind. Who wouldn't want to make their life better, after all, if they could? What she objected to was not the immigrants themselves, but the government for letting everyone in and not protecting their own. Or – more to the point – she objected to the way that EU rules about free movement just made everything worse and worse.

*

In the middle of the night, Cecily woke again. Then she lay back on the pillows and closed her eyes. She'd been dreaming a confused dream about her mother. She and

her mother had been looking for something in this house…
oh yes! The Italian vases.

"I just don't know why Victoria would want to take
them!" her mother kept on saying. "I mean, it's obvious that
they belong to the house!"

Even in her dream, Cecily had not been entirely happy
with this comment. To the house, yes, she had thought. *But
in some sense, mainly to me.* Because she and her mother
had both loved Florence. And the family all knew – even
Victoria herself must know full well – that spiritually, those
vases belonged to Cecily. And now she was awake, she still
felt like that.

After lying there for about fifteen minutes, going over
the events and conversations of the day before, she realised
that, yet again, she wasn't going to get back to sleep. So once
again, she reached for her cardigan, and tiptoed past the
smell wafting from the bathroom and down the stairs. In the
sitting room she went to the bookshelves by the fireplace,
and sought out the shelf housing her university books. Her
eye fell on her old copy of R. H. Tawney's *Religion and the
Rise of Capitalism*. It evoked in her such a strange feeling
that she pulled it off the shelf and, holding it in her hands,
paused to try to identify what exactly this feeling was.

It was nostalgia, mainly, she thought; a kind of sweet,
painful sadness. A nostalgia, maybe, for her student self;
for the river and for Magdalen's gardens; for that magical,
youthful sense of being on a quest for enlightenment: the
secret code. But perhaps that wasn't quite it, she thought
then. It was also a nostalgia for something else: something
she'd imagined would never be lost.

This author, R. H. Tawney, represented in her mind a past theme of Englishness; some lost virtue. The thesis of the book, if she remembered right, was that from the sixteenth century onwards, Protestantism had joined forces with incipient capitalism, and that this ideological alliance had produced not only the famous Protestant work ethic, but also an ideology which condoned and even encouraged unmitigated economic exploitation.

She also picked out *The Collected Complete Works of Daniel Defoe*. Then she spied two works by Mary Wollstonecraft, and she took them too. Then, carrying them over to the sofa, she wrapped herself in Victoria's super-soft blanket. It was a lovely blanket: totally synthetic, unfortunately (could such a thing be biodegradable?), but so very soft.

As she settled on the sofa, she realised that she could picture her memory of R. H. Tawney's general thesis as a sort of diagram: lines meeting and converging and travelling across the centuries. She had understood it like this: by the end of the seventeenth century, with Catholicism officially banished from England, the Catholic idea that social groups constituted mutually supportive parts of a single 'body' was gradually disappearing, as were medieval Catholic economic doctrines. Medieval Catholic economic theory, though it held labour as worthy, saw not only usury, but basically all trade as morally suspect. It condemned the practice of buying in order to sell at a higher price, requiring always – in theory – that commercial instincts be subordinated to the need for social justice. This movement spread across her mental diagram of the centuries (vertical lines) in a sweeping curve. Meanwhile (and in Cecily's mental diagram, this curve came in a different colour), the spread of Protestantism and its more individual approach to spiritual salvation had coincided with an ever more individualistic approach to economic gain. In fact, increasingly, as both Protestantism and capitalism gained ground, they began to change both the economic behaviours of English society and our economic and social theory.

She opened the book. It had been old even back in the 1990s; now the pages were deeply yellowed and a little clammy.

It was not only, Tawney was saying, that the seventeenth and eighteenth centuries saw growing emphasis on 'personal responsibility' in both the economic and the spiritual spheres. 'The pursuit of economic self-interest,' he wrote, was 'coming to be identified by the pious with the operation of the divine providential plan, which is the law of God.'[28]

'No question,' wrote one of Tawney's sources, a Puritan pamphleteer in 1654, 'but it [riches] should be the portion of the godly rather than of the wicked... for godliness hath the promise of this life as well as that to come.'[29]

The simultaneous ascent of capitalism and Protestantism saw spiritual salvation increasingly connected, in the public mind, to economic gain, Tawney seemed to be saying, and this trend also brought about change in public attitudes to the poor. Within Catholicism, a consciousness that Jesus himself had been poor and had asserted that riches were a hindrance to salvation meant that lip service had to be paid to the notion that the poor were in some way close to God, and that poverty was in some sense holy.

But by the end of the seventeenth century, many in Protestant England believed, like Milton's friend Samuel Hartlib (who himself enjoyed a pension of a hundred pounds a year granted by Oliver Cromwell), that 'The law of God saith he that will not work let him not eat. His would be a sore scourge and a smart whip for idle persons...'[30] Increasingly, Tawney said, the poor were no longer seen as being in some spiritual way closer to God, but quite the opposite. In fact, the 'growing individualism of the age' saw poverty as evidence of sin and of God's rejection. 'Like the friends of Job,' Tawney wrote, 'it saw in misfortune not the chastisement of love, but the punishment for sin.'[31]

The ideological zeal that fuelled the civil war of the mid seventeenth century that culminated in the Glorious Revolution of 1688, Tawney appeared to be say, ushered in an age of breathtaking cruelty. Those without property, already excluded from suffrage, were now increasingly excluded from the land as well, by enclosing landowners. There followed, as time went on, a succession of vicious Poor Laws which punished them for their exclusion. This was, on the whole, sanctioned by the Anglican Church, which was by now kept securely within the pockets of the Protestant nobility and gentry, who had acquired the rights to appoint vicars and pastors to many livings.

Cecily stopped reading and went into the kitchen to make herself a cup of tea. Through the window, dawn was slowly breaking. She could just make out the dim shapes of the trees standing, still waiting, about the lawn. It seemed to her, as she stood there, looking out of the window, waiting for the kettle to boil, that this particular Protestant-capitalist tradition of thought had been revived, via the Reagan-Thatcher era, in Anglo-Saxon culture today. The members of the seventeenth-century establishment quoted by Tawney might just as well have been modern Tories, who also attributed their wealth and fortune to some innate value of their own, while depicting the poor and luckless as worthless 'scroungers' who must be punished.

When she came back to the sitting room with her tea, she opened the Daniel Defoe. Within it, she found the text of a pamphlet that Defoe, the acclaimed author of Robinson Crusoe, had presented to Parliament in 1704. It was called *Giving Alms No Charity*, and in it he argued against giving financial support to the poor on the grounds that they were poor because they were lazy. ''Tis the men that won't work, not the men that can get no work, which makes the numbers of our poor,'[32] wrote Defoe. 'The crimes of our people, and from whence their poverty derives, as the visible and direct fountains are: 1. Luxury. 2. Sloth. 3. Pride.' He told Parliament, 'Good husbandry is no English vertue, it may have been brought over, and in some places where it has been planted it has thriven well enough, but 'tis a foreign species.'

Defoe, she thought, would fit very well in the Conservative cabinet of 2019. His quotes on poverty, and on the English people, could have come from the mouth of Dominic Raab, Priti Patel, Liz Truss, or indeed any of the authors of *Britannia Unchained* (dubbed, by some, the unofficial Brexit Party manifesto), wherein they had complained – sounding, to Cecily's ears, almost like Foxe complaining about the Catholic Church – not only about Britain's 'bloated state, high taxes and excessive regulation', but also that 'The British are among the worst idlers in the world. We work among the lowest hours, we retire early and our productivity is poor. Whereas Indian children aspire to be doctors or businessmen, the British are more interested in football and pop music.'[33] Here in Defoe, like in *Britannia Unchained*, there seemed to ring out that strange Protestant idea that it was somehow virtuous to want to accumulate money and somehow contemptible not to.

Thumbing on through the Defoe, she was struck, in 1724's *The Behaviour of Servants in England Inquired Into*, by the observance that England was now a country where there were 'ten thousand stout fellows who would spend the last drop of their blood against Popery but do not know whether it be a man or a horse'.[34] She lowered the book and sat contemplating the empty fireplace. By 1724, more than 150 years had passed since the first edition of Foxe's *Book of Martyrs* was published in 1559. Yet still, anti-Catholic propaganda seemed so powerfully to exercise the English psyche. Nearly two centuries after England's break with Rome, continental popery was still the bogeymen.

It was light, she saw, looking out of the window. Picking up the last book from her lap, and still wrapped in the blanket, she tiptoed through the dining room to the French windows. As quietly as she could, she slid back the old locks at the bottom and top, turned the loose bronze handle, leaned her shoulder against the cracked wood and pushed against the swollen old window. Paint peelings fell in a shower to the ground, like confetti, as it creaked open. And then she was out in the dewy garden, walking over to the bench where you could look out across the sea.

Sitting out in the early sea wind, she opened Mary Wollstonecraft's *A Vindication of the Rights of Men*. 'Security of property!' she read. 'Behold, in a few words, the definition of English liberty. And to this selfish principle every nobler one is sacrificed.'[35]

After reading this, Cecily flipped back to the introduction and checked the publication date. Wollstonecraft had published these words in 1790, one year after the storming of the Bastille and one year before Thomas Paine wrote his own attack on English social hierarchy, *Rights of Man* and one year before the Methodist William Wilberforce's first slavery abolitionist bill was rejected in Parliament after decades of campaigning by first Quaker and then Methodist Nonconformists.

'Security of property! Behold, in a few words, the definition of English liberty. And to this selfish principle every nobler one is sacrificed,' Wollstonecraft had written. And in her second book, *A Vindication of the Rights of Woman*, 'From the respect paid to property flow, as from a poisoned fountain, most of the evils and vices which render this world such a dreary scene…'[36]

At the time when Wollstonecraft was writing, only propertied men could vote, while the main function of the law, as articulated a century earlier by Locke, was to protect their property. Thanks to campaigners like Wollstonecraft and Paine – and to the French – by 1790 things were beginning to change. Nevertheless, it was not forty years later – the 1830s – that the first step in extending the franchise was taken. In the same decade, slavery was finally abolished. And it was not until nearly a *century* later – not until 1928 – that all citizens over twenty-one could vote, whether they owned property or not.

Meanwhile, as the argument for political equality was being won, the argument for economic equality was only just getting going. In 1884 the Fabian Society was founded, and by the early 1900s it was calling for universal healthcare and a minimum wage, the first of which was not achieved until after the Second World War, and the second not until Tony Blair's Labour administration in 1998.

Cecily put the book down, crossed her legs and looked out across the morning sea. Finally, she thought, she had located the England she had been looking for.

DAY 3

Wednesday 28ᵗʰ August 2019

Cecily didn't even hear the doorbell; she was so fast asleep. The first she knew of the plumber's arrival was voices coming nearer, down the corridor. It was comforting at first, to wake to these voices: the low one warm and melodious; the high one professionally modulated and husky, in a worldly kind of way. She felt safe in her half-consciousness, almost like a child drowsing in the presence of adult voices, until they came closer and closer, and gradually more distinct, and then suddenly it was clearly Victoria outside her door, calling, "Cecily! Your plumber's here!"

Florian sat up immediately. He rubbed his eyes and then leapt out of bed. Thank goodness for Florian!

Cecily was tempted to just sink back into sleep, but she supposed that wouldn't be fair on Florian. So she called out to Victoria, "Okay! We're coming!" heaved herself out of bed and fumbled in the pile of clothes she'd dumped on the chair last night, for something to wear.

It was only later, when she was making tea in the kitchen for Florian, the plumber and herself, that it occurred to her that it was strange that Victoria had not just shown the plumber into the bathroom herself. 'Your plumber'? What did she mean, '*your* plumber'? The house belonged to both of them! This thought bothered her so much that, although she did see, out of the corner of her eye, a shadow flit across the room, she hardly registered that it was anything unusual; she was too busy squeezing the teabags grimly against the sides of the mugs, and muttering about Victoria. It was only when she went to throw the teabags in the compost and, seeing that it was full, pulled it out from behind the other bin, that she saw it. A dark, quivering hump squeezed in behind the bin: a rat! And then it vanished, but she could hear it scrabbling somewhere inside the wall. She didn't scream, but she did recoil far more violently than she could explain. It must be some atavistic instinct, the horror that swept through her. It was just so… well, so *alive*! So very alive and terrified, and in *their* kitchen!

She was still jittery when she went out into the sitting room with the tray of tea. And there she saw Victoria and Diana sitting on the sofa together, poring over a vast book. Goodness! Why did Victoria always have to court Cecily's friends like this?

"My God!" Cecily said. "You won't believe it! There's a rat in the kitchen!"

Looking up, Victoria wrinkled her nose and said, "A *rat*?" in a tone that was half sceptical, half disapproving.

"Yes, it was horrible! It went somewhere behind the stove. I hope to God it hasn't got a nest back there."

"Euw!" Victoria grimaced, recoiling, as if it were somehow Cecily's rat. "Are you sure, though?"

"A rat!" Diana exclaimed, in amazement bordering on disbelief. "It wasn't just a mouse?"

The way they seemed to doubt her made Cecily feel ill-treated. Unable now to keep the irritation out of her voice, she insisted, "No, it was a *rat!*" Did they think she was making it up?

"God!" Diana commiserated, but her eyes had already returned to the book they were looking at.

And then Victoria turned the page, saying, "What do you think of this one?"

Diana leaned over the book on Victoria's lap, "Ooh, that's lovely! I love the teal!"

"What is that?" Cecily asked, stepping forward, unable to contain her curiosity, even though she was annoyed with them both: for being together, for doubting she had seen a rat, for making her feel left out.

"Oh, it's a book of fabric samples!" Diana said. "Victoria's doing up her house in London."

Of course she was! Victoria was always doing up her house, even though it was already perfect! Either that, or 'landscaping' her already perfect garden.

Cecily put down the tray and went over to look at the sample book. They were beautiful: soft, velvety materials in fashionable greens and blues. She glanced at the logo: 'Romeo Smith: luxury curtains'. "What's Romeo Smith?" she asked.

"They're just this little curtain company. They have a few really nice brands, like Orion, Bethany, that kind of thing." By 'nice', Victoria meant 'expensive', of course.

"But actually, you know," said Diana, looking up from the book and turning to face the window, "what I really like are the curtains *here*, in *this* house. And the cushions!" she added, pulling one onto her knee and beginning to stroke it. "You know what it reminds me of here? It's like… oh, what was the name of it? That house! Where William Morris lived…" She looked from Victoria to Cecily. "Do you know the one?"

Victoria, who was watching Diana with a cool, patrician indulgence, smiled. "Oh, you mean the Red House!" she said. "Yes, well, it's not surprising you get that vibe, as this house was actually built by Charles Voysey, who was part of that whole Arts and Crafts movement. That's why we bought these William Morris curtains and cushions: because he started the movement."

"Mummy made them, actually," Cecily corrected. She could picture her mother now: how she'd sat there at the sewing machine, pins in her mouth. She'd told Cecily that there were designs that really reminded her of William Morris at the cloth market in Padua; so much so that she'd actually wondered if they might have been an influence on him. Her mother, who'd brought those two vases back from Florence, long ago in the 1960s…

Victoria paused at this interruption, but then continued smoothly, "Because William Morris was part of the same movement, which actually went back to the art critic John Ruskin and the Pre-Raphaelites."

Diana looked blank, and Victoria added, "You know? Ruskin College? In Oxford?"

"You mean the Ruskin School of Art," Cecily said. Victoria ignored her, looking only at Diana,

"You know?" She asked Diana again.

"Oh, yeah!" Diana nodded and began to stroke the cushion again, "It's so lovely!" She said.

Diana was pretending to know. Cecily could tell that from the light panic that crossed her eyes, from the way she pitched her tone and the way she changed, as if trying to hurry the conversation on the subject. She knew Victoria would have perceived those things too. Cecily experienced a strange mixture of impatience (why didn't Diana just admit she had no idea who Ruskin was? What did it matter?) and protectiveness. Sometimes she wondered what it must be like for Diana, moving in circles saturated in complacent middle-class culture, when she had grown up in a completely different world. But how repulsive it was that someone like Victoria talked about the Arts and Crafts movement in tones of shared values, of ownership almost, when in fact most of what Ruskin and Morris had really believed was anathema to a Tory voter like her!

"Ruskin was quite a political radical," she said.

Victoria sighed – all but rolled her eyes – and turned to Diana on the sofa beside her, explaining, in forbearing tones, "I expect you know, by now, that Cecily once studied history."

"Was he?" Diana turned to Cecily, all excessive interest, wide-eyed; still in that annoying role of the eternally grateful and admiring guest.

"Yes," Cecily said. "He campaigned furiously against Victorian capitalism, and against the notion that financial inequality was in some way necessary or even desirable. He thought that access to beauty and comfort should be a right for everyone."

"Really?" said Diana. Her eyes fluttered saccharinely to Victoria and then back to Cecily.

"He was one of the leaders of the Pre-Raphaelite movement," Cecily continued, "You know, those medievally, Gothicky paintings of women with thick necks and long, frizzy hair?"

Diana laughed. "But he didn't design these cushions?"

"No, that's William Morris. He came later. But he was part of the same political tradition – in fact, he was even more radical as he was a socialist who campaigned for wealth and possessions to be shared."

Victoria had half-turned away, taking out her phone and checking it, to demonstrate that what Cecily said was of no particular interest to her.

And then Florian appeared. "Weren't you making tea?" he said.

"Oh, yes!" Cecily picked up the tray from where she'd put it down on the side table. "Sorry, I got distracted!

"Sorry!" she said again, when she arrived with the tray at the bathroom, where the plumber was wiping his hands. That evil, sickly smell now seemed somehow more pungent.

"So Mark here thinks he's diagnosed the problem," Florian said.

Cecily caught in a whiff of that sewage smell and felt a wave of... really it was like hopelessness; like that awful feeling of energy draining away that you got when you were about to faint. "Oh, but can we talk down here, away from the smell?" she said, backing up the corridor again with the tea tray.

The men followed her until they reached the landing at the top of the stairs.

"Sorry, you were saying?" she asked.

"Mark thinks it's a loose connection along the vent pipe," Florian said, and then turned towards the plumber for confirmation. "Right?"

The plumber took a mug. "Yep. Which means we're going to have to open up the wall."

Cecily looked at Florian, who was grimacing. "Oh dear," she said, "that sounds major."

Mark and Florian both raised their eyebrows and nodded grimly.

*

They were coming back from the beach that afternoon when Zac halted, quite suddenly, in the middle of the cliff path. "Boris has gone to ask the Queen to prorogue Parliament," he announced, eyes glued to his phone.

They all stopped and looked at each other. And then, not knowing quite what would be appropriate to say, they just carried on up the path, as if nothing was happening at all. It was all grotesque, Cecily thought.

And then, as they reached the clifftop minutes later, Zac shouted, "She said yes!"

"Really?" Victoria came to look over his shoulder at his phone.

"Yep!" Zac said. He did a little run and a jump, punching

the air and whooping. He looked like an idiot, Cecily thought. "The Queen said yes! She said yes!" he yelled.

"What? That quick?" said Florian in amazement.

"Just like that?" Cecily burst out. "Didn't she even want to talk, maybe, to some of her advisers?"

"My God, this country is crazy!" Florian gasped. He stopped and began to turn slowly around, his head tipped up to the sky.

"Yup. The prorogation is going ahead!" Zac said triumphantly.

They all just stood about there in the buffeting wind.

"The Queen said yes!" Zac shouted at Cecily, punching the air again. "Boris is a genius! It's checkmate! Now there's no way Parliament can stop Brexit going ahead!"

"Okay, okay, calm down!" said Victoria, smiling indulgently.

But Cecily found that there were actually tears pricking her eyes. Her stomach was falling away. It was exactly how she'd felt back when Parliament voted to trigger Article 50.

As they were coming off the windy cliff path and onto the gravel road, Diana ventured tentatively, "So it's not unconstitutional after all, then, I guess", looking from Cecily to Victoria.

"It's *entirely* unconstitutional," Cecily said through gritted teeth. She could hardly trust herself to even look at Diana.

But Victoria laughed and placed a hand on Diana's arm. "Really, I have no idea at this point!" she exclaimed.

"Me neither!" Diana re-joined. "But you know, at least it sounds as if at last things are finally, *finally* moving forward."

*

Although he was her son, Victoria couldn't for the life of her understand quite why Zac was so invested in this whole thing. This excitement of his about Brexit; the way he idolised the key players, following them on social media, savouring their names on his tongue: Jacob Rees-Mogg, Boris Johnson, Dominic Cummings, Arron Banks. He was almost like someone in love, the way he talked about them, and it was very hard for her to fathom. It reminded her of various other childhood passions of his: those Transformer toys when he was five, for example. He used to talk about them – their names, their special powers, their particular attributes – in these same tones of awe and simmering excitement.

Cecily turned and began walking on ahead, very fast, towards the house. Victoria and Diana exchanged expressions of concern, and then Victoria shrugged and turned out her palms to express to Diana that there was nothing they could do. Cecily was always melodramatic like this. She had a childish view of life: she saw *everything* as a battle between good and evil.

"I think I'm going to lie down for a bit," Cecily called behind her. She didn't stop to look back at them, and when she got home she went straight upstairs to bed.

When the others came in and found no Cecily anywhere downstairs, Diana turned, with an anxious face, to Florian, and said, "Oh dear – do you think Cecily is really upset?"

Florian, embarrassed, raised his eyebrows and opened out his palms. "Yeah, I guess so…" he replied, looking from Diana to Victoria, as if he expected them to explain something to him. And then he went off as well.

Diana turned again to Victoria. "Should I go up after her, do you think?"

"Don't worry about it," Victoria told her. "I'd just leave her alone for a bit. She's just very... well, to be honest, Cecily is always getting worked up about things like this."

After that, Diana went to her own room to read for a bit, which was a relief. It was almost like being at work, this mission she had set herself to cultivate Diana's affections. In fact, it was exactly like work; that was pretty much what she did all day: cultivate people and groups of people. It was essentially the same process. People always wondered how she knew so many people; had so many contacts. Many of them imagined that it just happened; that she just attracted people with some indefinable personal magnetism, and she never disillusioned them regarding their misconception. It was enough for her to know that it was nothing to do with magnetism; it was unrelenting vigilance: daily weeding and watering of a rota of her social contacts. It was a practice that she had begun in her late twenties, after she had met Dan. She'd learnt it from him, in fact. But while it came quite naturally to Dan, for her it involved quite a lot of effort. But it was so worth it! She'd found, over the years, that it was a very effective way to feel safe.

She went to find Dan, who hadn't gone to the beach: he'd stayed home to watch his boeuf bourguignon. He was out on the terrace, shelling peas.

"Have you heard the news?" she asked, sitting down on the wooden bench.

"What?" Dan looked up and scratched his nose energetically with the back of his hand. "You mean the prorogation?"

"Well, yeah," she said.

He nodded, reaching for another handful of peas. "Yeah. Looks like it's for real," he said.

"Zac is very excited, of course!"

Dan chortled. "Well, there we are," he said, nudging a row of peas out of their pod with his stumpy thumb, so that they fell, tinkling, into the pan. "The only question now is: do they actually want a deal or not?"

Victoria nodded listlessly. That was the strange thing about Brexit. It had become just a group of phrases which everyone felt obliged to repeat, even though no one really knew what they might mean in practice. A 'deal'; 'no deal' – both were proposals so lacking in detail as to be meaningless, and yet we found ourselves exchanging these phrases as if their meaning was something we could all understand. It made her feel like she was stuck in a circular conversation in which words had no real sense behind them, and as a result there was really nothing to discuss. It had been so long now: nearly three years in which the media had talked of almost nothing else and all the arguments went round in the same circles.

"Anyway," she said, "I've got a problem."

Sensing a shift of weight in her tone, Dan looked up at her. "Oh yeah?" he said, and sat back, and hung both arms over the back of the chair behind him. "What kind of problem?"

"There's a sewage leak in the bathroom, and Cecily will want us to pay half."

Dan frowned at her, not comprehending what the problem was. "How much?" he said. "Has she got quotes?"

"It's not just that," she said. "The wood on the French windows in the dining room is rotting. There's damp in the hall, and the roof is leaking. And there's some problem with the kitchen – she says there's a rat getting in."

Dan tipped his head to one side and grimaced. "Well… it's an old house," he said. "We'll need to get some quotes."

He still didn't get it.

"Yes, but the thing is, if we buy her out, we'll want to change things, right? I mean, we'll probably want to completely change that bathroom and the kitchen, for a start." She hesitated, watching him slit another pod with his thumbnail, before continuing. "You know? What's the point in paying to open up the bathroom wall now, and then close it again, when actually we want to knock out and redesign the whole room? The same with the French windows – I'd get rid of them, anyway. I want to extend the back of the house and have glass doors all across the back wall, that pull all the way back – you know, like we have in London."

Dan sat up, and rubbed his nose again. "I see," he said. "But wait: didn't you want *her* to buy *us* out, so that we could buy something else – like, in the South of France?"

Victoria looked at him. She waited for the obvious to dawn on him, but still he sat there, waiting for her to explain. Dan could be very slow sometimes. "*Cecily* can't buy us out!" she exclaimed. "They've got no money! Dan! Come on! Have you not even noticed what *car* she drives?"

Dan looked a bit sheepish. "Yeah – I guess I just thought maybe there was some family money saved."

"All gone!" Victoria said. "On her house. And she can hardly afford to maintain that. There's no way she can afford a second one as well."

Dan resumed shelling peas, a small frown forming between his eyes as he thought this over. She knew what was coming. "But then… so then why did you say that we should suggest she buy us out?"

Victoria sighed. How was it possible that he didn't understand? "Because it sounds nicer! You know? To give her a choice. It sounds better to ask her, 'Do you want to buy us out, or would you prefer us to buy you out?' Right? It sounds a lot nicer than just informing her that we want the place."

Dan nodded. "But what if she doesn't want to do either?"

"What do you mean?"

"Well, what if she wants to just continue to share it?" He looked up. "I mean, it's possible she'll say that, isn't it?"

Really! He was *so* dim!

"Well, *of course* she'll say that!"

"Yeah!" he agreed, but then looked confused. "Oh! She *will*? So what then?"

It was really unpleasant, the way he couldn't see anything himself: he made her lay it all out for him. It made her feel like a horrible person. "Well, that's why we want to stop paying for the maintenance." It sounded horrible, but that was because people had no idea. No idea what it had been like growing up in a family where Cecily was the golden child.

"What?" he said.

249

But at that point Diana came outside, looking lost. "Oh, there you are!" she said, and sat down next to Victoria. "What are you up to?"

*

Cecily lay on her bed, arms folded across her stomach, and looked at the ceiling.

It seemed incredible to her now, the way that, from the minute the referendum result was known, this country had become a different place. Overnight, Brexit had become a dangerous area, fenced with warning signs. And there were ancient Brexit landmines, we suddenly discovered, laid out all over the country, along lines where differences of region, class, education, and family history met. It was like... well, you heard about those places in the Balkans where Christians and Muslims had lived happily side by side for centuries, and then suddenly, in the 1990s, begun massacring each other.

That moment, outside, when Diana had said, "Oh, so that means it's not unconstitutional after all?" – Cecily had thought she would explode. *It means,* she had wanted to say, *that the Brexiters want to bypass our Parliament. It means they want to be free of all laws and constraints whatsoever, so they can loot and pillage the country undisturbed.* But she couldn't say that. It was taboo. It was literally taboo to say anything that was actually *true* about Brexit.

In the children's bedroom down the corridor, she could hear the girls arguing about something with Zac. Then shrieks and laughter, and more shrieks, and the thuds and bangs of children leaping and clambering across furniture. And then Julia again, shouting, "Oh for God's sake!!"

Cecily glanced down at her phone. Already, the slogan was gathering pace on the internet: 'Stop the coup!'

She stared out through the window, across the bumpy coastal road, at the fields sloping dramatically down towards the sea. This day was too momentous to be allowed to pass; to just follow on in the usual way. Didn't the Queen know that moments like this were steps on the slippery slope to dictatorship? One break with precedent here, one transgression there, and inch by inch, the nation would slip, so slowly that no one would notice, until they found themselves at the very bottom of the slippery slope. And once there, how would they ever climb back up? You only had to look at Hungary, or Poland. She'd heard again and again, all through her childhood, that the Queen's father had refused to leave the capital during the Blitz, and yet here she was now, nodding in the home-grown fascists without a moment's hesitation.

She turned to the books that lined the wall in front of her, hoping to distract herself. Yet more old books: rows and rows of dusty red hardbacks, they were, with thin, yellowing pages. Apart from a few incongruously bright and shiny contemporary novel shoved in among them, here and there, they must have sat there, unread for the most part, for fifty or sixty years or more. And yet more books piled on her bedside table. Her eye fell on Wollstonecraft's *A Vindication of the Rights of Men*, which she had brought back to her bedroom last night. Listlessly, she reached for it, more to divert her mind from the unbearable present than out of any actual interest.

Florian interrupted. He was in the doorway, rather rattled. "What are you *doing*?"

"I was just…" She let the book fall face down onto her stomach, and looked at Florian, hoping that he would intuit her need for him to put his arms around her and tell her it was all going to be okay. But he seemed tense, preoccupied. He was often tense these days: money worries, for one thing, but not only that. Sometimes, nowadays, she was afraid that with Brexit he'd had enough of England altogether and might one day decide to up and head off back to civilised Germany.

But he didn't intuit anything. "Just *what*?" he said gruffly. "I've got someone who will come and look at the leaky roof, but not for a couple of weeks. We'd need to come down for a weekend or something to start them off, or supervise. Have you talked to Victoria?"

She raised herself onto her elbows. "No, sorry… somehow there hasn't been a chance."

"Oh, for goodness' *sake*, Cecily!" Florian was about to say more, but then, noticing that he'd left the door open behind him, changed his mind and went back and closed it. He turned back to her then but, before he spoke, looked up at the ceiling, as if to collect his thoughts, or perhaps to collect some patience. "Cecily, you've really got to find a time to do it," he said sternly. He sounded, she thought, like a parent. "It needs to be done and we need to work out how we're going to pay for it all."

But actually, it just seemed crazy that he was talking to her about this stuff right now. She felt almost teenaged. Our democracy was being overturned and all Florian wanted to talk about was the leaky roof. That teenage sense of living in an intensely dramatic, important reality that no one else seemed to know about.

"Okay, okay. It's just this prorogation. I mean, how could they *do* it? Tell the Queen that they need to prorogue Parliament for *five weeks*, just to have their party conference, when that's never been necessary before, and anyway, for *weeks* they've been *publicly* floating the idea that they might prorogue Parliament just to get Brexit through."

Florian sighed. He was standing in front of the door. And now he leaned back against the closed door, saying, in gentler tones, "Yeah, well. It's happening all over, you know. Look at Poland: they've basically taken control of the entire court system, including the supreme court." He picked at the flaking old gloss paint on the door frame,, shaking his head. "Or Hungary," he added. "It's not just England. It feels like the end of liberal democracy all over the world. Politicians everywhere are trashing all of the rules. Big money is taking over, and installing populist puppets in government to make the laws they want. All the super-rich who want freedom from European regulations and tax-haven crackdowns; who want to buy a government that will allow them to fleece the rest of us…" He picked at the paint again, before continuing, "It's not even just neoliberalism. It's like a mafia. It's neo-feudalism. I mean, now it looks like we have both Russian and American billionaires employing big data companies like Cambridge Analytica in order to secretly affect elections, just like the overmighty feudal barons used to use the power of their patronage to make or break Kings. That was what feudalism was: an

253

international mafia network who called themselves nobility and controlled regions through their clients and retainers."

"But what I don't understand is why don't Diana and Victoria care that our hard-fought-for rules of fair play are being torn down in front of our faces?" she said.

He looked at her. "They don't care," he said, "because they don't know it's happening."

"But they *do*!" she protested. "They know the Leave campaign cheated in the referendum. They know the prorogation is happening."

"Do they, though? Most people don't know the referendum was bought. Most of the media didn't really report that. And anyway, even when they do report on this stuff, the English media represent it all as if it's just a game, as if it doesn't matter – and then move on to what the royal family are wearing or whatever. They make it seem as if there's no connection between our lives and dry constitutional issues like the legality of lying to the Queen to obtain prorogation."

"But there are 'dry constitutional issues', like 'sovereignty', that people somehow are excited about. Right? Why has this specious notion of sovereignty galvanised such support in the Brexit context when it's so obviously completely meaningless, because sovereignty always and only ever follows economic power; and yet genuinely important issues, like how the referendum was illegally bought by plutocrats, are brushed aside as pedantic quibbles? I just don't understand. I genuinely don't understand!"

Florian raised his eyebrows. "Well, but you *do* understand. It's money. It's money that buys the media talking points."

There was a silence.

"Maybe it's time to move to Germany?" he said.

Cecily's heart almost missed a beat.

Seeing her face, Florian pushed on, embarrassed that he had raised such a vast subject so lightly. "But anyway, the pipe in the bathroom needs to be fixed and the roof needs mending, and somehow we have to get Victoria to pay her share of it all."

There came a knock on the door then. Florian opened it, stepping back, and there was Diana, looking embarrassed. "Oh, er… sorry, I didn't mean to interrupt," she said.

Florian smiled; a strained smile, Cecily thought, but still friendly. "You're not interrupting," he said.

"Are you sure? Well, anyway, it's just that…" she leaned further into the room, as if trying to see Cecily better, "… well, Victoria suggested playing croquet, and I…" She tittered. "Well, I'm quite excited, because she said she'd teach me, and I've never in my life played croquet before!"

It was becoming quite maddening, Cecily thought: Diana's way, here in Dover, of constantly making the point that she had not grown up with the same opportunities and privileges as Cecily and her sister. "What – you mean *now*?" she said. She noticed that her voice did not sound very friendly. She had a sense that she was losing self-control.

Diana looked thrown.

"Well… now-*ish*…" she offered tentatively.

"I'll come and join you in half an hour or so," Cecily said, but she couldn't keep the brusqueness from her tone.

"Oh, okay!" Diana said, falsely, reproachfully bright, and turned quickly to Florian. "What about you?"

Florian smiled. "Well," he said, shaking his head, "I was going to sit in the garden and finally read my book. But maybe I will play instead. Are you setting it up now?"

Thankfully, thought Cecily, Florian had – in that way that men did – completely failed to notice the strained tones between the women.

"Soon, I think," Diana said.

Florian and Diana left soon after that, and, alone once more, Cecily picked up the Wollstonecraft and began to read. But then there came another knock on her door. This time it opened almost immediately, before she'd had a chance to answer, and there stood Victoria.

"Hi, I'm just here because Diana asked me to come and talk to you. She says she's worried she's offended you in some way."

What the hell? Cecily frowned. "What?"

Victoria sighed. "Well, I don't know what you said, Cecily," she said, shaking her head as if she couldn't quite believe what an uncomfortable situation Cecily had created, "but Diana is afraid she's done something wrong."

Cecily waved her hands to express how absurd this all was. "What on earth are you talking about?"

"Diana said you were kind of angry and you didn't want to play croquet. She thinks she's upset you."

"Oh, for goodness' sake!" Cecily felt like throwing herself on the floor and kicking her legs and screaming. You couldn't – at the age of forty-six – accuse your sister of trying to steal away your friend, however true it was.

Victoria now feigned the low, warm, anxious voice of someone who – for the best of motives – only wanted to get to the bottom of things. "Well… so what did you *say* to her?"

"What do you mean, what did I say to her? I don't need you to stick your oar in! I didn't say *anything* to her! I said I'd come out and play croquet in a bit. Because I'm really upset about this whole prorogation!"

Victoria nodded, still acting as if they needed her to pour oil on troubled waters. "Okay. I'll tell her you were just upset about the prorogation, that's all. So you're sure she didn't do anything wrong?"

"What do you mean, 'do anything wrong'? What could she do that's *wrong*? And why would *I* be the one to decide what's right and wrong anyway? It's not like I'm a teacher here and she's a schoolchild!"

Victoria closed her eyes and then opened them again and kept on nodding patiently while Cecily said this, as if humouring the diatribe of a child or a lunatic. "Okay," she said eventually, in a soothing, bedside voice. "It'll be fine! I'll just say that you were just upset about the prorogation."

"Because I *am*!"

Victoria held up both palms, as if to show that she had no weapon. "Okay! Okay! Calm down, Cecily!" she said. "Stop jumping down my throat! I'm only trying to help!"

But you're not! Cecily wanted to shout. And there it was again: that infantile fury of injustice and impotence. She wanted to thump the bed with her fists and scream. She wanted to throw things. She wished she'd never come. What had possessed her to come and stay here with a Brexiter – because, good friend or not, that's what Diana was – and her evil older sister?

257

As soon as Victoria had gone, she pulled Florian's pillow into her arms and hugged it tight. It was one of those '70s pillows, festooned with great, big, hopeful orange, purple and pale pink flowers on large lime leaves. Her mother had bought those pillows, forty years ago, when Cecily and Victoria were little girls in Clarks sandals and knee-length pelerine socks. She folded the pillow in two and squashed it behind her head. Then she opened the book. But her mind kept wandering.

The more she read of Mary Wollstonecraft's *A Vindication of the Rights of Men*, the more she noticed that it too reverberated with Foxe's language. Wollstonecraft used all the now-familiar religiously heated tropes of righteous rebellion that had beat their rhythm through the Reformation and the civil war and the 1688 revolution. Here was the same political language of 'slavery', 'servility', 'tyranny', 'darkness' and 'superstition' versus godly 'liberty'. It was curious how this politico-cultural tradition, this human rights tradition which Cecily traced back to people like Wollstonecraft, actually seemed to trace its way further back to the very same Puritan tradition as that of the Brexiters.

Wollstonecraft had originally written her *Vindication* in refutation of a conservative tract by Edmund Burke in praise of the eighteenth-century social status quo. In it, she mocked her adversary's 'slavish paradoxes', accused him of a 'servile reverence for antiquity', and identified in his writing 'a latent spirit of tyranny'. Sounding just like Foxe, she accused Burke of supporting a legal and governmental system that was 'settled in the dark days of ignorance, when the minds of men were shackled by the grossest prejudices and most immoral superstition'. In opposition to Burke, Wollstonecraft claimed that all humans were born with 'God-given' rights, which the inequalities of the existing social structure denied to all but those at the top of the hierarchy. Like all those in the Foxean tradition she founded all her claims, ultimately, on biblical revelation.

It did seem remarkable that both the language of eighteenth-century human rights campaigners like Wollstonecraft and that of the Brexiters should stem from the same Protestant tradition. The Brexiters, after all, detested human rights. They had made it clear that one of the goals of Brexit was to repeal the EU-instigated Humans Rights Act, and some even wanted to withdraw from the European Convention on Human Rights, even though the Convention was a predominantly British creation. Cecily knew why: the Convention empowered people to hold governments and corporations to account and Brexiters didn't want that: human rights got in the way of power. It was almost, she began to think now, as if the Brexiters wanted to return us to an eighteenth-century England, before people like Wollstonecraft got going. An England *post* civil war and yet *pre* French Revolution, where human rights had not yet been invented, and the purpose of the state was to secure the safety and prosperity of the propertied, who controlled the government, Church and an all those beneath through strings of patronage. To the world of Daniel Defoe, whose contempt for the poor and unemployed was echoed so uncannily in the writings of today's cabinet members.

Not five minutes had passed since Cecily picked up the book, before once again she was disturbed. This time it was Julia, bursting through the door and hurling herself onto the bed, stomach down. She squashed her face into the duvet.

"Julia? Are you okay?"

Julia wriggled a bit, but gave no answer.

"Julia? What's wrong? What's happened?"

"It's Olivia!" mumbled Julia's muffled, shamed voice into the duvet. Or at least, that was what Cecily thought she said.

"Olivia?" queried Cecily in amazement.

"She keeps going off with Zac! And agreeing with him!"

"Agreeing with him? What do you mean?"

"Ugh!" Julia sat up, crossly pushing her hair back off her face. "Whatever he says, she agrees with!" She looked at her mother, eyes teary and furious. "Or else she does this stupid laugh! Like this…" She mimicked a simpering, flirty giggle. "And she keeps wanting to do stuff with him all the time!"

"Ohhh!" Cecily said, watching her daughter. Well, she'd seen it herself: the way Olivia was so animated in front of Zac. And it was predictable, she supposed: he was an attractive boy, two years older, with all that bubbling confidence and good humour. Even if you knew that he would not be quite so ebullient, so sure of himself, if it were not for the sense of superiority that his expensive school had cultivated in him, even if you were fully aware of that, you couldn't deny that it was magnetic, that gravity-defying assurance of his. And Olivia, of course, was far too young to understand exactly where his aura of glamour came from. "Don't worry about it. She's just a bit bowled over by him, that's all. It'll pass."

"But he's so annoying! And she giggles at *literally* everything he says!"

Cecily grimaced sympathetically. "Where are they now?" she asked.

"They've gone off to the field. They've gone off to the field *without* me!"

"Hmm!" Cecily considered the problem, trying to identify a way to defuse it. "How about we all do something together?" she suggested.

"Like what?" asked Julia. She was grumpy, yet hopeful, her eyes on her mother.

"Well," Cecily began, not knowing how she was going to finish, until suddenly she had an idea, "Auntie Victoria was talking about croquet. How about we get everyone to come and play together?"

*

I t was a strange sliding of emotions that Diana felt, seeing Cecily appear in the garden with a tea tray. Victoria had been showing her how to lay out the trail of croquet hoops, while Florian watched, amused, from the chair where he was reading his book.

"Well, this is all very *Alice in Wonderland*!" he remarked, as Cecily came out of the house with the tray.

Victoria laughed, "Just you wait for the crumpets! Dan's decided to master the art of crumpets."

Diana felt relieved on one level: if Cecily had made tea for everyone, she must be feeling better. And Diana felt sorry for her, she really did. She felt genuinely sorry for all these bleeding-heart liberals, struggling as they were with Brexit. She knew, she understood, how much Cecily loved openness; the idea of us all being tolerant, open to other cultures, opening our arms to immigrants and everyone less fortunate than ourselves. She knew that about Cecily; she even loved her for it. But eventually, even people like Cecily had to realise that you couldn't just leave everything open. You couldn't walk around with your handbag open; you couldn't leave your front door open. And a country was no different.

Cecily's education and family money had cushioned her against all the trouble successive governments had welcomed in. London was now the money-laundering capital of the world, because we'd let global oligarchs buy up properties and open fake companies to do whatever they liked here. We had no manufacturing industry anymore because our governments had not valued it, not protected it against foreign takeover. Builders and plumbers and cleaners and carers had all had their wages driven down because of foreigners who could do the jobs cheaper because they'd left their families at home in countries where the cost of living was lower. The politicians – from all parties – had just allowed everyone and anyone to loot our country in any way they liked.

People like Cecily had been largely unaffected so far. But even they would come up against the reality sooner or later, because even if all of this 'openness' didn't yet threaten the livelihoods of those who had degrees and family money to put down on a house, it threatened their political and social standards. She had begun to realise that her mum was right: that there was a limit to how much relentless immigration a culture could absorb, and that our culture, a secular civilisation we had built up slowly, painfully and at great cost, was under threat.

It had taken us centuries to separate Church and state, but now religious intolerance brought in from other cultures was trying to join them up again. They were gradually altering the norms in our formerly secular country. How else did you explain the fact that Tony Blair's government had three times tried to pass an act that would have made it a legal risk to criticise any religious group?

And what was strange was that English society now did not apply its new deference to religion equally. No modern UK paper would dare to publish a cartoon satirising Allah or Mohammed, but would they have any qualms about publishing one satirising the Christian God, or Jesus? She'd read about a schoolgirl who'd won a court case against her school after it excluded her for breaking its 'no jewellery' rule by wearing a religious bangle. Some human rights group, which supported the girl, claimed the school had breached race, equality and human rights laws by not allowing her to wear it, and ultimately the court ruled that the school had to let the girl wear the bangle, as it was not jewellery but a symbol of Sikhism.[37] And yet wasn't there that Christian nurse who'd lost her job for wearing a crucifix around her neck? She'd had been wearing it ever since she got it as a confirmation present back in the 1970s. Diana's mum had shown her the story in the paper.[38]The NHS trust claimed that the issue was health and safety concerns around patients potentially getting hold of necklaces, although this woman had been wearing the crucifix safely for years and years. That nurse was told that the crucifix was not a 'mandatory requirement' of her faith, unlike Muslim headscarves, which could be 'exempted.' It didn't sound fair. How could we say that we were all equal before the law, with this stuff going on?

The real irony, when it came to Blair and his laws, was that nowadays no one dared to criticise any religion (Christianity excepted) anyway. None of us dared utter even the faintest criticism of Islam in particular. Here, in our post-Enlightenment country, you couldn't say that Islam was, in many of its contemporary forms, sexist, although it was absolutely no problem if anyone wanted to make such comments about Christianity. Just because religions claimed Gods behind them, that did not change the fact that they were ideologies and, like other ideologies, had to accept criticism, even if they didn't like it. They should not be allowed to intimidate critics via some chauvinistic notion of blasphemy. We ought to start sticking up for our secular state again, because otherwise, we were going to lose it!

One reason it was happening was that we were suddenly all so muddled. Things we used, as a nation, to understand, were now confusing to us. We were all so confused about what was race and what was culture and what was religion and what was ideology that we had muddled them all up together. Nowadays religion was often reclassified as race, which it wasn't, and opposition to religious doctrines or practices was redefined as race hatred, which it wasn't. When Diana had refused to send Olivia to the Hindu temple where she'd be made to sit behind the boys, for example, one of the other parents had suggested that she was racist (not to her, of course, but in a group chat; a friend had told her). But she wasn't being racist. She didn't like the Catholic Church, either, because it too was sexist and wouldn't let women be priests and forced women to bear the consequences of male ejaculations. She didn't like going to *any church at all*, in fact, even though she *did* believe in God, probably; but it got her goat that most of Christianity still continued to pretend that God was somehow male, for goodness' sake.

But here came Cecily, and she was relieved, for Cecily's sake, that she felt better enough to join them, and even bring out a tray of tea things. But still she also observed her approach with a lurching dread, because nothing had really been resolved. It was that lovely old tray again, she noticed, as she went forward to meet Cecily at the garden table.

"Oh, you've brought some tea! How lovely!" Diana said.

"It's just Tetley's; I hope you don't mind," Cecily said, moving mugs from tray to table. It seemed to Diana that she was avoiding her eye. "We always used to have a tin of loose-leaf Assam, the kind my mother used to buy, but I couldn't find it," she continued, her eyes still downward. Now she was peering into the willow-patterned teapot, to see if it was brewed.

"Oh, it's fine!" Diana said. She sat down on the bench with a heavy feeling in her stomach; an oppressive restraint that made her cheerful voice ring false even to herself. "You know, I was saying to Victoria earlier, I just love the picture on that tray!"

Cecily stopped pouring tea and looked at the tray for a minute. "Oh, this! The Constable!" she said. And then, "You were saying to Victoria?"

Victoria was on the other side of the lawn.

"Yeah, yeah. She brought me a cup of tea this morning," Diana explained.

"Oh! Did she?" Cecily said. There was a funny edge to her tone. Surely there wasn't anything wrong with that: Victoria bringing a cup of tea?

In the short, strained silence that followed, Diana contemplated the tray: the brave cathedral spire rising into the sky amid the departing storm clouds; the plodding carthorses stopped, dreamily, in the river to drink; and that mellow, yellow, post-storm sunlight slanting lovingly over the rain-wet meadow. Perhaps to fill the silence, or perhaps to try to find some connection with Cecily, she began, although she didn't know quite why, to describe it. "I like the gentle light. And the tumbly grass and blackberry bushes. It all just looks so unhurried and peaceful. And the cathedral with the rainbow – it makes me feel…" She stopped. She couldn't say, because she was afraid of Cecily's anti-Brexit scorn, that it made her feel – the cathedral spire rising heroically up into the post-rain sky like that – it made her feel, even though she had rejected Christianity long ago, an almost tearful longing, a nostalgia for a world in which God still resided in the church and still looked out for all of England.

"I always liked it too," Cecily said.

Diana had thought Cecily was going to continue, but she didn't. And yet, when Diana looked up, she found Cecily looking directly at her, as if there was something she really, really wanted to say.

But then Cecily looked away again, across the field to where Zac and Olivia were playing in the grass, and sighed heavily before saying, "Shall we call the children over to play croquet?"

At that moment Dan came out of the kitchen carrying a big plate covered with a tea towel. "Crumpets!" he shouted, and then, as an aside to Diana and Cecily as he approached the table, "They've actually come out quite well!"

At this, Olivia and Zac began to run back through the field, and Julia also appeared, rather suddenly, from the house.

"I'll be back in a sec. Just going to get the butter and Marmite and stuff!" Dan said, and, whisking up the Constable tray, he waddled off to the house.

As the children came back up the field, Cecily turned back to Diana and said, in a low, rapid, emotional voice, "But do you know, Diana, that the Brexit referendum wasn't won honestly? The Electoral Commission found that the Leave.EU campaign's spending exceeded its statutory limit. We don't even know by how much, or where all the money that went into the various Leave campaigns came from: Putin's Russia? Corporate America? It's hard to trace. And, you know the whole reason we have rules about how much spending there can be on political campaigns is so that we don't become a plutocracy. And yet it seems we have, because it seems that is what Brexit was: a referendum that was illegally bought with dark money."

Diana hardly knew what to say. She felt attacked. She opened her mouth to try to explain, even though she didn't see why she had to explain herself.

But before she could even begin, Cecily had started again. "And our Prime Minister has just lied openly to the Queen in order to gag our Parliament. I mean, Brexit was said to be necessary was so that all our laws could be made by our 'sovereign Parliament' – and yet this government wants to gag the very Parliament it was supposed to be championing, in order to push through a Brexit deal that will be good for no one except rich scavenger capitalists who want to pick clean the carcass of our fallen state."

Again Diana opened her mouth. But still Cecily hadn't finished.

"Yeah?" She said, in an aggressive, demanding tone, "The executive is literally gagging the highest representative body in the country: our democratically elected sovereign Parliament!"

Diana felt dazed. Her mind whirled, but there were no words or sentences within it. How to address all this, when everything Cecily had said was just words and none of it really meant anything? How to explain that the reason Diana had voted to leave the EU was *nothing to do with any of this*? It was because… It was because of that feeling she got from that Constable painting: that aching loss and nostalgia. Brexit was the only chance she had ever been given to express that longing. "But it's not like that for me," she said. "That's just not how I see it. And anyway, I mean – what's new? They've been lying to us for years and years: Tory, Labour, all of them…"

But she didn't have time to finish, because Dan was back, and Florian and Victoria were now coming over. Dan put the butter and Marmite down on the table next to the plate of crumpets and rubbed his hands, chuckling at the reaction he had caused.

Looking around at all of them with their croquet and their tea and their crumpets, Diana felt quite moved. There was none of it planned, it had just happened, and yet it was all so quintessentially *English*. "Oh my God, it's just so English! It really *is* like *Alice in Wonderland*!" she marvelled. Even though, it occurred to her after she had said it, this idea of England she was marvelling at was not something she had ever really known; was not something she had ever really seen, except in films.

"Yep – all we need is a few flamingos and a Red Queen," Florian said.

Everyone looked excited, amused to find themselves in such a stereotypical situation. All except Cecily, that was. Cecily had wandered off with Julia, and they were, with an odd kind of silent concentration, tapping a croquet ball back and forth between them.

*

At supper that evening, Zac groaned and dropped his head into his hands. "You wouldn't believe it! I have to learn the whole of 'Jerusalem' by next week!" he complained.

'Jerusalem', Diana wondered? What the hell was that?

"'Jerusalem'?" Dan asked, with his mouth full.

Watching him, Victoria winced. "You know – William Blake!" she told him, ever so slightly irritably. "*And did those feet in ancient time walk upon England's mountains green…*"[39]

Oh! They were talking about the hymn, Diana realised.

"Oh!" Dan exclaimed, almost at the same time. "I thought that was a hymn!" And then he shrugged, his eyes and cutlery both returning to his plate.

"So did I!" Diana said, laughing, thankful that Dan was there. He made her feel more confident. "I actually love that hymn!"

"What? You know it?" asked Olivia, staring at her mother in amazement.

Diana said, looking around at the other adults, "Everyone knows it! Because we used to have to sing it in school assemblies, that's why!"

"Yeah!" Dan re-joined, and began to sing, in a camp, fruity baritone, "*And was Jeru-u-usalem builded here, among these dark Sata-anic mills?*"

His voice subsided into a contented chortle, as Victoria grimaced and Zac groaned across the table, "Oh, God! Dad! Please stop!"

Diana laughed, thinking – not for the first time – that she really rather liked Victoria's husband. He was fun and unpretentious.

"I've never heard of this. I mean, I've heard of Blake, but not this hymn!" Florian remarked, looking amazed.

"Me neither!" Zac joined in, "I never knew it was a hymn either. They didn't tell us there was a tune."

It was true, Diana thought. There was none of that anymore. She'd ridiculed them at school, as a teenager, along with everyone else: those hymns with their ludicrous words ('*Veiled in flesh the Godhead see*') But now, in spite of all the nonsense, it was comforting to remember them.

"But a hymn would have been so much easier to learn!" Zac protested.

"Oh, do you want me to sing it again, then?" joked Dan, to more laughter and protests.

"But I had no idea that Blake wrote Anglican hymns!" Florian said, still in tones of amazement. "I thought he was an anti-establishment radical!"

"I think he was!" Cecily said, "He just wrote a poem. And it's meant to be a protest poem, I think."

"Yeah! Against the Industrial Revolution!" Zac said importantly. "The '*dark Satanic mills*'."

Had she known that, Diana asked herself, uncertain? Yes – she thought she had, in some vague way.

"Although there is a school of thought, I think I read somewhere, that says the '*dark Satanic mills*' are not so much the industrial mills, but the hegemony of the established Church and the oligarchic government," Cecily said.

"So why would he write a hymn for the established Church, then? If he was anti?" Dan objected.

"He didn't!" Cecily said. "That's what I mean: he *didn't* write it for the Church. He just wrote a poem. But later, like, a whole century later, somebody – some Etonian, I think, but I can't remember his name – put it to music and it became, ironically, a favourite hymn of the establishment."

Diana had not grown up in a household like this, where they talked in this way. In fact, she'd never been quite aware, until these few days in Dover, just how different a world it was that Cecily came from. This Cecily she was seeing now seemed quite a different Cecily from the one she thought she knew so well. Back in London, in their group of mums, they had never talked like this, either.

She was quite relieved when Victoria brought the subject back to more familiar ground, and asked Zac, "So how much of it have you learnt?"

"Hmm… umm… well… er…!" Zac said, making a big show of shiftiness and prevarication, his bright eyes flashing around the table. He was a fun boy, Diana thought, like his father. "Shall I see how much I can remember?" he asked suddenly, looking about with winning enthusiasm.

His dad grinned; his mum was watching him with smiling pride.

"Go on, then!" encouraged Dan.

"Let's hear it!" Florian added, kindly.

And Zac stood up, beaming. He seized an empty glass and tinkled a teaspoon inside it, even though everyone was already looking at him, and then he cleared his throat.

"Speech!" called Dan.

Zac drew breath, his eyes twinkling, and began reciting. But when he got to the words *'Bring me my arrows…'* he broke down into giggles, the prospect of pronouncing the word 'desire' proving too much for him. But he wanted, Diana could see, with both girls watching him, to say it, so that they would know why he was laughing.

"Okay, well, that was pretty good," Florian said, beginning to clap.

But before anyone else could join in, Zac recovered enough to shout, "Bring me my arrows of desire!" and then collapse back into his chair, covered in excited giggles.

Olivia was giggling too.

He really was quite an impressive young man, Diana thought. He had an air of natural, open, fun-loving confidence that was irresistibly attractive. You could see that, even when he was just being silly about his homework! It wasn't a phrase you often heard nowadays, but he had that confidence about him, that wholehearted can-do air; You could already tell, even though he was only thirteen, that he was going to be a 'leader'.

*

Victoria watched Cecily take another sip of wine and then replace her glass on the table. Her cheek rested glumly in one hand; with the thumb and forefinger of the other hand, she turned the glass idly around and around by the stem. She looked mentally absent, though her gaze was ostensibly fixed on the stem of the wine glass. And Victoria experienced a squeezing in her stomach. She felt almost as if she was Cecily, or Cecily was her: she could feel how Cecily felt, inside her own stomach. It was horrible. She leaned back from the table and tried to shake her shoulders loose.

Cecily had hardly said a word since she'd come out from sulking in her room that afternoon. She'd perked up a bit during the croquet game, as she'd been in the lead all the way and certain to win. But when Victoria had managed to slip past and hit the central pole right at the very last minute, she'd slumped back into her semi-silence. And since the wine came out, she'd mostly just sat there drinking, apart from that brief lecture about Blake a while ago.

Everyone else might think it was the prorogation Cecily was in a mood about. But Victoria knew her better. She knew it was really about Diana; about the way in which Victoria had so easily, within a couple of days, charmed her out of Cecily's sphere and into her own. Knowing this made her feel buzzy, triumphant, powerful. But it also felt bad; like it was not really the way she wanted it to be. It was just that she had no choice: the world was as it was, and she had to survive in it.

Besides, there was the past, when Cecily had always been the angelic little sister who ran to their mother every time there was the slightest disagreement, even though that mother had once been just Victoria's mother and no one else's. And in a sense, nothing had changed. Because here was Cecily being a goody-goody again, all hurt and shocked and self-righteous because of Diana, and because the Other Side had won the referendum. Only now there was no Mummy to run to; there was no judge to judge. There was only life, and life – as Cecily could somehow never learn – was not about wrong or right. How *could* it be?

*

At about ten, Dan suggested playing a few rounds of poker, and Diana piped up, predictably, all enthusiastic, "Ooh! I've never actually played poker!"

But Cecily excused herself, saying she thought she'd drunk too much and had better go to bed. And at that point, watching Cecily on the threshold of the sitting room, just before she walked through the door, pausing to rub one eye, Victoria felt another squeeze in her stomach. Cecily looked suddenly, horribly vulnerable, rubbing her eye like she used to do when she was little. It was a combination of this rubbing of her eye and the fact that, as she stood there under the light, you could see grey streaks in her hair.

Why couldn't Victoria just be generous and share the house with Cecily? Did it have to matter that Cecily wouldn't have the money to pay for all the changes Victoria and Dan wanted to make? Did it matter if she didn't pay half? Couldn't Victoria just go ahead and do it her way and pay for it all herself?

As she entertained this thought, she experienced a gush of relief; a golden, hazy, honeyed warmth spreading through her. There had been occasions when – fleetingly – they had discovered hidden channels of affection for each other. At their grandfather's funeral, for example, they had reminisced about how they used to come in here and make pretend gin and tonics in the tiny, sherry glasses, and talk about their pretend children. They had stood here in this room and laughed about the way their grandfather used to drop off at the lunch table, and then startle awake and glare around the table, as if daring anybody to have noticed. There were those brief moments – almost every time they met, in fact – when they clicked and a sudden tenderness and relief gushed up.

But those moments of sympathy were, in the end, only more disappointing because they vanished almost as quickly as they appeared. And though over the years Victoria had tried – they had both tried – a handful of times to meet up, to find more common ground, for the most part it eluded them. Cecily, Victoria knew, disapproved of Zac's school. She didn't need to say anything; Victoria already knew. And then there was Dan. Cecily looked down on him, Victoria knew that too; while, to be honest, Victoria herself found Julia unappealing. She was both shy and yet also forthright: an unappealing combination, in Victoria's view. And she was just like Cecily: superior.

And there was Florian. There was Florian. There was Florian. Not that Florian mattered. It wasn't something for the real world, or even that Victoria had ever actually wanted *him*. The way he talked, he partly bored and partly intimidated her. It was just his *presence* that reminded her, incomprehensibly, distressingly, of how it was possible to feel.

There was no one else, ever, who had made her suffer as wildly as Matthew had. After that, her life had cleaved into two halves: before Matthew and after Matthew. Not even Zac's birth was as critical a juncture. And even today, there were certain songs that, if she heard them, gave her weird, throbbing waves of pain and desire, almost like homesickness. And she could still see him: his face, aged twenty-three; that quick smile when he was feeling extrovert, with his friends, and that other smile – slow, dark, unwilling. He was actually kind of grumpy, Matthew, as a person; a bit dreamy and a bit grumpy. But with *her* – he made her feel… she shifted her chair. Well, it just wasn't something that happened every day. But what was strange was that over the years she had occasionally got nostalgic snatches of Matthew from other men. Just now and then, unexpectedly, like when you're walking down the street and you catch a breath of linden blossom. She got that Matthew rush in drips and drabs here and there from the presence of other men, and most of all from Florian.

She picked up her wine glass. Already that tenderness she had felt when Cecily rubbed her eye was fading, superseded by a series of images. She imagined Cecily walking through the house, renovated and modernised as she, Victoria, envisioned it: her new bathroom, her pizza oven, her heated pool and… oh, God! Because she could already see how Cecily would react. That withdrawn look on her face; the exchanging of glances with Florian. Victoria just knew that Cecily would think that every change she made was somehow in bad taste; in some way not in the spirit of the place. She would be sentimental about the old tiles, the old French windows; would see any change as an act of sacrilege… and she just wouldn't be able to bear it.

And besides, Victoria knew, it could never work, even if – by some miracle – Cecily *did* like the way she did up the house. It would never work if she and Dan just paid for it. Acts of charity on this scale were always invidious, breeding mutual resentment. And it hardly needed to be said that between Victoria and Cecily, there was resentment enough already.

*

Cecily woke. She was hot, her head was aching, and she felt nauseous and desperately thirsty. A hangover. Which was really all she needed. She reached for the water glass by the bed, and gulped down what was left inside it. She'd dreamt three times that she'd got up to get a glass of water. And in between those parched dreams she'd dreamt about… what was it? But she couldn't recall anything about the dream, except sadness.

There was something uncomfortably hard under her pillow. She pulled it out. Oh yes – it was the Blake book. A book about William Blake that she'd drunkenly taken to bed with her after that conversation at supper, although she'd only read a chapter or two.

Her head was throbbing, and she was still thirsty. She sat up and reached for her glass. She'd have to go and get some more water.

Having dug some paracetamol out of her sponge bag, and taking the book with her, she slipped out of the bedroom, past the sewage-bathroom and down to the kitchen.

Remembering the rat, she stopped outside the door, listening for any signs of the rat in the kitchen before entering, and even though she heard nothing, she deliberately flung open the door so that it banged back against the wall, and then she turned on the light before she went in, so that if by any chance it was there, it would have a chance to disappear before she entered. The last thing she wanted was to come face to face with it again.

She went in. There was barely time to even register that it was there, before it was gone: a k-thump and then a skidding hot smudge of fear, claws scratching on the tiles as it scrambled to vanish behind the fridge. It left the empty room thumping to the beat of Cecily's heart… or perhaps it was the rat's heart.

She backed out of the kitchen and sat down on one of the spoon-backed chairs in the dining room. Her mind was still reliving the k-thump of the rat falling off the table and onto the floor before it scuttled, terrified, behind the fridge. A warm, fleshy thud, like a small leather beanbag hitting the floor.

It was pathetic to be chased out of your own kitchen by a single rat. Taking a deep breath, Cecily rushed back in, grabbed the kettle, a teabag, a mug, and some milk from the fridge, and then carried it all as fast as she could out to the sitting room, where she plugged the kettle in. The feeling she had was almost as if they had been violated in some way. As if this were a violation of the rules, as if a rat getting into the fruit bowl on the table was a terrible subversion of the natural order of things. But of course, she told herself, a rat did not recognise any human notions about the natural order of things.

Settling herself on what had become her nightly reading spot on the sofa, with Victoria's blanket, Cecily broke out two of the paracetamol tablets. She swallowed one with a too hot gulp of tea.

She regretted – had regretted almost immediately – all that stuff she had said to Diana at the croquet game. At least, a part of her regretted it. She did desperately want to make Diana understand what Brexit was really about. It was just that she didn't know how to tell her this stuff without offending her, and now she was afraid that Diana might not like her anymore.

She looked down at the book about Blake that she had brought from the bedroom, which was called *Witness*

Against the Beast by E. P. Thompson. Next to it, on the shelf last night, had been a second book by the same author, entitled *The Making of the English Working Class*. She went and got that too. Returning to the sofa, she began to leaf, a little distractedly, through *Witness Against the Beast*, coming across a reference to a poem called 'The Everlasting Gospel' which Blake had written in about 1810.

'The everlasting Gospel': she turned the words over in her mind. The phrase was familiar. Where had she heard it? Somewhere outside, an owl hooted. She referred back to the book. 'The everlasting Gospel' had, according to Thompson, been a term used in the New Model Army during the civil war – over a century, that was, before Blake was even born. Sects like the Ranters, the Diggers and the Levellers, some of whom demanded universal male suffrage and who were ultimately side-lined by the propertied gentry leaders of Cromwell's army, had sung songs about the everlasting Gospel as they marched.

Curious, she began to read: 'There is not one Moral Virtue that Jesus Inculcated but Plato & Cicero did Inculcate before him what then did Christ Inculcate. Forgiveness of Sins. This alone is the Gospel & this is the Life & Immortality brought to light by Jesus.' Cecily had to read this three times, and even then, it was only with Thompson's help that she managed to make any sense of it. Blake was saying, it seemed, that Jesus did not invent moral virtues such as temperance and patience; the Greek and Roman moral philosophers had created and systemised concepts like these before his time. What Jesus had brought was something entirely different: not morality but *grace* –

or, in other words, God's forgiveness and redemption of our human imperfection.

Grace! She remembered grace from those Sunday-school sessions with the vibrant, dashing Mrs Spooner. 'God's grace', it was always called there. And as a child she had imagined it almost like sunshine: a benign, yellow warmth beaming down from the sky. But Graces had had lives before and outside of Christianity, and perhaps because of the word's classical associations Cecily also imagined grace as a person: a woman, of course; round-shouldered like a statue, and with expressive hands. And then sometimes grace was almost a fairy, like the Good Witch in *The Wizard of Oz*, granting wishes with sugary smiles and sparkles from her magic wand. But now it seemed to Cecily that grace was more like what had happened – those instances of connection – that first day up on the cliffs with Diana. Grace was what, in most instances, for most of her life, was missing.

She returned to the book. Morality, Blake seemed to be saying, was a human invention; only grace was divine. If we were saved, it was through the grace of God, and had nothing to do with any claims we might have to personal morality. Cecily sipped her tea. Outside the owl hooted again, and for a moment – as she looked up from the book and towards the dark night through the window – it seemed an utter madness that she should be here in the middle of the night, exercising herself over an obscure religious term. And even madder that she was not the only one. There was the man who had written this book, and nearly two centuries before that, there was the man who had written the poems this book was about, and then well over century before *that* there were the Leveller parliamentarians; they had all of them exercised themselves over this concept of 'grace' that was centuries and centuries older than any of them. But what did grace have to do with the real world outside: the owls and the darkness?

Reading on, she came across this verse:

The Moral Virtues in Great fear
Formed the Cross & Nails & Spear
And the Accuser standing by
Cried out Crucify Crucify

According to Thompson, Blake here was talking about how human moral systems set up some groups as judges over others. The Pharisees in the Bible, for example, the ones who judged and crucified Jesus with the help of the Romans, had set themselves up as the arbitrators of law and morality.

And Blake went on:

The Roman Virtues Warlike Fame
Take Jesus & Jehovah's Name.
For what is Antichrist but those
Who against Sinners Heaven close
With Iron bars in Virtuous State
And Rhadamanthus at the Gate

People who arrogate moral authority to themselves, Blake seemed to be saying, might claim to do so in the name of Jesus. But they are not acting in the name of Jesus at all. In fact, anyone who claims the right to judge who is righteous and who isn't; they are anti-Christian. Because heaven – i.e. God's grace – was meant to save sinners; not exclude them.

Blake was saying that those who claim to represent 'good', who claim the right to lay down the law, are modern-day 'devils' or 'Pharisees'. Their power-hungry claims to 'morality' were just what Jesus had rebelled against. And this, Thompson stressed, was a truly revolutionary message. Jesus, Blake claimed, sent his disciples *against* the powers that were; against the existing social order and the laws that it enforced. Jesus, Blake wrote, 'His Seventy Disciples sent *Against* Religion & Government'.

Here again, Cecily thought, were some of the same tropes employed by Foxe. More than two centuries before Blake, Foxe had cast the early English Protestants' revolt against Catholicism as a revolt in the name of Christ against tyranny, proud prelates and 'Pharisees'. Since then, both the parliamentarians revolting against Charles I and then the Whigs revolting against James II had used much the same kind of narrative. And now, in the wake of the revolutions in America and France, both Wollstonecraft and Blake used the same lexicon to rail against the English establishment. Cecily seemed to remember that these thought patterns had also emerged during the American War of Independence. They appeared to be incredibly deeply engrained within the Anglo-Saxon psyche.

But what was curious was that while Blake, just like Foxe, contrasted 'true' Christians with the corrupt, imperious power of Rome, the 'Antichristian' Rome that he was talking about appeared to be a different Rome from the one that Foxe had raged against. Foxe's Rome was the Catholic Church, but when Blake spoke of Rome it sounded as if he was talking about classical Rome:

The Roman Virtues Warlike Fame
Take Jesus & Jehovahs Name.
For what is Antichrist but those
Who against Sinners Heaven close

Yes – he appeared to be contrasting not Protestantism with Catholicism, in the usual way of Foxean tradition, so much as Christianity with classical culture; with the 'moral virtues' of Plato and Cicero.

She put the book down and sat listening to the empty room. Once, there would have been the ticking of the grandfather clock: that clock which her grandfather had wound once a week with a special bronze winder. Now there was no one to wind it, and now all she could hear was the wind in the trees, and then, once again, a single, wistful hoot of an owl out there in the darkness.

"I love this colour! Don't you love this colour?" she remembered Victoria once saying, bright-eyed and excited, to their mother.

They were here at Dover, in a toy shop. Perhaps one of them had had a birthday coming up. It was a poky little late 1970s toy shop with steps down from the street to the tiny, shop floor: shelves crammed precariously from floor to ceiling. And Victoria was stroking the fur of some soft toy: a dog, perhaps? Bright pink, soft, deep fur, it was, and Victoria was standing next to the shelf and stroking it. It was a new thing, then, perhaps, in the toy world: a dog with silky, hot pink fur.

"Oh," their mother had smiled, mild but also deprecating, "well, you know, I prefer natural colours."

Victoria's face fell; Cecily knew how she was feeling. It was as if she were feeling it herself: a cold draught pulling ghostly centuries of unspoken family values behind it. Their mother had had no idea quite how alert they were, Cecily and Victoria, to all the subtexts, to all the implications of parental approval and disapproval that hid between the lines. They understood perfectly both what their mother had said and what she had left unsaid: it was bad taste (bad taste itself a sign of spiritual deficiency) to be attracted to the 'unnatural' pink of the dog's fur. And this information was a cryptic clue; another tiny piece of the enormous puzzle that was the universe's secret, mystic core.

"So what *are* your favourite colours?" Cecily had asked their mother. And she knew that in asking, she was abandoning Victoria, leaving her alone in the cold. She could have admitted that she loved the hot pink too. But she wanted to step out of the cold draught and into the warmth of their mother's approval. And also, she just wanted to *know*: She wanted to access the gnostic wisdom of the household Gods. She wanted to know what these 'natural colours' were, even if her question provoked an angry glare from her sister.

"Oh, I don't know, Cecily," her mother said kindly. "Brown and green, I should think."

She turned back to the books. The eighteenth century was a society which, like most societies had, as E. P.

Thompson said in his other book, 'a structure of social relations fostering some sorts of expropriation (rent, interest, and profit)' while 'outlawing others (theft, feudal dues), legitimising some types of conflict (competition, armed warfare) and inhibiting others (trade unionism, bread riots, popular political organisation)'.[40]

But it wasn't only state violence that the rich employed to maintain their political dominance. The powerful classes also secured the complicity of the less powerful through far-reaching systems of patronage. The rich lawmakers also had all the purchasing power.

Blake's parents were hosiers. His mother's first husband had been a tradesman, and she herself was the daughter of a tradesman. Artisans and tradesmen, people of Blake's class, were, in the eighteenth century, financially dependent on the patronage of the wealthy, which meant they could not afford to oppose them politically. Blake's frustration with this situation, and his furious objection to the lower classes' dependence on upper-class patronage, Thompson said, was evident in his writing. 'The Enquiry in England is not whether a Man has Talents & Genius,' Blake wrote, 'but whether he is Passive & Polite & a Virtuous Ass: & obedient to Noblemen's Opinions in Art and Science.'[41]

Blake was hostile to artists who won favour with the rich and influential. On the title page of a copy of the fashionable court painter Joshua Reynolds' *Discourses on Art*, for instance, Blake wrote, 'This man was hired to depress art.'[42] The eighteenth-century upper classes educated their children in a language and a culture which were deliberately constructed so as to keep the lower classes excluded from power. An expensive classical education created a dominant culture in which a familiarity with classical mythology and complex grammatical taxonomy was an essential ticket for access. So when Blake spoke with scorn about the morality of classical culture, he was, Thompson said, also expressing resentment of the culture of powerful elites who used their exclusive classical education to exclude the lower classes from power. 'Greek and Roman Classics is the anti-Christ,' Blake claimed grandly. He dismissed not only the classics which formed the basis of establishment education, but also the cultural 'authorities' of his own age. He held in 'Contempt and Abhorrence'[43] Bacon, Locke, Newton and Burke – that is, some of the best-known establishment figures of the so-called 'Age of Reason', the rational philosophy of the eighteenth-century intelligentsia.

According to Thompson, Blake and other Nonconformists in his circle drew their subversive confidence in criticising the status quo from the antinomian Christian tradition, which, in fully embracing the Lutheran doctrine of justification by faith alone, rejected the authority of the established culture, the established Church, and the political establishment: three establishments which consisted of largely the same families. Blake and people like him were suspicious of the term 'reason' because in their experience it meant the reasoning of those who made and benefited from existing power structures. The 'reasoning' of the genteel was just a tendentious justification for the injustice of the existing social order.

Cecily moved over to the window seat and pressed her hot forehead against the glass. But it was not cool enough, and so she undid the latch of one of the Tudoresque lead windows. She could hear the night ocean heaving and roaring and sighing down below, and even up here, on top of the cliffs, she could taste the salt on the wind. She licked her fingers and ran them over her throbbing forehead, and then leaned out of the window so that the wind could blow it cool.

The antinomian Protestant tradition, Thompson proposed, constituted a source of confidence, and its biblical exegesis provided a language which relatively powerless people like Blake could use to express their opposition to the 'reasoning' of the upper classes. The antinomian tradition, for example, provided support for Blake's hostility to notions of the 'moral law' or Lockean 'natural law', both of which could be said to express a type of reasoning whose sole intention was to reinforce the legal status quo, weighted heftily as it was in favour of landowners. The antinomian tradition taught Blake to equate the reasoning of the establishment with the self-serving reasoning of the serpent in the Garden of Eden. Dissenters of the antinomian tradition, like Blake, Cecily understood Thompson to be saying, were in fact the spiritual descendants of – and maintained much of the passion of – the seventeenth-century Ranters, Diggers and Levellers who had fought for social justice in the civil war, but gained no rights in the aftermath.

By the end of the eighteenth century, the dominant culture in England had moved on from the turbulent religious zeal of the civil war. The established Church was ensconced in a cosy relationship with the established gentry, and religious Nonconformists were reviled by polite society as 'enthusiasts'; derided as naive, overheated troublemakers. Blake, the spiritual descendant of seventeenth-century evangelicals, returned the opprobrium, rejecting not only the established Church, but the establishment in its entirety: its 'reasoning' and all its works.

'If we accept the view that in most societies we can observe an intellectual as well as an institutional hegemony,' Thompson wrote, 'or dominant discourse, which imposes a structure of ideas and beliefs, deep assumptions as to social proprieties and economic process and the legitimacy of relations of property and power, a general "common sense" as to what is possible and what is not, a limited horizon of moral norms and practical probabilities beyond which all must be blasphemous, seditious, insane or apocalyptic fantasy – a structure which serves to consolidate the existent social order, enforce its priorities, and which is itself enforced by rewards and penalties, by notions of "reputability", and (in Blake's time) by liberal patronage or its absence – if we accept this large mouthful, then we can see that these antinomian sects were hegemony's eighteenth-century opposition."[44]

Cecily looked up from her book again. Looking out now, over the grey sea to the grey horizon, she could hardly tell when one became the other. They merged into one murky oblivion: a still, shadowy world over which only sound could move; only the rustling wind and the booming waves constituted distinct and animate entities. She got up and began to walk around the room.

Until this morning, she had assumed, somehow, that it was people like her, the left-wing intelligentsia, who were the heirs to people like Blake. After all, she and Florian saw today exactly what Blake had seen in the eighteenth century: how the powerful created not only the rules but also a narrative that sustained them. Today's rich had managed to establish the myth that low taxation, low regulation and small government meant that markets were 'free' and competition was 'open', when in fact what low taxation, low regulation and small government did was rig everything in favour of those with money. And Blake had been bitter, like she was. And yet… there was a distinct mood here, to Blake's writing, that she found completely alien.

It was just light outside. And, feeling the sea wind on her hot face through the open window, she had a sudden desire to be out there, on the cliffs. She found her boots, coat and scarf in the hall. Although it was August, the early mornings were cold, and the wind out on the cliffs could chill you to the bone. She let herself out of the front door and crunched down the gravel path and onto the cliff road.

Their house was the very last in a spaced-out row along the cliff road, and it was only a short stretch from their gate to the end of the road and the beginning of the wide, grassy clifftop path. These cliffs were one of the first places in the British Isles to be touched by the rising sun each morning. But as yet, the early, early light was still so dim that the scrubby clifftop grasses were still grey, as were the waves, far away down there.

She stood looking out towards the faint smudge on the horizon that was France. White surf broke, continually hatching and vanishing in little lines on the surface of the water. And the booming of the mass of water against the rocks down below seemed, as Cecily stood there, insistent; meaningful. It was an eternal song which both pacified you and made you restless, as if it were awakening you to the presence of something vast that you could not quite define. As if there were some message from the universe roaring in this endless movement of the waves.

If she had lived at the end of the eighteenth century, Cecily wondered, how would she have felt about the social injustice that so exercised Wollstonecraft and Blake? How would she have felt about the French Revolution? Where exactly would she have been positioned culturally and socio-economically? And which side would she have been on?

There were all those people in America who had voted for President Donald Trump. She'd read an interview just the other day, with a man, a Trump voter in Texas, who said he knew that Trump was a liar, a thug and a charlatan. Of course he knew! He said that that was exactly why he'd voted for him: "I just wanted to show them, all of them politicians, what I think of their liberal democracy and their liberal press and the whole liberal lot of them." Government policy in America, Florian was always saying, was controlled by the moneyed few who funded political parties. Democrat or Republican, it didn't matter; some big corporations funded both, for good measure. And as a result, since at least the 1980s, nearly all legislation – "whether on taxation, on antitrust, on regulation, on labour organisation; you name it," Florian would say – had served to assist the ongoing transfer of funds from employees to employers; from labour to capital; from the poor to the rich. Which was, perhaps, what that man in Texas was protesting against.

This man, Cecily recalled, had said that he was a fundamentalist Christian, and didn't believe in antibiotics or vaccination. He said that all doctors were in the pocket of the pharmaceutical industry. He rejected, in fact, most of modern science, including Darwin's theory of evolution. He rejected the political establishment, the accepted cultural hegemony (the press), and the science of his day. Which was like Blake, it seemed to her now.

Along the edge of the horizon, she could just make out a glimmer of gold.

And if Blake were in England today, she wondered, on which side of the divide – this Brexit divide – would he stand?

DAY 4

Thursday 29th August 2019

Diana could hear the children's voices out in the garden already when she woke up. What time was it? Perhaps it would be considered rude to stay in bed too late? She pushed back the cover and pulled on her cardigan.

Victoria was already in the kitchen making tea when Diana went in. She was in Lycra leggings, and trainers in such a perfectly pristine white that they looked as if she'd just this minute brought them back from the shop. "Good morning! Do you want a cup of tea?" she said. "I found the kettle in the sitting room for some reason. Think Cecily must have been wandering around in the night…"

"Yes, please," Diana said, and sat down at the old pine kitchen table. She ran her fingers appreciatively over its varnished surface. It was deeply cut with ancient black knife marks and notches, and the wood so dark and seasoned, it looked almost as if it had been embalmed with ancient oils. "In the *sitting room*? Why would she take the kettle in there?"

Victoria shook her head and shrugged. "Who knows…"

They both remembered, Diana thought, how glum and moody Cecily had been all the evening before. But neither of them wanted to bring up that subject.

"I love your trainers!" Diana said.

"What?" Victoria said. "Oh, these?" She looked down briefly at her shoes, and tipped her foot, so as to see the sides of one of them.

"They look so clean and new!" Diana marvelled.

Victoria smiled and shrugged, as if she didn't know why that should be, and then said, "I'm thinking of going for a run, actually. Just a quick one. Do you want to come?"

"Um…" Diana ran her hand through her hair, suddenly conscious that she was still in her pyjamas and feeling fuddled and sleepy. "Um… well…"

"I mean, not immediately! After we've had a cup of tea, you know. In, like, half an hour or so?" Victoria pressed.

Diana looked through the window behind Victoria. Outside looked too bracingly bright and real. "Oh… well, yes, maybe…" she said. The last thing she really felt like was a run, and yet she felt flattered to be asked.

They were back in the kitchen, just about to leave for the run, half an hour later, when Cecily came in. She looked, Diana thought, as if she'd hardly slept. Her eyes were all puffy.

"Morning – did you sleep well?" Cecily began saying to Diana, her voice croaky, but then, seeing them both in running gear, she looked from one to the other. "Oh!" she said flatly. "You're going for a run."

Standing there with Victoria, Diana felt guilty, as if she'd done something wrong. But actually, was there anything wrong with her and Victoria going for a run? The thought crossed her mind that it was becoming quite difficult to be around Cecily. "Is that okay?" she asked Cecily, laughing slightly – just slightly – to show that it was a bit silly that Cecily had put her in a position where she felt she had to ask.

And then the doorbell rang.

"Are you expecting the plumber again this morning?" Victoria said in a voice of solicitous interest, turning to Cecily.

But instead of going to answer the door, Cecily went towards the kettle. Diana and Victoria exchanged glances.

And then Victoria grimaced at Diana and went to answer the door herself. They could hear her letting the plumber in, saying, "I'll take you to my sister again, as she's the one that knows what's going on." And then she was coming back into the kitchen, saying, in a light-hearted, friendly tone, "Cecily, here's the plumber!"

Cecily turned away from the kettle. "Oh!" she said. "Hello… um…"

And, turning quickly to Diana, Victoria smiled and then rolled her eyes in the direction of the door, as if to say, *Let's go!*

So they did, Diana feeling uncertain that leaving Cecily with the plumber was quite the right thing to do. But then, well, the thing was that she and Victoria had got up much earlier. When they'd planned to go for the run, they'd thought they'd be back before – or soon after – Cecily woke up. And they still *would* be back within, like, half an hour, so surely it wasn't really a problem?

And it was quite a relief to be out of the house, Diana thought as they ran along the cliffs with the sea breeze blowing; away from Cecily's bad mood. As her feet beat a rhythm behind Victoria's on the chalk path, she decided that it was probably a good thing that they were all going back to London today. Relations with Cecily had become difficult and Diana felt… well, she was starting to almost feel differently about her. Perhaps it was temporary, but there seemed to be a layer of bitterness and negativity to Cecily that she had never been aware of before.

Looking out over the sparkling sea as she ran, she experienced a wave of nostalgia for the days when their friendship was inspiring, like a new morning. It had been a source of strength and satisfaction to both of them when they'd discovered that, though they came from such very different backgrounds, they felt the same about so many things.

There was the day when some Tory appeared on the news, talking about the "criminal classes", and only Diana and Cecily, out of all their friends, had noted the phrase. Diana had mentioned it the next day, and Cecily had been amazed and delighted: "Yes, I heard that too! And I bet he didn't mean the bankers who gambled away all our savings in the 2008 financial crisis, or the Tory Party, who've been passing government contracts and backhanders to their friends and donors…"

"No, or even all the MPs, from all parties, who helped themselves to taxpayers' money and then lied about it in the expenses scandal," Diana had said. "He just meant poor people."

They had felt like soulmates sometimes. But now it seemed to Diana that, in fact, they saw most things very differently, after all. This holiday, in fact, there was nothing but differences. The thing was – and Diana had realised this, but had never seen it as such a negative thing before – that Cecily was wilfully ignorant, even childish, about many things. Like most middle-class liberals, she had a guilt complex. She wanted to give everything away to everyone: council homes to immigrants and extra school support for their children, arts funding and political representation to minority cultures, special religious rights and representation to minority religions, support to Palestine and everyone else around the world who was oppressed, devolution to Scotland and Wales, development funding to the Third World, EU funding to Eastern Europe: something for everyone, and all paid for by the British taxpayer. For everyone, that was, except the boring old English. The English themselves got nothing. The way Cecily saw it, the Scots and the Northern Irish and the Welsh got their own budgets and Parliaments, but the English got nothing at all; nothing except privatisation and austerity and lectures on self-reliance. And though there were so many millions below the poverty line, the English were just supposed to keep calm and carry on, because apparently, though they owed everything to everyone else – because of the Empire, because of slavery, because of world conflict, because of the Union – they didn't actually deserve anything themselves.

It was guilt that Cecily had. But actually, it was really

just condescension: this idea that everybody, absolutely everybody, needed and deserved our help, because we were just naturally so superior. Diana had seen it in Cecily when she was round at her house once. A young man, one of those ex-convicts who sell household items at rip-off prices, supposedly as part of their rehabilitation into society, had knocked on the door. Fatally, Cecily had not told him firmly 'no' and shut the door in the initial stages; she had dithered. And dithering was what you should never do, as that gives them time to open up their bag and start pulling things out of it. Sure enough, that was what happened. In the moment she took to dither, there he was, kneeling down pitiably on the doorstep, and keeping up a constant stream of talk all the while, so that there was no way to interrupt and stop him pulling packets of dusters and tea towels and squeegees and floor cloths out of his big duffel bag. He had been given up to a foster home at the age of two, because his dad had abandoned them and his mum had no help with looking after him, he said. His eyes were down when he said this, following his hand as he laid out his goods, but then his chin flicked up and he fixed Cecily with soulful eyes, before dropping his gaze again and rearranging the microfibre cloths and the potato peelers in yellow and blue. His mum took him back when he was twelve, but she had a new husband by then, who was abusive, and by the time he was sixteen, he'd walked out and was sleeping on friends' sofas. And then he got into crime. Again he looked up at Cecily with those soulful eyes. "I just need to make a clean start," he said, "and doing this will help me get back into the job market."

All the time he was talking, he was bringing out cellophane packets of stuff; kneeling on the ground, glancing up, then down, and up, then down. It seemed to Diana, watching, almost as if he were acting – not in the sense that he wasn't telling the truth, exactly; more than likely, he was. But that he was trying desperately to stay in character, the way he used stock phrases, and intonation learnt from TV, as if he had no voice of his own; as if he'd had to take on a character because he didn't know who he really was. Diana had met people like that before: people with tragic childhoods and shattered identities. Maybe it was something trauma did to you.

"But if I buy something," Cecily asked, "sorry, I mean – do you mind me asking? – but if I buy something, then do *you* get *all* the money, or do you only get some kind of commission?"

He looked taken aback when she said that, and then wary, as if he suspected that he was going to lose the sale if he gave the wrong answer. Which maybe he was, in fact. He dropped his gaze and his forehead crumpled into an almost childlike frown of concentration, as if he were trying to work out Cecily's thought processes so that he could find the right answer. And all the while he moved his items around on the doorstep. Finally, he looked up and mumbled defiantly, "No, I get it all."

The way he said it did not inspire much confidence, Diana thought. And yet it was at that very moment that Cecily suddenly blurted out, "I think I could really do with some of those carpet scissors!" She was a bad actor.

He handed her the scissors before you knew it, and instantly there was a whole new energy, a whole new joy in the way he began packing his stuff hurriedly back into his bag.

But Cecily had got it wrong again: she hadn't even asked for the price, and the scissors were already in her hand. "How much is that?" she said belatedly.

"Twenty pounds!" he said, now confident, almost jaunty, as he continued packing away, avoiding her eye.

"*Twenty?*"

She looked so dismayed and incredulous that he immediately came back with, "Fifteen for you!"

They wouldn't cost more than a fiver in the supermarket, Diana thought. Two pounds in the pound shop.

Cecily sighed. "Okay, I'll just get my purse!"

"You're a good woman!" he said, as she handed him the money. And when she laughed, cringing slightly at his patronising male tone, he raised his eyebrows and gave her a grave, soulful look, saying, as he tucked the notes away, "I mean it – I can tell these things!"

There was a bounce in that young man's step as he went off, waving as he closed the garden gate behind him. But Cecily sort of slumped back, resignedly, against the architrave, and turned the carpet scissors over in her hands. She was constantly broke, Cecily. She and Florian had no money. That was why their garden fence was wonky. They only had a house at all, Diana suspected, because her parents had helped them to buy it. But it was only a three-bed, and they barely had the money to keep paying the mortgage, let alone do it up. She really couldn't afford to be buying rip-off carpet scissors that she didn't even need in the first place. But that was the trouble with Cecily. Although she hadn't the money, she still had the expansive mindset, the charitable aspirations, the superiority complex of the affluent London intelligentsia within which she had grown up. That was the trouble with Cecily. And in a sense, you could say that it was the trouble with the entire country: a fallen empire in a ruined house, still trying to dispense charity right and left to those 'less fortunate than ourselves'.

A seagull's cry swooped Diana out of her thoughts and, returned to consciousness, she realised both that she was really quite puffed, and that Victoria was far ahead up the cliff path. There she was, bright against the moor grass, in her white, white running top and her brand-new bouncy trainers, her blonde ponytail bobbing and swinging. Would Victoria mind, Diana wondered, if she stopped to catch her breath? She was unwilling to inconvenience Victoria in any way. She felt in awe of her, almost as if she were back at school and Victoria was one of the cool girls who – for miraculous and entirely inexplicable reasons – had condescended to favour Diana with her notice. Why she felt like that, she couldn't say, and though she could fully see how ridiculous it was to feel like that, it didn't change the fact that she did. So that, although she felt increasingly breathless, she was unwilling to cause Victoria to slow her usual pace. But even as she was thinking this, the distance between them continued to widen, so that, when Victoria disappeared around a distant bend, Diana decided that if she just slowed to a walk, or stopped for the tiniest moment, it was unlikely to make much difference.

She stopped and stood there, panting, heart beating, and then sat down on the cliff grass. She could see ahead, right in front of her eyes, a tall stem of grass swaying and bowing in the wind against the background of the glittering waves, which spread and spread, pooling out to the very edges of the expanding blue sky. Watching the grass stalk bowing and swaying like that, with the distant waves behind it, she felt engaged. She had an urge to capture the line of that stalk; its grace, but more than that, the strange dignity of its stoical, resilient submission to the vagaries of the buffeting wind.

She'd actually done some painting, last year. She'd given up her job and taken a breather for a while; it was the first time in her life that she'd done so since she'd left home at sixteen. But Steve earned really well nowadays (he had four large hardware shops), and she deserved a sabbatical. She was burnt out after all those years when Olivia was little. It was only the paid work she'd given up; if you looked at the whole picture, actually, she was still working as many hours as Steve was. She was still running the whole show: housework, washing, cooking, shopping, childcare, meal planning, holiday planning, birthday planning, household administration, school administration for Olivia, administration of Olivia's social and extracurricular activities, homework supervision, taking Olivia to dentists and shoe shops and clothes shops and doctors, administration for the school's Christmas and summer fairs, buying and making costumes for school plays and assemblies, present buying, present wrapping, tidying, tidying again... the list was endless. She was still juggling several briefs; only these were the silent ones, the invisible ones, the unpaid ones that were done by women.

She'd heard somewhere that women's unpaid housework would, if paid, be the world's fourth-largest economy. And that was only the *housework*! One tiny item on the list!

But anyway, she'd done a few paintings on her free Friday afternoons, before all the cooking and tidying and organising of the weekend began. And then she'd had an idea that she might find a scheme or grant through the local council which would enable her to display her work. Perhaps it was a silly idea – after all, who was she? A middle-aged nobody with no art training; no A levels, even. Just one daughter and a history of fairly low-paid jobs in first retail and then administration. When she looked on the council website, there was nothing on offer for her, an ordinary white, working-class British woman. The only arts funding she could find available was offered as part of Black History Month. She hadn't really minded because she'd never *really* expected that there would be any money available in the first place. And she had nothing against Black History Month; she had just hoped that there would be something for her as well.

But it was the same last month, when she'd tried to look into the possibility of sheltered housing for her father-in-law. The council website proclaimed that all people over sixty were eligible for sheltered housing, and that applications from all – regardless of ethnicity, religion, sexuality or disability – were welcome. There was, however, no housing currently available. Nevertheless, the website went on to say, there were several other housing associations in the borough that managed schemes. There were schemes, for example, for Asian, Vietnamese, African-Caribbean and other 'specific groups' of people. Diana could find nothing, however, for an unspecific white British widower with increasingly crippling arthritis. And once again, she had nothing against the Vietnamese, or any 'specific group'. Why should she? She was *glad* they had somewhere safe to live in their infirmity. She just wanted to know why there was nothing for her father-in-law. And she'd begun to think about the future, when all those free-movement Europeans got old. More than a million Poles alone had arrived in Britain since 2004, she'd heard. Would they get their own 'specific' housing too, one day? And when it came to Diana's turn, would there be anything left for her?

She could never speak of this to anyone; not even to Steve. This was what 'taboo' meant. She'd be a social pariah if she said any of this to *anyone* she knew. *And* she felt ashamed. These feelings – did they mean that she was actually a racist? She didn't *want* to be a racist. But then again, wasn't that what they always said about racists: just like male chauvinists, they themselves were always the last to know?

The *Empire Windrush*, her mother used to say, docked at Tilbury on the Thames in 1948; the same year in which the Labour government ratified the British Nationality Act, which gave every Commonwealth citizen the legal right to settle here, marking the beginning of a social revolution. The *Windrush* was as famous as the *Mayflower*, the ship that took the first colonists to America. "And so it should be," she'd said tartly, with a toss of her hair and an awareness of her own cleverness. "Both ships signalled cultural crisis for the indigenous people."

Diana, of course, hadn't wanted to hear stuff like

that back then. "Oh my God, Mum! stop!" she'd cried, in outraged tones. It wasn't just that it infuriated and shamed her back then, the provocative way in which her mother used that word, 'indigenous'. It was the entire subject: she'd tried to dissociate herself from it entirely.

She'd mocked her mother furiously at the time. But now that her mother was dead, she felt bad. Because there'd been a hurt and a fear inside what she'd said, that Diana should have addressed. Besides, she could finally see her mother's point. Back then it was the Commonwealth citizens arriving, but that was nothing compared to what was happening now that EU citizens could just come and set up home here as well. It was completely out of control.

Then Victoria reappeared from around the bend, raising her hand to shade her eyes from the sun, searching like a caricature sailor for sight of Diana. Diana scrambled hurriedly to her feet, waving energetically, and began to run as fast as she could back to Victoria, who, she saw quite clearly, was swallowing a look of hot annoyance into a smooth, welcoming smile.

"Sorry!" Diana called breathlessly, as Victoria came within hearing distance. "I was just taking a little break."

"No, no, it's fine!" Victoria said, glancing at her watch. "But probably we should be heading back. Do you want to loop round and go home the back way?"

Diana didn't know what Victoria meant by either 'loop round' or 'the back way', although they both sounded ominously as if they might involve a lot more running. But there was that thing about Victoria that made you want to please her. Besides, Diana was still very aware of her status as a guest. So she found herself committing enthusiastically to this plan, despite having no notion of what it entailed. "Yeah, sure! Let's do that!" she said, and Victoria, smiling, turned around and led the way off the coastal track and onto a path that trailed steeply downwards into a shady, more wooded area. Diana had a sense of dread as they trotted ever further downhill, flint pebbles skidding under their feet. She was all too aware that the further they descended, the further they would have to slog their way back up to reach the house again. She was not nearly as fit as Victoria.

In the event, however, Victoria took pity on her and they walked the very last stretch. They were halfway back up the hill when Victoria looked back at Diana puffing twenty metres back. She stopped and did some stretches, and then sat on the bank until Diana caught up and flopped down beside her.

"Sorry!" Diana gasped. "I'm really out of shape!" Her cheeks were burning.

And Victoria smiled and said, "It's quite tough, this bit!", although to be honest she looked fresh as a daisy, herself. She stood up. "We can just have a nice walk home for the last bit!"

*

Olivia leapt up the instant that Diana and Victoria walked into the house. Cecily was in the driveway, saying goodbye to the plumber, and the children were in the sitting room. Zac was on the sofa, flicking casually through *The Satanic Verses*, and the girls were at the table, playing Spit with a pack of cards. Olivia looked up, and then leapt up almost immediately. From her face, Diana already knew that something was wrong.

"I'll be back in a minute!" Olivia told Julia hurriedly, and then came towards her mum.

"You okay?" Diana asked.

But Olivia said nothing; just took her hand and hurried her out of the room and up the stairs.

"What's wrong?" Diana said again, once they were alone on the landing.

But Olivia sucked in her lips, shook her head, and pulled Diana into her bedroom and onto the bed. Only when she had gone back and shut the door firmly behind her did she join her mystified mother on the counterpane.

Diana was giggling slightly – she couldn't help it – at Olivia's urgently sombre demeanour. "What is it?" she asked.

Olivia drew a deep breath. "Well," she said, "it's something Zac said…" She drew breath again as if to speak, but then closed her mouth and said nothing.

Diana laughed again. "What?"

Olivia drew another breath and then said, frowning, as if she wasn't sure that she'd got things right, "I think he told a racist joke."

It was not what Diana had expected, and it seemed… well, just impossible in this day and age. But there was Olivia, watching her with such intense, needy gravity that she had to take her seriously. "Really?" she said doubtfully. "Are you sure? What did he say?"

"He said…" Once again Olivia hesitated, and then

screwed up her face with uncertainty. "'How long does it take a black person to poo?'"

"What?" It just seemed like a silly question. Except for... oh! Except for the word 'black'. "What on earth?" Diana demanded. Discomfort made her impatient, tetchy, because she didn't want to hear this kind of thing. "And then what?"

"'Nine months,'" Olivia said gravely.

"What?"

"That's the answer! 'Nine months'!"

"Nine months?" Diana didn't understand. And then she did. "Oh." It was an indignity, actually, that she should even have to hear this. She felt annoyed, as if she had been tricked into becoming implicated in something shameful. "Oh, for goodness' sake! Are you serious?" she asked, flipping, agitated, at the corner of the duvet. She felt ambushed. She found herself tutting testily. "That's horrible,"

"I know!" Olivia agreed hurriedly, anxiously. "I *know* it's horrible. I didn't *want* to hear it!" She looked terrified, as if she were afraid she might have done something wrong.

"No, no." Diana patted her arm to reassure her. "It's good that you told me. It's not your fault you heard it. It's not your fault at all, but... gosh! I wouldn't have thought it. I really wouldn't; an educated boy like that."

And then after a while, because it was so incredible,

"Are you *sure* that's what he said?"

Julia widened her eyes and opened her mouth, to demonstrate her indignation at being doubted.

"Mum!"

"I'm sorry... sorry..."

"Julia wasn't there," Olivia said. "She doesn't even know."

Of course! Julia and Florian. It seemed so strange that Zac could tell a joke like that when his own cousin and uncle were mixed-race.

They sat there in silence for a while on the bed, holding hands.

"I wonder if I ought to tell Victoria," Diana said, but then realised – even before she had finished speaking – that that would be impossible. Even had they been close friends, it would have been impossible, and in fact she hardly knew Victoria at all.

They lapsed into silence again, but then, feeling that she needed to extract them somehow, that she needed to put distance between them and that degrading secret, Diana said decisively, "Well, we're leaving today, anyway. So let's just try and forget we ever heard that."

But even this attempt to draw a line under it didn't help. Olivia began to wander around the room, picking up things and looking at them, and Diana, kicked into an adrenaline-fuelled overdrive, went over in her mind everything she remembered Zac doing and saying over the week, and everything Olivia had said about him just now. She played it all back in slow motion – word by word; picture by picture – as if in this way she might uncover some little sign or symbol; some key to understanding that had previously been overlooked.

She had just reached the point, last night, when Zac stood up to recite 'Jerusalem', when she was startled out of her thoughts by a crash and a squeal. And there was Olivia standing by the wardrobe, her hand over her mouth, and great big curves of shattered china shimmying across the tile floor.

Diana sprang to her feet, wailing, "Oh no! Oh, Olivia, what have you done?"

"I'm sorry! I'm sorry! I just…" Olivia now had both her hands over her mouth.

"What was it?" Diana cried.

"A vase!" Olivia said, pointing into the wardrobe. "Like that one!"

Diana ran over and looked inside the wardrobe. There was a huge, ornamental china vase there, half-wrapped in a blanket. She felt panic rising within her; an awareness that she was out of her depth: she had no idea how much this might matter. She'd never known people like Cecily and Victoria until she became an adult. Supposing that vase was worth hundreds, like that slavery plate Dan had talked about? Or supposing it was some family heirloom of great significance, passed down through generations? "What were you doing?" she asked again, this time more heatedly.

And Olivia retorted, more heatedly as well, defensive now, "I don't know! I didn't do it on *purpose*! I was just pulling out that box because it's got some kind of weird mask in it…"

But there was no point in getting into an argument about it, Diana realised just in time. And the problem was not so much the breaking of the vase as her own panic at the fact that she had no idea how to measure its significance. It wasn't fair to take out her fear and sense of inadequacy on Olivia. So she began to row back hurriedly, saying, in what she hoped was a gentle voice, "It's okay, it's okay… these things happen. It's okay. I just need to think what to do…"

*

As soon as the plumber had left, Cecily went marching in to find Victoria. She was furious! It was just so unfair! Poor Florian had ended up doing all of the work: of finding a plumber, of dealing with him – of everything! And Victoria had not shown the slightest interest. And now here they came, waltzing in off the cliffs: her good friend and her sister, two people who'd never even met two days ago – but in they came, all flushed and high on endorphins, and walked straight past her as she talked to the plumber in the driveway, as if she were a servant, there to arrange things with the plumber so that they could carry on with their leisure activities undisturbed. She never understood how it was possible that Victoria always did this to her. Why she would *want* to, Cecily couldn't even imagine! As she stood there in the driveway watching the plumber drive away, the sea breeze, turning, carried the scent of the still-flowering lavender; one of the scents of her childhood. This was what she most associated with that scent, exactly this: this childhood sense of unjustifiable, hopeless pain.

She found Victoria in the kitchen, looking in the fridge. And although she was resolved to stick to her guns on this issue for once, at the sight of her sister in her expensive trainers standing there in front of the fridge with her back to her, glowing and utterly self-possessed, drinking a glass of iced water, she blanched briefly. Even now, Cecily hesitated to confront her.

"So, Victoria," she said, in a bit of a rush because she was nervous, "I think we're all leaving today, so I guess we need to settle the bill for the plumber before we go."

She had thought she'd kept her fury out of her voice, but of course, Victoria could sense it. Victoria knew her inside out. Without closing the fridge, she turned around and eyed Cecily coolly, and then, with a smirk of fake concern, said, "Are you okay?" It was classic Victoria: this subtle implication that Cecily was in some way defective, sick or abnormal. And somehow this trick, even though Cecily could identify and describe it, still worked.

She could already hear herself sounding childishly defensive as she answered, "Yes, I'm fine." And then beginning to stutter as she went on, "But the work in the bathroom's still not finished: he's coming back this afternoon, and it looks as if it's going to cost a lot. He's talking about six or seven hundred at least…"

She stopped to check Victoria's reaction, but Victoria didn't react at all. She just continued to stand there, looking at Cecily expectantly, as if still waiting to hear what her point was.

"So when are you leaving, Victoria? And shall I just email you the bill? I imagine we're going to split it, right?"

Victoria continued to stare at her, and then responded, "Oh, I see!" as if she'd only just understood what on earth it was that Cecily was struggling to express. She tipped her head from side to side, wincing, as if weighing up how to address some difficult problem. "Hmm…" she said, and drew breath.

"What?" asked Cecily, mystified.

"Well, it's just that… I'm not sure if we can…" Victoria stopped and then gritted her teeth, drawing breath between them as if summoning the courage to break some painful piece of news.

"*What?*" asked Cecily again, this time more demanding.

"Well," Victoria began in a self-consciously gentle, reassuring tone, "I'll tell you what: let me get Dan in here as well!" And she disappeared from the room.

She was back in five minutes, with Dan beside her, looking oddly grave and formal. By contrast, Victoria seemed flustered, smiling and giggling in a way that was almost girlish.

"What?" asked Cecily, laughing as well now, but only out of nervousness and a need to pretend that this whole situation wasn't worrying and Victoria's inexplicable behaviour unsettling.

"The thing is," Victoria said, her eyes sliding to Dan and only then, reluctantly, to Cecily, "well, we're not sure if it really makes sense for us to contribute to any maintenance or repairs right now."

"What?" Cecily said.

Victoria was biting her lip. She didn't speak, but looked hesitantly at Dan, who, seemingly flattered by her apparent deference, cleared his throat and stepped forward slightly, taking Victoria's hand.

"The thing is, we were wondering if you'd like to buy us out of our half," Dan said. "Or, alternatively, if you wanted sell us yours."

Cecily was so surprised that she must have gaped at him, because, thinking she hadn't understood, he added, "Of the house."

It was like when you drop something heavy on your

313

foot and you have that moment of dreadful anticipation, in the time it takes for the nerve message to travel from foot to brain and register as pain, knowing it's going to hurt although it's not yet hurting. Out through the kitchen window, the sun was shining down gloriously on the still-dewy lawn.

"What… but this house was left for us to share," Cecily said.

They neither of them, Dan and Victoria, looked at each other when she said that. And although Dan drew breath as if to respond, he actually said nothing in the end, and closed his mouth again. After that, they both just watched her in silence, almost commiseratively.

"But I can't buy you out!" she said. Did they not know this? She'd thought it would be obvious.

They still didn't look at each other. But they both reacted by raising their eyebrows, indicating surprise. And Dan said, "Really? Are you sure?" in amazement.

Cecily looked from him to Victoria and back again. Something about Dan's voice didn't ring quite true. And then she realised that they did know; of course they already knew she couldn't buy them out.

"Or we could buy *you* out," Dan said.

They just wanted the house all to themselves. Cecily could see it. It would be like her grandfather, who had bought his siblings out. Victoria would be like their grandfather and continue the family line here, and the house would pass to Zac and to Zac's children, who would have guests and tell them how many generations the house had passed down through, and when this extension was built and when that tree was planted, and show people the anti-slavery plate. While Cecily would be completely forgotten in the history of the house. She wouldn't be the direct line of inheritance in the middle of the page; she'd just be a fainter line on the side of the family tree; one of the ones that petered out.

"But what if I don't *want* to sell it to you?" she had blurted out before she even knew it.

"Well!" exclaimed Victoria. She glanced imploringly at Dan, and then kind of shrugged and looked helpless, as if to suggest that there were no words adequate to meet a question as uncivil as Cecily's. "The thing is," she said eventually, "actually we were thinking of either buying you out or, if for any reason you didn't want that, just buying another place for ourselves." She stopped and looked at Dan with a show of reluctance and uncertainty before continuing, "But you know, if we *do* have to buy another place, then we won't really… you know… understandably, we won't really have the money to carry on contributing to the maintenance of this one as well."

Cecily understood, finally. If she wouldn't sell, then they wouldn't pay for anything. And if they didn't pay for anything, this house would simply fall apart, because there was no way that she and Florian could afford the upkeep on their own.

"The thing is," Dan began, assuming the voice of assured, patriarchal reasonableness, "that I think it's probably in your interest, really, to—"

"It's 'in my interest' to share this house with my sister like a proper family, the way our parents wanted!" Cecily burst out furiously. "And to have a sister who doesn't go stealing the family vases that are the thing I love most in all the house, and that everyone knows were clearly meant for *me*!"

*

t was at then that they all saw Diana moving behind the doorway. She must have been meaning to come in, but then turned away on hearing Cecily shout.

But before she could escape, Victoria called her back, smiling, solicitous. "Hi, Diana! I'm so, so sorry you had to hear that. Did you want something? Are you okay?"

"Oh… well…" Embarrassed, Diana turned and came into the room. She had her hands behind her back. "It's just that… well, I'm *really* sorry, I'm *so sorry*, but I've broken this…" Her hands emerged holding up two large pieces of china.

"Oh! What is it?" Victoria asked kindly.

"Oh, it's… I'm so sorry, but it's this vase that was in the wardrobe. There were two of them…"

Victoria's expression changed.

"I'm so sorry!" Diana cried again, adding hurriedly, "The other one's fine!" She was watching Victoria's face imploringly, but Victoria didn't see: she was staring, aghast, at the two pieces of china in Diana's hands.

"What? But *how* did you knock it over?" Victoria burst out, shaking her head in furious disbelief.

"It's okay, it doesn't matter!" Cecily interjected hurriedly.

But Diana didn't seem to hear her; she was looking at Victoria. "I'm so sorry, I—"

Victoria took one of the pieces from Diana's hand,

asking, in a tense, sharp way, "What size are the rest of the pieces?"

Diana blushed. She looked as if she wanted to sink into the ground. "I don't know. I mean, well, some of them are quite large. Yeah, mostly they're quite large," she said in a hopeful voice. But then after a moment she admitted, "Although I don't know. There are some really tiny pieces. I'm so sorry..."

Victoria said nothing.

"It's okay!" Cecily insisted in a horrified voice, "Diana! Really!"

Diana cast her a quick, tense smile, but her attention was still all on Victoria. She looked distraught. "Please, just let me know what I can do. I... I'll buy you a new pair – I mean, they won't be the same, obviously, but I'm sure I can find something really nice..."

Victoria laughed, a little shrill. "Don't be silly!" And then, with a sigh, as if making a great effort to rise graciously above the occasion, "It's fine. It's really fine. Let's just forget it ever happened. Really, it's fine." Almost with the same breath, she turned to Dan, saying, in a hard, tense voice, "You know, I think we should probably get packing, actually. It's time to go."

*

Diana hardly knew what to do after that. But she got out of the kitchen as fast as she could. She didn't know if she could face Cecily for a bit, after hearing her shouting at her sister like that. It was as if she were no longer the Cecily Diana had thought she knew, but a whole other person. And what an uncomfortable situation to be in, after hearing all that: to be dependent on Cecily for a ride back home!

She went back into the bedroom, where Olivia was now quietly performing walkovers: lying back on the bed, reaching her hands down to the floor, and then flipping slowly over backwards. Diana sat down on the other side of the bed and looked around at everything. The old jug on the bedside table, the one with folk designs on it, now seemed rather grotesque. Even the elegant, oriental-looking coffee pot looked wrong on a bedside table. There was nothing in it when she peered inside, except some fluff and a single, dead, curled-up spider. She went over to the fireplace, where she found, spaced along the mantelpiece, four small bronze Indian bowls engraved with swirling patterns. These also, when examined, contained dust and a quintet of desiccated insects. Next to them stood three elephants, each with its trunk linked with the tail of the one in front, and all carved out of some beautiful smooth black wood – ebony, perhaps? They were probably from Mumbai, Diana decided, where Cecily's great-uncle had been harbour master.

It all seemed to come from some other, foreign world, and as she ran her finger around the edge of a bronze bowl she felt a wave of sadness; almost helplessness. She couldn't wait to get back to her own home and to Steve, put on her slippers and turn on the TV.

And then when she looked at Olivia, Olivia looked at *her* and then made a face and shrugged, and sniggered, almost, so that Diana too started to giggle, and soon they were clinging to each other on the bed, giggling helplessly, even though they hardly knew why. But the broken vase was still all over the floor by the wardrobe.

"Oh, I forgot to get the dustpan and brush!" Diana cried, leaping up.

She went back to the kitchen to find it, hoping there'd be no one in there now. And there wasn't, but just as she was looking in the broom cupboard she heard, out on the terrace, Victoria's voice saying in a stressy, gaspy way, as if she were laughing but simultaneously on the verge of tears.

"I'm not being snobby or anything, but can you *imagine* her trying to buy a *replacement*?!"

Diana literally couldn't move. She felt a great lurch in her stomach, like when you're in a car and you go over the top of a hill. This was what she was afraid of. What she'd always been afraid of. This was why she preferred groups more mixed – like, in terms of nationality and class. With women like this, who'd been well-heeled middle-class forever, she was always afraid she would commit some kind of gaffe – something that she didn't even know about, but which would be obvious to all of them – and that they would laugh about it behind her back.

*

Victoria shut the boot and then went back to the house, opening the front door to call, "Dan, are you ready? Hey, everybody! We're leaving now!" She went round to the front of the car and climbed in, feeling suddenly exhausted.

And shortly after, Dan came out, carrying his computer and an unopened packet of beef. "I thought we'd take this back, since we never used it." He opened the boot.

Victoria eyed the cellophane-wrapped beef. This was what she'd got away from: this 'waste not, want not' carrying of food from here to there, expending – on principle – an effort totally disproportionate to the original cost of the damned thing. She felt an uprush of irritation towards Dan. There he was, so blithely male and untrammelled, bringing her more things to remember, more things with which to clutter up her days that were already cluttered with endless lists. What did he have to remember each morning beyond getting himself to work and back, and paying the car insurance? Whereas she had bills, holidays and weekends to organise, presents to buy, school letters, shoes and uniform, doctors, dentists, hairdressers, house and window cleaners, shopping, meals, washing, folding, tidying, and cleaning and more cleaning (because of course a cleaner only did the weekly stuff) and God knows what else to manage before she even started work! Sometimes she felt her head would explode with the number of things to keep up in the air simultaneously, and here he was, presenting her with a polystyrene tray of beef that she'd now have to fit into her evening meal plans. Because of course, once they were home, it was mostly Victoria who did the cooking. Dan only cooked for show, for pleasure, when there were people to admire him for it. She could see that the little pad on the polystyrene tray, under the beef, was soaked with blood.

"Oh, for goodness' sake! Won't it get blood all over everything in the car?"

"Well…" Dan began.

But she had had enough. She swept all thought of it away with an expressive wave of her hand. "Just leave it for Cecily, please!"

Registering the rising heat – almost panic – in her voice, Dan held up one hand and said, placating, "Okay, okay, I'm leaving it with Cecily!" and began backing back into the house with the tray of beef.

Dan and Zac were in the car with Victoria, itching to go, when Cecily finally came out of the house with Florian to say goodbye. She was red-eyed, no doubt feeling the poor little victim again, and she came up to the window and said sarcastically, "Well, safe journey. I hope you haven't forgotten to pack the vase that you stole."

Victoria didn't quite know how it happened; perhaps it was just that one word 'stole'. But whatever it was, it just happened, like a switch being flicked. "You have no idea, do you?" she said. She got out of the car and shut the door, so that Dan and Zac wouldn't hear what she was saying, as they wouldn't understand. "Why is it that you always think that everything is somehow yours? Did it never occur to you that *I* always loved those vases. That I remember those vases from before you were even *born*?"

And then she climbed back into the car and slammed the door. The last thing she saw, in the rear-view mirror as she pulled away, was Cecily standing there glaring impotently, hands on hips, looking ridiculous. And it was ridiculous. The *whole thing* was ridiculous. Victoria felt ridiculous *herself* as she drove off, hearing again in her head what she had just said. How could they – the two of them, in their forties – be arguing like this, talking exactly like children?

*

"What do we do?" whispered Olivia.

"Dunno. Let's just stay here for a bit," Diana whispered back.

But they couldn't hide in Diana's room forever. They had to get back to London, for one thing. So after half an hour or so, once they had packed and stripped the beds and done everything else she could think of to put the moment off, Diana timidly emerged to look for Cecily.

She spotted her on the stone bench round the side, that looked out over the cliff to the sea. The late-morning sun rode high in the sky and the shadows were short and stubby, crouched intensely under the bushes and at the bottom of the trees. Cecily was hunched, staring down at her feet, and seeing her like that, Diana felt her stomach churn.

"Cecily?" she called tentatively.

Cecily looked round, but didn't immediately register Diana. When she did, she pushed back her hair and stood up, saying, "Oh, Diana, I'm so sorry! I'm so sorry it's all been such a disaster!" There was not a cloud in the sky, and her puffy red face was incongruous in the golden sunshine pouring all around her.

"No, it's okay. It's not been a disaster. *Not at all!*" Diana found herself lying so spontaneously, and so *necessarily*, that it surprised her.

"Well," Cecily said, sitting down again, heavily, "but

it has!" She waved her hand listlessly. "I mean, me and Victoria arguing, and… and you and me kind of… well… all the toxic Brexit tension. And, well, I don't know if you've noticed, but the whole house is falling apart, and…"

"Cecily," Diana said, moving forward and sitting next to her, "I'm so, so sorry about that vase!"

"Oh, the vase!" Cecily waved it away with that listless hand again. She rolled her eyes, shaking her head. "Those vases – you know, we're having enough trouble with them already. Having one broken really makes no difference."

Perplexed, Diana tried to make sense of this. Failing, she asked, "What do you mean?"

"Oh, it's just…" Cecily began, but then stopped. She looked at Diana and drew breath. "Well, my mother left those vases to *me*. Not that I was going to take them out of this house or anything, but when we arrived here, well…" She stopped and drew breath again, letting before saying, "Victoria had hidden them in that wardrobe, for some reason. I think she was going to take them to London."

"Really?" Diana felt embarrassed. She didn't know what to say. The whole thing was… well… distasteful. "Did she *know* your mother left them to you?" she asked eventually.

"What?" Cecily asked.

"Did Victoria know that your mother left the vases to you?"

Cecily looked stupefied, and then, frowning as if she couldn't quite see the relevance of the question, explained, "Well, *yes*! Those vases came from a town in Italy where my mother travelled when she was young. And I went there too, when I was in my twenties, and bought her a matching candlestick."

Diana nodded.

But perhaps that wasn't enough for Cecily because she added, a little insistently, "I mean, it was *our* thing. Mine and my mother's. Italy, the Renaissance, all of that. Anyway, I'm so sorry you got dragged into all of that. Unfortunately, Victoria and I have just never had a good relationship, somehow. And now…" Her voice cracked in a sob, and she had to stop and swallow before she could go on. "And now – oh, it's just awful! – Victoria wants to force me to sell her my half of the house."

"Oh!" Diana said. This was big news, but still perplexing. "But how could she *force* you?"

"Well, you know, she's refusing to pay for any repairs. She knows I can't afford to maintain it by myself, so if she doesn't pay, the place will fall apart."

"But that will affect her as well!" Diana objected. Cecily's take on all this just didn't make any sense.

"Yeah, but she wouldn't care. She's loaded! She and Dan could buy another holiday home if they wanted, even without selling this one. But she wants to force me to give her this one because… well…" Cecily looked out to sea, saying, without looking at Diana, "Because she just hates me, I think!"

There was a pause while they both gazed out across the sloping fields to the water. The wind hassled the trees along the borders of the fields, so that their leaves glittered in the sunshine. You could hear the surf breaking down below.

"I guess it's also that this house has sentimental value to her," Diana suggested, and then added hastily, because she saw Cecily stirring in protest, "not that that makes it all right to try and drive you out."

"But it *doesn't* even have sentimental value to her!" Cecily burst out. "Victoria's never been sentimental about *anything*! And anyway, she always *hated* being part of our family!"

"Oh," Diana said. Cecily was so vehement that there didn't seem anything else she could say. And the last thing she wanted right now was to antagonise her friend. Because that was how it felt now: Cecily was her good friend. Somehow, her perceptions had shifted and her emotions had rearranged themselves, and once again she was feeling sympathy towards Cecily. She could still hear Victoria's voice in her mind, saying, *Just* imagine *what kind of vase she would have bought as a replacement!*

"Anyway," Cecily said, "I'm so sorry to drag you into all of this. And you probably need to be getting back to London." She placed a hand on Diana's arm. "I'll go and pack!" She stood up.

"No, not at all," Diana said, "I'm really not in a hurry. Let's talk some more! Maybe... I know – shall we have one last walk on the beach or something?"

*

t was as they were walking down to the beach that Cecily remembered what Victoria had said in that stupid speech she had made about how she'd '*always loved*' those vases.

It was just a lie. Never *once*, could she remember Victoria showing any interest in those vases when their mother was still alive. It was just typical Victoria being manipulative. She had always been like that, claiming that this wasn't fair and that wasn't fair and angling for attention.

They walked right up to the water when they got to the beach. It was so hot that they took off their shoes and let the frothy surge lap around their toes. It was a heavenly day; a gift so blue and gold and shining that it seemed almost wasted when Cecily felt so hopeless. The shimmering sea expanded luxuriously under the loving arch of the celestial sky, and way up there were seagulls squawking, salt white in the glittering sunshine, freewheeling.

"I know you're really upset about Brexit, as well," Diana said after a bit. "I'm really sorry about that…" She looked at Cecily and then looked away, and then down at her toes. Cecily thought she was going to say something else, but she didn't; she just wriggled her toes under the water.

Anger darted through her. What was the point in saying sorry if you didn't actually want things to be different? But then it passed. She was just too tired, after all that stuff with Victoria, to feel angry about anything any more. And in fact, she could feel an openness emanating from Diana right now for which, in her upset, she was more than anything just grateful.

"It's just that…" Diana, wiggling her toes in the surge, tossed her head and frowned. "It's just that I want to feel that I'm valued in my own country. Not to be constantly told that somebody else might deserve my place here more than me. You know? I don't think that's right. I *belong* here

– I was *born* here, for goodness' sake! My mum was born here; my grandmother. And I want my country to look after me, *because* I belong here! Is that too much to ask?"

What did she mean, Cecily wondered? Was she talking about the unmitigated capitalism that had been destroying the country since the 1980s? "What do you mean – like, housing and healthcare and education and all those things?"

"Well, yes!" Diana said. But she drew a big breath and stared out to sea, scanning the horizon as if there were something that she hoped to spot there. "It's like the elites," she said after a while. "The politicians and the media and the money people – they've all been there preaching about liberalism and tolerance and competition and immigration and how it's all good for us. But it's *not* been good for us, Cecily. It's been good for *them* – you know, they've got cheap plumbers and cleaners and everything. And it's maybe good for people from poorer countries who want a better life here. But it's not good for us. All we've got over the last sixty years or so is overwhelmed buses and trains and Tubes and doctors and schools and hospitals, and more and more competition and zero-hours contracts."

"Right," said Cecily. Wasn't this exactly where they had got to last time they talked about it? Up on the cliffs that very first day?

"I mean, they lied to us," Diana said. "They've been lying for decades that everything would get better and better for us but it hasn't got better. Not for us. Everything just gets more and more chaotic and cut-throat and insecure. You know?"

"But that's exactly how *I* feel!" Cecily said.

Diana's brow puckered, as if she thought Cecily must have misunderstood her. "They just lie to us!" she repeated falteringly. "They thought they could tell us that liberalism and globalism and immigration was all for the best and silence anyone who dared to disagree by shaming them as a racist or a xenophobe or a loser… you see?"

Cecily was looking at Diana, but hardly saw her, as there was something – less a thought than a sensation – coming over her. Further up the beach, she could see those boards with the pictures of St George and the Victorian bathers with which they had photographed themselves on the very first day.

She would not have used the words that Diana used – or, if she did, they would have different meanings. The term 'elite' for Cecily, in the context of Brexit, denoted a different group or a different set of ideas than those it seemed to denote for Diana. And yet, and yet… her own feeling of discomfort and disillusion seemed much the same as Diana's. And even her analysis of what was so wrong with the current socio-economic structure took the same shape, the same narrative – only the characters were different. Where Diana saw immigration as the problem, Cecily saw the problem in the fallacy of the 'free market', the idolatry of money as God. And where Diana blamed liberals, she herself blamed dark-money oligarchs in Russia and the US. But the story was essentially the same.

"But I'm not sure," she proffered tentatively, after a while, "that Brexit is going to put any of this right."

Diana stared ahead out to sea, and then turned to look at Cecily. "Me neither," she said, "to be honest." She kicked at the sand. "But I just… well, everything was wrong; we had to do *something*!"

There was silence, then. And as they stood there, a group of cold-water swimmers appeared from the right, about fifty metres from the shore. There were three of them in front and two more further behind: little heads bobbing along on the rising and falling sea, pushing their weak little way against its lurching motion.

"Oops!" said Diana, grimacing as they watched. "That one at the end is falling behind. Do you think they'll notice?"

"I hope so!" Cecily said.

They stood there watching. Eventually the penultimate swimmer turned around and swam back towards the very last one, and then the first three slowed and waited while the other two proceeded towards them. Cecily and Diana watched until the swimmers were all together again, and then they looked at each other and smiled. The wind whipped up quite suddenly, spattering them with spray from the waves. But Diana's eyes were kind. Cecily had that feeling again: that this – *this* – this connection now was all that mattered. And then the feeling was gone.

"Shall we go back?" she said. "I guess we'd better pack up and go."

When they reached the steep slope up to the cliffs, they turned to look out to sea one last time. And as they turned towards the glittering waves far below, the wind whipped up unexpectedly again, buffeting at them.

Supposing Victoria *had* always loved those vases? The thought suddenly occurred to Cecily, almost as if it had come riding in on that sweeping gust of wind. Supposing she really had? And then, as they headed across the gusty clifftop, it further occurred to Cecily that if Victoria had always felt that the vases were hers in a way, what did that mean: that Victoria had always known that *Cecily* loved them, but Cecily had never – not until this very moment – had any idea that *Victoria* did as well? She couldn't find the answer, but the question heaved in her stomach all the way back to the house.

As they approached the house, with its lavender bushes at the front, Cecily became aware of an ache in her chest; or perhaps it was in her throat. There was the gate, and the cherry tree that Victoria used to climb and hand her cherries. It was impossible that this house, which had always been Cecily's, could ever not be. Imagine coming to this gate and not being able to just lift the latch, swing it open, and walk in! As they went into the drive, she could see the lawn and the fields slanting dramatically down towards the sea. In one of those fields there used to be a horse pastured that she and Victoria were afraid of, because it had once tried to bite them. Cecily could see the August sun on the rustling trees that stood about the lawn as she and Diana crossed the driveway. It dripped down like golden syrup, from leaf to leaf through the foliage, and onto the ground in little golden pools between the shadows.

When she was at university, she remembered, she used to take a blanket and lie reading in that dappled shadow. The grass was itchy, and it had a sharp, green, earthy smell. She felt her throat aching quite definitely, and her breathing growing convulsive, and tears pricking and stinging her eyes.

When she went inside, this rising wave of nostalgia gained momentum. Supposing all of this – the old pink bergère chairs, the art nouveau tiles in the fireplace, the bookshelves – became Victoria's and not hers anymore? And when guests and grandchildren came, Victoria would tell them the stories of the house, and she would get them all wrong, the dates and stuff, and romanticise everything until it wasn't true, like the way she told everyone that their grandfather had 'rescued' their 'Jewish' grandmother. It was all of this: the old French chairs, the William Morris prints, the shelves and shelves of books, the light flooding in through the small windows like a Flemish Holy Spirit. And there, in the middle of the coffee table, lay the Constable tray with the rambling hedgerows, the dreamy water meadow, and the distant spire of the cathedral. The Salisbury Cathedral tray, on which their grandmother used to bring out fig rolls and garibaldi biscuits. All of this reminded Cecily of a vanishing England: a little staid, a little stolid, a little bumbling, but dedicated, ultimately, to some quiet but magnificent ideal which she could not describe in words.

"*There* you are! Are you ready to go?" Florian said. He looked bad-tempered. They hadn't told him they were going down to the beach, she realised.

It wasn't until they were in the car on the way home, and Florian turned on the radio, that a thought occurred to Cecily. There was a young black man on the radio, talking about racism in schools. "We were told, me and my friends, not to congregate in groups, because apparently we looked threatening. They didn't actually say we looked threatening because we were black; they didn't *say* it because, you know, they didn't want to come across as racist. They thought they were being delicate – you know, on our side – by not actually saying it. But whether they said it or not, we all knew…" he was saying.

"Yeah," Julia piped up, "I've had people laugh at my hair."

"Really?" exclaimed Diana in the back, sounding shocked. "But you're not even that… *really*? At *our* school?"

Julia was not very dark-skinned. That was what Diana had been going to say, before she changed it, Cecily thought. She felt some sympathy for Diana: the way she'd had to stop herself, not knowing what was okay to say and what wasn't; afraid to fall into some social trap. While Florian was three quarters black, Julia was three quarters white. Although why we used those clumsy terms of 'black' and 'white' to refer to people at all was a mystery, when we were actually none of us either black or white; all of us just varying shades of beige and brown.

In the driver's seat, Florian harrumphed. "Well, you think it's hard today. You try growing up mixed race in the *1970s*!" he said. "It was a thousand times worse! Racism was so normal, it went completely under the radar! Only black people even *noticed* it, and to be honest, we ourselves internalised most social attitudes so that even *we* didn't notice a lot of underlying racism. But if we ever dared to point out even those cases that we *did* notice, people would not only tell us we were imagining it, or mock us, they were actually *offended* – you know, literally *indignant*, like, *angry* – that we should have the temerity to complain."

"Sounds like being a woman," Cecily remarked.

"The other day," Julia said, "our teacher handed out instructions to some game, and in the instructions all the players were referred to as 'he.' But the teacher said nothing, and neither did anyone else. They didn't even *notice*."

"Oh, that kind of thing happens *all the time*!" Olivia said.

And then quite suddenly, out of nowhere, Cecily realised why Victoria had always known that she, Cecily, loved the vases, and yet it had never occurred to her that Victoria might too. It was because Cecily *had* been the favourite child, just like Victoria always said. She'd just never noticed. And when Victoria had complained, she'd felt indignant, as if Victoria were just making an underhand bid for power and attention. And of course! It made sense! It was always like that: the privileged were never conscious of their privilege. Why would they be? We were all born assuming that we were the centre of the world, that we were especially deserving of love, luck, respect and attention, and so if the environment in which we grew up allotted more of any of these to us than to others, we naturally assumed that it was because we merited them. Men found it hard to perceive sexism; white people found it hard to perceive racism; the moneyed found it hard to perceive the unfair advantages that money gave them in life. Victoria was right! Cecily had grown up believing, in some half-conscious way, that she was the favourite not only in the eyes of their parents, but also in the eyes of... well, the whole universe. Or God.

*

Victoria pulled over into a petrol station about two thirds of the way back to London. She poked Dan, who had dozed off in the passenger seat, his arms folded across his chest, his mouth hanging open.

"I'm going to get some coffee. I'm shattered. Do you want one? And can you drive the rest of the way?"

"Ooh, can you get me a Snickers?" Zac piped up from the back.

Dan stirred, frowning and turning his head from side to side like a waking baby, and then swallowed and opened his eyes, gazing, zombie-eyed and blinking, at the dashboard, and swallowing several more times before he said, indistinctly, "Hmmm."

She left him to wake up fully while she filled up the car, and then she knocked on his window. He wound it down, still blinking.

"Coffee?" she asked.

"Can I have a Snickers?" Zac asked again, eagerly, leaning insistently up against the driver's seat.

She smiled. "Okay!" Zac was lean. Thankfully, he had long feet and slender fingers like her; unlike his father, who tended to fat. And this was a source of pride and relief for Victoria. It meant she could have the pleasure of letting him indulge freely in chocolates and biscuits and all those other little sins that her own parents had rationed so stringently when she was a child.

They were playing The Commodores on the radio as she queued up to pay. 'Once, twice, three times a lady.' And as she stood there, her eye travelling idly over the chocolates at the counter, she noticed a familiar-looking flat red-and-yellow bar next to the Crunchies and the Flakes. Caramac! A favourite from her '70s childhood. She hadn't seen them for years! She and Cecily used to be crazy about them: that particular butterscotch taste. They used to get ten pence pocket money every Saturday, and when they got it they'd cross the road, as even quite small children were allowed out by themselves back then, and go to the newsagent's and blow it all on a Caramac each.

It must be the emotional music, and the emotional morning she'd had, but as she stood there, Victoria's eyes welled up. She thought the tears would be no more than a prickling of the moment and then recede, but instead she found that one had already escaped to trickle down her nose, so that she had to leave the queue and scurry away down the aisle of fridges of plastic-encased sandwiches, in order to get a hold. But the tears wouldn't stop until after she'd wiped her eyes, blown her nose several times, taken deep breaths, and made herself think about what she was going to make for supper and all the people she had to phone and email tomorrow morning. It came to her as she was heading back to the queue: a vague, unwelcome feeling of warning, like when an alarm clock goes off in your dream and you hear it but you don't yet fully recognise the sound.

It wasn't until after she'd paid and was seated in the car again that she knew what that sudden warning feeling was about. It was about buying the house from Cecily.

Back when she was trying to give up cigarettes, before she eventually managed, it would come upon her suddenly: an overwhelming urge to smoke. She'd have done two clear days, and at first she'd tell herself, *No, it will ruin everything; you will regret it afterwards!* But she wanted a cigarette so much, and that was the only really convincing imperative. Utterly compelling was the sense that, until she'd smoked one, she'd never be able to think about anything else. The

335

instant she lit the cigarette she'd feel wonderful. She'd congratulate herself on knowing how to enjoy life; to seize the day. But then invariably, when she'd finished it, she'd feel terrible. It was almost instantaneous: she'd feel completely, completely worthless.

*

As they were driving into London, they saw the demonstrators – heading towards Parliament Square, no doubt. 'Stop the coup!' their placards proclaimed urgently.

"What's this about?" Julia asked.

"They're protesting against the prorogation," Cecily said.

They were stopped now at the traffic lights, and so they all sat and watched the demonstrators file past.

"And who are *those* ones?" Julia asked, pointing to another group approaching with different placards.

"'No justice; no peace!'" Olivia read out.

"'No justice; no peace'," Florian repeated, as they all sat there watching out of the windows. "Is that group a counter-demonstration? Or are they all just part of the same thing?"

They peered curiously from one group to the other.

"I think it's all part of the same thing," Diana said.

Endnotes

1   Diana's mother, frequently referred to in Diana's thoughts, is a character inspired, in part, by David Abbott. *Dark Albion: A Requiem for the English* (2013). Many of her thoughts and ideas, and indeed those of Diana, also owe a debt to this book.

2   'William Shakespeare (c.1591), *Henry VI, Part Two*.

3   John Foxe (1563), Foxe's *Book of Martyrs*.

4   Marc Maron (2014), *Attempting Normal*.

5   Winston Churchill (1946), speech to the University of Zurich.

6   Chinua Achebe *Things Fall Apart* (1958.)

7   Migration Watch UK (2014), *A summary history of immigration to Britain*. Available at https://www.migrationwatchuk.org/briefing-paper/48/a-summary-history-of-immigration-to-britain

8   'In the Royal Borough of Greenwich...' Royal Borough of Greenwich (c.2011), *The people of Greenwich and how we have changed*. https://www.royalgreenwich.gov.uk/info/200313/population_and_demographics/2150/the_people_of_greenwich_and_how_we_have_changed

9   Winston Churchill's speech Strasbourg 12th 1949

10 Gordon Brown (2010), speech to the Citizens UK general election assembly. Available at https://www.youtube.com/watch?v=BFqrMP2HR1A&ab_channel=CitizensUK

11   Muslim Village (2012), *Non-Muslim politician wants to make London a beacon of Islam.* Available at https://muslimvillage.com/2012/03/20/20805/non-muslim-politician-wants-to-make-london-a-beacon-of-islam/

12   'The slave trade has been...' BBC World Service (date unknown), *The Story of Africa: Slavery.* Available at https://www.bbc.co.uk/worldservice/africa/features/storyof africa/9chapter2.shtml

13   https://www.theguardian.com/politics/blog/live/2016/jun/03/eu-referendum-michael-gove-questioned-on-sky-news

14   https://en.wikipedia.org/wiki/Foxe%27s_Book_of_Martyrs

15   https://en.wikipedia.org/wiki/Foxe%27s_Book_of_Martyrs

16   John Foxe (1563), Foxe's *Book of Martyrs.*

17   John Milton *Areopagitica* (1644)

18   William Blake *Preface to Milton a Poem* (1810.) The poem became better known as the hymn *Jerusalem* after it was put to music by Sir Hubert Parry (1916.)

19   https://www.historyhit.com/who-were-the-normans-and-why-did-they-conquer-england/#:~:text=The%20 Normans%20were%20Vikings%20who,the%20leader%20 of%20the%20Vikings.

20   John Milton *Areopagitica* (1644)

21   https://www.telegraph.co.uk/news/2017/03/27/cut-eu-red-tape-choking-britain-brexit-set-country-free shackles/?WT. mc_id=tmgoff_psc_ppc_performancemax_dynamicland ingpages&gclid=CjwKCAiA3KefBhByEiwAi2LDHN9saE 7FWdg4sQmMSnBgBI3PGmshrrG8vVKUlB3MhMtGL-1rs511AhoCqHsQAvD_BwE

22   Milton Friedman *Capitalism and Freedom* (1962)

23   Friedrich Hayek *The Constitution of Liberty* (1960)

24   https://www.salon.com/2001/12/15/enron_4/

25   https://www.bbc.co.uk/worldservice/specials/1624_story_ of_africa/page26.shtml

26   C. Wright Mills *White Collar: The American Middle Classes* (1951.) https://www.google.co.uk/books/edition/White_ Collar/71cSDAAAQBAJ?hl=en&gbpv=1&dq=C.+Wright+ Mills+Nobody+talks+more+of+free+enterprise+and+ competition+and+of+the+best+

27   https://www.olivercromwell.org/Letters_and_speeches/ letters/Letter_19.pdf;

28   John Locke *Second Treatise of Civil Government* (1690)

29   R.H. Tawney Religion and the Rise of Capitalism (1926)

30   R. Younge *The poores' Advocate* (1654) cited in R.H. Tawney *Religion and the Rise of Capitalism* (1926)

31   Samuel Hartlib *London's Charity Inlarged* (1650) quoted in R.H. Tawney *Religion and the Rise of Capitalism* (1926)

32   R.H. Tawney *Religion and the Rise of Capitalism* (1926)

33   *Giving Alms No Charity* (1704)

34   Kwasi Kwarteng, P. Patel, Dominic Raab *Britannia Unchained: Global Lessons for Growth and Prosperity* (2016)

35   Daniel Defoe *The Great Law of Subordination Consider'd Or, the Insolence and Unsufferable Behaviour of Servants in England Duly Enquir'd Into* (1724)

36   Mary Wollestonecraft *A Vindication of The Rights Of Men* (1790)

37   Mary Wollestonecraft *A Vindication of the Rights of Woman* (1792)

38   https://www.theguardian.com/education/2008/jul/29/ schools.religion

39   https://www.theguardian.com/uk/2010/apr/06/christian- nurse-loses-battle-crucifix

40   Preface to *Milton a Poem* (1810.) The poem became better known as the hymn *Jerusalem* after it was put to music by Sir Hubert Parry (1916.)

41   E. P. Thompson (1963), *The Making of the English Working Class.*

42   Quoted in E. P. Thompson (1993), *Witness Against the*

Beast: William Blake and the Moral Law page 113

43   Quoted in E. P. Thompson (1993), *Witness Against the Beast: William Blake and the Moral Law* page 113

44   Quoted in E. P. Thompson (1993), *Witness Against the Beast: William Blake and the Moral Law* page 113

45   E. P. Thompson (1993), *Witness Against the Beast: William Blake and the Moral Law.*